Bernard G. Lord.

CLOAKED IN DARKNESS

By

Bernard G. Lord

ISBN 0-7414-3755-4

Published by:

INFI∞ITY
PUBLISHING.COM

1094 New DeHaven Street, Suite 100
West Conshohocken, PA 19428-2713
Info@buybooksontheweb.com
www.buybooksontheweb.com
Toll-free (877) BUY BOOK
Local Phone (610) 941-9999
Fax (610) 941-9959

Printed in the United States of America

Printed on Recycled Paper

Published January 2007

Acknowledgments

I would like to thank Geoffrey, Ruth and Claire Mitchell for their descriptions of Brittany villages, countryside and coastal regions. Thanks also to Dave John for researching transceivers used by agents during WW II, and leading me to a wealth of background information on the internet about SOE.

Credit must also go to my wife, Margaret, for applying her editing skills and tolerating my many hours in front of a computer.

Chapter One

It was dark. It was wet. Annette Renard was crouched in a shallow ditch on the periphery of a field close to a railway line in Brittany, France. She felt cold, damp and tired, and her left calf muscle was beginning to cramp up. She would have to move in a minute or that muscle would go solid with tension and give her unbearable pain. She glanced along the ditch to her right as though she wanted permission from someone before making a movement. Erwan Cottereau was the person she sought, a black, amorphous form lying fifteen feet from her.

It was hard to distinguish Cottereau's features through the slashing rain and the deep darkness of the November night. His black oilskin-covered body melded into the mud of the ditch's bank. His face was blackened with chimney soot, and his thinly-gloved hands held a Sten gun. He had it set for single shots of the 9-millimeter bullets it fired. Erwan sensed that Annette wanted to say something, so he slowly crawled over to her, keeping his head below the top of the ditch.

"Are you all right?" he said in a whisper.

"I'm getting a bad cramp. I've got to move my leg; is that OK?" responded Annette.

"Yes, of course it is, in fact both of us can probably stand up safely. That German patrol isn't coming back, and they won't send another one out on a night like this to check the railway line," said Erwan.

They both stood up and stepped out of the ditch which was rapidly becoming water-logged. Erwan knew that Annette was feeling miserable in the foul weather, and her

1

apparent calmness belied her nervousness. This was her very first sabotage operation as a member of the French Resistance, although she was more of an observer than an active participant. She was not even armed.

"OK, Annette, you're really doing fine. Try and relax a bit. I know those krauts gave you a scare. They came close but I can guarantee that they didn't see us. If they had, we'd be dead by now," said Erwan with an attempt at a calming voice."

"Thanks a lot, Erwan! What the hell have you got me into? I must have been crazy to come on this caper."

"This isn't a caper, as you call it. This is serious business for serious patriots who want to throw the krauts out of our country, and don't you forget it," said Erwan, whose voice had switched from being calm to containing a strain of anger.

"Sorry, sorry, my liege, I'm just a little bit nervous."

"My liege? What's that supposed to mean? Now come on, we've got a job to do. We're going over to the railway line to see how Marcel is progressing with the plastic explosives. Keep low and move fast, but make sure you don't trip; we can't afford a sprained or busted ankle at this point. Follow me!" commanded Erwan.

They bent their bodies double and awkwardly covered the hundred yards of ground from the ditch to the embankment upon which the railway lines ran. There they crouched in-between a group of gorse bushes that gave less than meager protection from German bullets.

The bad visibility did not allow Annette and Erwan to view Marcel at work, but Erwan knew exactly what he was doing as he, himself, had laid charges before. In fact, Marcel had already completed his task and was in another thicket of gorse about thirty yards from that of Annette and Erwan.

The railway lines ran north-east and south-west, close to the small village of St. Léry which was about twenty-six miles west of Rennes. Marcel had clamped a percussion triggering device, called a fog signal, to the outside of the left rail of the track for trains running north-east up to the main line between Rennes and Brest. The trigger would

2

activate the detonator which in turn would fire the cordtex fuse that ran to the first charge and then on to the second one. The three-quarter lb charges were about four feet apart and of the plastic explosive variety. To be exact, the plastic consisted of cyclotrimethylene-trinitrame - called RDX by the British - mixed with beeswax to give it the plasticity for easy molding into a convenient shape. With the charges placed against the left rail, and a lot of luck, the south-west track would also be destroyed and the train derailed to the left, causing blockage in both directions, and a severe headache for the Germans.

Erwan laid down his Sten gun, cupped his hands and blew gently into the small gap between his thumbs that were drawn together and parallel. The cooing sound of a dove was produced. He repeated it five times and then listened intently for a response. He tried again, but no response. The seconds ticked by. He cooed a third time.

"OK, OK, I heard you. Stay where you are; I'm only a few yards away," said Marcel, in a stern whisper.

I don't believe this, thought Annette; *my life is in the hands of a boy scout making bird calls; it's pissing with rain and I'm shivering with a likely dose of pneumonia. I've got some gorse thorns sticking in my thighs and my boots are full of water. What am I doing here?* Annette extracted herself from the bushes and stood tall.

"Over here, Marcel, wherever you are," she yelled. Very suddenly Marcel's hot breath was in her face.

"Shutup, you stupid idiot! That German patrol's not long gone. It could have circled around and be only a hundred yards from us. For God's sake use your commonsense, and don't act like an amateur."

"But I am an amateur," retorted Annette, highly piqued.

"I've no time for this now," said Marcel. "Listen, the charges are all set, and we've got to get back to some better cover. There's a clump of trees on a small rise back beyond the ditch you were in. From there we should be able to see the train and hopefully its destruction. The train is getting close. I can hear it on the rails."

"I thought we were supposed to head straight back to my farm," said Erwan. "That was the plan. Those trees are in the opposite direction to the farm. You've got me confused."

"Well, the plan's changed," said Marcel. "Follow me, and keep close."

They quickly reached the trees and took cover but with Marcel having an unobstructed view of the railway line, albeit a blurred one through the incessant, sweeping rain. In less than two minutes the train could be distinctly heard, chugging slowly up the line from the south-west, heavily laden. According to Special Operations Executive headquarters in London, the freight train would be carrying spare diesel engine parts, torpedoes and 88-millimeter shells for the U-boat flotilla in the pens at Brest. But London was not always right; there was a chance that the torpedoes might be German sausages and the diesel parts cabbages for making sauerkraut. London's information was only as good as the agents in the field were at checking and double-checking what was heard and what was seen. It was 1941, and at this point in the war some of the intelligence gathered was based on wild conjectures or was miscommunicated.

Wherever possible, although often circuitously, the Germans used secondary railway lines for very important freight as main lines were often targeted by RAF bombers and fighters. But this night, the French Resistance would prove that German trains were not safe anywhere.

Partially concealed behind a massive oak tree, Annette strained her eyes to try and see the approaching train. Her heart was pounding again and her nervousness had returned. Erwan leaned, somewhat nonchalantly, against another oak close by, his Sten slung over his shoulder. The rain had caused some of the soot on his face to run, leaving white vertical streaks, turning him into a wild native painted for tribal war. Marcel lay on his stomach in front of Erwan's tree. At first he had tried to view the train through binoculars, but the lenses became blurred with raindrops so he put them back in their case and rubbed his eyes as though to clear the night away. He had a good idea where on the

4

track he had laid the detonator trigger and charges. In fact, they were about lined up with a pile of spare railway ties at the bottom of the shallow embankment.

Now the engine was really laboring as it struggled up the grade. Erwan thought of the engineer frantically working the valves to get the last bit of pressure out of the boiler, and of the stoker, stripped to the waist, covered in coal dust and heaving lumps of anthracite into the fiery mouth of the iron monster. He knew the driver and stoker would be French, probably hating their forced contribution to the Nazi war machine. He fervently hoped that they would not be killed or wounded in the impending explosion.

If Marcel has calculated the length of the fuse correctly, based on the expected average burn-rate, thought Erwan, *the first charge should not explode until the second freight car is over it. But the train is traveling so slowly; has Marcel considered that factor? Maybe the charge will go off under the first car or even the coal-tender. If the leading wheel-bogie of the engine does not successfully activate the fog signal trigger then the charges will not go off at all. In that case, two or three more U-boats would be repaired and stocked with fresh torpedoes, allowing the bastards to head out into the frigid North Atlantic and send another 50,000 tons of vital Allied shipping down into the expanding graveyard. Too many 'ifs', too many 'buts'.*

The train was a hundred yards away, then fifty, ...thirty, ...ten. Now it was over the trigger.

"Blow-up, you bastard, blow-up!" said Erwan, spitting the words out through clenched teeth. The seconds dragged by. "It's not going to go. *Merde alors! Merde alors! Gast! Gast!*" Erwan's mixture of French and Breton swear words suited the tenseness of the moment.

"Patience, patience, Erwan. Keep......" But Marcel did not finish his reprimand before a brilliant flash of white light revealed the front part of the train, and a pressure wave of damp air hit the three saboteurs a second later, with an accompanying roar of sound. Not long afterwards the spectacle was repeated as the second charge exploded.

"Magnificent! Magnificent!" yelled Erwan. "You're a perfect genius, Marcel."

Annette felt a surge of uncontrollable excitement as though she were witnessing a massive fireworks display. But there was more to come. On the roof of the third freight car two armed guards were sitting. Suddenly, the car beneath them was split open in all directions by another mighty explosion which hurled them upwards into the darkness, doing ugly, slow-motion aerobatics. Annette's feelings of excitement changed to horror as she experienced a fleeting image of a leg detaching from one of the guards and an arm from the other. She felt the blood drain from her face and her hands start to tremble as she realized that she was indirectly responsible for the gruesome death of these guards. She had never killed anyone before.

The scene of destruction enlarged as ten of the remaining fifteen freight cars derailed with a grinding, squealing, splintering cacophony of sounds. Some tumbled down the embankment, others flipped onto their side and slid up the tracks, breaking them loose from their ties and turning them into buckling serpents. Then fire spread back from the cars in the front of the train to those lying on the tracks and the side of the embankment. As the fire roared more shells exploded, and terrible screams emanated from inside one car where another set of guards must have been stationed. The night's blackness dissolved into an eerie light which the falling rain could not extinguish.

Marcel and Erwan were satisfied with the night's work. They felt no remorse for their actions. This was the enemy dying before them. If the Nazis did not want death then they should have stayed in Germany. France must be rid of these diseased thugs.

"It's time to get out of here," said Marcel. "I've seen enough to make my report to London, and this place will be teeming with krauts in half an hour. We're heading back across country to Annette's house from where I'll inform SOE headquarters of our success, and, of course, see our amateur, Annette, safely back in bed. Now come on! Erwan, lead the way!"

" But, but, how can..." started Annette until cut short by Marcel.

"Quiet! I've already told you that I'll explain things later. Now, for God's sake let's get going. Here, Erwan, you can carry my pack of tools and spare plastic, like a good sergeant."

Chapter Two

The background of the three saboteurs was varied and colorful. The leader had 'official' papers that called him Marcel Rambert. This was his cover name fabricated by SOE. In reality he was Major Claude Roland who had been called up into the French army as a reservist at the outbreak of the war in 1939. In civilian life he had been a schoolteacher at a high school in his home town of Marseilles, in southern France on the Mediterranean coast. He was born in 1916 and raised as the product of highly respectable, middle-class parents. He was their only child and very much spoiled.

Claude had an Uncle Charles, however, who was less than respectable, and, in fact, he showed criminal tendencies in his early twenties. To escape the law and keep the family honor almost intact, Charles was persuaded to disappear into the French Foreign Legion on the day Claude was born. When Claude was ten, letters addressed to him started to arrive from all over North Africa. In the letters, Uncle Charles described, in lurid detail, the desert battles in which he had supposedly fought against *ungodly natives*, even though in 1926 such natives were hard to find. He became Claude's hero, much to his mother's consternation.

Claude became a clever student and a fine rugby player, two attributes which led him to Grenoble University, a degree in physics and a teacher's diploma. Although he enjoyed teaching, extracurricular military interests, seeded by his wicked uncle's stories, led to his joining the army reserves in order to play soldiers at weekends and attend summer camps in Algeria. He rose through the reserve ranks to become an officer and eventually a captain by 1939. Claude had a swarthy Mediterranean complexion, black hair and an unruly mustache, and although he was not very tall - 5 feet 8 inches - he was strongly built with wide shoulders and muscular legs. Women found his face attractive, for although it showed a mature strength of a man in his twenties, it also had flashes of boyishness. His eyes, cheekbones, chin and mouth always reflected his mood, from being stern and threatening to happy and mischievous. He was an open book, and well read.

In November 1939, Claude's infantry regiment was sent to join the 94 French divisions facing the threatening Germans on the eastern border of France. Together with the French, there were 10 British, 22 Belgian and 9 Dutch divisions. Against this Allied total of 135 divisions were arrayed 136 German divisions, almost a perfect match. The *phony war* stayed phony until May 10, 1940 when the Germans launched their blitzkrieg offensive, seizing Holland, Luxembourg and Belgium in a matter of days, and thrusting into northern France across the Meuse river and through the Ardennes hills. The main French armies were split in two as the German forces punched through to the English Channel by May 20. Claude's regiment in the First French Army put up a plucky running fight but could do nothing against the relentless German armor and the screaming Stuka dive bombers. May 28 found Claude and his dazed, exhausted, depleted and disillusioned regiment lying in the dunes on the Dunkirk beaches, waiting to be annihilated.

Then two miracles happened. First, the German armor stopped advancing on Dunkirk; a major tactical error by Hitler. Secondly, and more dramatically, starting on May 27, an armada of civilian and Royal Navy boats, of all shapes and sizes, sailed bravely from southern England to save 340,000 British, French and Belgian soldiers from the German onslaught and take them to the relative safety of English ports. Captain Claude Roland was one of the fortunate to escape, but at a heavy price paid for by the

Frenchmen who valiantly fought a ferocious rearguard action in and around Dunkirk, buying time with their blood so that their comrades could return someday and cut off the head of the devouring Nazi monster. On June 4 the evacuation was completed. The French rearguard had nothing left to fight with, and Dunkirk fell to the Germans. 40,000 French soldiers were captured and became slaves in German labor camps.

Many of the French soldiers who escaped from Dunkirk opted to immediately return to France and carry on the fight, but soon they needed to be evacuated a second time from the major ports of western France as the Nazi noose tightened. On June 23, the French cabinet signed an armistice with Germany which brought all military action in France to a halt. However, a proud and stubborn man called General Charles de Gaulle, who had secretly fled to England on June 17, was determined to carry on the fight and liberate France one day. He and others set themselves up as the Free French government in exile and started to form the nucleus of a new Free French Army with those Frenchmen still in England.

However, it became obvious that the new army would not see action in France again for a very long time. This did not sit well with Claude Roland who wanted action now. Although the Battle of Britain, fought between the Royal Air Force and the Luftwaffe, was exciting to observe first hand, and the threat of German invasion during this period reached its peak, these events past, and Claude's life in early 1941 revolved around endless army training exercises in various parts of England and Scotland. He became very bored, very jaded. The foul English weather did not help, nor the strange English food, nor the instances of friction, caused by national bravado and cultural differences, between the men under his command and the local civilian population. He knew he had to get back to France somehow; to see his parents once more, if they were still alive, and to fight the occupier of his country directly.

* * * * *

It happened by word of mouth, almost a slip of the tongue, by a middle-aged Englishman talking to Claude one night in a pub in south London. Claude, whose knowledge of the English language was very good, was sharing his discontent of his inactivity with the stranger and how he wanted to rectify it. The fact that he had already consumed three pints of best bitter was evident in his slightly slurred words and the volume of his voice.

"I'll tell you what I bloody well want to do, *mon ami*, I want to take all the Frenchmen in Britain and parachute them into Normandy, every single bastard. Then we'd show the lousy Hun who's boss; kick 'em all the way back to the Rhine, the sods.

"No, no, wait, I've got a better idea. We should commandeer the Queen Elizabeth and Queen Mary, fill 'em with French soldiers disguised as civilians and sail them into Marseilles harbor, waving little flags and throwing streamers overboard as though on a luxury cruise. Then we'd grab our rifles, unload our tanks and take the city by storm. Next, on to Vichy to kick Marshall Pétain's arse and his traitorous collaborators out of office, shouting '*Vive de Gaulle!*' and then, how do you say, we'd all live 'appily ever after. So what do you think?"

"I think you need to lower your voice, and be careful what you say. There could be some big ears around us, and take what you're saying literally, all the way back to Berlin. I know you're joking, but they don't," said the stranger.

"Who said I'm joking," said Claude, belligerently.

"Sssssh, sssssh! Now listen carefully," said the stranger in a whisper, "and make no response to what I'm about to say. If you're serious about wanting to get back to France, come and see me tomorrow at my office. I'm going to write the address on this bit of paper. Look at it and commit it to memory."

Claude just managed to focus his tired eyes on the address and repeated it to himself several times. "OK, OK, Mr Cloak-and-Dagger. Got it!"

The stranger took back the paper, tore it into shreds and put the bits in his jacket pocket. Then he said, "Goodnight, nice to meet you, *Vive de Gaulle!*" slipped off his barstool and headed for the door.

The next day, Claude had a twenty-four hour pass so he went to the stranger's address in central London, expecting that it was all a joke, that all he'd find would be a bombed-out building. But it was not a joke. The stranger was Captain Anderson of the Special Operations Executive who was in the business of recruiting French-speaking agents for F section. He gave Claude background information on the SOE, but gave no specifics as to what exactly F Section did except that it operated in France. If Claude was still interested, Anderson could try and get him transferred from his regiment into SOE. This request would have to go through General de Gaulle himself, and that would be very difficult. There was no love lost between de Gaulle and the British-controlled set of agents operating in what he considered as his territory alone, France. But this time the General acquiesced, and a month later Claude was on a train to a secret location in Scotland for six weeks intensive testing and training. A further month after the training, Claude was parachuted into France to join a resistance circuit, or *réseau*, called Tailor, in the vicinity of Rennes, Brittany. Along with his posting went a promotion to major, but that carried no weight for Major Claude Roland had ceased to exist; he had become Marcel Rambert of Avignon, now working as a farm-hand in Brittany. His SOE code name for communication purposes was Bantam, but all members of the *réseau* would know him only as Marcel Rambert. For security reasons they would know little else about him.

* * * * *

12

Erwan Cottereau's background could not have been more different than Major Roland's. Erwan was born and raised in Brittany as a man of the land, just like his ancestors had been for the past three centuries and maybe even longer. His bloodline was pure Celtic, and, whenever he could, he spoke Breton not French, a language more easily understood by a Welshman than an actual Frenchman. His parents, who both died in 1939 when he was only twenty-two years old, left him the 400-acre family farm, which in peacetime allowed him a moderate living standard, but in time of war it was a struggle to make ends meet.

He ran a mixed farm; some wheat, barley, artichokes, cauliflowers, carrots, potatoes, a few cows, a few sheep. He had to provide the Germans with part of what he produced, but although they paid him, it was barely enough to cover his costs. To supplement his income he acted as a fish wholesaler. Once a week, or whenever he was able to get gasoline for his truck, he drove up to the fishing villages near St Brieuc on the north coast and purchased whatever fish were available; mainly cod, herring, monkfish, and occasionally oysters. He then traveled around the villages in his own area and sold the fish to the few remaining local fishmongers. In order to make the best use of his truck, on the northward journey he would load up with vegetables and fruit from neighborhood farms and sell them directly in St-Brieuc market or wholesale to green grocers in the town. He needed permits for his truck and the purchase of gasoline, plus a license to do trade as a wholesaler. These were not easy to come by, but the German authorities realized that, as a farmer, he was a source of their own produce supplies and grudgingly gave him the necessary paperwork for his secondary business. Because of the frequency of his trips to St-Brieuc and then up the coast to Plouha and Paimpol, the German road patrols were used to seeing his somewhat ancient and reluctant truck, and on most occasions just waived him through any road blocks as he flashed his papers.

He had an attractive young wife, Claudette, also a Breton, but no children. The farm was close to the village of

Basbijou, about twenty-five miles west of Rennes, four miles east of Mauron and two and a half miles north of the large forested area called Forêt de Paimpont, which is sometimes known as Forêt de Brocéliande in medieval legends. Erwan was not a sophisticated man like the Major, but he had had a solid schooling and was very practical. He spoke well and with very little of the local vernacular. If his farm had been considerably bigger, he might have been known as a gentleman farmer, for he had a considerable influence in the community. His open-air life had given him a rugged complexion, and manual labor had made him strong. His hair was jet-black and very unruly. He could not understand why brushing it once a week was insufficient to keep it tamed. Erwan's green eyes were powerful and piercing. Once they locked onto you, you felt they were reading your very soul. His voice was strong and deep when talking, but underwent a remarkable transformation into a rich baritone when singing in the bath, or when called upon in the local café to entertain with a folk song or a dubious ditty. He was just over six feet tall with a thin but wiry body. His thighs and calf muscles, although not big, were like tempered spring steel, ready to release their energy at a moment's notice.

Although his wife helped work the farm, he needed another full-time worker so he employed a local village lad. And then there was the Major, alias Marcel, who lived, ate and worked with Erwan as an additional farm-hand.

Marcel trained Erwan in the art of blowing up freight trains, and together they had severely damaged a total of five and attempted another two; the latter operations failed because of dud detonators, but it was all good experience for Erwan. Erwan also became proficient in the use of the Sten gun, not only firing it but stripping and assembling it under a variety of conditions. The gun had been only introduced in June 1941 and it still had teething problems. Although its 32-round box magazine promised a firing rate of 550 rounds per minute, the gun sometimes jammed if more than 30 rounds were put in the magazine. Erwan found this out on two separate occasions when retreating from a train-wrecking operation with German guards in hot pursuit. It was only covering fire by Marcel that allowed them to escape with their lives. The gun also had the disconcerting habit of sometimes firing by itself if dropped on a hard surface. Erwan treated the gun with the utmost respect and a little suspicion.

Annette Renard was a small blonde with a lot of spunk and a quick temper. A French father and an English mother had given her a first class education in Paris and other European capitals. Monsieur Renard was a diplomat in the Foreign Office, and, before the war, he and his family moved to a new embassy every three years or so. In 1936 he made his last transfer back to Paris, his home town, where the family had an elegant apartment. There he worked directly out of the Foreign Office headquarters from where he hoped to retire in four years time. Madame Renard taught English Literature at the Sorbonne as a full professor, and her interest in literature and teaching was passed onto Annette. In 1939, at the age of twenty-one, Annette brandished her newly acquired degree and secured a teaching post at a high school in the 17th Arrondissement. But the war changed everything.

At the end of 1940, Madame Renard considered Paris to be an unsafe place for Annette, so she persuaded her to go and stay indefinitely with a widowed aunt, her father's sister, who lived on the outskirts of the little village of Guillaume in Brittany, not far from Basbijou and Erwan's farm. Annette was reluctant to leave Paris, her mother and all her friends. Paris was excitement even though it was occupied by the Germans, and, more importantly, she was just beginning an amorous affair with a wild but attractive young man called Pierre. But she soon settled down to the country life in Guillaume. As a child and a teenager she had spent many summer vacations with her aunt so she already knew the area well and quite a few of the villagers. This helped her find employment teaching at the village school, for, soon after her arrival, the school's one and only teacher mysteriously disappeared. It was rumored that because he was a Jew he had been sent to a special labor camp. He never returned to Guillaume.

Being a qualified teacher and teaching in her mother tongue, French, was one thing, but trying to teach small children in the Breton language, without being a native of Brittany, was an entirely different proposition. Breton is a branch of the Celtic Indo-European language, and has a rhythm to it that makes it hard for a French person to imitate. In addition, learning the vocabulary requires much effort because the same word does not always have the same spelling, depending on the word that comes before it. Annette rebelled against this illogicality, and could not understand, as an example, why *'the father'* was spelled *'an tad'* yet *'my father'* became *'va zad'*. But Annette was determined to speak Breton as well as French in her classroom. The children needed, and wanted, to be bilingual.

Erwan was the one who came to her rescue. He welcomed the chance to be her Breton teacher, for it meant spending time with her on a regular basis. He was a very patient teacher, and Annette persevered so well that within two months she could have a basic conversation with her pupils and write simple sentences. Although from time to time they laughed at her pronunciation, they enjoyed correcting her, and thought it very funny that they could teach the teacher.

Erwan Cottereau had first met Annette when he was eleven. His parents knew her aunt and uncle well, and during her summer visits the two families would often go on picnics together in the Forêt de Paimpont, and take long bicycle rides to the coastal beaches and camp there overnight. Although Erwan and Annette became childhood sweethearts, at least during the summer months, their fondness did not blossom into love as they became young adults. Monsieur and Madame Renard were relieved at this because the class difference between them would have produced strained relationships later on. Farming and the Diplomatic Corps were not socially compatible.

It was Erwan who first persuaded Marcel that Annette might make a good resistance fighter. He could vouch for her loyalty and he knew she was quick-witted and physically strong. Whether she could stomach the killing would not be known until later. So Erwan approached Annette who immediately became interested in the proposition with unbridled enthusiasm, as though the whole thing would be just a bit of fun. Her innocence of what actually was involved worried Erwan, but he hoped she would mature quickly enough to satisfy other circuit members after a few resistance operations.

Chapter Three

The rain eased off and then ceased completely as the three saboteurs moved across bocage country to Guillaume, following high hedgerows to avoid traversing open fields. The sky cleared enough to reveal clusters of stars and a quarter-moon periodically showed its face from behind scudding clouds. Erwan had a strong desire to stop and absorb the beauty of the night, but the cold grip of his hand on his Sten gun told him this was no time for communing with nature. Eventually they came to a cart-track that led directly into the outskirts of Guillaume. It was too dangerous to walk down the middle of the track so instead they walked in the fields beside it, making use of the separating high hedgerow as natural cover. The fields were water-logged so progress was slow and difficult. Soon the cart-track ended at a paved road. They followed this for two hundred yards around the village then stopped at a small driveway that led up a rise to a fairly modern house. This was the house of Annette's aunt, Marie Renard.

"We'll go around the back into the orchard at the bottom of the garden," whispered Marcel, "and be very quiet. I'll lead." As they went forward, Marcel took a .380 caliber Webley pistol out from under his oilskin jacket.

As they entered the orchard he signaled for them to stop and crouch down on their haunches. Annette wondered what on earth was going to happen as Marcel carefully laid his pistol on the ground and starting making the same bird noises that Erwan used to call up Marcel at the railway. She could not suppress a small giggle. Beyond the orchard stood a large garden shed from behind which a figure very slowly materialized. It said nothing; just stood there menacingly. Marcel picked his pistol up and waited. Then from the shape came three short flashes of light.

"It's OK; that's André. Move forward into the shed," ordered Marcel. "André insisted on coming here for his transmission. He thought Erwan's farm had been under surveillance this past week, although I haven't seen any Germans snooping around. Perhaps André's getting a little jumpy. Anyway, that's why we came back here and not the farm after we blew up the train."

In a corner of the spacious shed, André had set up his transceiver on a small workbench. He was the wireless operator for Marcel's group, highly trained by SOE in Britain. The transceiver was a light-weight Paraset developed for MI6 and packaged in a simple leather suitcase; it only weighed 6 1/2 pounds. It had a power output of 4 to 5 watts and its receiver covered frequencies of 3.0 to 7.6 megacycles in one band. André used a 6 volt car battery as a power source.

"What the hell kept you?" growled André, briefly shining his flashlight in their faces. "The home station is going to be listening for me at midnight, that's in ten minutes time. Now for God's sake tell me what you want me to say, and keep it short. I've got to encipher it before sending it, of course. I heard your big bangs from here, and you know what that means. The krauts will be out with their radio direction-finders in every village close by, and I'm not too keen to have a bullet up my arsehole. Now what's the message? I want no more than 500 letters. Got it?"

Marcel had already been formulating the message in his mind as he trekked back from the night's sabotage. He needed to convey the location of the wrecked train, where it had come from, where he thought it was going, time of demolition, what he thought it had carried, and an estimate of what had been destroyed, including the number of enemy soldiers. To do that in words totaling no more than 500 letters was a challenge, but he knew that André's Morse code speed was about 100 letters per minute, and the golden rule was not to transmit for longer than five minutes at a stretch in order to reduce the chances of enemy detection.

With his left hand holding a flashlight, André wrote down the plain text of Marcel's message on a pad of paper. He then quickly enciphered it using an algorithm to jumble the letters based on a series of numbers that were indirectly linked to his pre-selected poem-code, a copy of which home base would use to decipher the message. On his last trip to England, working with SOE coders, he had selected some lines from Shakespeare's *Julius Caesar* as his poem-code. In Act III, Mark Anthony was grieving over Caesar's dead body after his brutal assassination, and saying:

O, pardon me, thou bleeding piece of earth,
That I am meek and gentle with these butchers!
Thou are the ruins of the noblest man
That ever lived in the tide of times.
....
And Caesar's spirit, ranging for revenge,
With Ate by his side come hot from hell,
Shall in these confines with a monarch's voice
*Cry **Havoc**, and let slip the dogs of war,*
....

André knew the lines off by heart, and prior to sending a message, he would select five words at random from the lines and allocate numbers to each letter in the words which would then become the transposition key for the enciphering process. To let the decoders in England know which five words he had selected, he would insert an indicator-group at the beginning of the message. André, an educated man, had chosen some of the lines from *Julius Caesar* because Caesar's character, to some extent, matched that of Hitler who wanted unlimited power through world domination. But, in particular, he loved the imagery of the words, *Cry **Havoc**, and let slip the dogs of war.*

André carefully set up a transmission frequency of 4.5 megacycles, and using his Morse key tapped out the encoded message at exactly his scheduled transmission time. On completion he signed off with his code name, Carotte. He then tore the pages from the pad that contained the text, the key and the enciphered words, and burned them with a match. He stamped on the ashes and smeared them into the dusty floor. André knew that if the Gestapo found those pages, their interpretation could possibly lead to the capture of other agents.

André quickly packed up his transceiver, shook hands all round, and left the hut without making a sound. Marcel put his hand lightly on Annette's elbow and guided her to the door.

"Does your aunt know that you've been wandering around the countryside in the dead of night doing nasty things to the Germans?" asked Marcel.

"No, she doesn't. Do you think I should tell her? I believe she's trustworthy, and she's going to find out sooner or later, if not from me then from someone else."

"That's true, but ease into her knowing gradually; sound her out with a few 'what if....', and 'suppose I ....' type of statements. Then, if she doesn't respond positively, you'll still have room to back off and leave her ignorant of your helping the Resistance. Now get to your bed, woman, before the cock crows. You did OK tonight, Annette. We'll be in contact." Marcel kissed her on both cheeks, as did Erwan, then they both departed back to Erwan's farm, leaving Annette the difficult task of entering the house undetected and climbing a set of creaking stairs to her bedroom.

The inside of the house was pervaded by an enveloping damp coldness that made Annette shiver as she changed into a pair of heavy flannel pajamas and thick woolen bedsocks. Even so, the bed sheets felt like thin layers of ice as she slipped between them. They were not made for humans to lie between; they were for polar bears. Her skin became a mass of blue goose-bumps, and her nipples became so hard and erect that she feared they would crack at the base and fall off.

Frost patterns had started to form on the inside as well as the outside of the bedroom windows, for after the heavy rain a cold front had swept into Brittany lowering the air temperature to freezing. There was, of course, no central heating system in the house, and the wood-fired boiler that was lit only once every two weeks to provide hot water for washing clothes had been dead for two days. Peat was no longer available for burning in the small open fireplace, and there was precious little dead wood left in the forests after the needs of the German military base had been satisfied.

Sleep would not come as Annette lay shivering. The moisture in her breath condensed as a white mist just above the top of the bedclothes. Her mind was a confused jumble of thoughts about the night's happenings. Her group had killed. She had seen contorted bodies blasted away. She had heard the screams of burning men, men she did not know, men who had wives, children, girlfriends, mothers.

Did I hate those men enough to do that to them? she questioned. *Could I do it again? Do I have the strength of purpose? Perhaps I'm just seeking thrills. Perhaps I have a sadistic streak in me. No, no, these men are evil; these men are the killers, the torturers; they deserve to die. But they're just soldiers, following orders, members of the honorable Wehrmacht. Oh yes, then why do they hang civilians? Orders again? If it's all the Nazis' fault, then why doesn't the Wehrmacht stand up to them, throw them out of power. I don't know, I don't know and I don't understand. And where's God in all of this? Sitting on the sidelines, of course. Having a good laugh at our stupidity, our insane actions and reactions. Stupid, stupid, stupid! So why shouldn't I sit on the sidelines as well, tell Marcel this game is not for me. He'd probably think I was a coward. Well, perhaps I am. I certainly felt scared in the trees waiting for the charges to blow. Nearly wet my pants, in fact. Yet, on the other hand, it was a little bit thrilling. Perhaps I'd do it again, if asked.*

Annette continued to argue with herself, making point and counterpoint until she became tired of it and moved on to happier thoughts. Those thoughts took her back to the time when she was only eleven, a young person of innocence to whom the world was only just being revealed as an exciting place; in particular, she thought of the huge, mysterious Forêt de Paimpont which she and Erwan had explored on long summer days. There was the time when they took a very special hike to the Fontaine de Barenton and he almost persuaded her to believe in the existence of Merlin and Vivian. She remembered the storm and the cave and the fire that they lighted. If only she could transfer the warmth of that fire into the cold sheets and blankets on her bed. Those were the memories that eventually soothed her into sleep.

Chapter Four

While Annette dreamed of her more youthful days, Paula Drysdale continued her night shift as an SOE signaller at the Grendon Underwood wireless station, known as Station 53a, near Aylesbury in Buckinghamshire, England. Although only nineteen, she was a very experienced signaller, having volunteered six months ago for an organization with the unlikely name of the *Field Auxiliary Nursing Yeomanry*, FANY for short. FANY was also known as the *Princess Royal's Volunteer Corps,* and was made up of intelligent young women who were trained in signals, coding, map reading and navigation, first aid, self defense, driving military vehicles and weapons handling. Her job was demanding, both mentally and physically, and the hours were very long. She sent messages to and received messages from SOE agents in Europe and Scandinavia. She lived and breathed Morse code. Even when not actually transmitting, her right hand was rarely still. Sitting at a table or reading a book, her fingers would grasp an imaginary Morse key and tap out words she was hearing or reading. Some would say that she had a nervous complaint but in fact she was just finely tuned to her occupation.

Working and living conditions at Grendon were Spartan. The signallers and coders lived in separate Nissen huts, eight to a hut, two to a cubicle. The huts were freezing in the winter and stifling in the summer. The food was barely edible and sparse, social life was nil, and if you were not working you were sleeping. Yet the resilience of youth somehow got them through the stress and strain The young women formed close bonds and gained satisfaction from the importance of their work.

Paula looked after André's messages, although she did not know his name, where he was, or what his messages said, for all were encoded. At the beginning of each shift, she picked up her 'skeds' (schedules) which told her the transmission times and tuning frequencies of her contacts. Yet transmissions were not completely anonymous, for each operator of a Morse key had little idiosyncrasies which could be discerned by an experienced listener. For instance, she recognised André by his extra long 'dashes' and his very staccato 'dots'. If she was listening for him and these characteristics were not there, she would become suspicious that it was not him and raise an alert that maybe a German was sending the message instead. This could imply that André had been captured and killed after revealing his codes and transmission details under extreme torture. On the other hand, it could simply mean that he was under pressure from a personal physical condition; maybe a heavy cold, lack of sleep, even a little too much wine. The judgment of the signaller played a big part in these instances.

Paula had tuned in to André's transmission frequency fifteen minutes before his scheduled time of midnight. She liked to have a little time cushion in case he transmitted early. This night he was right on time and his signal quality was good. Sometimes the signal was noisy or would fade in and out. Paula dreaded this condition for it would make interpretation of the Morse difficult; she might miss a dot or a dash and have to guess what the letter was or write down the wrong one. She might make so many guesses that she had to ask the agent to repeat the whole message on another frequency. This she hated to do because the longer the agent was transmitting, the bigger the chance of his capture and death. That was a massive burden for a young woman of nineteen to bear.

When the transmission was finished, Paula handed the encoded message to a clerk who immediately took it to another building where a coder deciphered it. The coder found no problems in the deciphering process; André's message was clear and made sense. But it was not always so. The best of agents or wireless operators sometimes made mistakes in their encoding or transmission to the extent that the coders at Grendon had to declare the message as an 'indecipherable', throw up their arms in frustration, and refer the message to a crack team in London. The London team would then work day and night, cajoling sense out of it with hundreds of complex manipulations, trials and tests. Their motto was 'no message shall remain an indecipherable'.

At 4:00 a.m. Paula finished her shift and braved the cold early morning air to walk back to her Nissen hut. There, she made a quick cup of tea on a primus stove and gulped it down. There was no milk for her tea and the sugar ration had been exhausted a week ago. The girl she shared the cubicle with was fast asleep; her shift started at noon, a civilised hour. In order not to wake her mate by putting the light on, Paula groped around in the dark to find her heavy flannel pyjamas and the opening in the bedsheets into which she slipped giving a sigh of exhaustion. It had not been a bad night; she had successfully contacted all the operators on her sked, both sending and receiving encoded messages. Her last thoughts before sleep were for the operators over there in enemy-occupied territory. She asked God to keep them safe; she was a fairly religious young woman.

Chapter Five

You will not find the name Forêt de Brocéliande on any modern map, for although it lives on through the ancient legends of King Arthur and, in particular, Merlin, The Enchanter, and Vivian, The Lady of the Lake, cartographers are pragmatic people dealing only with reality. They use Forêt de Paimpont to signify the area of 18,000 acres to the south west of the regional capital Rennes. The woods are the remnants of a vast primeval forest of pines, oaks, and beeches, containing lakes, streams and springs. Many Bretons, who know their history and culture, prefer the name 'Brocéliande' to 'Paimpont' because it imparts a mysteriousness, an other-worldliness to the woods they love. Their imagination feeds on the legends and myths when they wander in the wild forest until they, themselves, become enchanted, become adrift from reality, and expect to find a path that leads to an airy castle in an azure sky, where soft music is playing, beautiful faeries smile and handsome, wise knights are in attendance.

Because they were very young and untainted by reality, Erwan and Annette could feel the magic around them as they sought adventure in the forest on a warm summer's day. They were walking lazily down a small cart track in a dense part of the woods, where the tree tops bent over and entwined into a canopy to protect the delicate forest flowers and small forest animals from the hot sun. Yet the sun found entrance here and there and cast beams of bright light down to the forest floor. Through the beams a myriad of small, almost invisible, insects played, and dust particles from ancient foliage, disturbed by the passage of the young people, swirled upwards then downwards bringing the beams to life.

Annette suddenly stopped in one of the sunlight shafts, held her arms out sideways and inclined her neck upwards so that her face received full illumination. Her little eyes were tightly shut, but as she stood bathed in warmth she relaxed her eyelids and let the whole of her twelve-year old body commune with the sun.

"Come on, Annette, or we'll never get there before dark, and you know you're scared of the dark," said Erwan.

"No I'm not," replied Annette, aggressively. "I just like to feel the sun's warmth. It makes the forest less spooky and the shadows less threatening."

"That's a big word for a little girl, 'threatening'."

"I know bigger words than that," retorted Annette.

"I bet you do, with your swanky Paris education and your posh parents. I bet you know all kinds of things, even though you're only twelve."

"Well, you're only one year older, Monsieur Big Boots Erwan."

"At least I don't think of the forest as spooky in the bad sense. Maybe it's full of spirits and faeries and animals that aren't really animals, but they are mainly friendly. They won't kill you."

"What do you mean, an animal that's not an animal?" said Annette, confused.

"If you see a white deer it may be Merlin in disguise, or it could be Vivian. Sometimes a white sheep will come from behind a big tree and push you to the ground, particularly if you happen to be drunk. It's happened to my dad a few times, least that's what he says," explained Erwan.

"I don't believe you," said Annette, incredulously.

"Well, I don't care whether you do or you don't. You're only French and I'm a Breton, and I know about these things."

Erwan was proud of his Breton heritage and of the Breton language which he could speak very well. His local schooling gave him knowledge of his ancestors, and he had a natural interest in history that reinforced his teaching. He knew the Bretons came from Celtic stock that went all the way back to 600 B.C. when the Celts arrived and called the Brittany peninsula Amor, meaning the country by the sea. In 56 B.C., he knew the Romans marched in and stayed for four hundred years, calling the land Amorica, before yielding to the immigration of thousands of British Celts in the 5th to 7th centuries A.D.. The British Celts came from Wales, Devon and Cornwall where they were subjected to brutal dominance by the Angles and Saxon invaders. As the population changed so the name of the land changed to the French word for Britain, namely, Bretagne; hence to Brittany and the calling of its inhabitants, the Bretons. Erwan had trouble remembering all the historical details of the next 1000 years for many rulers came and went, sometimes bringing destruction, sometimes renaissance and peace: Charlemagne; Nominoe of Vannes, Duke of Brittany; Erispoe, King of Brittany; Norsemen, raping and pillaging; King Alain Barb-Tort; the Montfort dukes; Duchess Anne of Brittany (and her French Kings, Charles VIII and Louis XII); the permanent reunion of Brittany with France in 1532 under Francois I.

Annette was not all that interested in the history of Brittany, but she sensed that Erwan was about to launch himself into a lecture on the subject so he needed some dissuasion.

"Come on Big Boots, see if the mighty Breton can catch the little French girl," said Annette, throwing down the gauntlet for a race through the woods.

She sped off down the path as fast as her legs could carry her, and those legs were deceptive. They were spindly legs, thin and not quite straight, but they were strong and fast and supported a body that was light and well coordinated. Her blonde hair was worn in plaits secured at the ends by rubber bands. A simple white cotton blouse and short black skirt were just right for a warm summer's day, and her dainty toes showed through open sandals. Erwan followed after her, but not so swiftly, for he wore the clothes of a working farm lad and carried a small pack on his back, containing cheese sandwiches, galette biscuits and a bottle of cider. He was planning on having a little picnic with Annette once they reached their destination which was the legendary spring at Barenton, the Fontaine de Barenton.

"Wait, Annette, wait! Don't get too far ahead or you'll get lost. You don't know the forest as well as I do. Wait, can't you!"

"You'll just have to go faster, Big Boots, if you want to catch me."

Annette suddenly swerved off the main path and made her own way through an undergrowth of large ferns and brambles, then around saplings and large pine trees. She was oblivious to the small scratches her legs received from thorns and broken branches protruding from tree trunks. She giggled as she went, and swished her plaits from side to side thinking what fun it was to lead Erwan a merry dance. She ran on and on, deeper and deeper into the ever enveloping forest, not knowing or caring where she was going. Suddenly Annette's progress was stopped by a stream, which was lucky for her because it made her pause and think what she was doing.

Well, I suppose I'd better wait here for Erwan, she thought. *He's a slowpoke. I can't even hear him yet.* She sat down on a grassy patch near the stream and moved her hands backwards and forwards through the cool water. So the minutes went by and still Erwan did not come. She heard no sound from the forest. *Where was he?*

"Erwan, Erwan! I'm over here. What's taking you so long? Has Merlin captured you? Erwan, Erwan!" she said with a hint of worry in her voice. But she told herself that there was nothing really to worry about. All she had to do was retrace her steps back to the main path. *Let me see*, she thought, *is it that way or the other way? It's that way*, she decided, and headed off with confidence, but a few minutes later she was back at the stream. *Well, then, it was the other way.* So she tried again, but with the same result; arrival back at the stream. It was now time to put a little panic into her voice.

"Erwan, Erwan, I need you! I'm lost! Help! I'm by a stream. Help me! Erwan." She continued to shout, to scream almost. Then she heard a faint "Hello", then another and another.

"Erwan, is that you? I can hear you. I'm over here." Her heart was still thumping in her chest but her thoughts had become calmer. *It's not my fault I got lost, it's Erwan's; he should have kept up with me. He's a silly boy!* But Erwan still did not appear. Then worry came again. *Perhaps that wasn't Erwan's voice I heard; perhaps it was a spirit of the forest, the ghost of a druid, an evil faerie, an angry Merlin. What shall I do? What shall.........* But she didn't finish that thought for suddenly a large ball of greenery bounded out of the woods onto the stream's bank with a ferocious, anguished cry.

"God help me! God save me!" shouted Annette, and tears started to well-up in her eyes as she thought her last moments on earth had come.

"It's me, it's me, Annette! Only me!" said Erwan, pulling back the large ferns that covered his face and upper body. "How do you like my disguise; a green forest demon? Got you scared, didn't I? That'll teach you to run away from me."

Annette became furious and launched herself at Erwan's waist sending him backwards into the stream. But her momentum also carried herself into the water, and there they sat for a few moments before they both burst out laughing. Then, good-naturedly, they started to splash one another until they were both thoroughly soaked and the laughter had abated. Slowly they stood up, grinning from ear to ear, happy to have found one another again.

"Come on, young lady," said a fatherly Erwan, "it's time to find the Fontaine de Barenton. Remember? That's what our hike is supposed to be about. Now follow me, and closely. Try not to make too much noise. This part of the forest is privately owned. Right now we're trespassing, and if we're caught, we'll be thrown into the dungeon of Comper Castle and die a horrible death."

"Well, that's better than being turned into a slimy toad by Merlin," retorted Annette. "Toads normally end up in the boiling water of a witch's cauldron."

Ten minutes later they came out of the darkness of the forest onto the public footpath. They found a sun-drenched patch and stood there awhile drying their damp clothes as they took a drink from the cider bottle in Erwan's pack. The soft scents of the forest, the stillness of the proud, towering trees and the lush green undergrowth took Annette into a magical world of nature, a connection to a higher being. She thought of her home in Paris with its bustling streets, stale smells, the clanging and banging noises of countless people. She preferred this beautiful forest, and thought Erwan was very lucky to live close by. Perhaps she should marry him, and then she could come and live on his farm and come into the forest every day. But, she was only twelve.

"We've still some way to go to the Fontaine so let's get a move on. Have you been there before?" asked Erwan.

"No, I haven't. Even though I've spent every summer vacation with Aunt Marie and Uncle Albert in Guillaume since I was seven, they never took me into the forest. I think they are a bit afraid of it."

"Grownups worry about the ghosts and the old stories they've heard," said Erwan, with a slight sneer in his voice.

"Tell me about some of the old stories, Erwan, the ones you don't believe in," requested Annette, "and especially the ones about the fountain we're going to see. Come on, Erwan, tell me, tell me!"

"I didn't say I didn't believe them. Some I believe, some I don't. Some people tell the story one way, and others tell it a different way. But you ask about the Fontaine de Barenton; what do you know already about its legend?" asked Erwan.

"Not much really, except that's where Merlin first met Vivian, and she was a pretty cunning lady and pinched all his spells and things."

"That's sort of true. But let's start at the beginning; first, who was Merlin. Some say he was the son of a royal nun, Princess of Dyfed, who lived in a monastery in Carmarthen, Wales, and at birth was given the Welsh name Myrddin."

"That can't be right," interrupted Annette, "nuns don't have babies."

"Well, they did back then, in the 6th century."

"Good grief, I bet they got into a lot of trouble," said Annette with astonishment. "So who was the dad?"

"It was either an angel or an incubus."

"What's an incubus? Something you ride in?" queried Annette.

"Don't be silly! It's an evil spirit that descends upon sleeping people, especially women, and has sex with them."

It took a full minute before Annette responded to that statement.

"Well, if you expect me to believe that, you're out of your mind. What a load of rubbish." Annette was more embarrassed than incredulous for she feared that Erwan might ask her if she knew what having sex meant. She was not one hundred percent sure; that was her problem, and such uncertainty can be embarrassing for a twelve-year old from sophisticated Paris talking to a country bumpkin.

"You don't *have* to believe it. Anyway, because Merlin had a supernatural father, he, himself, had supernatural powers. King Arthur of Britain was quick to make use of these special powers, so Merlin became his counselor and prophet; helped him unite and govern his country. He also persuaded Arthur to set up the Round Table and its Knights, then suggested that they should dash around the world looking for the Holy Grail. Merlin normally used his powers for the good, but sometimes life got on top of him. Then he liked to retreat into a forest and meditate. He really loved forests. That's why he came to Brocéliande; it drew him like a spiritual magnet, and here he met Vivian, The Lady of the Lake, and fell in love with her, totally and absolutely. Guess where they first met?"

33

"That's not hard to figure out; I'll say the Fontaine de Barenton," said Annette with surety.

"Right first time, and there it is, a few hundred yards more and we're there. I'll race you." They ran neck and neck for a way, but the speed and exuberance of Annette took her to the winning post first, where she stood breathless, hands on hips, and closely observed the fountain.

"Is that all there is to it, a group of old stones surrounding a pool with bubbles coming out of it?" exclaimed Annette, obviously very disappointed. "I expected a fountain gushing at least fifty feet high. Where's the magic? I don't see any, I don't feel any."

"Use your imagination. See the beautiful Vivian, only fifteen years old, a faerie from the Other World, maybe a Celtic water goddess, standing here tempting Merlin to tell her all his secrets, all his spells. And hear how he does just that, not all at once, but little by little over several visits, traveling to and fro between the Fontaine and King Arthur's Court. He relinquishes all his power to Vivian, even builds her a crystal palace that floats in the air and can be seen as a reflection in Lake Comper, if you're very lucky. Vivian is the love of his life, although, it is said, her love for him was not so strong. Then what does she do after sucking him dry of all his magic. How does she show her gratitude. She imprisons him in nine magical circles from which he cannot escape. That's a girl for you; can't trust 'em!

"You probably know all about her other tricks: her fancy sword Excalibur which she loans to King Arthur until his death, her being foster mother to Sir Lancelot who has his evil eye on Queen Guinevere, her trip to Avalon at Arthur's funeral. All standard legends."

"Certainly, I know about the Round Table and Excalibur. Who doesn't! But the Fontaine de Barenton, I did not know about. What else can you tell me?" asked Annette.

"The water from the fountain can cure madness, and people, over time, have come here to worship. So drink some; it'll stop you having silly moments."

"I don't have 'silly moments'. Drink some yourself! I'm not going to. With those bubbles coming up, it must be full of poison."

"OK, don't drink then, but splash some of the water on that stone platform. That's Merlin's perron."

"If I do, what will happen?" said Annette, quizzically.

"A big storm will come up and soak us."

"Well, that's just more rubbish," said Annette, chuckling, "but to prove it's rubbish, I'll do as you say." Annette bent over and scooped up handfuls from the fountain stream and threw them on the perron. "Now, we wait a few moments, and watch for thunder and lightning, and a howling gale with torrents of rain, I suppose." Annette folded her arms and, with a defiant stance, looked up through the trees to the sky. But the sky remained blue and cloudless.

"There, you see. Nothing! Not a drop. So much for the magic water and the magic perron. Rubbish!" declared Annette, strongly.

"Beware, the day is not over yet. Have patience." Erwan sat down on the perron, opened his pack and handed Annette a sandwich.

"Is this a magic sandwich, made by Merlin? Will it turn me into a faerie? I hope so because then I would seduce you and take all your cows and your pigs and your corn and lock you up in magical circles."

"Careful! If you're not a nice little girl I'll leave you here in the forest to rot. But before I do, there's something else I want to show you, one of my own secrets. We've got to go deeper into the forest to see it, and you mustn't tell anyone else about it, under penalty of death? Do you understand?"

Annette stared at Erwan for a moment, her eyes showing excitement and inquisitiveness at the thought of a new adventure. "I promise not to tell a soul, not a single one."

"Good, then we'll go in ten minutes. Here, have some more cider."

They traveled south east, deeper and deeper into the forest, sometimes taking small footpaths, sometimes making their own way through heavy undergrowth. Erwan worried that they were trespassing on private property and that ferocious dogs would seek them out at any moment. He dismissed his worries by damning the owners. *Why should these rich, upper class snobs have all the forest to themselves? Selfish pigs!* he thought. He had the makings of a good socialist.

After two miles they stopped in a clearing for a short rest and a drink. The going had been hard and even Annette, with her initial boundless energy, was beginning to flag. The summer afternoon was drawing to a mellow close. The forest light became a soft, misty gold where it broke through the branch canopy, and the shadows deepened, melding shapes into an impressionist painting. The air was still, at peace with all it touched, a soothing balm.

"Are we lost?" asked Annette, in an offhand manner, not wishing to show the small concern she had.

"Of course not! We're close now. Another five minutes or so," replied Erwan with assurance. "Come on, let's go."

Fifteen minutes later Erwan found the indicators he had been looking for; two small menhirs about twenty feet apart. "Come and look, Annette."

"What? These two big stones? Have we come all this way just to look at two tall stones? You're mad!"

"They are not just stones, they are menhirs, prehistoric stones, maybe placed here by druids as a monument to some special high priest. Menhir, a Breton and Welsh word, from 'maen', meaning a stone, and 'hir', meaning long. But you're from Paris, you wouldn't know that."

"Huh! You're not so smart. I'm learning Latin and Greek; far more useful than your silly old Breton language."

"Really! OK, say some Latin."

"Amo, amas, amat, amamus, amatis, amant. How about that!"

"What does it mean? Bet you don't know."

"Oh, yes I do, but I'm not going to tell you, so there," said Annette, pouting and frowning.

"Suit yourself. Anyway, we haven't come here just to see the menhirs. They are only markers for something big. Come and stand behind this first menhir and look over its top towards the second one; they are only about four feet high so even a little squirt like you can see over. Keeping the same line of sight, look beyond the far menhir. What does your eye come to?"

"Well, there is a big rock outcrop which you can see anyway without worrying about the menhirs. Lots of rocks; big ones, little ones, all piled up very high and partially hidden by young trees and gorse bushes."

"Exactly," said Erwan, "lots of rocks, so we need to pick one particular rock to find what we're looking for. OK, I'll stand behind you and show you what I mean. Line of sight, over the menhirs, passed the small beech tree, through the gap between the two bushes and then, bang, your eye hits a tall, smooth rock shaped like a bishop's hat. Got it?"

"Well, there are lots of rocks a bit like that. It's a bit confusing, but is it the one with a thin crack going across it about half way up?" asked Annette.

"Yes, that's it. Good! Now remember my method of finding it. You might need it one day. Follow me."

They walked over to the sighted rock as Annette's excitement mounted. *Is it hidden treasure; maybe a buried body; something really dangerous; something really nasty?* she asked herself. Erwan had a broad grin on his face as they stood before the rock, but Annette's expression was one of disappointment. *Was this another let-down like the Fontaine de Barenton?*

Erwan moved to the left side of the rock and started to clear away by hand a lot of loose small rocks, dead branches, and leaves piled up between the edge of his rock and the main rock outcrop, which was set back about two feet.

"What on earth are you doing, Erwan? You're like a big dog looking for a buried bone."

"You'll see in a minute. Hold on!"

Slowly an opening appeared, big enough for a man to get through. Erwan bent double and disappeared through the opening. Annette stood dumbfounded.

"Erwan, where've you gone? I can't see you. What's in there?" she asked anxiously.

Half a minute later Erwan re-appeared, a triumphant look on his face.

"It's my cave, a huge cave, a secret cave. I found it a couple of years ago. Great, isn't it? Go on through the opening; I'll follow."

Annette edged through the opening but after she was a few feet into the cave she stopped. She had stepped from the sunlight into almost perfect darkness. She could not see a thing; she felt unbalanced and more than a little scared. Then Erwan gave her a push in the back so that he could step in beside her.

"Let your eyes get used to the dark before going farther in, Annette. It's not so black as you think in here. The opening lets quite a lot of light in and there's another light source right at the end of the cave."

Slowly their eyes attuned, and Annette moved her head around to get a good look at her new surroundings.

"This is fantastic, Erwan! What a super hideout. The place is huge. Must be twenty feet to the roof and thirty feet wide. You could hide a whole band of robbers in here. How far back does it go?"

"I'll show you. Follow me and watch your step; there's a bit of a slope and mind you don't twist your ankle on all the small rocks."

The end of the cave was about one hundred feet in, ending abruptly in a smooth, vertical face, but with a hole going up through the roof down which a welcome beam of light shone.

"Good grief, it's even got its own chimney, and the sides are blackened. Someone must have had a fire in here," observed Annette.

"Right! It was me, and probably lots of other people have too over the past 8000 years. Look, there's a pile of wood left over from my last visit and some old newspapers to start a fire if we want one. Plus, if you put your hand up that crack in the wall behind the wood, you'll be able to feel some tin cans. My emergency food supply. See what a good Boy Scout I am; always prepared."

"Do you think druids lived in here? How about Merlin and Vivian? I bet they came in here to make love. Perhaps a wounded deserter from Napoleon's army used it and died a lingering death. Did you find any skeletons the first time you found the cave? Come to think of it, how did you know the cave was here?"

"Well, it was quite simple really. My grandfather and great-grandfather used to be iron ore miners in Brocéliande in the nineteenth century. Not only did they work the known mines around Paimpont and Les Forges, but they also went prospecting all over the forest looking for new sites. My grandfather kept a survey book showing all the places that had been checked out; it was like a detailed diary. My dad's got the book now and I've read all of it. Using the book, my dad and I have hiked around to several of the explored sites, and I've found a few all by myself. This cave was one of them. No seams of ore were found here, so it remained just a cave. The two menhirs were mentioned in the survey book, so they were the big clue that let me find the cave quite easily."

Annette was impressed by Erwan's detective work in finding the cave, and she began to think that he was a lot smarter than she had originally thought. She might even take him to Paris one day to meet her city friends.

Suddenly, the cave near the entrance seemed, momentarily, to be filled with light.

"What was that?" yelled Annette. "Don't tell me Merlin is about to appear." Then, a few seconds later, a low rumble was heard.

"Could be a late afternoon storm brewing," said Erwan. "I'll go to the entrance and take a look out. If it is a storm starting, we know who caused it, don't we Annette."

"What? No, no, don't be stupid. I know what you're thinking." They both went to the entrance quickly, their eyes now being totally adjusted to the cave's very dim light. Another flash and a louder rumble, then another and another.

They slipped through the entrance and looked towards the sky. It was darkening rapidly, and then the first rain drops fell, big ones. Another flash and two seconds later a hefty bang, rumble, bang. It was, indeed, going to be a powerful storm, courtesy of Annette.

"Now do you believe the tales I've been telling you? It was *you* who put the fountain water on the perron. It was *you* who made this storm," accused Erwan, but with laughter in his voice.

Annette looked at him seriously and for a few moments believed what he was saying. Then her face beamed with a huge grin as she canted it towards the heavens and let the cool rain bounce off her skin. It felt cleansing and pleasurable.

"Of course it was *I*! Didn't you know that Vivian and I are distant cousins? You be careful how you treat me in future or *I'll* lock you up in magic circles and leave you to rot," proclaimed Annette.

They stood in the rain and listened to the storm. The scents emanating from the forest changed from the dry, soft muskiness of summer to a more lively, fresh odor. Somewhere in the broad expanse of the forest, the lightning was picking out a proud, tall tree to strike and consume with fire. Maybe one close to them would fall victim and be enveloped in flames that would spread to neighboring trees. A raging forest fire might follow, unless the heavy rain immediately quenched the danger. They stood, with excited imaginations, until they were absolutely soaked and their bodies became chilled.

"Let's go back into the cave and warm up. I could light a fire. What do you say?" said Erwan.

"I agree. I'm starting to shiver. Do you have any matches though?"

"Of course, they're in my pack that I left by the wood pile. Didn't I say I was a good Boy Scout?"

"You certainly did! But if the matches don't work, I'll get Merlin to give us a hand. We know he and Vivian are around here somewhere."

They squeezed back through the cave entrance, found the wood, the paper and the matches and commenced to build a fire. After a little coaxing, the fire burned brightly, sending wisps of smoke to the ceiling and out through the natural chimney in the rock. Shadows from the wavering flames were cast onto the cave walls, making ever-changing phantom shapes in which they could see animals, dark castles, demons and frightening faces. Erwan and Annette sat close together in silence, steam rising from their drying clothes. They ate the last of their food and gulped down the last of their cider. They edged even closer together until their thighs and shoulders touched. Then Erwan put his arm around Annette's upper back and gave her a squeeze. She did not object, in fact, she enjoyed his closeness, and hoped the storm would not pass too quickly. She did not want to leave the cave or the forest yet.

* * * * *

At 5:0.a.m. Annette awoke with a start. She was confused. Was she a girl only twelve years old or was she a young woman of twenty-three? Had she just returned from Erwan's secret cave in the forest or did she help blow-up a German train the night before? The coldness of her bed returned her to reality. The cave was a dream, the train was not. The rest of her night was spent tossing and turning in fitful semi-consciousness. She worried what tomorrow would bring.

Chapter Six

As was usual after a train sabotage, the following day saw hordes of Germans scouring the surrounding countryside, woods and villages for saboteurs. Road blocks were set up, and anyone in a car, on a bicycle, on a horse or just walking was stopped for questioning and examination of their identification papers and any items they were carrying. Even children were stopped and searched on their way to school. This action traumatized some children, but others thought it just a big joke and made smart remarks to the German soldiers.

"What 'ave I got in me bag? Why, I've got a big bomb and if you open me bag, it'll blow your balls off." Such remarks were dealt with by at least a heavy smack across the child's head and a kick up the backside.

Annette had to go through a road block just fifty yards from her house as she bicycled to teach school. However, her obvious charms and feigned innocence got her through the block quickly, but not without a more than friendly pat on her bottom by a leering corporal. Her school bordered the village square of Guillaume, and she could easily have walked to it from her house, but Marcel wanted the Germans to get used to seeing her on a bicycle. Her Resistance work would take her to different villages in the area to meet others in the circuit for operation planning and to deliver liaison messages. Transportation by bicycle was ideal for this purpose, and a permit for its use had been easy to obtain.

As Annette cycled across the cobblestones of the village square she subconsciously scanned its surroundings to see if everything looked normal. The scene was barely lit by a low, watery sun somewhere in a steely-gray sky. She saw three women entering the most important shop on the square, la boulangerie, to get their daily ration of bread. Groceries were being unloaded from a van outside la épicerie. Father Nicholas was opening the heavy doors of St-Mark's church and looking for customers for the first mass of the day. A proud seagull, that had flown inland to escape bad coastal weather, sat perched on top of the majestic church spire, wondering where he should forage for food. The half-timbered, 18th century, Mayor's house already had its green shutters open and showed a light in a bedroom window. The other houses and shops around the square showed little or no signs of life. Annette thought how solid they looked with their walls made of granite or limestone, and frost-covered roofs of impermeable slate. Yes, at the moment everything looked normal, but no doubt German vehicles would soon be shattering the peace.

She arrived at the school at 7:55, five minutes before the official start time, yet ten children were already waiting in the playground outside the locked door, creating much noise and jostling one another to be first in line. Once inside the schoolhouse the children calmed down, and Annette sat at her desk, which was on a raised platform at one end of the room, and busied herself marking some composition papers written by the older students the previous day. The rest of the class arrived in ones and twos, each time allowing cold gusts of wind to chill the hallway and classroom as they opened and closed the main door.

The schoolhouse was a very simple one-room building, constructed in 1785 from pink granite that was obtained from the Côte de Granit Rose region along the north coast. The front of the school had four steps from its main wooden door down to the children's playground. Wrought-iron railings embedded in a low wall surrounded the playground, and a double iron gate opened out onto the village square. A small toilet was attached to the outside of the school building and a cold-water pipe and faucet stood close by. The water supply froze in the winter and ran dry in the summer, but, nevertheless, it was considered to be one of the grand amenities of the school. The only heating in the school was a portable, paraffin-burning, convection heater, but today it was not lit; the monthly ration of fuel had already been exhausted. The ages of the twenty-one students ranged from five to eleven, but because there was only one teacher and one classroom they all sat together. However, Annette had placed them according to four age groups so that she could conveniently teach them different subjects at different learning levels, simultaneously. It was not an ideal arrangement, but the children understood the difficulties and cooperated well.

Annette finished her marking and looked up to survey the class. It was a sad sight. The coldness in the room had turned the children's noses and earlobes blue, had stiffened their hands and legs and drained the luster out of their eyes. They were thin. They were hungry. They were barely clothed. Finger nails were dirty and faces unwashed. Mucous from runny noses had to be wiped on the sleeves of thinning woolen sweaters as no one possessed a handkerchief. And they all came from very poor families. Many had lost their fathers fighting the Germans in May 1940. Their future was uncertain at best and sure to be filled with pain, suffering and death.

Annette looked at each boy and envisaged him a young man in military uniform, for whether or not France and her allies won or lost the war, there would be other conflicts, other killings, other maimings. And the girls would become widows and don dark clothing as they worked and worked and worked to put bread on the table for their own children who, in turn, would go off to war. As in the past, so in the future. She felt heavy with sadness but somehow managed to urge a smile from her blue-tinted lips and get on with her task of teaching.

But first the attendance register had to be taken in the customary way by calling out each pupil's name in alphabetical order and waiting for the response. The tenth name on the register was Jacob Stein, and when Annette called his name there was no reply. She called it again and looked over to his desk. It was empty.

"Does anyone know where Jacob is? Has he gone sick? Has anyone brought a note from his parents?"

The class were silent. No one seemed to have any information about Jacob's whereabouts.

"Jules, you live next door to the Steins, don't you?"

"Yes, Mademoiselle Renard."

"Well then, surely you must know something?" insisted Annette.

"No, not really; I mean, not exactly," said Jules, hesitantly.

"That's not much of an answer. Either you do or you don't, which is it? There's nothing to be afraid of; I'm not going to bite you."

The class sniggered a little, and Jules felt the stare of their eyes as though they were condemning him for what he was about to say.

"At eight o'clock last night, I looked out of our window because I heard a truck. It stopped next door at the Steins, and four German soldiers got out and one man in a black coat." Jules went quiet.

"And what then, Jules? What happened next?" Annette asked the question although she feared she already knew the answer.

"There was banging and shouting next door. And I was a bit afraid. Then there was more banging and shouting, so I asked my dad what was going on in the Stein's house, but he just shrugged his shoulders. Some time later I heard noises in the street and I looked out of our window again. The Germans had flashlights and I could just see Jacob being pushed up into the back of the truck, followed by his mother and father. None of them wanted to go in the truck, but the soldiers had guns and were very rough with them. Monsieur Stein carried a small suitcase; and that's all I saw. The truck drove away, and then I was told to go to bed."

Annette sensed that several in the class had become uneasy, and she wanted to reassure them.

"Children, I'm sure the Steins will be back in a few days time. Monsieur Stein is a civil engineer and he is probably needed to solve some problems in Rennes. Please don't worry about them. They'll be all right"

"They won't be back, Mademoiselle Renard. They're Jewish," said a little girl in the front row. "My dad says they never come back."

Annette did not know how to answer that in a truthful way, for she, herself, did not know the real truth.

"Well, children, we're just going to hope that the Steins stay safe, and that we shall see Jacob again very soon." She knew it was important to carry on normally, so she completed calling the register in order to start the day's lessons.

"We're all going to do arithmetic today, but each group will have a different exercise to suit their level. The little ones will have small numbers to add and subtract, and the older ones some nasty multiplications. We'll take an hour doing this, and then we'll have a few of you come up to the blackboard and show your workings. Now doesn't that sound fun?" The response was a series of loud groans. "And if you all do well we'll go outside and have a game of football in the playground to warm you up. What do you say to that?" This time the response was mixed, some cheers, some further groans.

Paul Chrétien put his hand up to speak. "Yes, Paul?"

"Mademoiselle, it's freezin' out there, and my maman says that I must not cut my knees on the cobblestones playin' games, and she gets very cross when I do 'cause we don't have no more bandages."

"Paul, you should say, 'we don't have any more bandages', not, 'no more bandages'," corrected Annette. "And since when has a little cold weather stopped us having fun outside? You can be the referee, Paul, then your delicate knees won't get hurt."

Annette walked around the class distributing the arithmetic exercise papers and pencils. The papers were on the point of disintegration, they having been used and erased a dozen times or more, and most of the pencils were mere stubs. Even so, to use paper and pencils was a luxury; more often than not chalk-on-slate was the writing medium. The children settled down quickly and their numb little minds were bent to solving the mysteries of mathematics.

Annette busied herself preparing further future lessons, but her mind was not wholly concentrated. She could not help thinking of the inconvenience and, for some, the terror of having to go through a road block. Some of the locals would be detained because their papers were not up to date, or incomplete, or maybe even false. Then they would be taken to the Gestapo offices in Rennes and interrogated for hours, sometimes days.

She thought of Marcel and Erwan; *had they got back to the farm safely. What of hostages? Had the Germans already randomly picked some men and women, young and old, to be threatened with execution if someone did not come forward to reveal the saboteurs. Maybe a collaborator was, at this very minute, sealing the fate of Marcel and Erwan. Perhaps I'll be implicated as well.*

An hour had just past by when Annette heard some kind of vehicle screech to a halt outside the school. She walked to the window and saw a Kubelwagen - a jeep-like vehicle - with three German soldiers and an officer in it. In addition, there was a black Citroën pulled up behind the transport. Her heart starting pounding as she feared the worst, but she returned to her desk and took some deep breaths to calm herself. Two of the soldiers took up a guard position by the Kubelwagen; the officer entered the playground, came up the steps and into the schoolhouse. He walked down one of the aisles between the apprehensive children, gave Annette a military salute, *not* a political 'Heil Hitler', and announced himself.

"Mademoiselle, I am Major von Kruger, administrative commander of the German Army for this district, at your service. May I speak to your pupils?"

Annette was taken aback by his politeness. He was handsome, young and had a kindly smile. His good French accent indicated a higher education. "Well, yes, I suppose so, but speak slowly. Their Breton is good but not all of them are fluent in high French yet."

"Thank you." He turned to face twenty-one pairs of staring, frightened eyes.

"Children, I want to speak to you about a very bad thing that happened last night. One of our trains carrying important German goods was blown-up by some wicked men, some terrorists. They killed innocent soldiers and also two of your countrymen who were driving the train. We have to try and catch these people, so that they'll not do such a terrible thing again. Will you help me? I really want you to help me. It is a big job for me to do alone. So what do you say?"

The children continued to stare but gave little indication of understanding what von Kruger was talking about. "Did any of you hear the explosions? Did you look out of your bedroom windows and see any men running after the big bangs? What did your mother and father say about it this morning at breakfast? Anyone? Anything?"

After several seconds an eight-year old boy put his hand up to speak. He had a brazen look on his face and his lower jaw was set out in a defiant fashion, as though someone had dared him to respond to the German.

"I 'eard the big bangs, sir. They woke me up, but when I looked out the window I saw nothin'. It was black and pourin' with rain. How d'yuh 'spect us to see anythin' in that weather? You're not thinkin' straight, sir. And this mornin', not at breakfast, cause there weren't any, me dad says that was a grand 'splosion and 'ow we needed a lot more like that to get rid of the Nazis, and then he said ...." but the boy was interrupted by Annette.

"Fine, Pierre, that'll be enough."

Von Kruger looked sternly at Pierre for a while then slowly put his hand in his great-coat pocket and took out a small package. He walked up to Pierre's desk as the class remained frozen expecting physical punishment of some kind, and threw the package onto the desk.

"Breakfast for you, Pierre; six pieces of chocolate, courtesy of the German Army," said von Kruger with a gentle smile. "Does anyone else want any breakfast, but the information needs to be better than Pierre's to get it?...... No?...... No more brave boys?...... How about a brave girl then?...... No?...... In that case I'll leave you to your charming teacher. Good morning, children." Von Kruger, still smiling, left the schoolhouse swiftly.

Annette sidled over to the window to watch the Germans leave. But they did not, even though von Kruger and the soldiers climbed back into the Kubelwagen. Instead, another man, a civilian in a black leather overcoat, got out of the Citroën and approached von Kruger. Soon they were arguing fiercely then the civilian threw up his arms and headed for the school. He crashed through the main door into the hallway and then flung open the classroom door. Annette instantly knew who he was as he stood smirking inside the door. Gestapo! She shuddered inwardly. There was going to be trouble. She just knew it. How could she protect the children?

Like von Kruger, the Gestapo man, Hauptsturmfuhrer Eichmann, put his hand in his pocket, but instead of chocolate he took out a leather strap with a heavy brass buckle on the end of it. He proceeded down towards Annette between the desks, and at each desk he raised the strap and brought it crashing down with the buckle making a sickening impact, metal on wood, and in some cases, metal on flesh, for some children's hands were not removed quickly enough as they were approached from behind. Each time the strap flashed through the air he shouted, "I want information, I want information!" Many of the younger children started to cry, some screamed out as their small bodies trembled in fright.

Annette's anger was immediate; the blood rushed to her face and took adrenaline to every part of her body. She ran to the man like an unleashed lioness defending her cubs, roaring as she went, "Stop that you bastard! Stop it! Stop it, I say or I'll kill you." And she meant it.

She launched herself at the man with flailing arms and kicking legs. She connected with his left shin and made a grab for the strap which she succeeded in wrenching from his hand, causing the buckle to scratch his palm and draw blood. He recovered from the swiftness of her attack and went on the offensive. First, he pushed her away from him with an ugly snarl, then he stepped towards her, grabbed her left arm, spun her around and took hold of her hair with a vicious jerk, snapping her head back. Holding onto her hair and twisting her left arm behind her back he marched her to the far wall in front of the class. Her chin hit the wall with a crack, causing the teeth in her lower jaw to cut into her upper lip. The children let out a loud gasp, and three of the older boys ran forward and started pummeling the man in the back, but their small fists had little effect. Suddenly the man stiffened as he felt someone grab the back of his shirt collar and twist it until he started choking.

"Let the girl go, Eichmann, or I'll break your neck! This really isn't the way to get cooperation out of these children or their teacher. Try using a little intelligence, a little subtlety. I know it's hard for people like you, but try. Now I don't want to pull my gun on you but I will if I have to." Eichmann released his hold on Annette and turned to face von Kruger. "Good. Now we're both going to walk quickly but calmly out of here, and these children will not be interrogated again. Got it? So you go first; move!"

As von Kruger moved away he turned his head towards Annette and quietly said, "I'm sorry, Mademoiselle, for this incident. There is no excuse for it."

Annette did not respond but licked the warm sweet blood trickling down from her upper lip as she sat down at her desk and looked caringly at the children. Then she remembered that some of them had hurt fingers, slashed by Eichmann's strap. She took a small first-aid tin from her desk and went to examine their wounds. Ointment and a plaster made the wounded feel better, but all of them were badly shaken by the event. Their faces were white, their eyes disturbed and a few were still quietly sobbing. Annette tried to cheer them up.

"Right class, what's the good thing that's come out of the last ten minutes? Let's ask Pierre. Pierre, do you still have the chocolate, or is all of it already in your tummy?"

"I've still got it, Mademoiselle Renard. I was going to take it home to my family."

"That's a good boy, Pierre, but because your classmates are very upset right now, how would you like to share the six pieces with them? What do you say? Good idea?"

"Well," said a very reluctant Pierre, "I suppose I could, but how are we going to cut six bits into twenty-one bits. Don't you think that's too difficult?"

"Thank you, Pierre, and don't worry about the cutting; I've got just the thing in my desk for that little job. Class, give Pierre a cheer for being so kind." The cheering and the chocolate eased the children's trauma, even though the amount of chocolate per child was barely visible.

Word spread quickly through the village about the trouble at the school. Soon mothers were in the schoolhouse, reassuring their children and themselves that everything would be all right. Even some shop-keepers arrived bringing treats; small loaves of bread, a few apples, a dozen carrots. The trauma past and the schoolday continued.

Chapter Seven

That evening, as Annette and her aunt, Marie, sat down to a bowl of thin potato soup, Annette broached the subject of armed resistance to see how Marie would react.

"Last night's saboteurs are going to get us all killed. Did you hear that the Nazis have taken five people hostage in Basbijou? If the saboteurs don't give themselves up within forty-eight hours, they're going to start shooting the hostages," said Annette.

"Well, that's their standard practice. That's the price we have to pay for hitting back," responded Marie. "It's the new warfare; everyone is in it, soldier and civilian alike. If I were a bit younger I'd join the Resistance myself."

"Really? Would you? Well, I'm not so sure. The Resistance member is classed as a hero; the civilian hostage dies almost incognito. They don't go into the history books."

"So what," said Marie, "the dead can't read their own epitaphs. It's not important. All I know is, if your Uncle Albert were still alive, he'd join the Resistance without blinking an eye. He was a feisty old man, as well you know. He would consider this war just a continuation of the 1914 to 1918 slaughter in which he did more than his fair share. Wounded three times and almost gassed to death. He had no love for the Germans."

Annette thought Marie had made her views on the Resistance clear enough, but before she could ask her next question, Marie said, "If *you* were in the Resistance I'd say good luck to you. Well, who am I kidding; I already know you're in it. Why else would you get up in the middle of the night then return several hours later, and leave a trail of mud and leaves all the way up the staircase carpet. You've got to cover your tracks better than that or the Gestapo will grab you in no time at all."

Annette gave a deep chuckle and was relieved, but surprised, to know that she had her aunt's support even though her knowing made her, effectively, an accomplice and put her in danger. Why her aunt was so supportive mystified Annette considerably. Most women of Marie's age who had lived through the Great War, particularly the 630,000 French war widows, were still exhausted from the anguish, the sadness and the futility of those dark years.

On June 28, 1914, Gavrilo Princip, a member of a small group of Serbian nationalists, assassinated the heir to the Austro-Hungarian throne, Archduke Franz Ferdinand and his wife in Sarajevo, the Bosnian provincial capital. This was an act of defiance by a small political group against the oppressiveness of the Austro-Hungarian Empire. The Austrian government blamed the Serbian government for this belligerent act, and sought the support of the German government. The German government was not all that concerned until the Russians became upset at the treatment of their ally, Serbia. But France was an ally of Russia and Britain was an ally of France, all sealed by formal alliances. After Austria declared war on Serbia on July 28, Russia began to mobilize which caused Germany to do the same thing. The guns were pointed and loaded when Austria declared war on Russia on August 5, followed by Britain and France declaring against Germany and Austria on August 12. The Great War had commenced, but the old men of wisdom and courage in the warring governments and armies, had forgotten, by this time, what had started the conflict that quickly became a colossal tragedy. The crime in Sarajevo could have been simply settled locally by suitable punishment of the terrorists. The war could have been stopped before it even started, but national pride got in the way of commonsense. Pride, diplomatic bungling and arrogance killed 1,718,000 Germans, 1,700,000 Russians,

1,200,000 Austro-Hungarians, 1,385,000 French and 703,000 British before the war whimpered into an armistice. Annette remembered how sick she had felt at the grotesqueness of these numbers when first she researched them for a history paper at university. The numbers of the dead, when added to those of all the other nations of the world involved, amounted to a mountain range of corpses; nearly 8 million killed. The total number of wounded amounted to a staggering 21 million. Of these, thousands were doomed to spend the rest of their miserable lives without limbs, without eyes and with gasping, gassed lungs that barely functioned. On top of this horror were the civilian casualties from direct action, disease and privation. The carnage was so great that the exact numbers will never be known. Madness, total madness. Annette feared that the lessons of history had not been learned; that the age of slaughter continued, unabated; and she was being caught up in it.

* * * * *

A few miles away at Erwan's farm, Erwan and Marcel were having a conversation in the hayloft about Annette's suitability to be a Resistance member.

"I don't think she's going to be any good," said Marcel, "in fact, I think she'll be a grave liability if we keep her on."

"That's a bit strong," responded Erwan. "We haven't given her much of a chance yet; one operation, that's it. What exactly worries you?"

"She seems to treat our work as a bit of a joke. She's not serious enough and because of that she could get other members of the circuit killed. How would she stand up under torture by the Gestapo? Would she crack straight away? Does she have determination? Does she hate enough? And she's had no military training; never fired a Sten or a revolver, or stuck a knife into anyone. That's what worries me."

"Well, come on Marcel, lack of training is not her fault, and that can be easily rectified. Remember, I was very green six months ago. I think her attitude last night was more nerves than flippancy. She joked around a bit to hide her true feelings. And as for coping with torture, well, who knows how any of us would react. You and I haven't had to face that test yet, thank God. No, I think she's got potential, and I know she's brave when she has to be; remember, we've grown up together. She's a tomboy, a daredevil."

"OK, maybe you've made some good points. I'll give her a couple of months. We'll get her on three or four more operations and then decide her future. Also, she needs to work with some other groups in our circuit so I can get their opinions of her. But before that, give her some arms training. I don't want her going on another operation defenseless.

"On another subject, I've got to go away for a few days and I don't want to tell you exactly where, for security reasons. But the thrust of the trip is to try and improve relations and communications between the many different Resistance groups and circuits. Things are getting fouled up. We've got de Gaullists and communists antagonizing one another, competing for the same arms drops, not sharing information and even falsifying it just to get ahead. Different source reports getting back to London about the same troop and material movements are contradictory. It's a mess and it's got to be rectified. We've got to keep politics and petty jealousies out of all operations, or we're all dead.

"Now I can't tell you any more at present, so I'm going to the kitchen to scrounge a little dinner from Claudette and then hit the sack. Last night was a long night, and I'm going to slip away before dawn. I hope to God that this lousy weather improves."

"*Bonne chance*, Marcel! Tell my wife I'll be over shortly to sup on whatever is left after you've gorged yourself."

Erwan was left alone in the hayloft, which also served as the hiding place for the group's guns, ammunition and explosives. André kept his transceiver and repair kit in another undisclosed place; extreme secrecy was one of

André's idiosyncrasies. Erwan pushed aside some bales of hay and retrieved the arms cache stored in a World War One metal ammunition box. He lovingly took out his Sten gun, and although he hadn't fired it on the previous night's operation, he nevertheless thought he'd strip it and clean it. Gun cleaning was his obsession. He had to strain his eyes to accomplish this task, for the only light that he had came from a weakly-spluttering hurricane lamp.

* * * * *

Outside, the weather over Brittany provided a clear but windy night with a waxing moon, still small but adequate for aiding the passage of bomber pilots. To the north, squadrons of the RAF and Coastal Command were flying over the English Channel on their way to bomb the German battlecruisers Scharnhorst and Gneisenau and the heavy cruiser Prinz Eugen, all confined to the docks at Brest. Starting in March 1941, over 300 bombing raids would be made on these battleships, damaging them but not destroying them. The RAF were so persistent because the Scharnhorst and Gneisenau had played havoc with convoys of Allied merchant shipping crossing the Atlantic to keep Britain alive and fighting.

Another group of RAF bombers was flying over the Brittany countryside just west of Rennes, on their way to bomb the port and U-boat base at St. Nazaire.

Claudette stepped outside the kitchen door to listen to the steady, deep drone of the planes and to watch their silhouettes form as they were caught in the moonlight, restless hunters in search of a quarry. She knew they would suffer in their quest and many would not return. The aircrews would sit in their shaking coffins, some terrified, some resigned to their fate, as they ran the gauntlet of exploding flak and screaming German night-fighters. She sensed the hell the combatants went through night after night, and wondered why it had come to this. *Why could not all these young men, on both sides, just stay at home with their wives and sweethearts? Why do they listen to the rantings and ravings of politicians and militarists? Don't any of them read history?* Her thoughts were confused and sad.

She stayed outside until the droning faded away. *Poor St. Nazaire, would anything be left of it after the war,* she wondered.

Chapter Eight

In the following weeks Erwan trained Annette in the practical details of sabotage and subterfuge. She learned quickly how to handle a Sten gun, a revolver and a knife. Although there was little ammunition available for mere practicing, she showed she was able to hit a one-foot diameter target at fifty yards consistently with the Sten, standing up and lying down. So as not to draw attention to herself, she mainly just fired single shots at the edge of the woods, so that the noise would be construed by the Germans as someone out shooting rabbits. Erwan taught her a few judo throws, how to stick a knife up under the ribs into the heart with a clean, forceful thrust, and the gentle art of garroting with rope or wire. Although she practiced the latter with relish on a gatepost, Erwan feared that her small height would make this maneuver disastrous should she actually have to perform it on a person.

Marcel knew that, although Annette had learned good basic skills, one day she would need to go to England to receive far more detailed training if she were to become a top class field agent. But for now, as a supporting member of a sabotage group, she had enough knowledge to allow her a fighting chance of survival.

Annette's early equivocation about becoming a Resistance fighter was settled early in December when she received a sad letter from her mother in Paris. Her father had been taken away by the Nazis to perform forced labor in a factory somewhere in Germany. His crime was a nebulous 'political agitation and communist sympathies'. Annette knew that the chances of seeing him alive again were very slim. It was common knowledge that older men did not last very long performing hard physical labor on the meager food rations given to them. Her sorrow quickly turned to anger, and her anger to hate. She was ready to enter Resistance work with determination and a thirst for vengeance.

On December 7, 1941, the Japanese made a grave mistake; they bombed Pearl Harbor, causing a state of war to exist between them and the United States from that date forward. The sleeping giant became truly awake. Then on December 11, Hitler declared war on the United States, and on December 12 the US Congress voted unanimously for total war against Germany and its ally Italy. The dogs were loose.

The people of Brittany rejoiced at the news, for they had longed for America to enter the war ever since September 1939. French faces brightened in the shops, in the cafés, in the bars. Smiles were seen and laughter heard, even in the presence of Germans. But Hitler knew that America was not yet a strong military power, and he was convinced that he could conquer Russia before having to deal with a serious threat from the western allies. Success in his North Africa campaign was also boosting his confidence of invincibility. But good news for the Nazis made them a more dangerous enemy to the French civilians. They assumed they were all powerful. They could do whatever they liked. They were masters, all other people were slaves. The Gestapo became more brutal, more sadistic, and what little honor was left in the occupying Wehrmacht could not counteract the inhuman nature of the Nazi thugs.

Chapter Nine

Christmas Day, 1941, and snow lay on the ground in Brittany providing a soft, clean tranquillity to the countryside. Around Erwan's farm the sun's radiance sparkled on frost-covered walls and gates, and glinted through icicles hanging from gutters and tree branches. The sunlight was warm enough for the cows to be outside their barn either feeding directly on bales of hay or foraging through the snow for juicy blades of grass. But inside the farmhouse it was far from warm, except, that is, in Claudette's kitchen.

Today there would be a holiday celebration, no matter how meager the foodstuffs, the wine and the gifts. Erwan and Claudette were to throw a Christmas party to which Annette, Aunt Marie, Marcel and André were invited.

The guests arrived at three o'clock, and while Claudette was putting the finishing touches to the dinner preparations in the kitchen, in the lounge Erwan produced some homemade alcoholic cider that quickly loosened tongues, although André's, as usual, was mainly motionless. As the cider was being drunk, Claudette entered the lounge with a plate full of her specialty, savory crêpes. These were consumed in no time at all, and Annette asked whether there were anymore. Claudette flushed a little at this discourteous remark and said, "Sorry, supplies are limited; don't you know there's a war on." The group fell silent for a few moments after this reminder, but Erwan quickly rectified that by recharging their glasses with more cider whose supply did not cause a problem.

To add tradition and color to their little party group and to give a sense of local and national identity, Erwan had requested that the ladies wear Breton costumes. This they did, as far as they were able. Marie's costume was a family heirloom, a full-length, red velvet dress, with a large vee-neck that showed a white cotton under-blouse. The vee-neck, hem and sleeve cuffs were adorned with exquisite embroidery of a most intricate black and gold pattern. Upon her head she wore a delicate lace coiffe, covering the top, back and sides and tied under her chin. This garment was over two hundred years old, and had been worn by Marie's ancestors at pardons and weddings, a pardon being a religious festival honoring a local saint at which indulgences would be given to pardon the sins of the past year.

Annette wore a simpler traditional dress of blue cotton and with embroidery only around the sleeve cuffs; a typical peasant's costume. Upon her head she had a white linen coiffe, and white shoulder protectors spread out like small wings from around her neck to the top of her upper arms. Her feet were tortured in a pair of wooden clogs, although these were quickly discarded for sturdy but comfortable winter shoes. To emphasize her peasant nature she had tied a string of onions to a tasseled cord that was wrapped around her waist. But the onions were also soon discarded and taken into their rightful place in the kitchen.

Claudette also had a very fine Breton costume which she went and changed into after she had finished preparing the dinner. Hers was fairly similar to Marie's except the front of the dress was protected by a pretty silver pinafore and she wore a linen coiffe not a lace one.

When Erwan decided that enough cider had been con-sumed, he requested everyone to go into the dining room and be seated. Then, with just the right amount of ceremony, Claudette carried the entrée and vegetables from the kitchen to the table. These consisted of two small chickens on separate plates, a bowl of mashed potatoes, one of runner beans from the summer crop that had been pickled, and one of turnips. Two small dishes of Claudette's special but undefined sauces and a bowl of gravy stock were available, as desired, to add piquancy to the chicken. It was not a meal fit for a king or even a court jester, but, given the times, Erwan and Claudette felt proud that they were able to entertain in such a manner. Erwan sat at the top of the long oak dining table, Marcel on his right, Annette his left, with Marie, André and Claudette at the other end. Erwan carved the chickens and poured the wine, a Sauvignon Blanc from the Loire that he had been hoarding since 1938. Claudette said a very quick and perfunctory grace, and then everyone devoured the dinner in absolute silence. Once it was established that not a morsel of food remained, and after a replenishing of wine glasses, the conversation started to flow, with Marie's voice being the predominant player. They talked of childhood, of peacetime vacations, of politics, of heroes and heroines, of cows and sheep, of love and death; everything except the Resistance.

Claudette did her share of talking, but in the process seemed to stare, alternately, at Annette and then at Erwan, as though she wanted to ask them something not related to the topic at hand, something more personal. What kind of question was she afraid to ask. The observant Marcel picked up on this tension in Claudette, even though his brain was more than a little alcoholic. Suddenly Claudette broke through her fear, and, flashing her eyes from one to the other, asked Annette and Erwan if they would like to revisit the time when they were sweethearts. Annette blushed and Erwan looked uncomfortable.

So that's it, thought Marcel, *Claudette is actually a little jealous, even now years later, of their childhood romance. Is this going to be a problem? I mean, we've got to work together, out there, where emotions mustn't get in the way of the job.....But that explains some of the dirty looks Claudette gave me when I kept on throwing them together on training exercises in the forest....No, no, you're reading too much into a few furtive glances and what might be just an innocent question. Claudette is a lot more mature than you're thinking. Let it go! Don't worry, at least, not yet.*

"Of course I'd like to go back to that time," said Annette, "who wouldn't, but not just because of the family fun with Erwan, because of the whole carefree, happy world of that period. Good God, look where we are today! Who likes the present times; they stink, they stink." Claudette gave an unsure smile and wished someone would change the subject. Erwan did.

"Come on people, don't go morbid on me. We're having a good time right now, aren't we, *aren't we?* For heaven's sake let's not get nostalgic. To get you smiling again we're going to have a musical interlude, this very moment, after which Claudette, my beautiful, loving wife, will go into the kitchen and make some of her scrumptious dessert crêpes. How about that? All in favor say 'aye'!" Everyone responded 'aye' to Erwan.

He got up from the table, went to his bedroom and came back with two of his prized, old-fashioned musical instruments, a biniou and a bombarde. The former instrument is a member of the bagpipe family, and the bombarde is a little like an oboe. Typically, it supports the biniou by playing the melody of the piece being performed an octave lower.

Erwan handed the bombarde to André and together they tuned up, standing well back from the top of the table. Smiles quickly spread across the faces of the audience, and, jokingly, Annette put two fingers in her ears. The musicians agreed on what pieces of Breton folk music they should play, and the concert began. It was tuneful music, even though the biniou was a droning instrument like other forms of bagpipes, and a few missed notes turned into squeaks. Their repertoire was exhausted after eight pieces, so then it was repeat time but with a difference. Erwan handed out copies of the words to the folk songs they had just played, and urged everyone to sing along, in the original Breton language of course. Marcel, being from the south, did not know Breton so he murdered the difficult words, but nobody cared. They all sang lustily, and as one of several encores, Erwan and André formed the head of a procession and led the group, playing and singing, around the room, then into all the other rooms of the farmhouse. They returned to the dining room out of breath, a little hoarse, but glowing with warmth and happiness.

As they rested back on their chairs, Claudette went smiling to the kitchen to make the promised dessert crêpes. Fifteen minutes later she reappeared holding high a plate of the sweetest things on earth, and was greeted with a loud cheer. Erwan magically produced a bottle of dessert wine, Quarts de Chaume of the Coteaux du Layon, to go with the crêpes, and all was contentment. However, one important item was missing; there was no coffee to bring the meal to a conclusion.

More conversation flowed so easily that nobody noticed the time until André suddenly said, "It's seven o'clock; past curfew and I'm in trouble. I must leave immediately."

"Since when did missing curfew bother you, André?" said Erwan. André responded with just a grunt, rose from the table somewhat unsteadily and gave thanks to Claudette and Erwan for a Christmas Day that he would long remember.

"Good God!" said Marie. "You think you've got a problem, André. I've just realized we've missed the last bus to Guillaume. Now what do we do? We don't have our bikes here. Erwan, you're a kind man with a truck. Can you run us home?"

"I'd love to but my tank is just about empty, and you can't buy gasoline on Christmas Day."

"Claudette, you're stuck with Annette and me for the night. So who's going to sleep with whom?" said Marie, with a small giggle.

Claudette did not respond immediately, so Marie provided the solution. "I know, Annette can sleep with you and Erwan and I'll snuggle in with Marcel. That's a good way to keep warm. Perfect!"

Claudette reddened as she took Marie seriously. "No, that is not a good arrangement. I will not have Annette in our bed. That is stupid. Annette can sleep on the sofa in here and we can put a straw mattress down for you, Marie, in the attic. I have plenty of spare blankets."

"I like Marie's idea better," said Erwan, grinning from ear to ear. "Two women around me will double the warmth, and who knows what it'll lead to; all kinds of possibilities."

"Oh, no, Erwan, that will not be, and that's final. Annette sleeps on the sofa," said Claudette, raising her voice in agitation."

"OK, OK, it was just a joke, a little Christmas friendliness," retorted Erwan. "Let's go and see André off."

André went out of the kitchen door, mounted his bicycle and set off without lights across the farmyard in a precarious state of instability. After five wheel rotations he crashed, skidding on some very juicy cow dung. A stream of abuse thundered loudly into the night air, which was repeated again when André placed his left hand firmly into the offending dung as he heaved himself off the cobblestones. The scene was witnessed by the others standing at the farmhouse windows, and the amused group gave an encouraging cheer when André finally regained his composure, remounted his trusty steed and made it out of the courtyard into the lane.

"Where is André headed to tonight?" asked Marie.

"That is unknown," said Marcel, somberly. "He keeps on the move; that's why he's still alive."

"Come on everyone, back to the table, there's more cider to be drunk, games to play and love to be made," said Erwan with a laugh, as he pinched Annette's backside. But the day's festive spell had been broken with André's departure as most of the remaining group thought of his dangerous ride back to his present home. There would be patrols out looking for curfew breakers. He could easily be shot in the darkness by a trigger-happy, scared German soldier.

Marcel and Erwan turned serious and played a game of chess; Marie fell asleep in an armchair; Annette found a book to read while Claudette busied herself in the kitchen, washing dishes, cleaning the floor and feeling depressed.

By ten o'clock everyone had gone to bed or their makeshift resting place. But by midnight Annette was still awake;

the sofa had broken springs and was very narrow. As the house cooled, Annette started to shiver and shake. *To hell with this!* she said to herself, wrapped the moth-eaten blanket around her and went in search of Marcel's bedroom. Marcel was also restless and immediately heard the latch on his door click as Annette entered. Within five seconds she had located his bed in the small room and hovered by his side. He knew who it was because her blonde hair harbored small pieces of light gathered from stars reflected through the uncurtained window pane.

"What do you want?" whispered Marcel.

"I want warmth and anything else you've got to offer," replied Annette, with distinctly accentuated chattering teeth.

Marcel lay still, pondering the situation. If she entered his bed, he would be breaking one of his own golden rules, and there would be no going back. If she did not, she would hate him in the morning, and anyway he could already feel his passion rising. Annette settled the matter for him as she lifted up the bedclothes and slipped in beside him. He did not object.

Chapter Ten

Communication between Resistance members was always a problem. Using the telephone was dangerous; sending letters or leaving notes with a third person was equally dangerous. Face to face verbal communication of the next Resistance activity and its planning details carried the least risk, but was by no means foolproof. A meeting between members had to look as though it were a natural occurrence, carrying no clandestine overtones. Care in selecting the place and the time was paramount. A village café and bar was a good place because it was a public rendezvous where locals went on a regular basis to follow innocent pastimes, like playing chess or cards, talking about farm matters or family problems. Marcel, Erwan, André and Annette used a café in Guillaume and one in Basbijou as their meeting places, although Marcel, more often than not, just gave Erwan information and instructions while working together at the farm to pass onto the others. The café in Guillaume was called La Chatte and the one in Basbijou Le Chien. La Chatte was situated on the village square, close to the church, and Le Chien was next to la boucherie, the butcher's shop, in a street that joined Basbijou's square. Both places had owners who, it was thought, could be trusted implicitly, but that was not the case with all of their customers.

In 1941 certain Bretons were still members of the pro-fascist political party called PNB, Parti National Breton, which wanted a Brittany independent from France and saw the German invasion as a means to an end, at least initially before the Nazis committed brutal crimes against the Breton populace. It was important to know who was or had been a PNB member in your village, and whether they were in earshot of your conversation in the café. Also there might be other informers in your vicinity, paid by the Gestapo, or being blackmailed to provide information in order that a son would not be sent to a forced labor camp in Germany. So conversation needed to be guarded, if not actually in code, with important items being given quickly in a whisper.

Noon, on Saturday, January 3, 1942, saw Erwan and André sitting at a table in Le Chien playing chess while Annette looked on. They each had a glass of hot cider beside them, and Annette was smoking a Gauloise. There was little heat in the café, requiring the door to be firmly closed most of the time. It was almost full, so the noise level from all the conversations and the clatter from activity in the kitchen was quite high. A fourth person was sitting at Erwan's table, Maurice, a middle-aged man, dressed in farm overalls with an undersized black beret jauntily resting on his head. He talked in quick, witty one-liners and simple-minded puns that disturbed the players but made Annette giggle almost the whole time.

"You know why the queen can move in any direction over many squares?" asked Maurice.

"Shut up!" growled Erwan.

"Yes, I thought you'd want to know; because she's just had a one-knight stand and needs to quickly find a bishop to hear her confession."

"Ha, ha, ha!" sneered André, but Annette laughed and gave Maurice a playful dig in the ribs.

Encouraged, Maurice then asked, "Now, how about the king, why can he only move one square at a time?" Both André and Erwan looked up from their game with evil eyes.

"You're asking for trouble, Maurice," said Erwan. "And there's an arms drop, Sunday, tomorrow, 2:0 a.m.," continued Erwan in a whisper.

"No, you've guessed wrong, you big clown. It's because in the queen's eyes he's just a mere pawn and needs to be confined to his castle."

"Good, very good, Maurice!" said Erwan, with a forced laugh. "And let's hear some more laughter from you Annette; those two krauts in the corner are looking this way." And then, very quietly, "Get your group to my farm by 1:0 a.m., Maurice. Bring ten fully armed men."

Annette laughed as commanded and even pretended to wipe a tear from her eye as her laughter subsided. Then under her breath she said, "Don't you mean fully armed men *and women?*"

Erwan picked up on the comment. "If you do bring women, make sure they've got some pretty big muscles; we'll be lifting and lugging some damn heavy canisters." Erwan's eyes dropped down to the chess game again, then he made one move and very loudly shouted, "Check!" André clicked his tongue against his teeth, thought deeply for five seconds then made a move that got him out of check. A wisp of a smile spread across his face.

"No problem, Erwan," then, in a whisper, "and seeing it's an air drop I'll bring the ground-to-air equipment, OK?"

"OK," responded Erwan.

One of the German soldiers sitting in the corner rose and made his way over to Erwan's table. The café proprietor, Pierre Chirac, tried to intercept him with his bill but he wasn't quick enough. The soldier looked down at the board and the players. In German, he told André how to put Erwan in check with two moves. Not knowing German, André looked at him blankly. The soldier repeated what he had just said but more loudly, sufficient for the whole café to hear. Annette sensed that this could get nasty for she knew that André had a quick temper. Her German was good enough to do a fair translation and this placated the soldier for the moment. But André did not do the moves demanded of him; he just continued to stare with his lower jaw jutting out defiantly. The German took this as insolence and clenched his fists. Then with a wide sweep of his right forearm he knocked over all of the chess pieces. André was on his feet in a flash, and he would have been at the soldier's throat had not Chirac come between them and gently steered the

German away with an offer of a free carafe of wine. The German hesitated, but then the other German soldier took hold of his elbow and quite forcibly led him back to their corner table. The carafe was produced and the Germans relaxed somewhat, although the confrontational one kept glancing over at André as though he were committing to memory his face and features for future reference.

Erwan calmly set the chess pieces in their places for the start of a new game, quietly saying, "I think it's time we left. Go slowly; no eye contact with the Germans, just be normal and smile a bit." As they left the café, they gave a cheery *adieu* to Chirac and the other customers they knew as though nothing had happened.

Outside, a watery sun was trying to brighten the cobbled streets of Basbijou, but the air was cold and damp. Quite a few villagers were going to and fro buying the week's provisions, eking out their meager money supply on their meager rations. However, living in a farming community they were better off than city dwellers, for what food the shops did not have, could, in many instances, be bartered for at local farms.

Erwan had been given a small shopping list by Claudette so he quickly melded in with the other villagers. Likewise, the others did not hang around outside Le Chien very long because they knew they were probably under observation by the two soldiers inside the café. They mounted their bicycles and took off in different directions.

Maurice had not been on his bicycle more than ten seconds before he realized that his bladder was uncomfortably full. To rectify this, he dismounted outside le pissoir in the center of the village square, and, slightly bent over, entered. He unbuttoned, and with a satisfied smile on his face looked down at his strong and steady stream. Maurice was a native of Basbijou and very proud of its public urinal, particularly seeing that he had contributed to its renovation in 1935.

The residents of Guillaume, on the other hand, had lost their pissoir, and therefore continued to suffer shame and humiliation whenever it was spoken of. The French army were to blame. One day in 1937, a column of tanks was traversing the square when for some inexplicable reason one tank wanted to go its own way. To the horror of some villagers in the square, it headed for their pissoir and aggressively smashed it to the ground, driving through it and over it. One lone occupant emerged through the cloud of dust and debris, stunned and with his trousers around his knees. Maurice had been a witness to this event and still laughed about it whenever he found himself in a public urinal.

Having completed his urgent mission in the beautiful Basbijou pissoir, Maurice mounted his bicycle, with a smile on his face, and headed for home.

Chapter Eleven

Moonlight placed its eerie mantle over the fields and hedgerows at one-thirty on Sunday morning, as fourteen members of the Resistance took up their positions on the northern edge of the Forêt de Paimpont awaiting the arms drop. The group was split up into seven pairs, each pair would work together in retrieving the arms canisters after they landed, carrying or dragging them into the shelter of the forest prior to opening them and dividing the arms up according to the arms dispersal and storage plan.

The airplane making the drop was to be an Armstrong Whitworth Whitley B Mark V night bomber, powered by two 1145 horsepower Rolls-Royce Merlin X engines that gave a somewhat lumbering cruise speed of only 185 miles per hour. The fuselage floor was specially modified with a large hatch through which arms canisters and other supplies could be released. Before leaving Erwan's farm, André had received a communication from Grendon that the plane was on its way from somewhere in southern England. Unless the plane was shot down or developed engine trouble, the drop was on.

Erwan and Annette were operating as one of the pairs, so they lay together in the forest's undergrowth, but with a clear view of the field into which the canisters were supposed to fall, at least according to the plan. In fact, it would be a miracle if they fell into that particular field because of the many varying parameters that affected their descent, such as release point, release height, and wind drift.

Fifty feet from Erwan, André stood behind a large oak tree adjusting a new toy. The toy was an S-phone, an ultra-high-frequency secret radio-telephone powered by batteries, developed but under refinement by SOE. This enabled intercommunication between an agent in the field and an aircraft or ship. André had never used the S-phone before, and as far as he was concerned it was still experimental. He was a diehard Morse code lover, but because London had ordered its tryout, André reluctantly agreed to its use. Marcel had been able to give him some instruction on how to operate it, based on a limited training session he had had during his last recall in England.

The S-phone was strapped to André's chest, and because it weighed 15 pounds, he felt as though he were going to fall flat on his face the whole time. Also, he did not like the idea that he had to stand out in the open and rotate himself until he was lined up with the incoming aircraft in order to get suitable reception for a two-way conversation with the pilot. It sounded like suicide to him. On the plus side though, he did appreciate that because the device used a sky wave beam tilted upwards, the ground wave was minimized, so making detection by an enemy monitoring station very difficult. In an earlier radio transmission, he had been told by Grendon that the Whitley would locate the approximate drop-zone by dead-reckoning navigation and then circle it at 500 feet until the pilot heard André's voice guiding him to the exact spot. If the S-phone failed, the backup plan was for André to run into the middle of the field and use his flashlight as a Morse code indicator by repeatedly sending the letter "V" - three short and one long set of flashes.

Marcel moved quietly over to André and said, "You see that gap in the high hedge on the far side of the field about 100 yards away, get there now and keep still. I think the hedge on either side of you will give reasonable cover; at least you won't be on the skyline. There's still fifteen minutes to the plane's ETA, but just as soon as you think you hear it start talking. You've got a range of about six miles for a plane at 500 feet. I don't know how good the pilot's French will be so you'd better use English; I know yours is good.

"If you hear the plane but can't communicate with it for any reason, don't hesitate to run to the middle of the field and use your flashlight as the backup method. OK, good luck; go, go!"

André broke cover and moved off around the edge of the field in an unhurried fashion. He did not like this; this was not his usual modus operandi. He was used to sitting in a small room surrounded by friendly walls and a roof that gave him some sense of security. Out here in a large field, alone, he was scared stiff. The bright moon cast complicated shadows from the hedgerow he was following, and a light wind rustled the hedge leaves whose motion was magnified in the shadows. Every movement could be a German soldier about to open fire and tear André into shreds. He told his imagination to be quiet. He was going to be all right because he had a bunch of good comrades hiding in the forest, armed to the teeth, protecting him. But his heart was pounding like a jack-hammer. He wondered whether the pilot would hear his heart over the S-phone. What a joke that would be.

He reached the gap in the hedge, climbed the small embankment upon which the hedge stood and crouched down, trying to make himself invisible. Barely a minute had past when he thought he heard the dull drone of engines in the distance. He stood up, put the earphones on, activated the S-phone and spoke into the mouthpiece in a normal voice.

"This is Carotte calling Foxtrot. Do you hear me? Do you hear me? Carotte calling Foxtrot. Come in please. Come in please."

No response. He repeated the sign-on but in a louder voice. Still no response. Now he could hear the plane distinctly, but he saw no shape in the moonlight against the clear starry sky. He repeated the sign-on once more, but all he received back was crackling static, even though he rotated his body and the antenna through 360 degrees. The antenna was a vertical rod that formed a T-junction with a smaller horizontal rod that came out of his phone chest-pack.

Then he suddenly realized what was causing the problem. It was the hedge on either side of him making a blind spot as he swept the antenna passed it, and, as luck would have it, the plane just happened to be on a course straight up the line of the hedge. His theory sounded a bit far fetched for surely his ultra-high-frequency gadget could shine through a bit of foliage. Maybe, maybe not, but when the plane starts to circle, at some point the antenna should have a clear line for signal transmission. He was not going to wait for that; time was running out. He had no alternative but to head for open space right in the middle of the field. He scrambled down the bank, and, clutching the S-phone pack close to his chest, ran as fast as he could to the center of the field. By the time he got there his earphones had fallen off his head and were trailing through the grass. He quickly put them back on and hoped they weren't damaged. Once more he spoke into the mouthpiece.

"Carotte calling, Carotte calling Foxtrot. Do you hear me? Do you hear me?"

Silence, then, with ears straining, André heard a voice, very faint, but definitely a voice. He smiled one of his rare smiles and even gave a quiet chuckle.

"OK, Foxtrot, I can just hear you. Welcome to France! Now I'm going to talk a lot of nonsense, continuously; anything that comes into my head just so you can get a beam on where I'm located. I'll stand still, you circle and find where the signal strength picks up then turn to port and fly down the beam until the signal is a maximum. Then, *voilá*, here I am, good to see you. But you don't need me to tell you how to do this stuff. You're the expert, I'm the novice."

"This is Foxtrot. Message received, Carotte. Good to hear you. Will start circling now. Keep talking," said the Whitley pilot.

Marcel had become worried and confused as he crouched at the edge of the forest. He had seen André get to the gap in the hedge and then obviously try to use the S-phone. He had cursed when André headed for the center of the field because that must have meant the phone wasn't working. So then he should have started to use his flashlight, but he didn't. What the devil was he up to, he thought, for he could distinctly hear the plane now. He crept along to where Erwan and Annette crouched anxiously."

"What the hell is André up to? We're going to lose that plane if he doesn't damn well signal it right away," growled Marcel. "You'd better get over there and see what's up, Erwan, and move like the wind."

"OK, I'm off." Erwan didn't need any further encouragement. He ran upright as fast as he could, even though that gave him a bigger profile for the enemy to see should they be in the neighborhood. He reached André without incident.

"Has your flashlight packed up as well as the phone?" gasped Erwan, almost out of breath as he clutched André's forearm for support.

"What do I need my flashlight for, I've got the pilot on the phone? We're having a grand conversation. Can't you see his silhouette as he circles? Now bugger off and let me concentrate on getting him right overhead before he does the release."

The pilot circled one more time, flying lower as he did so.

"This is Foxtrot, Carotte. I can actually see you now. This moonlight is giving you a beautiful complexion. I'm going to drop the canisters now, seven of them, and then buzz off back to Blighty. Nice chatting with you. *Bonne chance, mon ami!*"

André kept his eyes on the plane and saw seven objects tumble out, fall about a hundred feet and then have their descent slowed by mushrooming parachutes. The canisters swung like giant pendulums before crashing into the ground with considerable force. Four of them landed in the field where André and Erwan were standing, but the other three were a bit off target and came to earth in the next field over. The Resistance did not waste any time. As soon as the canisters were down, they broke cover and ran doubled up with rifles or Sten guns slung across their backs. For a few minutes they fussed over which pair should have which canister. Three pairs had to climb the gate of the next field to find the strayed ones. Annette ran to Erwan, and together they took hold of the straps at each end of the canister nearest to them, lifted it a few inches off the ground and walked laboriously towards the edge of the forest. They had walked about ten yards when chaos erupted.

Annette saw it first as small flashes of light coming out of the forest, then the air was whining and bits of the field mysteriously jumped upwards in puffs of dirt and glistening frost. Hot lead was seeking their bodies. She and Erwan, reflexively, dropped the canister and threw themselves on the ground behind it. As they did so, they heard someone on their right give an ugly but short scream as the person was thrown backwards by a bullet's impact. Intuitively, Annette knew it was André.

Annette was sweating from running and lifting the canister, and from the fear that comes with being under fire for the first time. So she welcomed the cool, moist, frosted grass on her face as she lay hugging the field. Erwan slowly raised his head to peep over the covering canister and saw more flashes.

"Sorry, Annette, we're in a tight spot. Must be a German patrol; just stumbled upon us."

"Like hell!" said Annette. "Some traitorous bastard gave them a tip-off. But what do we do now? We're stuck right out in the open. We don't stand a chance." Erwan did not respond immediately. He was not a rapid thinker.

But Marcel was. He and his partner were carrying a canister that had fallen only ten yards from the right hedge when the chaos started. In front of the hedge was a ditch, shallow but deep enough for a man to crawl along unseen. After the first burst of gunfire, Marcel and his partner made a successful dive for the ditch and edged along it to the forest. His plan was to try and outflank the Germans by reaching the forest, filtering through it and then pick them off one by one. He hoped that another pair of his men on the far side of the field were in a position to formulate the same plan so both flanks could be attacked. But it was only a hope. He knew that a frontal assault across the field would be suicide. His plan gave them the best chance, but he was not able to tell the other members of the group what he was going to do. Anything could break loose.

Marcel and his partner crawled along the ditch as fast as possible, but it was slow going because the bottom of the ditch was a mixture of mud, ice and water. It was hard to get a grip and Marcel knew that time was running out. The Germans might emerge from the forest in strength at any moment and finish off whomever was still alive in his group. So he got out of the ditch and ran along side it, going like a hare. His partner followed suit. They had almost made the edge of the forest when, out of the corner of his eye, he saw a figure running fast, firing from the hip and yelling something incomprehensible. Whoever it was possessed either extreme bravery or extreme stupidity. Marcel had no option; he had to draw some of the Germans's fire to try and give the charging lunatic a chance. He unslung his Sten and fired short bursts at where he thought one of the Germans was located. The response came quickly; a stream of bullets pummeled the bank of the hedge just behind them, off the mark but too close for comfort. Marcel increased his stride then took a flying leap into the undergrowth at the edge of the forest, unscathed. He gave a quick glance back into the field but saw no movement, although there was a still form about twenty yards from the forest. It could be the fallen lunatic, thought Marcel.

Marcel's partner crouched beside him and gave the thumbs-up sign. They moved deeper into the forest to gain more substantial cover from the large tree trunks before moving along to seek out individual members of the German patrol. The firing became spasmodic and then stopped altogether. This was not good, for Marcel needed gun flashes to locate the enemy. He froze in position behind a tree with his partner about fifteen feet to his right behind another tree. The perfect silence was uncanny; no zephyrs rustled leaves or branches; no forest animals scurried about their nightly business. It was as though the steely moonlight wanted all to rest, all to be peaceful. Momentarily, Marcel's brain was distracted by that age-old philosophical conundrum, 'If a tree falls in a forest and no one is there, does it make a sound?' Marcel smiled at the foolishness of this thought occurring in a situation like this where his life hung by a thread.

There was a sound just ahead of him, small but distinctly metallic. A shadow moved. It must be human, thought Marcel, so he opened up with single shots in the shadow's direction. Then all hell broke loose. Gunfire seemed to be coming and going in all directions; from the forest into the field; from the field into the forest, although not so heavily, and from deep in the forest to the edge of the forest. Marcel did not have time to think what it all meant for another shadow was moving in front of him. He fired again but the shape came closer and took form. He fired again but nothing happened, just a trigger click. Then he saw a bayonet flashing in a moonbeam about five feet from him. A bayonet on the end of a rifle versus a jammed Sten gun were not good odds for Marcel. He should have sought the cover of the large tree that was close by to his right, but instead he acted as though he were on the rugby field again by leaping forward and crashing his left shoulder, low, into the knees of his assailant. He felt a quick burning pain on top of his head, and then heard a sharp crack like a small pistol going off. He lay still for a few seconds, dazed, with his left forearm under the ankles of the German who had gone flying over his back. Then a hand was helping him get to his feet.

"Thanks, Pierre, but look out, I only tackled the kraut, I didn't kill him," said Marcel.

"No, but I did."

Marcel could now see the face of his helper. "You're not Pierre! Who the hell are you? A forest phantom?"

"That's a good guess. I'll explain later, but now follow me or you're likely to get shot by one of my men."

Marcel was hesitant at first but, still being a little dazed, did what he was told. Suddenly, Pierre was in front of both of them with Sten gun leveled. "*Arretez!*" he shouted, not worrying about how loud his voice was because there was so much noise going on in the rest of the forest anyway; shots, screams, breaking branches, commands yelled in German, commands yelled in French, a truck's engine starting up, a loud explosion.

"It's OK, Pierre, it's me, Marcel, and a friend."

"Call me Jean," said the friend. Then, "There's another group of three Germans over there still firing at your group in the field. Let's get them. Keep close. All the other krauts are engaged with my men."

The Germans never knew what hit them as Pierre and Jean gave a three second burst from close range. Then the gunfire stopped, save for a few seemingly random shots from the field. It was almost peaceful again.

"I think we've probably got them all," said Jean. "Now you'd better get your survivors to quit firing from the field. I don't want my men going out there until it's safe. And hurry, there will be another German patrol coming to see what's happening shortly. You can bet on that."

As Marcel went out of the forest, he put his hand to his forehead because something seemed to be trickling into his eyes. It felt sticky so it wasn't sweat. He touched the crown of his head. Very sticky and warm, indeed. *Obviously blood, and quite a bit of it,* he thought. *So that's where the German soldier's bayonet had gone, a glancing blow to my skull. No wonder I went groggy. No time for first aid now, it'll have to congeal by itself. But I've lost my damn beret. Sod the krauts!*

"Hold your fire, hold your fire! This is Marcel! I repeat, Marcel! Stop your firing!" Marcel waited a few seconds and then stepped farther into the field, but he saw no signs of life so he walked over to the canister closest to him. As he did so, a figure slowly and suspiciously stood up with Sten gun ready to fire. It was Annette. Marcel breathed a small sigh of relief but did not express it in words.

"Come on, we've got to move this canister into the forest quickly. We'll talk as we go," ordered Marcel. They staggered with their heavy load through the frosty field, so brilliantly lit by the moon.

"Erwan took off towards the forest about half a minute after the firing started, but I don't think he quite made it," said Annette. "I watched him make his wild charge like a man possessed, but then he was in the shadow of the trees and I lost sight of him. He might be hit or he might be OK. And I'm sure André got it. I believe he's lying somewhere over to the left. I heard him, or someone, give a nasty scream of pain as he went down."

Marcel was impressed with the steadiness in Annette's voice. She had just been under intense fire, had seen some of her comrades killed or wounded and yet had given him a cool, calm, factual report. Yes, he was impressed with her courage and professionalism.

They reached the heavy shadows near the edge of the forest, and heard a faint cry for help. Annette's sharp eyes searched to her left and almost immediately spotted a moving form. She prayed that it was Erwan.

"Over there to the left; someone's moving," said Annette.

"OK, I see him. A few more yards then we'll dump the canister and go back to see who it is. We've got some unexpected help waiting just inside the trees; they'll look after this stuff for a while."

Jean had been tracking Marcel's movements and now stepped out of cover to help him with the heavy load. At the same time, some of Jean's men went into the main field and the adjacent one to help in the recovery of the other canisters, while those that remained kept a close vigilance for the arrival of more German soldiers.

Annette was the first to reach Erwan who was sitting up and holding his right leg. "Come on, Erwan, let's go. We're sitting ducks out here. What's up, can't you walk?" said Annette with little sympathy in her voice.

"*Merde alors*! Of course I can't walk. Do you think I'd be sitting out here counting my toes if I could. I took a bullet in the calf muscle. The whole leg's gone numb. Can't put any weight on it," said Erwan in an angry voice.

"You're lucky you haven't got ten bullets in you, you suicidal maniac," said Marcel, angrily. "Trying to make

Claudette a widow, were you? OK, Annette, you get the other side. We'll take an arm each over our shoulders and get him into cover," said Marcel.

They went a little way into the trees and laid Erwan down gently. By this time, Jean's group and those still alive from Marcel's group had brought in all seven canisters and were busy opening them.

"Now hold it right there!" commanded Marcel. "Keep your hands off those guns until I know who the hell you are, and what you were doing in the forest during the arms drop to *my* group?"

"I'll answer the second part of your question first. We were in the forest stopping you being annihilated. You should be damn grateful. Your perimeter security was lousy; no lookouts, no trackers. Rommel could have come into the forest with ten Panzer divisions and I doubt whether you'd have noticed him.

"As to who we are, well, for now I'll only explain briefly; we've got to disperse. We're the remnants of the unofficial Renoir circuit that operated in east Normandy. The circuit was betrayed by an insider, and all except we fifteen were taken, tortured and then shot. We managed to escape and came cross-country until we found a place to hole-up. We have to live off the land. Our Resistance identities are blown, our papers and permits useless. We arrived in small groups ten days ago at the Forêt de Paimpont which seems a good place to hide and operate from, as long as we can get support from the local inhabitants. If you've read the underground newspapers recently, you'll know that more and more groups are doing what we're doing; taking to the countryside, the forests, the mountains. We're being known as the Maquis, after the dense scrublands found along the Mediterranean coastline and on Corsica."

"Are you from what was an independent communist group?" asked Marcel.

"Yes, exactly. London doesn't control us; not like you. We made our own papers, our own plans, reported to no one but our group leader."

"Yeah, well perhaps that was your downfall. We've got to have an overall control organization that knows what everyone is doing, irrespective of your politics. We've got to have a coordinated Resistance throughout all France, even Vichy France. We've got to support one another, share information, share equipment and arms. That makes sense and that's what de Gaulle wants," emphasized Marcel.

"You could be right, but first let's finish this night's operation together. We'll talk more later," responded Jean. "We'd better do a head count now. How many do you think you've lost?"

Marcel went around the group checking faces. "We're missing five out of fourteen," he said, "and three are wounded."

"I've lost two, killed. I guess our group wins," said Jean, pointedly, but Marcel let the jibe go.

Together the communists and the de Gaullists retrieved their dead and buried them quickly in the forest, noting the location. The graves were shallow and were not indicated by the customary cross. Marcel and Jean did not want the Germans to find the bodies, and maybe later they could be retrieved and given a proper burial in a proper graveyard. Annette was right; André was one of the dead and Maurice was another. She would miss Maurice; he made her laugh. The German dead were left where they lay. No German wounded were found.

Although Marcel did not like it, he agreed to split up the arms and equipment equally between the two groups. London control would be furious at this, but if Marcel could persuade Jean's group to accept London control, and so become *official*, maybe all would be forgiven.

Thirty minutes had now past since the moonlight battle, and Jean was getting more and more nervous so he dispersed his group back into the depths of the forest, their new home, carrying the rewards they deserved.

While the arms were being shared, Annette suddenly remembered André's S-phone pack. She knew that under no circumstances must it fall into enemy hands, and those who retrieved André's body must have removed the pack from his chest and left it out in the field where he had fallen. But why take the time to unstrap it, she asked herself. Perhaps the antenna, headphones and cables were in a jumble and too much to deal with as well as the carrying of the body. At the risk of high personal exposure, she went back out into the field to find it. She searched back and forth for what seemed an eternity, and was just about to give up when she spotted part of it. The pack was there with a bullet hole through it, and the antenna was bent double like the drooping stalk of a dying flower. She quickly picked it up and almost dropped it again for André's blood still lay wet and slippery on its surface. The earphones and microphone mouthpiece were nowhere to be seen. She thought about leaving the damaged pack; it obviously would not work again, but then thought, no, not a good idea, the smart Germans could probably figure out how it was designed and make a replica. So she took it with her back into the forest.

Annette's next problem was really difficult. Somehow she and Marcel had to get Erwan back to his farm, not only carrying him but also their share of the dropped arms - four Stens, two pistols, ammunition, six hand-grenades and some plastic explosives, all of which weighed heavily on their backs in sturdy canvas packs.

The hike back to the farm was exceptionally strenuous work. Erwan almost fainted a couple of times from the pain in his leg as it banged against objects that Annette and Marcel failed to see, as they part-carried and part-dragged him along. After what seemed an interminable two hours, they arrived exhausted, with sore arms, sore backs, and drenched in sweat.

Claudette was awakened and immediately showed a foul temper, berating Marcel and Annette for what they had let happen to her beloved Erwan. Eventually she calmed down as she dressed Erwan's wound and put him to bed with a glass of hot cider. The bullet had gone clean through his calf, causing considerable bleeding, but, it was thought, no bone damage. The nerves in his leg had come back to life after being in a state of shock. Whether the family doctor should be called in or not was undecided. Marcel wanted to wait two days before making a decision, to see whether infection was setting in. However, Claudette had other ideas; she was going to get the doctor tomorrow at first light.

While Claudette fussed over Erwan's wound, Annette cleaned up the gash on top of Marcel's head and pulled the skin together with six stitches. She had never pushed a needle, threaded with simple cotton, into anyone's scalp before, but tonight had been the first time for many things, so she took it in her stride. Marcel, on the other hand, was highly nervous and winced with pain at each jab of the needle. The worst part was not being able to see what Annette was actually doing with her sharp little weapon.

Even though Annette was thoroughly exhausted, Claudette would not allow her to stay at the farm for the rest of the night. She left for Guillaume on her bicycle, and only the cold night air kept her from falling asleep as she rode.

Marcel hid the new arms in the barn, then threw himself into bed, his mind still racing with the night's near disaster. He persuaded himself that it was only a *near* disaster because the objective had been accomplished in that the much needed arms had been successfully dropped and retrieved. The cost had been seven men killed, out of twenty-nine, and three wounded. He had lost men before, many men, during the battles with the Wehrmacht in the retreat to Dunkirk, yet tonight's losses somehow seemed more personal; André's loss certainly was. He had been Marcel's link to the one small country that remained free, a lifeline for help and encouragement. With André dead how would he contact London? He had André's Paraset transceiver in the barn, but he was by no means competent in encoding and decoding messages, setting up the correct transmission frequency and in dealing with the mysterious idiosyncrasies of the whole system. But that was a problem for much later in the day.

Chapter Twelve

At Wireless Station 53a, Paula Drysdale was becoming anxious. She had tuned in to André's frequency according to her Sunday midnight sked and waited, and waited, and waited. André did not sign in; how could he, he was dead. Now although Paula had experienced delayed transmissions many times before, this time her intuition told her there was something radically wrong. Maybe her worry had been heightened by the rumor that wireless operators were being located and captured by the Germans in large numbers, in fact, the statistic was spreading that over the past year three out of four had 'disappeared'.

Paula sat patiently for a whole hour but then she had to move onto her next contact after telling her shift supervisor of the missed sked. The supervisor informed the coding department which then sent over the standard coded message for Paula to try and initiate contact with André in three hours time; that would be Monday, January 5 at 4:0 a.m.. Paula knew the contact coding for André by heart, but procedure required that she await official sanction before trying. There was a grave danger in her sending an initiating message because, if André and his transmitter had been located, the Germans might be listening in if he had spilled the transmission frequency to them. Hence the three hour wait; maybe in this time the Germans would decide that Grendon was not going to transmit and retire for the night. It was a cat and mouse game.

The three hours past, then, calming a racing pulse, Paula sent out on André's frequency the short initiation message.

But no response; no André. With a slightly sick feeling in her stomach, she continued her night's work. This was the third operator in six months that she had 'lost'. She should have become used to the sadness by now, but she had not.

Chapter Thirteen

The following day, Monday, bore the full brunt of the arms drop aftermath. The countryside, the villages and the woods were full of Germans; on foot, on motorcycles and in armored vehicles, stopping every Breton and questioning them at length after the discovery of fifteen dead German soldiers in the Forêt de Paimpont. Luckily the shallow graves of the killed Resistance fighters were not found, but the nearby fields showed distinct markings where the heavy canisters had landed, and tell-tale tracks of frantic human activity in the long grass and ditches were obvious. It did not need a German forensic scientist to put together the likely scenario of the night's arms drop and ensuing gun battle; a Wehrmacht corporal could have figured it out.

Annette got to school over an hour late because of the roadblocks, but she need not have worried for only half the class was in attendance, and those present sat subdued at their desks, wary of what the day would bring. News of Resistance activities traveled fast in Guillaume, and many mothers were fearful of what would happen to their children if they went out on the streets with so many nervous Germans present. Home was safer than school today.

Annette sat in front of the depleted class and made an effort to teach. She was totally exhausted, both physically and mentally, from last night's frightening and chaotic events. She could barely keep her eyes open from lack of sleep, and her head ached and ears still rang from the sounds of gunfire that had been all around her just a few hours earlier. Every muscle in her body felt strained, every joint throbbed from the extreme exertion of lugging laden arms canisters into the forest and supporting the wounded Erwan as he limped back to his farm. She wanted rest; she wanted quiet; she wanted safety. Instead, fear arrived in the shape of Hauptsturmfuhrer Eichmann. Annette was the first to see him as he slunk through the classroom door behind the children. He stared at her, she stared at him. No greetings were exchanged. Her stomach churned, her heart rate leapt up. She placed her hands on her thighs just above the knees and squeezed tightly to help control her fear and her anger.

What will he do? thought Annette. *Will he use that strap and buckle again to hurt the children? What should I do to protect them? What does he want anyway? It's probably me he wants, the way he's looking at me. Questioning, that's what it is. He's going to take me to Gestapo Headquarters in Rennes, the bastard, and torture me until I break. Think girl, think, what'll I do?* The seconds past slowly. All her fear now turned to anger. *That's it; you've got a sheath knife in your desk. Remember, you put it there after his first visit; you knew he'd be back one day. If he lays a hand on any child, I'll charge him with the knife. I'll stab him or slash him before he gets me; surprise is on my side. I killed a Nazi last night with a bullet, I can do it again with a knife.*

As Annette rationalized her intended actions, she slipped her hands onto the edge of the desk lid and waited, observing Eichmann the whole time. Although evil intentions covered his face and one corner of his mouth twitched nervously, he made no threatening moves against the children. Instead, he walked up and down the lines of desks quite calmly. The children turned their heads to look at him as he passed by. Some were terrified, some just apprehensive and one or two looked defiantly at him. Still Eichmann said nothing.

"Eh, Monsieur Nazi, what you want in 'ere? Can't you see we're busy doin' sums and things?" said Pierre, the bold one in the class, who emphasized his admonition by sticking his tongue out at Eichmann. "Now why don't you just bugger off and leave us alone," continued Pierre.

Annette thought this was it. *Eichmann will explode. I'll have to make a grab for the knife in the next five seconds.* She partially lifted the desk lid and felt for the knife. Her tiredness had evaporated, adrenaline had taken over. Yet still Eichmann remained calm, except for a savage stare thrown at Pierre who received it with a chin thrust outwards and upwards. Then Eichmann moved to the front of the class and stopped before Annette.

"Good morning, Mademoiselle Renard. I trust you slept well. I thought I'd just sit in on your class for a while and see what I can learn. I am always open to my continuing education."

Annette was caught off guard and had no immediate response to Eichmann. He turned and selected an empty desk at the back of the class and squeezed onto its seat. For ten minutes he sat silently, his arms rigidly folded. Not once did he take his eyes off Annette. She carried on teaching, but her tenseness returned and became almost unbearable. The children sensed her grave unease and tried to support her by being models of good behavior.

Then suddenly Eichmann stood up and left.

Chapter Fourteen

While Annette was going through her ordeal with Eichmann, Erwan had a less sinister one with the local doctor who had been summoned, as promised by Claudette, to check his leg wound as he rested in a bed in the spare bedroom. Erwan did not like the fuss and was less than gracious with the doctor who, however, was not perturbed because, over the years, he had learned that Erwan's rough character had a well-meaning base.

"You're going to live, Erwan," said the doctor, "and most likely continue to worry your wife half to death. I don't know how you got this wound, and I don't want to know. Your nocturnal activities are your affair. Claudette, please change the dressing every two days for the next week, and check for any increasing redness around the periphery of the wound or puffy swelling. That would be a sign of infection. If that happens, get word to me at once. I'll leave you this small pot of antiseptic ointment; use it sparingly at each dressing change. And finally, stay off your feet for at least four days, Erwan. No plowing, no hedge cutting, no chasing your cows. You've got Marcel and the boy for that. So, good day to you, Erwan and Claudette."

Erwan did not like the idea of staying off his feet for a few days. He had planned to make a trip to St-Brieuc tomorrow with a truck full of assorted vegetables and to bring back a load of fish. He would have to postpone that journey until his leg was healed because he could not risk a road inspection with a bandaged leg; that could lead to too many questions. He thought that perhaps he should

91

familiarize Marcel and Annette in more detail with his little wholesale business, so that they could step in when needed. Perhaps even Claudette should get involved, although he thought that she may not be a tough enough bargainer when dealing with fishermen and vegetable retailers.

An half an hour later, Claudette allowed Marcel to go up to Erwan's temporary bedroom. Marcel explained that he would rather talk to Erwan alone. Claudette just shrugged her shoulders as a sign of condescension, and went out into the farmyard to feed the hens.

"You're dead lucky, Erwan, or should I say you're lucky not to be dead. Either way, no more heroics on our next operation; use your head not your heart. But, as you know, we've got a couple of big problems.

"First, the communication problem. André's death leaves us without an expert radio operator. I tried to set up the Paraset and make a quick transmission to Grendon early on this morning. But either my brain is muddled from lack of sleep or I don't know as much as I thought I did about procedures. I couldn't raise anyone. I tried encoding and sending by Morse. No response. Not surprising really; I haven't much of a clue about the code that André used. He did mention something about a poem-code once, but he never told me what poem or what code; said I was safer not knowing. Anyway, I made up my own code. Simple Boy Scout stuff; shifting the letters of the alphabet five steps to the right. The boys and girls in Grendon should have been able to figure it out quite easily. Then I broke the rules and tried voice on the emergency frequency. Still nothing. With all the German activity out there I just cannot risk a further transmission. They'll home in on us and then we'd all be cooked."

"I doubt they'd detect us," said Erwan. "They'd need to get within 200 yards of the transceiver while we were sending in order to catch us, and we'd spot their big detection van well before they got that close. We've got good visibility of all access roads and lanes from the hill where my barn is located."

"Maybe so, but with you in bed and me using the set who's going to watch for Germans? Your most intelligent cow?"

"We could try that," responded Erwan with a wry grin, "but I was thinking of someone more attractive, like Annette."

"Not a chance! I don't want her hanging around the farm in daylight. That would be abnormal and therefore suspicious to any passerby. Anyway, she teaches all day, remember. And can you see Claudette allowing her up here; she'd get more than a cold shoulder. You saw the way Claudette looked at her when we staggered back here in the middle of the night with her wounded beloved between us. If looks could have killed, Annette would have been a goner. No, we have to find an alternate radio operator, and fast. London needs to know the outcome of the arms drop and our losses, but, in particular, they need to know about our new found friends, the guys who stopped us all being wiped out. Jean and his merry men. Essentially they are a rogue group of communists without any central control, splintered from a bigger group that was somehow betrayed and scattered.

"Now I've got nothing against working with communists; we all have the same goal, but the SOE big boys in London may not see it that way. They are *politically sensitive*, to put it politely. However, I intend using them, no matter what London says. So, first, I have to find them again; find Jean or anyone of them who can lead me to Jean. We left them in the forest doing a disappearing trick with their share of the arms, so in the forest I guess they remain."

"And how do you intend finding them in 18,000 acres of woods? By walking every path whistling *The Marseillaise*?"

"I'm not going anywhere near the forest at the moment, and I only hope that Jean's group had the sense to go way deep into the woods well away from where we had the skirmish with the Germans. No, what I think will happen is that Jean will come searching for us. At the moment, he needs our help more than we need his. I don't know whether you noticed in the dark, but his group looked in bad shape;

half starved, poorly clothed for the winter, and generally exhausted. They've probably been on the run for days, carrying just what's left of their weapons. They probably had to destroy all their support gear once their cover was blown; all their identity papers, true or false, maps, permits, the lot."

"And how exactly will Jean find us? That'll be almost as hard as we looking for him?" questioned Erwan, wincing as a sharp pain traveled up his wounded leg.

"I told him the name of your farm and roughly where it was," said Marcel. "I had to. I had no option. I knew it was risky, but I also knew we'd have to make contact sometime or another."

"My God, you're right it's risky, damn risky! What happens if Jean and his twelve men come strolling up the lane to the farm in broad daylight, waving to the neighbors as they do so. Tongues will wag and the Germans will be up here in a flash."

"Now don't be stupid, Erwan. That won't happen. These men are seasoned Resistance fighters. They know how to move around as silent as shadows. Jean will probably get the lie of the land over the next few days, and then he, and he alone, will approach under cover of darkness."

"Well, I hope you're right. Remember, their group has already let themselves be betrayed once. Who's to say they don't have another traitor in their midst ready to pull us down too? And another thing, there were two strange coincidences last night. First, the German patrol just happened to be in the very spot where the arms drop was made. Then, secondly, Jean's group just happened to be in the very spot where the Germans were lying in wait for us. Think about that, Marcel."

"Yeah, yeah, I already have. For now I'm going to trust Jean; we really do need his men. We're five short, and to continue our operations we've got to have replacements. But don't worry, I'll be making some checks. I no more want a lingering death in the hands of the Gestapo than you do.

"Back to the question of communications. It may be a long shot, but perhaps Jean has a trained radio operator in his group, or, at least, somebody with more knowledge than I have. If so, we'll introduce him to the Paraset in your barn and hopefully raise Grendon. Then I'll put in an urgent request for an airborne pickup. I want to take Jean back to London headquarters with me, get him known, in the flesh as it were, to the controllers and bosses. I have to get formal permission to link up and use Jean and his bunch of communists in the fun and games of our sabotage work. If SOE has any bad information on Jean, they'll tell me about it after the meeting. But if they think he's loyal and can eventually fit well into the organization, they may want to send him on some crash training courses to learn our methods.

"If all goes well and green lights flash, we'll have to forge new papers and dream up cover stories for Jean and his men while in London. That means we'll need photographs of them to be made before Jean and I are picked up. That's going to be a difficult job. As you know, I have an SOE field camera but I don't have a well-lighted studio that goes with it. But I'll think of something.

"Next problem. Assuming Jean makes contact, we'll then have to take on the role of group support. You're a man of the forest, where can they best hide until they're ready to diffuse into the various communities around here? I mean, they'll eventually have to get jobs; on farms, in stores, in small workshops, wherever they can lead a normal, unnoticeable life. I bet you know a few places, Erwan; caves, old mines, quarries, that sort of thing? Speak to me."

A deep frown came over Erwan's brow and the corners of his mouth turned up in a grimacing smile. He seemed agitated.

"I didn't think my question was all that difficult, Erwan."

"It isn't," hissed Erwan through clenched teeth. "My backside's gone numb sitting like this, and I can't feel my good leg. I hate lying in bed, so I'm going to get up and hobble around. Give me a hand, will you. To hell with doctor's orders."

"You really think you should? What if you slip and open up the wound?"

"Well, I won't have to, will I. Now come on, give us a hand. Your shoulder is just the right height to be my crutch." Erwan slowly swung his legs out of bed, and with support from Marcel stood up and moved around the room.

"Do you want me to rub your backside to bring it back to life?" asked Marcel.

"I don't think that'll be necessary. I'm very particular about who does that; you're not on the list."

"Thank God!" And they both laughed.

"OK, I've been thinking. Hiding places for our friends. I know one for sure; a nice big cave in a rock outcrop, deep in the forest. Another one I have in mind is a steep hill with a lot of trees and very heavy undergrowth. The hill will give them the high-ground advantage in any shoot-out, if the heavy undergrowth fails to provide concealment."

"That's good, that's good, Erwan. Yes, but how are we going to show them the locations? You can't lead them there with your leg."

"Well, I couldn't lead them there without my leg."

"Very, ha, ha, funny, smart ass."

"Annette's the solution. Years ago I showed her the cave, one beautiful summer's day. We did a little hike to the Fontaine de Barenton, and then went on to the cave. We spoke of Merlin and Vivian and other legendary people as we walked. The forest smelled of a million scents, the insects buzzed lazily and birds preferred to doze rather than fly through the warm, soft air. It was a perfect day."

Erwan looked out of the bedroom window and his eyes glazed over as the memories flooded back.

"Don't get sentimental on me, Erwan. How many times has Annette been to this cave of yours?"

"Just the once, I believe, unless she tried to find it again on her own. But no matter, I can draw her a map and remind her of the landmarks used to find the place. She's a smart girl and never forgets details."

"Good, very good. We'll get Jean's group into the cave just as soon as possible, and when you're fit enough again for strenuous walking and climbing, you can split the group and take half of them to the hill area."

"OK, boss. All this assumes Jean actually does make contact and does need us. He could, instead, just decide to operate on his own, or go back to Normandy and link up with another communist group."

"You're a real devil's advocate, aren't you, Erwan?"

"If I knew what that meant and it's good to be one, then I am."

"One day I'll explain it, but for now I order you back to bed, then I'll go and get on with some farm work. There are hedges and fields out there needing attention, and livestock to feed. If we don't work, we don't eat. I'll let myself out and give Claudette a kiss on the way."

"You may get your face slapped if you try. She's been mightily depressed lately. I don't know what's wrong with her. I seem to annoy her. She's taken to disliking Annette, and she hates the war."

"I'll turn a little charm on. Perhaps she's got a numb backside as well. I can fix that," said Marcel, with a twinkle in his eye, "but, of course, only with your permission, Erwan."

Chapter Fifteen

Marcel was right. Jean remembered the name of Erwan's farm and its rough location. Early Thursday evening, four days after the arms drop, Jean arrived at the farm as cold rain poured from a blustery sky. He stood on the doorstep, bedraggled and shivering, a Resistance fighter who appeared to have very little fight left in him. Erwan welcomed him, found him some dry clothes, and, wrapped in a blanket for additional warmth, gave him a substantial, if simple, meal of steaming potatoes, cabbage, carrots and three rashers of bacon. He ate like a starving man, and afterwards drank cider hot enough to cause sweat to breakout on his forehead. Now all he needed was rest, but somehow he managed to stay awake long enough for Marcel to question him and layout the immediate plans affecting his group. Jean agreed to everything, mainly because he was too tired to disagree and argue about a different course of action. At ten o'clock he thankfully stretched out on the sofa and was asleep in five seconds. At four o'clock the next morning, Marcel awoke him, as planned, so that he could return to his group in the forest while darkness still lingered. He took with him as much food as he could carry and a bizarre assortment of old clothing that would give a small amount of warmth to a lucky few of his group. Marcel wanted Jean to move his group to the vicinity of Folle Pensée, the village south of La Saudraie, but to remain well hidden in the forest.

Marcel's prayers were answered; Jean *did* have a man in his group, called Igor, who used to be an expert radio operator with a de Gaullist group before he changed his politics and sought out Jean's freelance communist gang. He had been London-trained over a year ago, and was very familiar with coding practices and procedures of that time. However, because Jean never communicated with anyone but his own men, and therefore had no need of a radio operator, Igor's Morse talents had not been used of late. Jean was to bring Igor to Erwan's barn that night, Friday, for an attempted transmission to Grendon at midnight.

Jean's men had divided into four groups of three and had hidden themselves in close but different locations in the forest. The forest undergrowth gave the men some measure of protection from the winter elements, and they had made bivouacs from dead branches laced with ferns.

During the day, Marcel cycled over to Marie Renard's house in Guillaume to give her a message for Annette. Annette was to come to the farm before dark, after she had finished teaching school. It was important.

By late afternoon, Annette, Erwan and Marcel were sitting around the table in Claudette's kitchen, the warmest room in the house. Erwan's leg was mending well; he was able to walk on it, but slowly and with a limp. For a change, Claudette was very amiable, and once or twice even put her arm around Annette's shoulders as she moved around preparing the evening meal. Marcel brought Annette up to speed on the week's events, and Erwan showed her a map he had drawn for her to use in finding the cave where Jean's group was to hide. Annette was less than enthusiastic about going on a cave hunt with a group of men she did not know, whose morals and trustworthiness had yet to be defined.

"You're assuming a hell of a lot, aren't you? Let me get this straight. You want me to follow Jean into the Forêt de Paimpont and link up with his fully armed desperadoes. Then to lead them to a cave which I've only visited once when I was twelve with Erwan, the world's best cave finder. But this world's best cave finder is not coming with me. Oh, no! He's got a leg problem. Instead, he's drawn this superb map on a bit of scrap paper which will magically direct me straight to the spot. Sure, sure! .... You've got to be out of your minds. I'm not going! And that's that!"

"Now calm down, Annette," said Erwan. "Where's your spirit of adventure? I'm going to give you more than this map; I'll write out some detailed directions for you. You start at Folle Pensée village and take the well-defined paths to the Fontaine de Barenton. You must remember the first part of our little hike; it was only about ten years ago. From the Fontaine, I admit, it was rather difficult to progress through the dense woods to the cave, but, as I say, I'm going to write down the details, step by step. Then, once you're close, you'll spot the two menhirs and home in on the cave entrance with no trouble at all."

"Really! You think so! Well, I'll tell you what I think; I think if we're not picked off by a German patrol in the first ten minutes, or savaged by the hounds of local landowners, we'll spend three weeks going around in circles pursued by Merlin and his lady-friend. Then, if by chance, I should find the cave, the men, relieved to be in a dry, cozy sanctuary, will become too familiar with me, a lone, helpless woman, and commit diabolical acts."

"So your answer is 'yes', you'll go," assumed Marcel. Annette did not answer immediately but sat, head down, staring at the table top. Slowly her head came up, and slowly a smile spread over her face.

"Of course I'll go. When?" asked Annette.

"Tomorrow, very early, before dawn," said Marcel. "You'll stay here tonight. Jean's coming later with one of his group who happens to have been a trained radio operator in the past. We hope to contact Grendon at midnight, but the outcome of that should not affect your plans to find the cave tomorrow. The operator will hole-up in the barn for the next few days, receiving and sending messages to do with our short term planning. I can't come with you to the cave; I've too much organizing to do. Don't ask me what."

After a small evening meal that still left a hole in their stomachs, the group, and, surprisingly, Claudette, sat around the kitchen table playing cards, amicably. Then, because of her early start tomorrow, Annette took to her makeshift bed. Erwan and Claudette were not far behind, leaving Marcel with his thoughts and a howling wind that found gaps in doors and window frames.

Chapter Sixteen

Around 11:00 p.m., Friday, Jean and Igor arrived at the farm, cold and tired, to be greeted by Marcel who took them into the kitchen and warmed them with the usual reviving drink; hot, spiced cider. Once the blood was flowing again, Marcel led Igor into the communications center, also known as the cow barn.

The ex-radio operator was fearful that his expertise would be out of date, but as soon as Marcel said that André used a poem as the basis for his encoding messages he felt happier. It seemed that nothing in the communications world had changed, although it took him a little while to figure out the usage of the Paraset, a new transceiver to him, which he fell in love with straightaway. But Igor soon realized that there were a few major problems. What poem-code should he select, or would the British want to select one for him? Whatever it would be, first, he had to make contact with Grendon on the fixed frequency of the crystal employed in the Paraset. To do this he had no alternative but to use a simple coding method like the one Marcel tried, the Caesar cipher. He thought Marcel had failed because Grendon could not authenticate his message. He had not included the secret security code that André embedded in all his messages. Marcel, of course, had no knowledge of it. Neither had Igor, so he had to think of another way that Grendon could authenticate his transmission. He needed to mention in his initial message a piece of knowledge that would prove his identity to be bona fide.

His mind went back to his London training and the code name of his instructor, Wimpole. But that name could possibly be known by the Germans. He thought of the instructor's sister. He had dated her a few times. *What was her name? Monica? Yes, that was it, Monica.* But there was also a finite possibility that the Germans would know her name as well. Then Igor thought of Monica's dog. *That's it, her damn dog, the one that sank his foul yellow teeth into my leg. I'll never forget his name. Brutus, black Brutus. The Germans won't know about him, that's a certainty. And I'll couple this unique knowledge to my old operator code name, Priam; they should still have that in their London records.*

"Marcel," said Igor, "I need a book of poems or a novel; a good piece of literature, something the British would be familiar with. What's Erwan got in his library?

"I wouldn't exactly call it a library, but he does read quite a bit in the wintertime. Let's see now.......Well, I think he has a book of Molière's plays, and Zola's *Germinal*, and I know he has some Guy de Maupassant's short stories."

"Better to use something English," said Igor. Grendon will need to get hold of a copy quickly, or London, if they retransmit the message to the 'Brains Trust' in the big city.

"I really don't know much about English novels; I taught physics and mathematics, but I'll try and rouse Erwan, or rummage on his bookshelves myself."

Marcel did the latter, for Erwan was fast asleep, snoring and snorting like a pig at the trough. With the aid of a flashlight he scanned the small bookcase in the living room, looking for any English volume. He was about to give up when he came upon a book of Rudyard Kipling's poems. He was surprised that Erwan's limited literary interests stretched into the English domain, but then he connected Erwan to the influences of Annette, and Annette was half English. He hurried back to the barn with the book of Kipling's poems and gave it to Igor who quickly selected *Mandalay* as a suitable coding vehicle.

Now Igor had to work fast to concoct a message that told Grendon who he was, what had happened to André, and setup the procedure for subsequent transmissions using *Mandalay* as his poem-code. He also had to explain that he did not have a security code. Of course, he could not mention the name *Mandalay* directly; that would be a huge security risk for later transmissions. Instead, he embedded in the message:

...........*First, understand the road that RK liked to travel*..............

Igor hoped that a smart, literate coder in Grendon or London would immediately home in on the initials RK and deduce that they could stand for Rudyard Kipling. From there it was only a small journey down a popular, oft-repeated road, namely:

...... *On the road to Mandalay, Where the flyin'-fishes play* ......

The word *First* in the message referred to the first verse of the poem which would be the context for the poem coding. Not only was *Mandalay* a poem but also a song that used to be sung in Victorian music halls by pukka Indian Army sergeants. Consequently, how could a British encoder fail to miss Igor's obvious reference. The Germans, on the other hand, never having had a decent empire, would not understand what Igor was talking about if they intercepted his message. Igor also said in his message that in four hours time he would listen for confirmation from Grendon that they had understood everything. Using the agreed upon poem-code, he would then transmit a further message of high importance.

Chapter Seventeen

Paula Drysdale was not only conscientious about her scheduled work but she also acted on her own initiative at other times. That is why she had continued to listen in every midnight on André's old frequency just in case he should make contact. Her hopes were not high, so when she picked up a 2-minute message early on the morning of Saturday, January 10, she was astounded and thrilled. So much so that she rushed the encoded message over to the coding building herself and demanded, politely of course, that it be immediately decoded. She sat with the appointed decoder, Mary, and watched her struggle with what she had given her.

"What the devil is this stuff supposed to be? This operator's file says he uses text from Julius Caesar for coding, but I can't figure how. He hasn't defined the five words that were his coding basis, and I can't pick out his security code or his operator code name. This is an indecipherable. I'm going to flash it up to London for help."

Paula then explained that it was highly likely that the message sender was not the one defined in their system but a substitute.

"You mean it might have come from the Abwehr? Now you tell me!" said the irate decoder. "Bloody Hell!"

"Look, don't get pissed off at me, I'm only the dumb person who sends and receives messages," retorted Paula. "Let's keep calm and do our best because I think this message is important. All right?"

Mary and Paula looked at one another in silence for a few moments. Both their faces showed signs of strain and a lack of good sleep. Then gentle smiles slowly transformed their mood.

"OK, ducks, sorry, you're right. Easy does it," said Mary in a Cockney accent.

Mary dispatched the message to London with an *Urgent* tag on it, then settled down to apply her considerable brains to the problem at hand. Paula gave her several minutes to think alone then offered a suggestion.

"If the sender does not have an approved poem-code, he'd have to fall back on some other independent method, wouldn't he?"

"Absolutely, my dear Mrs. Watson. I've thought of that. That's what all these scribblings are. I'm trying to apply other methods but so far I can't crack it."

"I believe the new operator is not a beginner. His Morse was very good; clear and fast. Does that help?" asked Paula.

"Not one bit............Hang on, though! Look at this! I don't believe it! Talk about simple-minded." Mary roared with laughter. "He's using the Caesar cipher which is damn funny because he's supposed to be using a *Julius Caesar* poem-code. And I believe his alphabet shift is five letters to the left. How about that! We've cracked it, duckie. Give me a minute and I'll have the whole thing written out in plain text."

Paula and Mary puzzled over Igor's decoded message, and, although they now understood all of the words, they could not immediately decide to whom RK referred, and knew nothing about a dog called Brutus who was linked to an instructor called Wimpole. This was a job for the London office. However, Paula and Mary agreed that in three hours time - one hour having gone by since Igor's transmission - Paula would make contact with Igor, saying his message had been received and understood, and that he should use the poem he had selected for all future transmissions. Paula's reply would use the Caesar cipher if London had not figured out the name of Igor's poem by then. Paula returned to the signals building and continued with her scheduled work, but her mind was partly on the letters RK. Whose initials were they?

Paula was an avid reader, particularly of classical literature. She was going up to Oxford University to study French and English Literature before the war intervened. Her mind raced through all the names of French poets and authors that she knew, because surely the new operator would use a French text. But there was no RK. She tried another memory scan of the lesser known literati, but no one was there. She became mad with herself and thumped her clenched fists on her thighs. Another precious hour went by. She wished she could talk to her father; he was good at this kind of thing; always doing crosswords. *That's a stupid thought*, Paula said to herself, *he's been posted to India; sweat and flies. India, India...........Oh, my God! It's Rudyard Kipling, RK. Not a Frog but a Limey poet. So what's the poem? Something about a road that Kipling or someone liked to travel; a road, a road? Got it! Paula you're brilliant, even though I say it myself. How does it go? "........Come you back, you British soldier; come you back to Mandalay!..........On the road to Mandalay, Where the flyin'-fishes play, An' the dawn comes up like thunder outer China 'crost the Bay!"..........Well, I guess I don't know it all, but that's not a bad start.*

Paula immediately telephoned Mary on a scrambler line and told her the good news.

"You're kidding, Paula! Get away! You're really smart, Paula. Well done! I'll get the information up to London. What a laugh, they'll be really peeved that little us in Grendon cracked the RK bit first. But it's still the middle of the night and it might be tricky for London to get a copy of Kipling's poems. They've also got to track down Wimpole and Brutus to see if your new operator is authentic. Look, we'll stick to our original plan. I've got a simple reply message for you to send in about an hour using Caesar ciphering. I'm coming over with it right now. See yuh!"

* * * * *

At 4:00 a.m., Igor was still in Erwan's barn and tuned into Grendon. He was very nervous because he really should have changed his location to minimize detection by the Abwehr. However, he rationalized that his initial message had been very short, and the poem-code one he had prepared was not much longer. Paula's message was received with much joy. Marcel and Jean's circuit had a lifeline again. Igor quickly decoded it, guessing that it was in Caesar cipher with the same shift as his first message. He knew Grendon or London could not have got *Mandalay* organized in just four hours. Next, Igor transmitted Marcel's poem-encoded message requesting an airlift for him and Jean to England as soon as possible. Igor would listen in at 2:00 a.m. every night for SOE's confirmation and detailed arrangements. Paula acknowledged receipt of Igor's message and passed it through to decoding to await arrival of Kipling's *Mandalay*.

Chapter Eighteen

When five o'clock came Annette was not ready to be woken up, but prodding and cajoling by Marcel brought her round, albeit with a lot of cursing and malcontent. She and Jean slipped into the darkness as a cold January wind froze their cheeks and made their joints ache. Soon, brisk walking towards the forest pumped lively blood through muscles and brain making them warm and alert. On their backs they carried packs of clothing and food to supplement that taken by Jean to his men the previous night. Gloved hands held a Sten gun at the ready. They knew if they had to use them they would probably die, but just the feel of the hard metal provided a little confidence.

After about an hour and a half they quietly walked through Folle Pensée and into the edge of the forest. From there Jean led the way to where his men should have been waiting. They were not there. They were not there an hour later.

"This is becoming a problem, Jean. It'll start to get light in another hour and it'll take at least that time to find the cave."

"Don't worry, don't worry. They'll turn up soon. I'm used to waiting in our business; you should have learned that by now also," said Jean, calmly.

"*Merde!*" said Annette, forcefully, "something's gone wrong. I'm going to scout around a bit; go deeper into the forest. They could well be holed up a mere hundred yards from us and we don't know it."

She found a small path and stealthily went down it, trying not to tread on any fallen branches that would crack under her weight and announce her presence. Her eyes penetrated the darkness, sifting the degrees of blackness, left and right, looking for any unnatural form. Nothing. Suddenly, after a farther fifty yards, her face seemed to run into a brick wall followed immediately by her head being jerked backwards with a horrifying crack of her cervical vertebrae. Something covered her mouth and nostrils and pressed hard into her cheek bones. She could not breathe. There was also a coldness on her throat below her chin. She was going to die. A light flashed in her eyes and a gruff voice in front of her whispered:

"'ello, Mademoiselle, you're up early, and we almost killed you."

Another man standing behind her released his left hand from her mouth and removed a knife from her throat. She staggered forward and gasped some deep breaths. It took several seconds for her heart to stop pounding and much longer to regain her composure.

"You stupid bastards! What the hell do you think you're doing. You almost broke my neck. You damn well better be Jean's group," said Annette, hoarsely.

"Sorry for the rough welcome, but you could have been an undesirable. And where's Jean? He's an hour late."

"No we're not; you're the ones who are late. We've been freezing our arses off on the edge of the forest waiting for you at the rendezvous point."

"*This* is the rendezvous point, Mademoiselle."

"Balls, you've got it wrong!" Annette was about to argue further, but changed her mind. "OK, OK, we haven't got time for this; just follow me," ordered Annette.

Within ten minutes they were all united with Jean. Annette took command and led the cold, tired and disgruntled group to the Fontaine de Barenton, endeavoring to appear confident of her pathfinding capabilities. That was the easy part. From the Fontaine to the cave was a nightmare. Annette lost her way four times, even though, afterwards, she conceded that Erwan's map and instructions were fully detailed. She blamed herself and, to a certain extent, the weather and the lack of support from the rest of the group. Landmarks were missed or overgrown with bracken; paths had been washed out by the rain; she misread some instructions due to a weak and intermittent flashlight.

But she carried on, determined, oblivious to the masculine criticism. She would show these so-called hardened warriors what she was made of, a mere woman, but not so mere. Anyway, she thought, they were dependent on her to find the sanctuary of the cave where they could regain their strength and feel safe. This half-starved, bedraggled, pathetic group of men were not so tough. Who the hell were they to criticize her. She was risking her life for them. Her thoughts fluctuated between pride in what she was doing and the fear of failure. But she persevered, and eventually found the menhirs and then the cave, just as dawn was breaking. There was a rapturous smile on her face, with a hint of smugness, as she ushered the men through the cave entrance and gave them a guided tour.

Once inside the cave the tension in the men's bodies gave way to extreme exhaustion. They were even too tired to eat any of the new stock of food, but instead threw themselves down on the cave's hard sandstone floor, covering themselves, as best they could, with the odd items of clothing and blankets that Jean and Annette had stuffed in their packs before leaving Erwan's farm. Within five minutes most of the men were sound asleep at the far end of the cave, partially illuminated by ever-strengthening light streaming down the hole in the roof; the hole which Annette remembered acted as a chimney for her and Erwan when they lit their fire so many years ago to dry their rain-soaked clothes. She smiled at the thought, but quickly came back to reality as she scanned the bodies lying around her.

What an assortment, she thought. Young, old, long hair, balding, tall and thin, short and fat, ugly, handsome. All had grimy faces. Hands she could see looked raw and sore, fingernails broken with black dirt under the ends. One young man had his pants torn off below the knee, and his lower legs wrapped in bandages that no longer provided protection but instead were a perfect source of infection. She wanted to go over to him and play Florence Nightingale; she *did* have some clean dressings, but she shuddered to think about the state of his wounds; she would also need some boiled water, some antiseptic, maybe a needle and thread for closing the flesh; the latter items she did not have. What were the stories of each of these men? Where were their homes? What had they done? How many Germans had they killed? Did they like killing or did they loathe it? What did their womenfolk think, left behind to feed the children, to make a little money, to be cold and lonely? Questions that would remain unanswered, at least for the present.

She found Jean and gently poked him awake.

"Jean, Jean, I've got to get going. Marcel and Erwan will want to know that we found the cave. When your men wake up you'd better post a guard outside. Don't make too much noise. You'll need water. There's a small stream about fifty yards away. Go left outside the cave entrance; you can't miss it. There's plenty of small, dead wood around, but I wouldn't light a fire in here until nightfall; a lot of smoke out of the chimney in daylight would surely attract the wrong kind of people. Here, take these matches for lighting a fire tonight, and you could probably use these bandages and ointment; some of your men could do with a bit of first aid. I'll try and return tonight with more supplies and clothes; might even bring some soap; my nose tells me your men could do with a good scrub. Oh, yes, I almost forgot; here's some money, courtesy of Marcel. The bank's getting low so only use it for necessities. Even though I'll be bringing supplies to you when I can, I can't guarantee my regularity, so one or two of your men will probably have to go to village stores for what is really needed. When they do, impress upon them to act normally but say as little as possible. Our villagers are notorious for their inquisitiveness; they've got very long noses."

"Of course, and thanks, Annette. Thanks for everything. I'm sorry the men have appeared less than appreciative, but they've had a lot of trouble and despair over the past weeks. It's no fun being on the run the whole time; you get very twitchy."

"That's all right, I understand. I've got a pretty thick skin. So, I'm off now. *Bonne chance!*"

Chapter Nineteen

Annette picked up her empty pack and quietly left the cave, stepping into full sunlight that warmed her spirits. For a few moments she stood absolutely still, looking and listening for any signs of human life in the vicinity. Not only did she not want to go crashing into an early morning German patrol, but to unexpectedly meet a local person would arouse that person's curiosity about her presence in this place at this time. All seemed clear so she carefully made her way back through the forest, endeavoring to cover the tracks made earlier by Jean's men. After doing this for about a hundred yards from the cave's entrance, she decided that was good enough, and that she could relax a little. The air was crisp and its coldness condensed her breath and made her cheeks and nose tingle. She felt good although she should have felt tired; maybe the success of her mission buoyed her up and gave her extra energy.

Twenty minutes went by quickly when suddenly there was a noise behind her. She turned and slowly bent her knees until she was in a fully crouched position. Her eyes darted left and right but saw nothing unusual. *Maybe it was a deer moving through the undergrowth*, she thought, *or a fox slinking back to its lair after a night's hunting.* She was about to stand up again when she noticed a short broken branch lying across the path she had just trodden. It was fairly thick so surely she would have noticed it as she passed over it, but she could not remember. She looked left and right again, puzzled. Then a large pine cone hit her shoulder and another one landed beside her. This time she looked upwards instead of sideways. Her eyes settled on a group of five pine trees over to her left, tall ones with strong, dense branches. Everything seemed normal, yet there was some movement high up. *Probably squirrels jumping around,* Annette thought. Her eyes widened. "I don't believe it," she whispered to herself. Then again but louder. About thirty feet up she saw two legs with large boots on, dangling in space. Presumably there was an upper body attached to the legs, but she could not see one. She changed her position slightly until the full body came into view, suspended, as if by magic, between the branches. The body spoke.

"Good morning, my dear. Very pleased to see you. 'Fraid I'm a bit stuck. Sorry, you probably don't know what I'm saying. 'Fraid I'm bloody English. Lousy at French."

A smile slowly spread over Annette's face. She gave the body a gentle wave of recognition.

"I understand you Englishman, and don't swear; there's a lady present. And don't speak so loudly. Not everyone around here is your friend."

Although half-English, Annette had not used that language for many months, and it would take a little while for her mind to automatically think in English. For now she thought in French, and then consciously translated her thoughts into English, and, of course, when she heard English she had to first translate it into French before understanding.

"I beg your pardon, miss; I'm new around here. Sorry if I hit you with that cone; just trying to get your attention. I think I'm in need of a bit of help. Been up here since midnight and I think my balls are frozen off."

"Please? What balls? I don't understand."

But Annette knew what he meant. As a schoolgirl, her English pen-pal had taught her many English swear words, and all the impolite but colorful expressions for the naughty parts of the body. But there was no time for further friendly banter. Annette's mind raced ahead to solutions for this unexpected encounter; one that she cursed. She could not cope with this; hadn't she enough to contend with. She had to get back to the farm and report to Marcel.

She looked up at the Englishman again. Obviously a flyer who had baled out of an aircraft. She could see that his parachute had caught in the branches and was supporting him somewhat precariously. *Although he seems to be smiling the whole time, perhaps that is a cover-up for pain*, Annette thought. *His right shoulder is dangling unnaturally and dried blood is caked on his face. Blood's actually dripping from his left hand so it must be very badly injured; probably lost some fingers and the blood flow has not congealed.*

Mon Dieu! thought Annette, *he could bleed to death. I must get him down somehow. But how? How? I can't do it alone. I'll have to go back to the cave and get Jean to help. It's too far to the farm.*

"Englishman, listen! I have to leave you for about forty minutes to get help. Try not to move too much."

"OK. I promise to stay right here. And you can call me Jimmy. We need to be properly introduced."

Annette took one more look at the Englishman, and, as she did so, he slumped farther forward in the parachute harness, his eyelids fluttered briefly and then closed. He had fainted. Annette threw caution to the winds and ran back to the cave, not caring about the noise she made as she crashed through the ferns and broke off the lower branches of trees. She entered the cave and shook Jean awake. In a state of semi-consciousness, he grabbed for his gun and lurched to his feet, thinking the Germans had found them. Annette calmed him and told him about the complication that had fallen from the sky.

"Do you have any rope, Jean? We need rope to get him down. We've got to make a sling or something to lower him gently to the ground. If we just cut him loose he'll fall to the ground and break his neck. Well, have you got any?"

"No, I damn well don't! Apart from guns, we've been traveling light. Why would we haul a coil of rope around."

"OK, OK! Let me think a bit. Anyway, rope or no rope, wake up a couple of your men and come back to the flyer with me. Time is really critical; he may be dying."

There were strong objections from the two selected *volunteers* until they learned the full story, then they were only too pleased to help in the rescue.

As they hurried through the forest, Annette thought of a possible way to get the flyer down. She had loved climbing trees ever since she was a young girl, and she was still agile and light. They certainly needed some rope, but not having any she would have to improvise using some of the shrouds from the parachute. She would cut four shrouds from just above the parachute harness, then climb up to where the parachute canopy was held and cut the other end of the shrouds. She would knot the shrouds together and then halve their length by doubling them over to give increased strength. At one end she would make a big loop and pass it over the flyer's head and shoulders and let it rest underneath his buttocks. The other end she would throw over a thick branch directly above the flyer and let it fall to the ground. She hoped to God that the flyer had regained consciousness, for he would have to grasp the makeshift rope above the loop and allow the bottom of the loop to snag his backside. She would need another person up the tree to help in the slinging process and to hold her as she leaned out from the tree's trunk. Then, the two men on the ground would pull on the shroud rope to take the flyer's weight while Annette cut the remaining shrouds loose from the harness. The freed flyer would then be gently lowered to the ground and be made very happy. At least, that was her plan. She and the rescuers arrived under the suspended flyer, and put her plan into action.

Annette expected problems, but was almost disappointed when no major ones occurred. The whole process went smoothly, apart from stifled cries of pain from the flyer when he tried to grasp the rope with his injured hand as well as his good one. He collapsed when on the ground, and it was only then that Annette saw he had lost two fingers on his left hand, cleanly cut off right at the knuckles. His whole hand was wet with blood, with drips falling off frequently. However, even in her hurry to leave the cave, she had had the foresight to know that she would need one of the bandages she had given to Jean. She now used that bandage to dress the bloody hand and apply pressure directly to the bleeding part. She was in two minds as to whether or not a tourniquet should be put around the wrist to help stem the bleeding. She had heard that you had to be very careful when using tourniquets because, if applied too tightly, you could cut off circulation completely and do irreparable limb damage. She was no expert, so she decided against a tourniquet. There was no doubt the flyer needed immediate medical attention, but that was not likely to happen.

While Annette was doing the bandaging, her helpers had climbed the tree again to retrieve all parts of the parachute that had remained suspended. There was a double incentive to do this; first, to remove all evidence from German eyes that one of their enemy was in the area, and, secondly, the parachute silk could be put to good use as barter for food in local markets.

It was decided that the flyer should go back to the cave to regain a little strength, to be made warm and to be given some water and food. His heavy flying jacket and fur-lined boots had saved him from hypothermia during the freezing night. And luck had played a big part in his survival. To fall into the trees in this part of the forest on this day and to be found by Annette, a very smart and plucky young woman, was evidence that the Fates were sometimes kindly.

Annette went back to the cave with her flyer's rescuers mainly to act as interpreter and to see that he was made as comfortable as possible. The flyer's hand was not his only problem. He said that his shoulder felt as though a red-hot poker had pierced it, but he tried to dismiss the pain as being just a strain from crashing into the branches of the trees that arrested his fall. Annette sensed otherwise, for he had difficulty in putting any weight on his right hand when he went to sit down on the cave floor; in fact, his whole arm collapsed when he did so.

"Englishman, let me take a look at that shoulder of yours. I don't think it is good. Now no arguments. I'm just going to slip my hand inside your jacket and shirt and feel around a bit. I promise to be gentle."

Her actions raised a few cheers and some deep sighs from the men gathered around her, inspecting the newcomer. One said that he had a shoulder problem that definitely needed her attention. It took but a minute for Annette to diagnose that the flyer had a broken collar bone. She looked around for an old shirt in the bundle of clothes not yet distributed, found one and tore it into a shape suitable for an arm sling. This adequately supported the flyer's forearm to take the load off the broken bone, but that put both of his arms out of commission and he desperately needed to light a cigarette. He shuffled his bottom on the cave floor until his back was against the wall.

"Fair maiden, in my right jacket pocket you'll find a full packet of cigarettes; Players to be exact, and some matches. Be a love and light one for me and I'll remember you in my will. Then dish out one each to these lucky lads standing around and take one yourself. No, on second thoughts, you take three for yourself. You've more than earned them."

"Thanks, Englishman, I'll enjoy them later. Here, here's yours, burning nicely. Enjoy it," said Annette, slipping the cigarette between his chapped and swollen lips. He pursed his mouth and inhaled strongly, held the sweet smoke in his lungs for as long as he could and then exhaled slowly, grudgingly. He repeated the process until the cigarette was totally consumed, rested his head back against the wall and closed his eyes; he had found a temporary relief.

"Englishman, don't sleep yet! We need to know who you are and where you've come from. I have to go soon and report to my....... er,........ er,....... how you say, er, boss, yes, that's it, big boss. He likes to know everything."

Without opening his eyes, the Englishman said, "I'm James Alcock, Squadron Leader, DFC, of the Royal Air

Force, serial number 5011360. That's all I'm obliged to give you by the Geneva Convention."

"What are you talking about, Squadron Leader Alcock? You're not a prisoner of war. We're on your side, you know, well, at least up here in Northern France. Can't you tell us more? Maybe we can contact England and ask what to do with you. Are you a pilot? Bomber or fighter? Where's your home base? Where did you fly to last night? If a bomber pilot, what happened to the rest of your crew? Did they bale out? Are they likely to be in this area? Come on, if we're going to help you we need to know these things," demanded Annette, sternly, but then she gave a small laugh. "Excuse me, but you have a funny name, Alcock. What does it mean?"

"I can assure you that it is a fine Anglo-Saxon name which does not have any direct links to my anatomy. But forget my surname; just call me Jimmy."

"OK, Jimmy, then give me some answers. I need to know more about you," insisted Annette.

"Right-ho! I'm a bomber pilot. My squadron of Halifaxes attacked St. Nazaire last night. The flak was heavy and my plane was hit, although not too badly. Nevertheless, I lost an engine and two of my crew were killed. We headed for home, a base near Bristol, but we were losing fuel pretty quickly. I ordered the rest of my crew to bale out, but I hung on until the last moment before jumping. Must have been about midnight. I didn't see the plane go down. Might have gone on for quite a few miles before taking the final plunge; could have made the Channel, I suppose."

"Could the rest of your crew that baled out have landed near here?" asked Annette.

"I doubt it. They'd be much closer to St. Nazaire. I stayed at the controls for quite a while after they jumped. Well, that's about it, and here I am, wherever 'here' is."

"I can't tell you exactly. The Germans might still capture you and torture information out of you about us. I'll just say that you're not too far from Rennes. Also, right now, I won't tell you my name or those of the men around you, although you probably heard some of them as we got you out of your favorite tree and walked here. Now, I really must get going, but I'll be back later. These men will look after you. I suspect one or two of them speak a little English, but don't expect them to say so. If not, then communicate with hand gestures. Oops, sorry! I forgot your hands aren't working too well. Really sorry!"

* * * * *

Annette left the cave once more and was able to get back to Erwan's farm without incident. She found Erwan, Marcel and Claudette in the kitchen, eating scrambled eggs and drinking a glass of fresh milk. She was ravenous and joined in the meal energetically, slowly revealing the dramatic events of the night in between mouthfuls. Marcel gave considerable deep thought to Squadron Leader Alcock's condition and what, eventually, should be done with him.

"You say, Annette, that he can walk OK, although the jarring motion makes his hand and shoulder become painful. Well, too bad, he'll have to put up with that. He obviously needs a doctor to look at him, particularly his hand; he could get gangrene in it unless it's properly cleaned and dressed. So he can't stay in the cave, which means he'll have to come here and be cared for. There's no other immediate solution. Of course, it's yet another risk we're taking."

For some time Claudette had sat quietly absorbing all that was said, but she had become more and more agitated by what she heard. Her eyes showed fright as she flicked them from person to person. Her hands, clenched into fists with white knuckles, rested on the edge of the table. Her lips were drawn tight, but then burst open and issued a torrent of scathing words.

"No, no, no! He shall not come here! Never! It is impossible. *I* can't take anymore of your dangerous games; yes, that's what they are, games, terribly dangerous games. You all want to be heroes, well I don't; I've put up with enough and I'm frightened to death. You go out in the middle of the night with your guns and your hand grenades, and I never know whether Erwan will come back to me. You allow a man who looks like an escaped convict to come into my house, eat my food and maybe cut my throat. You keep an illegal transmitter in the barn and let another total stranger come in at midnight and use it, sending messages to God knows whom. Annette uses this place as though it were her own home, sleeping here, sleeping there, creeping in, creeping out. And now, ... now you want to bring a wounded Britisher here, dripping blood everywhere, with every German between here and the coast looking for him. If they catch him here, we'll all be shot or worse. I tell you, I've had enough!"

Tense silence prevailed, then Erwan slowly moved his hands to cover both of Claudette's. He gently caressed them using his thumbs and looked understandingly into her watering eyes.

"I'm sorry, my love, I know it's hard for you, but we're all frightened too. And it's not a game, it really isn't. We've got to struggle against the Nazi bastards, or they'll be here for a thousand years, making us their slaves and slowly wiping us out. We mustn't make it easy for them. No matter how small our efforts, I believe each one will affect the outcome, will help the Allies. Try and believe that. Come on, give us a smile, just a little one. Come on!"

A glimmer of a smile lightened Claudette's troubled face, but, nevertheless, she released her hands from Erwan's, slowly stood up and quietly left the kitchen with a mixture of embarrassment, lingering anger and resentment.

"I think she'll come round in the end," said Erwan, softly. "She's tougher than she just sounded. But back to our problem; I agree with Marcel, we have no choice but to bring the Britisher here."

"What about you Annette, what do you think?" asked Marcel, wanting full agreement.

"Definitely, he must come here, and you can call him Jimmy; sounds more friendly than 'Britisher'."

"Good, that's settled then. Annette, you bring him back with you tonight after making your second supplies trip to the cavemen. Perhaps Jimmy can squeeze into your bedroom, Erwan, on an old straw mattress. Let's get your doctor out early on Sunday morning to check him out. I'll get Igor to let London know about our new complication, and suggest they airlift Jimmy to England along with Jean and me. I hope they can do that soon. God, I hate being responsible for wounded warriors; I've had too many die on me."

Chapter Twenty

That night, Annette found the cave again, and delivered a further set of supplies scrounged from friends and neighbors by her Aunt. This time Jean's men were most appreciative of her efforts, and, having rested well, had regained their strength and liveliness. Annette's cheeks had a thousand kisses planted on them by her admirers. Jimmy, on the other hand, was not so good. His hand throbbed severely and he kept on becoming light-headed. However, he was able to walk slowly to the farm, guided in the darkness by Annette and Jean. Once there, he collapsed on a mattress in Erwan's spare bedroom and slept soundly until Sunday morning.

When the doctor arrived at the farm, he could not hide his anxiety about Jimmy's hand, but said that there was presently no sign of gangrene. He cleaned and redressed the severed fingers, and made a point of *not* asking what the plans were for Jimmy's future. While at the house, he also examined Erwan's leg which was healing nicely, and gave him permission to resume all reasonable activities.

SOE in London reacted quickly and positively to the request for an airlift as soon as possible. Perhaps Squadron Leader Alcock was classed as a V.I.P, and was likely to have some important intelligence about the St. Nazaire raid.

A lift would take place on Monday night at 2200 hours.

Chapter Twenty-One

The SOE had a love affair with the "Lizzie", the affectionate name for the Westland Lysander, or, to be more precise, the Lysander IIIA (SD) version, the SD standing for Special Duties. It, or rather she, was a slow-flying, high-wing monoplane with a dual cockpit that gave an excellent field of vision. However, its appearance was rather comical, resembling a pregnant duck with its legs permanently down and feet covered with oversized spats or mudguards.

The initial version entered service as an RAF ground support combat aircraft in 1938, equipped with three 0.303 machine guns, two in the wheel spats and one in the rear cockpit. As an alternative to the guns, sixteen 9 kg bombs could be carried on racks attached to the spats. This version did not meet with any success due to its slowness and light armaments. But because of its low landing speed of 45 mph, and short takeoff and landing distances on almost any type of terrain, it was ideal for the cloak-and-dagger operations of SOE. Thus the IIIA (SD) was evolved, discarding all guns and adding an extra 150 gallon fuel tank to beef the range up to 700 miles.

In order to quickly drop off and pick up agents or other persons, a ladder was fitted to the port side of the rear cockpit which could carry two or, with a squeeze, three passengers and associated equipment. The SOE had three squadrons of Lizzies and their daring pilots transported more than 800 agents into and out of the fields of France, at night, between 1941 and 1945.

The winds were high on the night of January 12, 1942, almost gale force coming from the south west, and the Lizzie pilot had his hands full crossing the Channel from RAF Tangmere, his base in southern England near Chichester. For him it was almost a head wind, and he could not get anywhere near his basic cruising speed of 165 mph with the plane's Bristol Mercury XX, radial, air-cooled engine. 870 horsepower just wasn't enough. From Tangmere the pilot had set a course to Guernsey, one of the Channel Islands, which, if he found it, would give him a very good fix before turning south towards the Brittany coast. Although flying was hard work, the pilot seemed happy enough either singing the latest Vera Lynn song, or telling his passenger dirty jokes. Not that the passenger was really receptive to communication of any kind. His sole occupation was keeping the contents of his stomach where they should be, and not putting them over the cockpit floor.

It was a beautifully clear night with but a few clouds and a moon and stars that swayed and pitched in unison. Unfortunately, the moon was waning in its last quarter. Normally, SOE flew their agents on or close to the time of the full moon in order to have its maximum illumination for finding the landing zone. But the next full moon was not until February 1, and this would be too late to pick up the wounded Squadron Leader who needed proper medical attention as soon as possible. In this case, the rules had to be bent, and the pilot's eyes had to be a lot sharper.

A thousand feet below, the Channel was churning with white caps on the large waves, angry at the wind for not letting it sleep. The pilot thought of bomber crews unfortunate enough to have to ditch into such a seething cauldron of foam and coldness; their chances of survival would be nil. As the pilot approached the Brittany coast, he put the Lizzie into a steep dive in order to get down to about two hundred feet. This height would drop him below the German radar sweeps. His passenger thought his last moment had come, and he let loose with all the expletives his mother had not taught him. He was not aware that the pilot had crossed the coast on a southerly heading well west of Dinard to avoid German flak.

Now navigation became difficult, and the Lysander did not carry a navigator. The pilot had to do it all; fly and read a map perched on his thigh all at the same time. To see the map he had to juggle a flashlight, which, if dropped, would be hard to retrieve. The trouble with flying so low was that it restricted map reading; landmarks came and went too quickly to be recognized, and the range of vision, port, starboard and ahead, was much reduced. Consequently, once clear of the coast the pilot climbed to one thousand feet again to get his bearings. But even so, the country below consisted of many little villages with hardly any lights showing, narrow roads, small lakes, and small woods. Distinguishing features in the dark was difficult, but soon the pilot gained confidence when, with a little help from the moon, he pinpointed the string of lakes and adjoining rivers west of Dinan. Near Caulnes he spotted the railway line that went down to Montauban and on to Rennes, which appeared as a large black mass well to the east. Directly south he could see another large black area which he guessed was the Forêt de Paimpont.

Although the pilot had landed agents in this general area before, he had not made the acquaintance of the specific field for tonight's rendezvous. However, his friends on the ground were supposed to place a series of oil lamps in the field marking the least hazardous section for landing on. They were also supposed to flash the letter 'L' in Morse code if it were safe to land.

The Lizzie passed over the northern edge of the forest but the pilot did not see any welcoming lights.

"Where the hell are they?" said the pilot. "I'm sure I'm in the right area. Yes, over there is the main road passing through Mauron; well, at least it *could* be Mauron. Bloody hell, this is getting tricky! I'll have to go lower and circle. Keep your eyes skinned, Joe. This is your show, you know. I don't want to do all the work. At least the wind has dropped;

we might even be able to land in one piece, if we can find the bloody field. Hang on, time for the merry-go-round."

The pilot banked the plane until its wings were almost vertical and then proceeded to fly in ever increasing circles. Joe, the passenger, was beginning to find his wings *and* keep his stomach; in fact, he was beginning to quite enjoy the violent maneuvers.

* * * * *

On the ground waiting anxiously were Marcel, Erwan, Annette, Jean and Squadron Leader Alcock. They had positioned themselves in front of the hedge over which the Lizzie would fly as it landed. The field selected for the landing was three fields north of the one where the supplies drop had taken place earlier that month. Given that the Germans had been present then, would they be present again tonight? In selecting tonight's field, Marcel was betting that the Germans would apply the logic that lightning and the Resistance do not strike twice in the same place. And the Germans are a very logical people. The French, on the other hand, are good at reverse logic, which works a fair percentage of the time. However, Marcel protected his bet by having five of Jean's men patrol the edge of the wood. He kept Erwan and Annette in support just a few yards away from him.

"Where's the damn plane?" growled Marcel. "It's late, damn late! We can't keep those lanterns out there much longer. It's a dead give away."

"It'll be here," said Alcock, with confidence. "I know the squadron that runs these operations; their pilots don't give up easily, believe me. He probably encountered severe head winds."

Alcock had an exhausting pain in his broken shoulder, and his hand was throbbing mercilessly. The moonlight showed his face to be ashen, and his eyes seemed sunken in their sockets from lack of sleep and fatigue. It was imperative that he be lifted tonight.

"I hear something," said Jean, " very faint but definitely something; an engine maybe."

"And maybe it's Erwan's cows in the next field chewing the cud," replied Marcel, attempting a little humor to dispel the tenseness.

"It's getting louder. I'm right," said Jean.

Erwan and Annette had also heard the noise and pointed upwards. A few seconds later the Lizzie passed over them but headed for the forest.

"Jesus Christ, he's missed us!" screamed Annette. "He's gone, gone! I don't believe it! Can't he see the lights? He must see the lights, he must." Then a shock of guilt ran through her body. "Oh, my God, I forgot to flash the signal to land, and I've got the flashlight right in my hand. Come back, come back, please come back."

Marcel also realized that the code letter had not been flashed, and rushed over to Annette in a furious temper.

"You stupid woman! You dumb idiot, why didn't you send the code letter?" said Marcel, and grabbed the flashlight out of Annette's hand.

"OK, OK, I'm sorry, I'm sorry."

"Calm down Marcel; it was my fault. I distracted her," said Erwan, instinctively protecting Annette from Marcel's verbal abuse.

"Oh yeah, doing what?"

"The plane's coming back; look, it's circling," said Annette, with relief.

Marcel flashed the code letter frantically, and then repeated it frequently. The rhythm of the Morse flashes soothed his temper, and, as the plane definitely seemed to be lining up for a landing, a small smile of satisfaction spread over his face.

In the Lizzie, the pilot was very active. He had finally seen the landing lights, after circling a couple of times, but without seeing the code letter, he dared not land for that meant there was trouble on the ground. He would have to abort the mission. *Bloody hell*, he thought, *I've put a lot of effort into this caper, must I really go home empty-handed.*

"God damn it! Blast! Hang on, Joe, I'm not finished yet. I'm going around again. You down there, give us the signal boys and girls. I haven't got all night!"

No sooner had the pilot uttered these reprimanding words than he saw the flashes. "That's more like it! Joe, we're cleared for landing. Whoopee! Just hope it's not all mud in that field down there; I'd hate the boys back home to call me a stick-in-the mud."

But Joe wasn't listening; he had other things on his mind, such as his very imminent transition from being in a relatively friendly place into one where the enemy wanted his death, where survival depended on his own wits and a lot of luck.

The pilot lined himself up with the lights that formed the L-shaped landing strip and checked his altimeter for the last time. From now on it would be seat-of-his-pants flying; he already had beads of sweat on his upper lip. He mumbled to himself for reassurance, "Slats and flaps down, landing lights on, adjust throttle and attitude, tricky crosswind now, keep correcting drift, speed 70 mph,........ 60,........ 50,...... that should do it. Over the final hedge now,....... searching for the ground. God, I hope it's frozen hard."

The wheels touched, bounced and touched again before the plane settled. The ground was solid, although bumpy, but that was to be expected; it was only a farmer's field. The Lizzie waddled down the field losing momentum until the pilot could turn it around and taxi back to where he first touched down. Then a small burst of power swung the plane around for a quick take-off. The pilot cut the throttle back to idle, praying that the engine would not die as the human cargo was deposited and a new one picked up.

The agent used the ladder on the port side of the fuselage to reach the ground, after he had lowered some critical packages and bags that had traveled with him. While he was doing this, the new passengers, Marcel, Jean and Alcock hurried out to the plane, immediately followed by Erwan and

Annette. The pilot stood under the plane's wing and welcomed his superior officer with a lazy RAF salute.

"Good evening, sir. Flying Officer Evans at your service. I trust your are well and looking forward to a nice trip home."

"Cut the crap, shall we, and help me up into your flying duck," said Alcock, but first he turned and kissed Annette on both cheeks.

"Thanks a million, Annette, you saved my life and I'll be eternally grateful. If you get tired of the Resistance, come to England and join the WAAFs. You're a sparkling diamond. God bless!" He then turned to the others and offered his right hand from inside his shoulder sling. He was part way through giving further thanks to them when Evans cut him short.

"OK, sir, we've really got to get going. Time is of the essence unless you want a German bullet up your backside."

Alcock was assisted into the second seat in the cockpit and strapped in while Marcel and Jean said their good-byes. Marcel gave Annette a particularly warm farewell to compensate for his roughness to her over the flashlight incident. It was a tight squeeze for Marcel and Jean on the floor behind Alcock, but they were used to tight spots in their line of business. The pilot released the brakes and opened the throttle fully; it had been four minutes since he landed, an average time, but no time was short enough for him. The Lizzie was quickly airborne and rose gently into the night, hoping for a safe passage home.

Annette and Erwan looked around for the agent, Joe, but he had already disappeared like a vanishing phantom. He did not need them; he was self-contained and knew exactly where he was and what he had to do. Erwan helped Annette shoulder one of the heavy packs brought by Joe, and together they set off cross-country to the farm.

As she walked, Annette felt a warm satisfaction about her part in helping the Squadron Leader escape. He had said that she'd saved his life. That pleased her. She had never saved anyone's life before, and it gave her a sense of her own value. It was neither smugness nor pride that she felt, but a quiet happiness, a calming, a release of tension. She decided that saving people was far preferable to shooting them.

Chapter Twenty-Two

The Lysander had a successful flight back to RAF Tangmere, although the air turbulence gave the passengers less than a comfortable ride. As soon as the plane landed, an ambulance whisked the Squadron Leader away to the station infirmary for initial medical evaluation. Subsequently, he was sent to a London hospital for reconstructive surgery on his hand.

Marcel and Jean were quickly but quietly driven to SOE Headquarters in London; Norgeby House in Baker Street. Here they underwent an extensive de-briefing of the separate operations they had been involved in over the last four months. Jean, in particular, was grilled for several hours on end, almost as though he were an enemy and not a Resistance fighter. This was because London knew very little about his loose-knit communist group or the Renoir circuit to which it was attached. The story about his group's betrayal in Normandy had to be checked; the resistance methods his group used had to be compared with those of SOE's; his knowledge of weapons and the latest "dirty tricks" gadgets had to be surreptitiously ascertained; his leadership capabilities, mental stability, aggressiveness, dedication to the cause and many other aspects of his character had to be evaluated. Until proven otherwise, a cloud of suspicion would hang over him. Proof as to whether that cloud could be lifted or not would be drawn from Jean's performance during intensive training courses he was required to attend in Scotland and England.

Marcel, of course, was a true blue member of Section F, fully trained and much respected. Apart from telling the SOE "interrogators" what he knew of Jean, his main mission in London was a shopping expedition. The circuits in western France were woefully short of weapons, explosives, money, transmitters, first aid supplies, warm clothing, maps, false identity papers and food ration coupons. Marcel wanted more supply drops by the RAF or coastal smuggling by the Royal Navy. He pleaded and cajoled but promises were slim. SOE was still finding its feet, and competition for resources with the real armed forces and the Special Intelligence Service, SIS, was fierce and very political.

* * * * *

On his third day in London, Marcel was summoned to a meeting with a high-ranking staff member of the Operations and Training Department in a small flat which was a five minute walk from Baker Street. He had no idea what the meeting was to be about.

"Sit down Marcel, sit, sit. Glad you could come. Sorry about the sparseness of this room. Bit dark and dingy, ain't it. Still, I bet you're used to all kinds of privations working out there in the field. Cigarette?"

"No thanks, I don't smoke," responded Marcel as he sat down on a wooden chair that was no more than a rough plank with four legs on it.

"Good, good, I like that. You probably need to keep your lungs in tip-top condition for chasing Jerries through the woods, or do they chase you? Eh? Eh? But enough of that. You can call me Charles, Marcel."

Charles was an ugly man with a greasy nose. His short and rotund stature prevented his feet from reaching the ground as he sat in his chair, consequently, he frequently went through a squirming motion to try and relieve the load on his backside. His face wore a perpetual grin, so it was hard to know when he was actually attempting to be humorous and when he was serious. To be on the safe side most people did not laugh when he was talking. Although Charles's demeanor was not pleasant, he was very, very clever. Educated at Eton and taking a first class honors degree at Cambridge in Politics, Philosophy and Economics made him an ideal staff member for the SOE. In addition, he had many good contacts in high places, inherited from his father who had been a conservative cabinet minister. Marcel had met many men like Charles in both England and France, and so was not intimidated or annoyed by his affected language and behavior. If anything, he was just quietly amused by him.

"I need not say that everything we talk about in this splendid room is top secret; top, top, secret. You understand, Marcel? You talk and I'll shoot you! Good.

"So what's it all about, eh? Well, SOE needs a big one. We need a big success right now or we'll be on the way out before the summer. We know we're good but nobody else does. We're viewed as a group who thinks a lot and delivers only a little. So what we're going to do is blow up a damn great supply dump south of Rennes. Won't that be fun!"

Charles produced a map from his briefcase beneath his desk and laid it out on top. Marcel leaned forward as Charles prodded the map with a fat forefinger.

"The dump's right here. The Jerries built a line off the main Rennes- St. Nazaire railway to take not only ammo but tanks, armored vehicles, anti-aircraft guns and God knows what else into this area. The goodies are then off-loaded from the rail cars and dispersed into staging sections. When Hitler decides who needs what, the equipment is assembled, reloaded and shipped either by road or back onto freight trains. The place is heavily defended and heavily camouflaged.

"Now, do you know this place, Marcel?"

"I've passed by in the vicinity a couple of times but never really got close to it. The Germans discourage sightseers with road diversions and identity checks by Waffen SS."

"That's good. Assuming you're willing to join our little party, you'll get to know the area like the back of your hand.

So now for a few details. This is going to be a joint RAF-Resistance operation; bombs from above and plastic from below. Twenty Resistance men will penetrate the defenses and judiciously lay explosives against piles of ammo and some of the biggest tanks you can find. The plastic will have delayed fuses, set or wired. The men will retire to a safe distance and wait for the arrival of a squadron of RAF heavy bombers. You blow the plastic when the bombers are overhead and down come the bombs. Talk about Guy Fawkes night! What a magnificent show!"

"Wait, wait! If we're using plastic, why do we need the RAF? We can handle this job alone," stated Marcel, emphatically.

"There are several reasons why we need the RAF, the main one being that their 500lb bombs pack a bigger wallop than your bits of plastic, and there are tons of armored steel vehicles to be torn asunder. But, of course, their bombs will only be effective if they hit the target, and that's where the bangs and fires caused by your boys play a big part. They'll be acting as markers for the bombers who'll need as much help as they can get in pin-pointing the target.

"Secondly, if you attacked the dump alone, the Germans would know that it was a Resistance operation and take reprisals against French civilians the following day. There would be a massacre, which, in turn, would be partly blamed on the Resistance by those Frenchmen who prefer to sit safely on the sidelines. So the RAF will be your cover story, if you will. The RAF raid will hide your contribution to the war effort.

"Now, the raid will cause total confusion amongst the German soldiers guarding the dump. It will blast open further holes in the perimeter defenses and allow your men to trot into the dump again and finish off anything the bombs missed. The Germans won't notice you amidst the fires, smoke and bedlam that will reign supreme. Of course, perfect timing will be of the essence."

"Yes, you're right, but the essence might be the smell coming from the burning bodies of my men if we're too early or the RAF too late," said Marcel, with a cynical smirk on his face.

"Just take a good Swiss watch along with you and you'll be fine; absolutely no problem at all," countered Charles.

"Then perhaps you'd care to come along with us; you could be the official timekeeper."

"I'd love to, old boy, but loud bangs make me nervous and upset my intellectual capabilities, not to mention my stomach. Somebody has to do the deep thinking back at base, and that's me. No, I'm sure you'll do a fine job, and such a joint operation will show just how well SOE can cooperate with the "real" armed forces. It'll be a beautiful, bright feather in our political cap.

"So, that's about it for now. I'm glad you're enthusiastic about this operation. Now I'll turn you over to the detail planners on my staff in the flat below. I'm sure you have a thousand questions which they'll answer to your complete satisfaction. It was fun meeting you, Marcel; I always love talking to a real, live agent. Better than talking to a dead one, eh, eh. You get that one?"

"Yes, I get it, sir."

Charles pushed a button underneath his desk and his secretary appeared promptly to escort Marcel to the flat below where he met the two main planners of the operation; both were military men, one seconded from RAF Bomber Command and the other from the Royal Engineers. It was a fruitful meeting with Marcel making useful input. He came away feeling much better about the operation, even believing that it could be a success. However, he emphasized again that if he were to support the attack on the dump with at least twenty men then those men needed to be armed to the teeth. He demanded an arms drop before the operation - plastic explosives and detonators, Sten guns, Bren guns, hand-grenades, commando knives, mortars.

* * * * *

Jean was to go on two training courses, one in the wilds of Scotland north of Fort William, where he would be subjected to vigorous and difficult physical exercises, and a second one on a private estate, commandeered by SOE for the duration of hostilities, on the south coast of England. The latter course was designed to evaluate the mental toughness and personality of potential field agents, to find weaknesses and strengths. If Jean passed both courses he would be offered employment as a full field agent with SOE in France. If he failed there would be no offer, and he would have to remain in Britain until the war was over, because he would know too much about SOE's modus operandi to risk him being returned to France as an ordinary civilian.

Jean had a few days to kill before going to Scotland, so he and Marcel ventured forth from their small hotel and did some limited sight-seeing in London, or what was left of it. Although the height of the blitz had past, the Luftwaffe was still killing and maiming Londoners and attacking other strategic targets throughout the country. Jean found out first hand what it was like to spend a night underground in the fetid air of a Tube station, confined with hundreds of inwardly scared but plucky people, young and old, trying to get some sleep before surfacing at dawn to see if their homes and shops were still standing. They looked exhausted, hollow-eyed and emaciated from the daily struggle, not knowing when, or if, it would ever end.

Jean had not been to London before or any other part of England, so he was determined to see as much of the city as conditions would allow. He mentally compared Westminster Abbey with Notre-Dame, St. Paul's Cathedral with the Sacré-Coeur, and Buckingham Palace with Versailles. He also compared the girls at the Windmill Theatre with those at the Folies-Bergères; all were objects of beauty.

But his time in London was soon over, and Jean headed by train to Glasgow with four other SOE candidates, all of whom were British. This was just as well for Jean's command of the English language, although adequate, did not stretch to understanding broad Glaswegian, whereas one of his companions was himself a Scot and obligingly translated the directions of a railway porter as to how to get to the platform for the Fort William train.

Left in London, Marcel was kept busy with more intelligence meetings at SOE headquarters, and arranging for him to be parachuted back into France some time close to the next full moon, which was on February 1. Originally, Marcel was to take back with him new, SOE-forged, *cartes d'identité* (identity papers) for Jean's men, but he left France without the men's photographs for the documents. The photographs were essential, therefore it was decided to use a reliable forger in Rennes to make all personal papers, permits and food coupons. This involved much risk not only for the forger but also his supporters in the city registry offices where the new, fictitious birth certificates of thirteen fully grown men would have to be surreptitiously recorded.

* * * * *

Two days prior to Marcel's anticipated journey back to France he visited James Alcock in a convalescence hospital fifteen miles north of London. Alcock had had two successful operations on his wounded hand, which had escaped becoming infected. Although his manual dexterity was reduced, he was pleased with what he could still do with his remaining fingers, and he expected to return to flying duties very shortly.

Alcock was pleased to see Marcel again, and heaped many more thanks on him for all that he had done. In particular, he wanted to send a thousand hugs and kisses to Annette, who, he believed, should be sent a *Croix de Guerre* by General de Gaulle. This was not a moment of passing praise, for much of his time he thought of her courage, resourcefulness, patience and sympathetic nature. He vowed to seek her out after the war and repay his debt to her.

Chapter Twenty-Three

When Erwan and Annette arrived back at the farm after seeing the Lysander safely off, they went straight into the barn to unload the heavy packs sent from England. They were surprised and thrilled to find an S-phone in one pack, just like the one poor André had used so effectively during the last airdrop on the night he was killed. As she gazed at the device, Annette felt a heaviness in her heart as memories of André were rekindled; his quietness when with a group of people, introspective but not morose; his intense concentration when receiving and sending messages, as though he were talking to God; his comical, drunken bicycle ride across the farmyard after Christmas dinner and his close encounter with a cow pat.

To erase the bitter-sweet memories she helped Erwan delve into the second pack. There they found a bundle of French franc notes, not a fortune but an essential commodity for the survival of the men in the cave. Money bought food, clothing, medical supplies and fuel. Money was needed for bribery. Money was needed for travel. In an occupied country, money could save your life. In the same pack were found three pistols, one with a silencer, a box of bullets, a commando knife with a vicious-looking eight-inch blade, a Michelin map of Brittany, and, strangely, a small book of French poetry. Annette picked up one of the pistols and held it in the palm of her right hand, gently moving it up and down as though weighing it. Then she flopped it into her left hand and back again into the right.

"It has a nice feel to it, Erwan. I want to take it home. If any German comes to get me, I'll get him first."

"Oh, no! Definitely not, far too risky! The gun stays here for use on sabotage operations only," said Erwan, with a hint of anger.

"Come on, Erwan, I'm not a child anymore. Please?"

"I said no, and that's that." Erwan realized he had roughness in his voice, so after a few seconds he reached out and gently held her left hand while he took the gun from her right. "I would worry the whole time it was in your house. The Gestapo occasionally do a sweep through the village making random house searches. If they found this, you and your aunt would probably be shot. I would lose my best friend."

The light from the lantern in the barn was just strong enough to show the sincerity in Erwan's eyes, and the soft response on Annette's face as she gave a small sigh. "Erwan, you're very sweet. Almost sweet enough to love." Erwan gave a short laugh.

"Brother-sister love?" he questioned.

"Of course, as always." Annette knew what Erwan was trying to say. "You're married, Erwan; that's the only type of love we can have, isn't it?" Erwan still held her hand, feeling its coolness and a little tremble running out through the fingers.

"Can I ask you about Marcel?"

"Marcel? What about Marcel?"

"Well, is he like another brother to you, or is there something more between you?" Erwan was remembering the very fond farewell they gave one another before Marcel climbed into the Lysander. Although Erwan could not see it, Annette blushed at hearing this unexpected question.

"Don't be silly, Erwan. I like him most of the time, yet he can make me angry. When he calls me a *stupid woman*, I really get mad. I certainly don't love him. There is no grand passion, believe me. To tell you the truth, parts of his character worry me. He has mood swings, and there seems to be an aggressiveness waiting just below the surface. I'd say he could be quite cruel, even to his friends." But Erwan was skeptical at her response.

"What about Christmas night? You went to his room; you must have made love?"

"We did not, really, we did not, believe me. I was freezing cold. All I wanted was someone's body heat. And I was dead tired. Cold and tiredness do not allow for a romantic union."

"So, you're still a virgin?" asked Erwan.

"What? What? Why all these immature questions about romance and sex? They don't go with these items around us; the guns, the bullets, the knife. Romance and weapons of war are not a good match."

"Maybe so, but we still need some romance in time of war or we'd all go insane," replied Erwan, not really knowing what he was trying to say.

"Right now, I don't need romance and I don't need sex. As for my virginity, well, that's my business. All I'll say is that I'm twenty-three and I've lived in Paris, the city of love and light. So you figure it out. The subject is now closed, and I want to go home, if you don't mind."

Erwan could not mistake Annette's peevishness and chided himself for his clumsy questions, but he had wanted to ask them for a long time.

As Annette was leaving, Igor entered the barn to listen into Grendon and decode any messages, but none came. Annette took most of the money with her, intent on buying food with it for Jean's men. She would make another delivery in two days time, and after that Erwan's leg would be fully healed so he could take over liaison duties. It was time for Jean's men to earn their keep by planning and executing acts of sabotage while their leader was away in Scotland, eating haggis and drinking malt whiskey.

Chapter Twenty-Four

The following morning a tired Annette had to face her class and pretend that nothing out of the ordinary had happened the night before. One or two of her pupils looked at her quizzically when a vacant expression appeared on her face followed by the whisper of a smile. *What was she thinking about? Why does she seem happy? Teacher normally thinks about nothing but reading and writing and sums and being cross with us.*

In fact, although tired, Annette was relatively happy because of the success of the Lysander pickup. No one was shot, no one was hurt. And part of her smile was for the conversation with Erwan in the barn; the talk of love and virginity. She knew from her late teenage years that Erwan wanted her love, not just her friendship. She saw him suffer in his unrequited emotions, but she could do nothing about that. She was sorry for him, but only to a certain extent, for had he not found a wife, a woman of his stock, of his farming life, someone more compatible than she, a Parisienne.

"Mademoiselle Renard, you didn't give me the list of sums we have to do. Mademoiselle? Mademoiselle?" said an almost tearful little boy in the second row. "Mademoiselle, please, the list?" Annette was awakened from her meandering, personal thoughts by the insistence of the boy's question.

"Yes, yes, I heard you Jean-Paul. You should know by now that each of you don't have a list because of the severe paper shortage; there's one per row. Whoever has the list in

Jean-Paul's row please pass it to him, so he can copy the sums onto his slate. Good heavens, what a fuss Jean-Paul!"

The grating, squeaking sound of chalk-on-slate as the children did their sums ensured that Annette's mind remained focused on the class, and did not drift off again into her night-time activities with the Resistance. There was one train of thought, however, that combined her two distinctly different occupations. That was the question of a substitute teacher. Sometimes Resistance plans would call for her to be away from school, and on such occasions another teacher would have to stand-in for her. A few days ago, Annette had arranged for Madame Binoche to be her substitute. She was a kindly person with a good sense of humor, and she had had some teaching experience. Although sixty years of age and a little arthritic, she could still move quickly up and down the aisles between desks, meting out discipline when needed. She had been widowed by the First World War, and her one child, a son, had died of la grippe, or influenza, in the epidemic of 1918. Annette thought that this would be a good time to tell her pupils about Madame Binoche who, fortunately, was no stranger to most of them for she lived in their village. The news produced a mixed reaction; some cheers, some groans. Then the sounds of chalk-on-slate continued.

The morning progressed well until a half an hour before lunch break when, as before, Hauptsturmfuhrer Eichmann entered the classroom and sat in an empty desk at the back. Annette stared at him, grimly. He stared back. Nothing was said. But then he did something that had not occurred in his previous visit. His prolonged stare turned into a sheepish smile, and he lowered his eyes as though embarrassed. This action worried Annette; it did not fit his character as she knew it. The ugly, aggressive, sinister Gestapo man was showing a softer side, which she did not trust. What was he up to, she asked herself, and gave an involuntary shudder. Then he left quietly. His visit had only lasted two minutes but it hung in the air; the children felt it as a foreboding, a coldness, a fearful thing. Annette broke the tension.

"All right, everyone, the nasty man has gone, and to celebrate we'll have lunch early. Take out your caviar, your cold roast beef sandwiches and your Camembert. *Bon appetit, mes enfants.*" But all the children could produce from their ragged pockets were small lumps of gray bread, a few thin carrots, and a dry biscuit, which the health authorities said contained a protein supplement.

Annette looked at each of the children as they ate their tasteless, nutritionless, meager rations. The war had been on for over two years now, and in that time she had seen a steady decline in the health and appearance of almost every child. Some had boils on the nose and back of the neck, miniature volcanoes waiting to erupt a flow of pus. Others had flaky, sallow skin and cracked lips and hands, victims of painful chilblains caused by living in unheated houses and having poor blood circulation. The younger ones had spindly legs and arms that seemed to have no muscles on them. Teeth were yellow with dark areas where caries lurked, ready to cause excruciating pain leading, eventually, to an extraction by a mother wielding a pair of pliers with tears in her eyes. There were no dentists in the local villages. Yet somehow, despite their emaciated bodies, the children still played running games, still jumped and hopped and wrestled. Above all, they still showed spirit, dampened, maybe, but not extinguished.

That the children were alive at all was due to the food rationing program, the objective of which was to give everyone the same, albeit inadequate, share of what food was available. Food rationing had been in effect since the beginning of the war, and had been implemented by the issuing of the all-important *carte d'alimentation* (ration card) and its accompanying colored stamps which were called "tickets", an English word. The English, in an effort to keep the *entente cordiale* alive, called their stamps "coupons", a French word. The whole food rationing process revolved around a massive bureaucratic core. First, to obtain a ration card, a person had to register with the authorities. Next it was necessary to register with your usual local baker, butcher, dairyman and grocer, followed by a trip to your mayor's office to receive your allocation of tickets. At all these places you stood in line for hours waiting on the services, condescendingly given, of a very minor civil servant or a tradesperson wallowing in his or her new-found petty power. Finally, you stood in line for several more hours to reach the counter for your ration of bread or meat or milk, et cetera, only to be told that it had all gone and to come back tomorrow or the end of the week.

Annette's mother had written to her from Paris describing the severe shortages there for most citizens; the daily allowance of bread was down to 180 grams, the weekly meat allowance only 90 grams. People slept overnight in shop doorways in order to have a good position in the queue when, and if, the shop opened the following morning. Those Parisians who were rich could afford the black and gray markets to sustain an almost prewar life style; those who wanted to become rich ran the illegal markets without any qualms of conscience. Later, it was established that during the occupation the mortality rate in Paris had risen by 40%, indicative of the fact that most citizens could not or would not deal with the criminal element but were determined to 'make do', as best they could, with the rationing and accept the consequences of poor health and even death.

Annette realized from her mother's letter that, in regard to the food supply, it was easier to be a country dweller than a city dweller. Vegetables and fruit were not rationed, and, although the Germans requisitioned much of this food source, supplies in small villages remained almost adequate for local people. In fact, many villagers with a garden plot could grow their own vegetables, and those that were not consumed were used as barter for eggs and chickens, milk and meat. Yet even with these advantages, Annette knew that most of her children went to bed hungry every night, suffered vitamin deficiencies, and were never seen by a doctor, let alone counseled by a child psychologist for the emotional trauma they went through almost daily from seeing such sights as hostages hanging from trees, hearing gun shots and explosions, and wondering whether they would return from school to find their mother dead or bleeding on the doorstep.

"Right, children, lunchtime is over and your stomachs are bursting with good things. It's time to sing some happy songs, so think about what you would like to sing while I play you some sweet and gentle music on our piano. I believe you'd enjoy some Claude Debussy; remember, we spoke about him and his life a few weeks ago?"

Annette walked over to the upright piano in the corner of the room, lifted the lid over the keyboard and sat down on the piano stool. The music for *La Cathédrale Engloutie* was already positioned on the stand, for she had been practicing it the day before, after class. A strong beam of sunlight from a nearby window gave Annette's seated form an enveloping aura. The strands of wool in her red sweater sparkled as though laced with silver, and her short, wavy blonde hair was a crown of incandescence. She transfixed the gazes of the children like a goddess as she half-turned to face them and explain what she was about to play.

"I want you to imagine a beautiful but mysterious church deep down in the ocean. The church is very old and so big that it is a cathedral, just like Notre-Dame in Paris. The cathedral is seen through waving clusters of seaweed that reach up to the ocean's surface, and the seawater currents, drifting backwards and forwards, seem to blur the cathedral's shape and details. So the image is not clear; it is only a dreamy impression. The music starts slowly with low notes then drifts higher and louder as though the cathedral is moving upwards, reaching for the sky. But the ghostly image cannot escape its watery grave and sinks once more to the ocean bed as the music fades away to nothing.

"To help you imagine what the music is trying to tell you, shut your eyes as I play. Now relax and listen, but no peeping at your classmates."

Annette elicited softness and dreaminess out of the piano as she played the piece, for she was an accomplished pianist, and understood the mood that Debussy wanted to create.

However, not all the children were accomplished listeners, and many eyes flickered open and closed. Some of the smaller boys exchanged funny faces, while others took the opportunity to propel loose objects across the room. Annette finished the piece, and the mysterious cathedral lingered for a while.

"Now it's your turn, children. What do you want to sing? Something the whole class can sing together, please. So, what's it going to be? Don't be shy!"

"Mademoiselle Renard, let's sing *Frère Jacques*," said a loud voice from the back, "and do it one after the other."

"What a good idea, Monique!"

"No it's not! It's silly. It's girl's stuff," contradicted Henri, a dominant male.

"Ignore Henri everyone; we'll do it. I'll split you into three groups, one, two three, to take the three parts. We've done this lots of times, so group one, please start."

Frère Jacques, Frère Jacques,
Dormez-vous? Dormez-vous,
Sonnez les matines. Sonnez les matines
Din, din, don. Din, din, don.

As group one started the second line, group two started the first line. As one started the third line, two started the second line and three the first line. And so on, composing the round or musical canon. Unfortunately, the groups sang at different speeds, and instead of there being a crisp, decipherable ending, cacophony reigned. The children considered it all a big joke that needed repeating ten times. And Annette let them do just that for she loved their laughing and giggling, their temporary release from sad times.

But the singing did not rest there. Annette let the children choose some other favorites from their repertoire; *Une Souris Verte*, (A Green Mouse); *Sur le Pont d'Avignon*, (On the Bridge of Avignon); *Que Fait Ma Main?*, (What is My Hand Doing). They sang lustily if not too tunefully, and without self-consciousness. Annette allowed them to act out the words of *Que Fait Ma Main?* which led to some boisterous interaction according to the following:

What is my hand doing?
It caresses: soft, soft, soft.
It pinches: ouch, ouch, ouch.
It tickles: tickle, tickle, tickle.
It scratches: scratch, scratch, scratch.
It hits: whack, whack, whack.
It dances: twirl, twirl, twirl.
And then.....it goes away!

The boys in the class, of course, took the interaction to extremes as they sought out a girl to caress and another boy to whack. Annette barely maintained control, and decided that this particular children's song should be avoided in the future.

Calmness eventually returned, but then the silence was broken once more when Monique, of her own volition, climbed on her desk and started to sing the French national anthem, *La Marseillaise*; her tone was sweet but firm, expressing an innocence that was becoming lost in the turmoil of war.

Allons enfants de la Patrie/Let us go, children of the
fatherland,
Le jour de gloire est arrivé./Our day of glory has arrived.
Contre nous, de la tyrannie,/Against us stands tyranny,
L'étandard sanglant est levé,/The bloody flag is raised,
L'étandard sanglant est levé./The bloody flag is raised.
Entendez-vous, .../Do you hear,....................

Annette was not prepared for this sudden manifestation of patriotism by one so young. She did not know what to do. Her bitter-sweet emotions were a mixture of fear, pride, sadness and anger. The child's voice, in fact, was a reflection of what she was feeling. But why was Monique doing this?

What was her spur? Annette had not yet heard that over the weekend Monique's father had been taken by the Germans and sent to a forced labor camp in Germany.

Outside in the village square, several people had stopped and gazed at the school building when they heard what the brave, little voice was singing. Some smiled, some frowned, some worried what would happen to the child and her teacher if a member of the authorities heard her. The singing of the national anthem was strictly forbidden. Fortunately, the child did not know all of the verses so she had already concluded her act of defiance when a Vichy gendarme bicycled passed the school windows. The gendarme was a Nazi collaborator.

In the classroom, Annette helped Monique down from her desk top and gave her a long hug; both had watery eyes and Monique could not suppress small, heart-rending sobs.

To get the class back into a more academic frame of mind, Annette thought that she could give a little history lesson on the birth of La Marseillaise and the derivation of its title.

"Does anyone know who wrote the national anthem?........ It's gone very quiet. Anyone? Anyone?.........No, well, I'll just have to tell you then. It was composed in only one night during the French Revolution of 1792 by Claude-Joseph Rouget de Lisle, a captain of the engineers and an amateur musician who was stationed in Strasbourg. After it was played at a patriotic banquet in Marseilles, copies of the music and words were given to the revolutionaries who sang it lustily as they entered Paris. Later, the anthem was given the title La Marseillaise because volunteer army units from Marseilles loved to sing it. Now, there is a twist to this bit of history. Would you believe that the composer, Rouget de Lisle, was a royalist; that is, he *liked* kings and queens to rule over him. Even so, his music gave the revolutionaries something powerful to sing. Then he made a big mistake; he refused to take the oath of allegiance to the new constitution. So he was thrown in prison and almost had his head cut off. What do you think of that tale?"

The children liked it, especially the part about Rouget almost having his head cut off. "Blood, blood, blood!" shouted three of the boys.

After school, one of Annette's pupils requested her help in putting the chain back on his bicycle which was kept padlocked in a rack just inside the gate to the playground. She willingly bent her bicycle expertise to the task, but after five minutes the chain was still proving difficult and she was covered in black grease. Suddenly, she felt the presence of a third person, so she looked up from her crouched position and saw a German officer smiling down at her through the school railings; his Kubelwagen, with driver, was parked close by in the square.

"Can I help, Mademoiselle Renard? It is a cold day to have your hands contacting metal. I see yours have gone blue already," said Major von Kruger.

"No, I'm perfectly capable of doing this myself," said Annette, curtly.

"I'm sure you are, but an extra hand never hurt anyone. Please, allow me to enter and help you."

Annette still heard the words of *La Marseillaise* in her head, and here was one of the tyrants whom Monique had so poignantly sang about. How could she accept help from the enemy; it would not be right. She tugged on the chain to try and get it fully over the front sprocket. She was almost there when it slipped and a sharp link cut into her forefinger.

"*Merde, merde, merde!*" she exploded, as she watched the blood flow. She sucked on her finger to clean the wound which caused grease to be smeared all around her mouth. The grease did not have a pleasant taste.

"Now, you really must let me help you. Here's my handkerchief. Wrap it around your finger and squeeze the wound to stem the blood. Come on, Mademoiselle, don't be so stubborn. I'm not an ogre, you know."

Reluctantly, Annette accepted the handkerchief, but with it on her finger manipulation of the chain was even more difficult. She looked into von Kruger's eyes but she did not speak. His help was now definitely needed, for it was getting dark and both she and her pupil were shivering with cold. Von Kruger took over.

"Here, hold this end of the chain with your good hand while I ease the connecting link through it and lock it in with the circlip. *Voilà!* I think the young boy has an operational bicycle again. Together we have fixed it."

Annette waited until the boy mounted his bicycle and saw that it was fully functional for his ride home. Then she turned and started to walk away, but knew that not to offer any thanks at all would be very ungracious, and she remembered that von Kruger had acted kindly towards her before when she was threatened in the classroom by the Gestapo. On the other hand, there was an unwritten rule: give the occupier a sullen silence when spoken to; an act of contempt if not of anger. This time Annette did not obey the rule.

She turned her head and quietly said, "Thank you, Major. Good afternoon."

"Please, don't go yet. I have something to ask you, in fact, I drove out here to specifically see you. I assure you, it is important." Annette fully faced the Major and endeavored to be expressionless even though her heart rate had quickened.

"Can we go into the school? This wind is very cold, and you don't seem to have sufficiently warm clothing on," said the Major, considerately and sincerely.

Annette hesitated, for she was, indeed, getting colder and colder, but if she were seen by a villager going into an empty school alone with a German, collaborationist suspicions would be aroused. "No, Major, please say what you've come to say out here." Von Kruger reluctantly agreed and immediately got to the point of his visit.

"Has the Gestapo man, Eichmann, bothered you again since I marched him out of your classroom?" Annette worried that this was some kind of a trap being set. She played for time in order to gauge what her answer should be.

"Why do you ask?"

"I'm the Administrative Officer for this area, and part of my duty is to keep tension between Germans and French to a low level."

"Don't you mean between *you* the *occupier* and *we* the *occupied*?"

"I don't have time to play word games with you, Mademoiselle. Just answer my question," said the Major, curtly.

"The answer is 'Yes', he has been to my class twice more and intimidated us."

"How does he intimidate you? Does he physically assault you or any of the children?"

"No. He just sits at the back of class and glowers, menacingly. The children become frightened and expect to be hit by him at any moment." Annette did not want to mention that his staring had turned into a sexual leer towards her.

Von Kruger looked agitated by her reply, and gave a small hiss through his teeth. "Eichmann is not supposed to enter schools without one of my staff being present, and, even then, he must have a bona fide reason for the intrusion. If he comes again, you must inform the French police who will immediately inform my headquarters. I will then take appropriate steps. Is that understood?"

Annette had understood what he said, but could not understand why he said it. Why should a Wehrmacht officer worry so much about her and her pupils? And since when could the Wehrmacht *take steps* against the Gestapo? The Gestapo did whatever they wanted to do; their thugs did not kowtow to the officer corps, whom they despised.

"Finally, Mademoiselle, please be careful. I fear for your safety." Von Kruger gave an informal salute by touching his hat with two fingers, followed by the suspicion of a bow with his upper body. He returned to his car and gave the driver further instructions. As the car passed Annette, Von Kruger gave her a warm smile and a small wave.

Annette was confused by his parting words. How was she to be careful, and careful of what? Their conversation had given her time to study von Kruger more closely. She decided that he had a handsome, kindly face; deep blue, honest eyes; a strong chin and straight nose. His smart uniform seemed to clothe a lithesome body that was athletic but not overly muscular. She thought that he was probably quite intelligent and culturally sensitive, although that was only an intuitive feeling. She did not like to admit that she quite liked von Kruger.

Chapter Twenty-Five

Annette was getting tired of making supplies deliveries to Jean's men in the secret cave. It was a long and difficult walk through the forest, particularly when the evening dusk deepened into night. She had to concentrate on looking for landmarks; if she missed one, she could go round in circles for hours. In addition, after a full day of teaching, her mood was not usually very benign.

Thank God this is the last trip for a while, she thought, as she approached the Fontaine de Barenton. *From now on Erwan can exercise his spindly legs. Damn this heavy pack! It's cutting into my shoulders, and something hard is pressing on my spine; must be one of the pistols. Hey, Merlin, come on out from behind that tree and give us a hand. I bet you're having a good laugh at my expense. Yes, yes, in your day nice young ladies didn't stoop to being beasts of burden, did they. They had gallant knights in shining armor attending to their every desire, their every whim. Huh, just listen to me talking to a phantom; I must be going mad.*

As she continued down the narrow path in the twilight, she sensed that she was not alone. There was someone following behind her by a hundred yards or so, and it wasn't Merlin; Merlin never broke dead branches with his feet, or had a wheezing cough. Annette stopped dead in her tracks and turned, but the dim light only allowed her to see a vague moving shape. The clouds of condensing breath from her mouth became thicker as her chest heaved in and out with anxiety, if not fear. She knew that the likelihood of another person being in this part of the forest late on a January day was remote, unless that person had an evil intention, and only she could be the object of that intention. Should she wait for the person and confront him, or her, or should she continue walking as though having another person behind her was of no consequence? But, if the person were going to attack her for any reason, the latter action would put her at a disadvantage. She would not know when and how an attack would be launched. She decided to wait and let Fate take over.

She did not have to wait long. Her stalker was the devil himself, Hauptsturmfuhrer Eichmann, who approached with a sneering grin on his jaundiced face.

"Mademoiselle Renard, what a pleasant surprise; good evening to you," said Eichmann, and held out his hand which Annette pointedly ignored.

"Why are you following me?"

"Me? Following you? Yes, of course I am. It's my job to follow people. I need to see what they get up to, especially when it's close to curfew time. At five o'clock I can arrest you, which I will unless you cooperate."

Eichmann leaned forward and grabbed her left biceps in an iron grip. She winced with pain and tried to shake him off.

"Now, now, I said cooperate. What's in your pack and where are you going with it?"

Annette's brain raced. *This little thug is going to do me harm*, she thought. *Fight back! But how can I get to the pistol in my pack. No, not an option; can't be done quickly enough. Can I crash him on the ground in a judo throw and kick his testicles in? How about a karate chop to his throat or two forefingers in his eyes. Erwan has shown me these unarmed combat tricks, but I don't think I've the confidence to try them out right now. And where's Eichmann's support? Gestapo normally operate in pairs, and in an open, hostile forest like this, I'd expect there to be at least half a dozen of the bastards lurking behind the trees or bushes.*

"Take your pack off and open it up," demanded Eichmann. "Come on, come on."

He turned her round and ripped the pack from her back, almost dislocating her shoulder with his viciousness. He pushed her heavily to the ground and unlaced the pack flap. Then he upended the pack and quickly disgorged its contents onto the forest floor. He separated the items with his foot for better examination, giving a maniacal laugh as he did so.

"You French bitch! Bitch, bitch! Look at this: a knife, a pistol, two hand-grenades, a map, food, money! Good God! you'll hang for this. You'll hang slowly, but only after I personally torture you to within an inch of death."

Annette saw the fury of the man, that it was mounting, that he was capable of anything. But she also was becoming furious, although she kept a cool head. No man had ever assaulted her like this, and this little slimy toad would pay dearly. She made a quick lunge for the pistol, got it and pulled the trigger at point blank range, and pulled again and again. Click, click, click, then silence. The terror on Eichmann's face dissipated into a wide grin of yellow, broken teeth.

"But first, my lovely, you have to put bullets into the gun. You French fail at the simplest of things, although some say you are experts at love. I don't believe that, but let's find out, shall we. While the blood is hot, let's find out."

Eichmann seized Annette's shoulders and rolled her onto her back. He tore open her jacket, revealing underneath a thin black sweater, which was well-shaped by her breasts that pulsed up and down in her struggle to free herself. But Eichmann was sitting astride her, pinning her hips to the ground as he clawed at the sweater, determined to rip it off. Annette tried desperately to grip his wrists and stop his invasion, but his sexual arousal was so great that restraint was impossible. Her last defense before rape was to go for his eyes with her fingers, but he quickly backed his upper torso away from her outstretched arms and sat in an upright position for a few seconds. It was then that she heard a loud crack which echoed around the pines until it died away. Then

Eichmann slowly pitched forward across her chest and buried his shocked face in the dirt next to hers. He lay still and heavily on her so that she felt trapped. She managed to move her head slightly, and out of the corner of her eye she could see the back of Eichmann's head. Blood was oozing from it and running down and around his neck. Her pumping adrenaline gave her extra strength to squirm out from under him. She was shaking as she stood up to the extent that her legs almost gave way. Fear and shock gripped her for several minutes as she found a tree trunk to sit down on.

She stared at Eichmann's body, expecting it to show signs of life. She picked up the commando knife that had been in the pack and slowly approached Eichmann. She bent down and rolled his body over, which revealed a small hole in his forehead surrounded by blood and gray matter; a bullet must have entered the back of his head, passed right through and exited at the front between his eyes. She looked down at her opened, torn jacket and saw more of Eichmann's head spattered over her sweater. A wave of nausea swept over her, so she took her seat again on the tree trunk and looked around her. Eichmann was dead. Someone had shot him in the back of the head. Someone was close by with a gun. Was she next? Would she be shot? It was now quite dark and the assailant could not be seen. Five minutes past and still the marksman did not appear. Although totally alone, in a dark forest with menacing shapes and a dead body, Annette composed herself and started to think logically.

Who would kill Eichmann in this place at this time? she asked herself. *Obviously he doesn't want to kill me as well. I'm a sitting target perched on this log, and I'm still alive. That is very good. So who's the killer? Erwan? No, although it's possible that he might have changed his mind about risking his leg and accompanying me to the cave, saw Eichmann ahead of him, attempting to rape me, and got a very lucky shot off. Two things wrong with that theory. Surely he would have cried out to distract Eichmann when he saw what was happening. There was no cry. Secondly, if he had fired the shot, he would have rushed forward to make sure that Eichmann was dead, and if not, finish him off. Then he'd help me get rid of the body. Good God! The body! What do I do with the body? I've got to bury it. But how; I've nothing with which to dig a hole. My hands? I don't think so.*

Annette became more preoccupied with how to hide the body than with who had put a bullet neatly through its head. The best she could do, as a temporary measure, was to drag Eichmann's foul form into the undergrowth, well away from the path, and throw leaves and branches onto it. This she accomplished without too much trouble. Then she used some small rocks to act as markers near the path and again in the vicinity of the body, so as to help her locate it on her return. The next decision was difficult. Should she continue on to the cave, deposit the supplies, then return and get Erwan to help her dig a deep grave for Eichmann, or, go to find Erwan directly, return and do the burial, then go on to the cave. Either way it would be a lot of hard walking for one night, and she was already feeling exhausted, mentally and physically. After wrestling the options, she decided to find Erwan first because there was the chance of him being able to carry on alone to the cave, if his leg held up, and deliver the supplies. That would reduce dramatically the amount of walking she would have to do otherwise.

She put the supplies that Eichmann had strewn on the forest floor back into her pack. Next, she tried to return to a pristine state the area on the path where the vicious struggle had taken place; although she was sure that the Germans did not have a team of forensic scientists that would be unleashed to search for tell-tale hairs, broken fingernails and slivers of skin. Eichmann was not a Himmler whose demise warranted any special efforts. She quickly played her flashlight over the area to make a final check that nothing of hers remained and hurried out of the forest.

* * * * *

Later, in the village of Folle Pensée a noisy Kubelwagen was started up by its lone occupant. *If* Annette had seen the vehicle speed away she might have caught a glimpse of the driver, Major von Kruger. This would have prompted a string of puzzling questions in her mind. What was von Kruger doing alone, after dark, in this isolated place? Whom had he been visiting and why? Is it possible that it was he who was the third person in the horrifying drama that had taken place tonight beneath the witnessing trees? And if it were he, why would a German officer track and kill a fellow German? But Annette was a mile away from the Kubelwagen as it departed, so these questions did *not* bother her mind.

* * * * *

Annette found Erwan bedding down his cows for the night, and excitedly related her brush with death and the glorious slaying of the monster, Eichmann. He confirmed that the shooting was not his doing, although it would have given him great pleasure had it been so. For the time being, this would remain a mystery, along with the identity of the collaborator who caused the air drop disaster.

Erwan and Annette successfully found Eichmann's body, and with two heavy spades penetrated the hard, frost-laden ground to make a suitable grave, not the standard six-feet-deep type but sufficient to fool any searching German patrol or wild animal.

Erwan's injured leg was able to take the stress of walking, so he insisted on taking the supplies to the cave while Annette returned home. Annette was truly thankful, for the shock of the night's events had penetrated her outward composure, and periodically caused waves of trembling to invade her body. As she fell into bed, exhausted and cold, she gave a worrying thought for Erwan's safety.

Chapter Twenty-Six

Jean's men had now been in the cave for six days. Their recuperation had been rapid, thanks to the food and warm clothing supplied. They were becoming restless for action once again. Several had ventured out into the forest and the surrounding countryside. Two of them had already found work on local farms, even though they lacked official papers. Farmers were short of young workers for laboring-type jobs so they did not ask probing questions. One young Resistance fighter became the group's poacher. Under cover of darkness he selected his targets; chickens, eggs, ducks, a lamb, scraps of food left on kitchen tables. He rationalized his thievery quite simply: 'To fight and die for these people we need feeding, if they don't give it, we steal it.'

Another fighter with a thirst for wine and bad coffee spent some time in La Chatte, the café in Guillaume. He was a sociable person, and in talking to the local people he was able to glean useful information about many things: employment opportunities, German strength and activity in the area, who was in the black-market, who was not to be trusted, which side were the French police on, how to get transport. But he could not be too inquisitive, so he couched his questions carefully, nonchalantly, almost as though he did not care whether he got an answer or not. Nevertheless, he ran a grave risk from informers.

Having left Annette to return home through the forest, Erwan reached the cave with the further supplies without too much trouble, even though the darkness tried to hide the path to be taken. All of the men slept in the cave at night, out of the cold and damp, although two of them rotated guard duty a few yards away from the cave's entrance. During the day the group split up. Those with farm work left early to hike north out of the forest. Four others took up defensive positions in the woods some distance from the cave, prepared to reveal themselves and fight any German patrol that approached dangerously close to the cave's location. Two remained in the cave doing 'household' chores: cleaning weapons, doing exercises to keep warm and planning minor acts of sabotage.

During Jean's absence in England, a man called Philippe took over command of the group. He was a strict disciplinarian, respected, confident, with a strong physique and a remarkable tolerance for pain. He was thirty years old. The minor acts of sabotage that Philippe organized, based on his men's ideas, were designed to create nuisance and aggravation for the Germans. These acts included cutting telephone lines, felling trees across roads, slashing tires on German vehicles, and dynamiting electrical power substations. But Philippe was very worried about the lack of official papers for his men and requested Erwan to find a solution. Like Marcel, Erwan knew of the forgery ring in Rennes, so he made discreet inquiries about whom to contact and the costs involved. He preferred to wait for Marcel's and Jean's return to France before sending the individual fighters off to the forger in Rennes. But first, cover stories for each man had to be concocted, and Marcel was good at that.

Then a perturbation in the plans occurred.

* * * * *

On the night of January 30, Igor sat, half-frozen, in Erwan's barn and received a message from Grendon which, when decoded, read:

'The chickens will not, repeat not, be coming home to roost as planned.'

Erwan, sitting beside Igor, knew exactly what this meant; the parachute drop of Marcel and Jean was canceled. That was clear enough but it raised several questions. If not as planned, when? Would they be returning at all? Was the circuit to be disbanded? Had security been breached in London? In France? Clarification was urgently required.

Igor sat staring at his Paraset, urging it to speak some more, but apart from the one simple message there was nothing. He became very suspicious. Had the Abwehr been listening in to his transmittals, and were they about to pounce on him? Did Grendon know this and had prematurely shut down? Perhaps it was a trick. Maybe the Grendon message was really a fake, broadcast by the Germans. If so, the Abwehr had broken his coding method.

Igor decided not to wait around to find out. He hurriedly packed up his transceiver and bicycled to his safe haven, another farm about three miles away. This was his prearranged plan, to be executed in case of an emergency. The emergency had happened.

Erwan left the barn and went to bed. His wife swore at him as he let cold air swoop under the blankets and his freezing feet touched hers. Sleep did not immediately come to Erwan, for he was confused and worried. The circuit's resistance activities had fallen into a vacuum. What should he do about it?

Chapter Twenty-Seven

The following day, Saturday, Erwan awoke refreshed and clear-headed. Gone were the worries of the previous night caused by the message from Grendon. The plan for Marcel's and Jean's return had changed. So what? *The best laid plans of mice and men often go awry.* Erwan could accept that; he was a farmer, often dependent on the weather which was always changing his farming plans. He would stop fretting and execute Plan B, which was a trip to the Saturday market in St-Brieuc with a load of winter vegetables. This would be an opportunity to introduce Annette to his wholesale business operation; vegetables and fish. He would show her the best and safest truck route to the coast, and let her meet all his contacts in the fishing villages as well as those at the St-Brieuc market.

The truck was already partially loaded with vegetables from his and other farms, and, with Claudette's help, he quickly made it a full load by transferring barrels of potatoes stored in his barn into the truck. Claudette had made some sandwiches for him as he would be away all day. She handed these to him, along with a bottle of her cider, gave him quite a passionate kiss, which was a surprise, and waved him good-bye. Erwan did not mention to her that he would first go to Guillaume to try and persuade Annette to come with him. Claudette would not appreciate them being together on such a trip. Annette jumped at the chance of a day's adventure.

Erwan's truck had seen better days. It was fifteen years old and sounded it. The gearbox alternately growled and whined, as though it were in severe pain. The engine burned more oil than gasoline, as indicated by the volumes of blue smoke that exited the exhaust pipe. The carburetor had given up trying to provide the correct air-to-fuel ratio, and the brakes really had no intention of stopping the truck at speeds greater than 20 miles per hour. Nevertheless, Erwan was its master, and his knowledge of the truck's temperament enabled him to more or less control it, and get it to perform the duty he asked.

They followed the quiet backroads up through Mauron, Merdrignac and Moncontour to St-Brieuc, a distance of about fifty miles. The Brittany countryside was coated with a heavy frost that sparkled in the winter sun, knowing that by noontime its short life would be over as it turned into cold water droplets. Annette had her window partially open and she breathed deeply the fresh, clean air. It was cold enough to sting her cheeks and bring out a rosy glow in them as she marveled at the beauty of the fields, the moorland and the woods. Erwan's eyes were elsewhere; directly on the road ahead and filled with an intense concentration as he strived to control his mechanized beast. Several times he barely escaped ending up in the deep ditches on either side of the road. He said few words but occasionally whistled a popular song to show Annette how composed he was, how she could rely on his impeccable driving skills. After two hours, they slowly entered the ancient and picturesque town of St-Brieuc, capital of the Côtes d'Armor département, situated between the ravines of the Gouët and Gouëdic rivers near St-Brieuc Bay on the English Channel. As the truck gingerly navigated the narrow streets, Erwan could not resist giving Annette a little history lesson.

"Because you're not really from these parts, you should know that the town is named after a Welsh monk, St-Briocus, who tried to evangelize the region in the 6th century. But religion didn't stop the town's inhabitants being put to the sword by all kinds of so-called noblemen and foreign pillagers, like the Spaniards in 1592. And of course there were the standard plagues to deal with, one of the worst being in 1601. Then we had Bonaparte and the Chouans. Now we have the Germans; Lord help us! Who'll invade us after they're gone? Russians, Indians, Africans?

"Look, there's the estuary and the fishing port. Boats should be coming in soon. Sometimes I buy my fish there and sometimes I go farther up the coast to Plouha. It all depends. But first, to the market place and a bit of dealing with the local vegetable sellers. Remember the people I deal with and what prices I get. Some of them can be tricky."

After only an hour, Erwan had sold all his vegetables and for a good price. It was winter time and supply was low, prices high. Annette enjoyed the market scene, the bustle, the bargaining and the friendliness, even though the shadow of occupation was not far away. Off-duty German officers and other ranks wandered from stall to stall, behaving well but nevertheless providing an insidious threat.

From St-Brieuc they drove north along the rugged coast, passing through quaint little fishing villages, and seeing who was selling the catch of the day. Just passed Plouha, Erwan decided he was hungry for lunch. He pulled off the road, stopped and pointed to a path that led to the edge of the cliffs.

"Come on, Annette, grab that pack; it's got sandwiches and a bottle of cider in it. Claudette was in a good mood this morning; she made the sandwiches herself. I'm starving, so what say you to scrambling down the cliffs to Bonaparte Beach and having a picnic?"

"Sounds a great idea. Lead the way," agreed Annette.

"The cliffs are very high here; over 200 feet so the view from the edge is very dramatic. You should be here in a storm when the sky and sea are angry at one another. Thor and Poseidon don't get on well together."

They had not gone very far when they heard a shout coming from behind them. Across the road, in the front garden of a small house, an elderly woman was frantically waving what appeared to be a piece of red flannel.

"Stop, you imbeciles, stop!" she shouted. "Do you want to get killed."

Erwan and Annette stopped walking and stood confused. They did not really understand what the woman was trying to say. They were about to proceed farther down the path when the woman hobbled across the road and yelled more loudly than before.

"Mines, you fools! German mines! Don't move or you'll be blown to bits."

This warning had the desired effect. Erwan and Annette froze in place, feeling terrified and stupid at the same time. The woman walked slowly and carefully to where they stood and commanded them to follow her back to the road.

"I'm sorry, Madame. I am very stupid. I should have guessed that all the approaches to the cliffs would be mined. We owe you our lives. Thank you a thousand times," said Erwan, taking her hand and gently shaking it in both of his."

"You young people don't think enough. Didn't you see the danger signs? Just ignored them, didn't you. Now get in your truck and leave. If a German lookout in that post on the hill has seen you, he'll send a patrol to arrest you. Now go, go!"

They reached the road without having their legs blown off, and the woman started towards her house.

"Madame, a moment please," said Erwan. "I would like you to accept this bottle of cider. We thank you again."

The woman stared at Erwan with twinkling eyes set in a creased and weathered face. She smiled and gave a small laugh, grasped the bottle eagerly and continued to her house. At the garden gate she waved to them with her free hand as they climbed into the truck, then she held the bottle to her lips as though to drink.

Erwan and Annette sat in silence for a while, still shaken from their near disaster.

"Don't worry, Erwan, the threads of Fate did not want us today. Here, your sandwich. Eat and enjoy; I am. I must thank Claudette for making such a tasty one when I see her next."

"Better not do that. She thinks I came alone. You know how she is. She has the green-eyed monster inside her."

"Jealousy? You think she's jealous of me?"

"Always has been, and you know it; if you don't, you must be blind."

"Yes, I know it," answered Annette, coyly, "but what can I do about it?"

"Do nothing to provoke her. She can have very dark moods, almost dangerous moods."

"Come on, Erwan! What's she going to do? Kill me?" Erwan did not answer this. Instead, he bit into his lunch with gusto.

"You're right, it's a good sandwich, but I wish I had some cider to wash it down." They finished their food, satisfied but wanting more.

"We'd better get going. The fishing boats should have returned to Plouha by now. I think that'll be the best place to buy our fish today. We'll go straight to the harbor, buy blocks of ice and then look for Jacques Carnac's boat. He's a fair man."

For Annette, it was hard work loading the blocks of ice; a school teacher does not have much of a chance to develop strong arms and shoulders. But what she lacked in strength she made up for with enthusiasm. The catch was not good today, partly because Jacques had stayed close inshore in an area that had become overfished. The French fishermen did not venture far from home waters for fear of aerial attack by British and German planes. The former sometimes mistook the boats for armed trawlers on their way to protect a German coastal convoy. The latter thought every boat was trying to reach England with escaping Allied airmen. Erwan had to be content with a barrel of cod, two barrels of mackerel and one of assorted flat fish. Jacques's wife had gathered a fair number of oysters from a safe, rocky area near the headland, so Erwan bought a hundred of these then quickly got back on the road to St-Brieuc. It was already early afternoon, and he wanted to get back to Basbijou and Guillaume before the fishmongers closed. If he did not, he would have to keep the fish, albeit well iced, in the back of his truck until Monday. Sunday was the Sabbath so the shops would not be open.

The unexpected happened five miles south of St-Quay-Portrieux; a German roadblock.

"No problem," said Erwan, "they know me and my truck and what I carry. They'll just wave us through, although they'll probably want to see our papers. It's unusual though, a roadblock on this stretch of the road, and on a Saturday."

They waited in line to be checked by two Wehrmacht soldiers, one thin, one fat. The fat one examined papers while the thin one stood a little back, nervously holding his automatic. And even further back stood a leather-coated, leather-gloved civilian, except that he did not look very civil. Annette immediately sensed that he was a member of the Gestapo. She stiffened in her seat as her traumatic experience in the woods with one such animal rushed into her consciousness. Erwan put his hand on her knee for reassurance, but it did not help much. Then it was their turn to be checked.

"*Guten Tag, Karl. Wie geht's?*" was the limit of Erwan's German. He pretended that he knew the fat soldier. "Where's Johann today? Haven't seen him for a while? On a spot of leave, eh? Back in the glorious fatherland?

"OK, Karl, this is my new partner. Good looking, eh? Hard worker as well. She'll be making a few trips by herself in the future, so you'll be seeing more of her."

The fat soldier's name was not Karl, so he immediately became flustered. Also, he spoke no French so he had no idea what Erwan was talking about. Not so the Gestapo man who stepped forward and snatched Erwan's papers from his hand and examined them thoroughly. He reluctantly returned them, went around to the other side of the truck and gave Annette's papers the same concentrated examination. He seemed satisfied.

"Open up the back of the truck," the Gestapo man ordered. This surprised Erwan, for he had only ever been searched once before. He thought that they must be looking for someone in particular; an escaped POW or a member of the Resistance. Little did they know whose identity papers they had just approved. Erwan laughed inwardly as he went round to the back of the truck to untie the canvas flaps that were part of the cover which was draped over the truck's simple tubular frame. The contents of the truck were separated from the cab by a plywood wall.

"Behold the bounty of Mother Nature plucked from the cold, cruel sea," said Erwan with a dramatic flourish of his left arm. The Gestapo man did not appreciate Erwan's satiric tone, neither did he appreciate the strong fishy smell that hit him full in the face. He was obviously not a seafaring man, and he did not intend to inspect the fish barrels personally; instead he ordered the fat soldier to clamber into the truck and search for weapons by plunging his bare arm into each barrel. The fat soldier did not enjoy this activity on two counts; first, the fish were packed with loose ice that froze his arm; secondly, the fish were very slimy and looked at him, accusingly, with dead, staring eyes. But he finished his task and reported that no weapons were present. The Gestapo man grimaced, disappointingly, and told Erwan that he was free to proceed. Erwan wasted no time in getting back in his truck, and with a thumbs-up to Annette drove off with a sigh of relief.

What they never knew was that fifteen minutes later three men in a Citröen, that had been four cars behind them at the roadblock, were forcibly dragged from their vehicle, beaten, and thrown into a Gestapo van that came in from a side road. The men, who were members of the Resistance, were taken off to a local Gestapo building where they suffered a brutal and ultimately fatal interrogation.

Erwan and Annette arrived back in Basbijou in time to catch the fishmonger and sell their load before closing time. The fishmonger, in fact, had no option but to extend his hours by customer demand as word spread of his display of fresh fish. By six o'clock not even a cod's tail was left in his shop. Erwan took a tired but happy Annette back to her home, then he returned to Claudette and presented her with a dozen oysters and some of his hard-earned cash.

Chapter Twenty-Eight

The coldness of the January night seeped into the bones of Lieutenant James Wainwright as he stood, frozen in place, at 0300 hours on the bridge of his motor torpedo boat holding station two miles to the seaward of the Cherbourg Peninsula. Although swathed in two thick woolen sweaters and oilskins, and wearing fleece-lined seaboots, the cutting northerly wind still found chinks in his armor sufficient to shiver his lean 5 feet 11 inch-body. And the wind was wet with spray gathered up from a moderate sea that slipped easily around the boat as she prowled along at 6 knots on her quiet auxiliary engines. The spray and the perpetual dampness were worse than the cold; nothing was really dry, not clothes, not bedding, not charts or logs, not benches, not binoculars, not even the toilet paper. Everything was covered in a cold condensation. The lieutenant's one solace was a steaming mug of hot cocoa which he held in his bare hands, lovingly, and which he sipped slowly as though he wanted it to last all night. Occasionally, he paused in his drinking to wipe his mouth free of the thin deposit of sea spray that would otherwise add a little saltiness to the cocoa. His face had prominent cheek bones and an aquiline nose whose nostrils sprouted strong black hairs. He was clean-shaven, but, having jet-black hair, his chin usually showed a dark shadow which could easily grow into a formidable beard, if allowed.

James Wainwright, at age twenty-three, was the commanding officer of a Vosper motor torpedo boat (MTB), with pennant number 9339. Her crew of two officers, two petty officers and six ratings was one of three MTBs lying off the French coast, waiting to pounce on German E-boats returning from raids on Allied convoys on the other side of the English Channel. The Germans would be tired and battered from jousting with the convoy escorts, carrying dead and wounded, and hoping to make a safe landfall in Cherbourg harbor. But like the Allied sailors, the German crews were all very young and very tough, and no matter what their condition, they would put up a stiff resistance.

But first, the E-boats had to be found in the darkness of the sea and the sky. Even though mariners had coined the name "the narrow seas" for the English Channel, there was water enough to be lost in. And Jimmy Wainwright knew it. He and his crew had spent many hours on many other nights patrolling the French coast, sent on operations, supposedly carefully planned, to seek out the enemy and strike swiftly, only to find nothing but disappointment in the moody, empty sea.

Supporting the three MTBs were two motor gun boats, MGBs, which, although not equipped with torpedoes, carried more guns for attacking the enemy in face to face situations. The two types of boat were very similar in overall length, the MTB being 72ft 6ins and the MGB 70ft, but their displacements differed. The MTB weighed in at about 47 tons whereas the MGB was typically 31 tons. Both boats could leap through the seas at 40 knots on main engines, with the wooden, hard-chine hull clear of the water over much of its length as the mahogany frames strained under the dynamic loads.

The five boats ran silently in V-formation with the MGBs at the back, port and starboard. This night there should have been another two MTBs and a third MGB in the formation, but, at this point in the war, boat availability and engine reliability were not the best. Two MTBs had to return to port twenty minutes after departure with seized engine shafts, and the third MGB had a total electrical failure while it was still at the dock. These failures left three crews highly frustrated, if not demoralized. They had been ready for action, their blood hot and pulsing, ready to get at the enemy. And now, nothing, just a pint of beer and a warm bed for the night; and tomorrow all their mates would jeer at them, expounding on the 'great fun' they had missed, all, that is, except those who would be dead or badly wounded; they would remain silent.

"Message from the SO, skipper," reported the telegraphist, breathlessly as he clambered onto the bridge. He handed Wainwright a limp piece of paper which he read quickly with the aid of a shielded flashlight.

"Your writing gets worse and worse, Baker. You must have a bottle of gin down there by your Morse key. What's this word?"

"Don't rightly know, sir. It decoded as 'plunket'."

"No such word, Baker. What do you say, Coxs'n? You're a man of vast useless knowledge; what does 'plunket' mean? Anything?"

"Last time I looked, skipper, it meant a grayish-blue woolen fabric."

"Does it now! I'm impressed Petty Officer Morris. Take the rest of the night off."

While this banter was going on, Wainwright strained his eyes to read the whole message. He was amused by the thought that it had come all the way from the Senior Officer, Lieutenant-Commander Francis Cadogan, DSO, RN, leader of the flotilla, on his port side and ahead by only fifty yards. Cadogan had decoded a message from the base commander, re-encoded the relevant parts and sent it to all boats whose telegraphists had then decoded it.

Why not just shout the message from one boat to another, thought Wainwright. *There's no enemy closer than the gun batteries at the entrance to Cherbourg Harbor, and they are probably fast asleep by now.*

Wainwright, not being a Royal Navy career officer but only a volunteer in the RNVR, did not always do things by the book. He preferred a direct approach to getting things done; using one's initiative not bounded by red tape. At times his methods got him into trouble.

"OK, Coxs'n, change course ten degrees starb'd, if you will," ordered Wainwright, who then proceeded to tell the rest of his crew the gist of the message.

"Stay alert everyone. We've just got confirmation from a Coastal Command recce plane, assisting one of our convoys under attack off the Isle of Wight, that the E-boat attackers have broken off and are headed our way. Five or six of them. And another bit of info, source unknown; there's a dense fog bank forming along the French coast northeast of Le Havre. The SO wants us to run closer to the coast and cut back to 3 knots. Engine room, I hope we can do a quick crash start on mains if we contact the E-boats. Stay on your toes."

The five boats barely made way at 3 knots, and the only sound was a gentle chuckle from the bow as it parted the surface of the sea. Wainwright was glued to his binoculars. He held them firmly but lovingly to his eyes, for without them he might as well be blind. To see the enemy before he saw you could be the factor that allowed you to survive. The darkness of night merged the sea and the sky, and only the sharpest of eyes could distinguish the horizon and search for a discontinuity in it that might be an enemy vessel. If only the low pressure weather system which covered the sky with a thick layer of cloud from 10,000 feet upwards were not present, the night would have been lit with a moon that was almost full. That mystical light would have aided the search, but, on the other hand, it would have also helped the enemy to see *them*. Wainwright scanned the night; to port, to starboard, to port, to starboard, his eyeballs aching and watering with the strain. Occasionally he rested for a few seconds and wiped his eyes and the eyepieces of the binoculars.

He did not search alone. His navigator, Sub-Lieutenant William Matthews, stood in the wheelhouse not only repeating the actions of his CO but also looking shorewards seeking coastal landmarks. He used his own personal binoculars because the Navy could only spare one pair per boat, and, naturally, the captain commandeered those. Matthews was a meticulous navigator, never content with just dead-reckoning techniques but always seeking a good fix to confirm his position on his nautical chart. He was somewhat of a nervous type, never truly satisfied with his performance. But Wainwright trusted his abilities, although he sometimes chided him, 'Billie, you worry too damn much; your face is starting to twitch. If you say that's where we are, I believe you, I believe you.'

Behind the bridge in his twin gun turret, Able Seaman Gunner White ignored his two 0.5 inch Vickers machine-guns, and, like the CO, added his eyes to the search for unfriendly forces, although he did not have the assistance of binoculars. He viewed the process as a competition. If he spotted an unnatural shape anywhere on the sea before the skipper did, he proudly announced his finding and let a cocky grin spread over his face. Wainwright never felt piqued at this, but, on the contrary, he praised White for his sharpness, and let the rest of the crew know that White could put a feather in his cap.

In addition to the straining eyes, the crew's ears were primed to listen for any foreign sound. They knew the faint, whispering sound of their two Ford V-8 auxiliary engines and those of the other boats in the flotilla as they idled along. But the sound they were listening for was the rhythmic pounding of Daimler Benz diesel engines, each delivering 2000 brake horsepower, three of which gave the E-boat a speed comparable to that of the MTB, even though it was a longer and heavier boat.

The crew saw nothing and heard nothing. Wainwright thought of lowering the hydrophone, an underwater listening device, but the last time he used it he heard nothing but static crackling up the microphone cable. Then of course there was the type 286 radar box which was a marvelous idea, but, at this point in time, usually gave all kinds of conflicting information and obviously needed further development. So eyes and ears remained the best instruments on board.

As they headed east, Wainwright spent most of his time looking to port because that was the direction the E-boats would come from if their base was Cherbourg. But maybe their base was Le Havre, or Dieppe, or Boulogne.

Because of the uncertainty of an engagement, Wainwright was not fully primed for battle. He almost felt relaxed, yet he knew that as soon as he saw the enemy his stomach muscles would tighten and his mouth would go dry. That would be the beginning of fear, an emotion he had experienced many times during the last two years. But when the firing started, when he saw the colored tracer bullets coming straight for his eyes, the fear would disappear and anger take its place. An aggressive determination would flood into his body which was almost too difficult to control. The other crew members would have similar feelings, almost as though a central agency controlled their thoughts and actions to behave as one entity. Maybe it was the many hours spent together in training exercises. Maybe they were all natural aggressors, born to hunt, born to kill. For now, however, Wainwright was not thinking of killing anyone; in fact, he was thinking of the pretty little blonde Wren he had danced with the night before in the Dartmouth Community Hall. He remembered her pale blue eyes, her warm, soft body pressed into his, her sweet, discreet perfume that drugged his senses with desire.

"Skipper, dead ahead!" yelled Gunner White. "Horizon disappeared. Could be a fog bank."

Wainwright quickly returned from the dancehall to his more hostile environment. "By God, White, you're right! It could indeed be a fog bank. A thick one too. That's what you call substantial condensation. Hard to tell how far away it is; maybe 1000 yards, maybe more. The message we received said it was northeast of Le Havre. Damn Met-man got it wrong again; God bless his rain gauge!"

This was no time to get lost in a choking fog with E-boats in the vicinity. Had the other boats seen the bank? Must pull alongside the SO and find out what action he wants to take.

Wainwright pushed the telegraph lever forward to ask for more speed, and told the coxswain to close the gap with the

SO's MTB. Once level, the SO shouted across that he had also seen the fog.

"OK, Jimmy, we're not going into that lot. It's time to turn anyway; we're about three miles north of Cape Barfleur and need to prowl back towards Cherbourg. Change to a heading of 280° true and keep it at 6 knots. That should keep the bank behind us." By this time the other MTB and the two MGBs had gathered within hailing distance of the SO and understood the new instructions. "Right then," continued the SO, "turn to port now and pick up your stations; stay on auxiliaries of course." But Gunner White thought otherwise.

"Observe the fog bank immediately, sir. I see a large shape breaking out of it, about 090°," said White calmly but emphatically. The boats delayed their turn to port.

Silence, while all crew members stared at the fog.

"I see nothing. You could be mistaken, White," said the SO. "Sometimes a moving fog will swirl around and form a shape that appears to be very real, only to disappear after a few seconds."

"Begging your pardon, sir, but this was no ghost. But I admit, the fog seems to have swallowed it up again," said a disappointed White. Silence again, as the boats and crews waited for some further development that would take them out of limbo.

Coxswain Petty Officer Morris heard it first. "Heavy ship's propellers, Captain Wainwright. In the fog, I'd say."

"Confirmed, Coxs'n," said Wainwright. A steady, low frequency pounding. Must be a big one."

"I can also hear it," said SO Cadogan, in a whisper as though the enemy might be eavesdropping. "We'll continue to drift on 090° until she comes right out of the fog. We need to know what we're dealing with. Ten to one she's part of a German convoy, and that means she'll have plenty of escorts."

The waiting seemed interminable to the tense crew members. Would there be action? Would they survive it? Would the engines hold up? Would the guns work or jam? Would the torpedoes launch or misfire? Who would die, who would be wounded? The questions were there but answers were put on hold. And still they waited in the cold, inhospitable night.

"It's there," said Cadogan, "there's a shape forming, and, by God, I think it's turning into a good-sized tanker. Bloody hell! We've got lucky. She must be about 500 feet long overall, which gives her close to a 10,000 tons unladen displacement.

"Right! Jimmy, Charlie, Jean-Paul and Tony, Plan A. You know the drill, and this ain't no practice. MGBs get over on her starboard beam, undetected at slow speed, if you can, then crash start your main engines, open up with all your guns and charge in. Make a lot of noise; you're the big diversion, remember. MTBs, we'll run silently to her port beam, then I'll launch my torpedoes at about 1000 yards while you other two hold off. If I miss, you have a crack, successively. If I hit, hang on to your fish as there has to be more juicy morsels in that fog that'll come out when the fireworks start. After that, it's going to be the usual; every man for himself and death to the enemy."

Wainwright thought Cadogan's last remark a bit too dramatic, but then, that was Cadogan. All he needed was a black patch over his right eye, a telescope in his left hand and he would be a reincarnated Vice-Admiral Horatio Lord Nelson. But Cadogan was RN so Wainwright made allowances for his hero worship of the glorious naval figures of the past.

The MGBs slipped quietly off to port, 5631 having an all-Canadian crew with Lieutenant Charlie Wilcox as CO, and 5639 of the Free French Navy, Lieutenant Jean-Paul Demont, CO. Then the three MTBs slowly turned to starboard to get on the landward side of the tanker. Wainwright hated the slow speed. He wanted to dig his spurs into the sides of his vessel and urge it into action, for he now knew he was committed and his nerves were steady; the butterflies in his stomach had melted away. He gave no further thought to the humanity on the ship he was about to attack. They were simply the enemy.

The SO led his MTBs around in a wide circle until they were abeam of the tanker at 1200 yards, then the three of them spread out in line abreast and waited for the diversionary attack to erupt on the tanker's other side. They did not have long to wait. Suddenly there was *son et lumière* reaching the ears and eyes of the MTB crews; the MGBs had opened up, sending red and white tracer shells from their 20mm Oerlikons and 0.5inch Vickers guns arcing gracefully towards the tanker, burning the night away. But SO Cadogan did not have time to enjoy the show; he and his coxswain were busy positioning his MTB for firing the torpedoes. Cadogan had to estimate the speed of the tanker to give an offset for the torpedo trajectory, and give course corrections to the coxswain to align the fore and aft sights of the aiming device with the tanker. It was essential to have the torpedoes strike the target at right angles to cause the maximum damage.

The Germans were slow to react to the attack on their starboard side, which gave Cadogan time to order the main engines started and for him to increase speed to 12 knots. At 1000 yards he did a final sighting check, but, simultaneously with this, the Germans sent two starshells high over the attacking MGBs, turning night into a day of eerie, pale-green brilliance. The cat was out of the bag and into the pigeons. Cadogan uttered a strong navy expletive and pulled both torpedo triggers. His fingers were crossed for the impulse cartridges in the 21-inch torpedo tubes to detonate correctly and send the fish on their way. With relief he heard the muffled detonations and sensed the pressure build up in the expansion chambers.

"Come on, come on!" yelled Cadogan, "where are you fish? Get out of your tubes, for God's sake."

The torpedoes lumbered out of their tubes on either side of the bridge, their propellers, wreathed in smoke, whirring on their rear end. That was it; the die was cast. The torpedoes were alive and committed, and Cadogan could do nothing else to affect their destiny. He watched the bubbling trail of the fish for a few seconds as they moved their 500 lb warhead at 35 knots towards the tanker, then he called for hard a-port and retreated to 2000 yards to await results.

Wainwright had, of course, seen Cadogan launch his fish and leave the immediate scene. Still the Germans did not know that they had company on their port beam; the MGBs were doing a superb job keeping the tanker's crew fully occupied, although they were suffering for it. Wainwright had estimated that if Cadogan's fish found the target they would do so within 40 to 60 seconds. The wait was agonizing, rather like the hell of an innocent prisoner standing in the dock awaiting the return of a jury. 30 seconds,......... 40 seconds,......... 50,......... 60.

Wainwright's thoughts homed in on a crisp decision. *I'll wait 20 more seconds and then go in farther to 400 yards. We've got to get this tanker, God damn it! Time's running out. Jerry will discover us any moment now. OK Jimmy boy, let's do it.*

Wainwright spoke into the voice pipe, "Give me main engines stoker, and fast. I'm going to increase speed to 25 knots and get in closer."

The Packards spun up and Wainwright advanced the three throttles on the bridge while he gave Coxswain Morris the course to steer to keep abeam of the tanker. At 400 yards he pulled the torpedo triggers, but only the port one fired. He cursed loudly and yelled at the seaman standing close to the misfired tube.

"Hit it hard, Seaman Jackson; you know the drill. And hurry, before we ram the bloody Hun."

"Aye, aye, sir."

Jackson wasted no time in giving the back of the tube a series of hefty clouts with a mallet. It worked; detonation, then the reluctant fish was on its way. But the MTB was now only 200 yards from the ship and still closing.

"Port wheel full, Coxs'n. Take us out of here," said Wainwright, as he advanced the throttles to maximum speed.

The surge of power took the boat to 40 knots, and the whole crew felt the exhilaration, the relief, the excitement as blood pumped faster and faster through their bodies. The shackles of tension were broken; they were alive and loving every moment of it.

As they went round in a wide sweep with the bow well clear of the water, Wainwright looked back over the stern at the wake. They were leaving a sea of boiling white foam behind them, angry but beautified by phosphorescence. He looked for Cadogan's boat, but could not immediately find it.

In fact, the SO had slipped into the edge of the fog, using it as a thin veil of concealment. He and his crew were more than disconsolate, for by now they knew with certainty that their fish had not found the target. MTBs carried only two torpedoes; they could not reload and try to redeem themselves. The crew might have felt a little better if they had known that their port fish had passed forward of the tanker's bow by only four feet, and that the starboard one had malfunctioned; it never found its correct running depth, but just went deeper and deeper down to Davy Jones's locker. It did not even have the decency to explode when it hit the seabed.

* * * * *

As he stood on his bridge, the German captain was totally engaged in directing the fierce battle with the MGBs on his starboard side. If his imagination had been a little more open to the unexpected, he would have checked his port side from time to time. As it was, he did not even hear the engines of Wainwright's MTB above the continuous gunfire, and his eyes, half-blinded by the light of the tracer shells, would probably not have been able to see the torpedo trails if he had looked to port. Too late, the first fish quickly got the captain's attention as it struck amidships with a roaring explosion that sent a fountain of water, laced with torn, hot metal, high up into the air. The bridge structure crumpled as though made of paper, and the captain, along with his helmsman, died in a matter of seconds. The second torpedo passed harmlessly behind the stern but that was of no consequence, except to the Lords of the Admiralty who had to account for its cost. One fish had been sufficient to deliver a crippling blow to the tanker, although it had a lingering death.

Chapter Twenty-Nine

That part of the night's operations that was at all coordinated now came to a rapid close. Each CO took action more or less independently of the others, responding to evolving circumstances as he thought best. Communication among them was not possible; there was no time for discussion. Cadogan's MTB leapt out of the fog on hearing Wainwright's torpedo strike the tanker, and Cadogan saw it well on fire but still very much afloat. In a few seconds he was up to 40 knots and charging towards the tanker, intent on raking it with gunfire. He saw that Wainwright had the same idea and that their boats were on a convergent path. In fact, Wainwright's plan was a little more dramatic than peppering the burning hull with his peashooter bullets. He wanted to zoom around the tanker's stern and drop a depth charge to blow it right off. It was *his* tanker now; *he* was the one who had put a hole in it, and, by God, *he* was going to be the one to finish it off.

Suddenly, another starshell illuminated the scene, and another, and a third. Cadogan and Wainwright had no idea where they came from and did not really care. They had only one focus, one purpose; to send the tanker to the bottom as it breathed out great clouds of oily black smoke laced with red and yellow flames. But they should have cared about the starshells because the source was an armed trawler that had just poked its bow out of the fog. Soon it let loose with its 37mm gun and then its 20mm. The former aimed at Cadogan, the latter at Wainwright. The shells fell short, so the young MTB captains remained ignorant of the presence of another enemy vessel. The two MTBs came closer and closer to one another.

"Jimmy, for God's sake, break to port! Can't you bloody well see me?" yelled Cadogan, knowing full well that Jimmy could not hear him, and confused as to why he was heading for the vessel's stern area.

But Wainwright had not seen Cadogan's MTB, and cut right across her bow at 40 knots, missing her by inches and drenching her with vast volumes of wake. It was only Cadogan's last second cutting of all his throttles and the coxswain's spinning of the wheel to starboard that stopped both boats being smashed to bits. Cadogan stood on the bridge, his face stinging from the impact of the icy cold sea and his body shaking with fury and fright. The coxswain, who had been thrown to the floor by the vicious turn to starboard and the impact of the breaking wake, staggered to his feet, blood streaming from a gash on his forehead. Cadogan let the whole crew know what he thought of Jimmy Wainwright's driving.

However, his cursing was cut short when, to his horror, he saw tracer shells demolish the gun turret and engine room companionway on Wainwright's boat. Only then did he turn his head and follow the tracer stream back to its source as shells continued to blow up boiling fountains from the surface of the sea. Cadogan reacted instantaneously. Even before he had finished shouting his orders, the coxswain had swung the boat around and was heading at full speed for the trawler, while the gunner on the Vickers twin blasted away hoping to silence the enemy guns. But it was a difficult task at 1000 yards, for the searing light from the incoming tracers half-blinded the gunner. Nevertheless, his grim determination paid off for the 37mm stopped firing.

As Cadogan was wishing he had another torpedo, yet another starshell rose up, not from the attacking trawler but bursting through the top of the fog bank from an unknown inner enemy. The eerie green light lit up the whole area and revealed to Cadogan that he had some much needed help. On his starboard quarter he saw the third MTB, 9340, only 50 yards away, going at full speed for the trawler.

Tony Richardson, 9340's CO, was yelling a war cry and waving his right arm in circles as though he carried a sword and was leading a cavalry charge. When Richardson had seen Wainwright's torpedo strike the tanker, he had had a tinge of despair because that meant he might have to take his torpedoes home with him unless he found another target. But now he was happy, even though it was only a trawler that he could devour. And devour it he did. One torpedo was enough to send the trawler to the heavens in a thousand pieces.

Meanwhile, Wainwright, still in the dark about what his SO was doing, reached the tanker's stern and dropped a depth charge within feet of it, daring Fate to blow his boat up with the enemy's. The 400 lb explosive was set for a shallow detonation. Wainwright missed disaster by a hair's breadth, twice over. First, he misjudged the distance to the tanker and came so close that he could have reached up and touched the tanker's hull. Secondly, the detonator on the depth charge was, by pure luck, a bit slower than the average, which allowed the MTB to be on the periphery of the gigantic explosive eruption instead of in the middle of it. Even so, the boat still rose up as though on a tidal wave, twisting and turning in agony. Yet she survived the concussion and the sea surge, but the tanker did not. Its stern structure was split in two and peeled back in two halves, revealing interior compartments and two, lifeless crewmen draped over some machinery.

Wainwright did not have time to witness the final flooding of the tanker and its death throes as it slipped, almost graciously, under the waves, stern first. Neither did he see three surviving crew members leap into the spreading fuel oil, seeking a last chance at life, and hoping that the fuel would let them swim through it before catching fire. Wainwright and his crew had their own problems.

Gunner White required immediate attention. Although badly wounded, somehow he had carried on firing his guns as they approached the tanker to lay the depth charge, until the shock and pain from a smashed left shoulder and arm caused him to pass out. Two of the crew extricated him from his turret, that was now just a jumble of twisted metal, and carried him forward and down to the messdeck. In the process, they discovered that his left hand was not with him, and they could not immediately find out where it was. After Wainwright had turned the bridge over to Sub-Lieutenant Matthews and told Coxswain Morris to circle slowly at 10 knots, he went down into the engine room to directly assess the damage.

Petty Officer Motor Mechanic Bartlett was a man with a thousand things to do, but he had concentrated his mind on the two most important ones. One of the three Packard main engines was running rough, and he had shut it down to investigate the problem. One of the three rudders was jammed and needed inboard disconnection, if possible, so that it would float free and not input a bias to the steering. Two shells had penetrated the wooden hull just above the waterline, which meant that the sea slopped into the engine room in turning maneuvers or when the boat bounced through a wave. The aft fuel tank had taken a shrapnel hit and had leaked a few gallons of petrol before the tank's self-sealing property took hold. The floor of the engine room was awash in a mixture of seawater, petrol and oil. The air was hot and stank of fumes and vomit, the latter being provided by Leading Stoker King who suffered from chronic seasickness. He should have taken a factory job to help the war effort, a job where the room did not rock and items stayed in their place. Add to the heat and the stench, bad intermittent lighting and deafening noise and you will understand why Petty Officer Bartlett was not the happiest of seafarers.

"How's the situation, Bartlett? Everything under control?" asked Wainwright, somewhat too cheerily for Bartlett's liking.

Why doesn't he open his bloody peepers and nostrils, thought Bartlett, wiping sweat and grease out of his eyes. *Or does he need me to make a bleedin' written report to the bleedin' Lords of the Admiralty.*

"Oh, it's a piece of cake, sir, as our RAF friends would say. Everything is just purring along, sir, everything except the center engine and the starboard rudder, and, oh, yes, the aft fuel tank is not feeling too well." Bartlett said this with a very straight face, and Wainwright responded with a short smile at his facetiousness.

"Good; do your best. You're the man to get us home."

Wainwright went forward to see the condition of Gunner White, but in the wireless communications office he found a scene of devastation that stopped him short. An exploding 37mm shell had killed Telegraphist Baker, instantaneously, and destroyed all his equipment. Seaman Jones was bent over Baker, looking for signs of life. Wainwright did a quick check himself; pulse, breathing, eyes. In the process, his hands became smeared with blood for the body was grotesquely mangled.

"He's dead, Jones. Find a tarpaulin and cover him, if you please." Wainwright continued forward to the messdeck where White was laid out on a bunk, being attended to by Stoker Blanford. Wainwright could see right away that White was in a bad condition and might not survive the trip back to base. Blanford had put a tourniquet on his upper left arm to stem the blood flow that should have gone to his hand, if he had one, but which now trickled out of his wrist area where tendons, cartilage, bones, nerves, arteries and veins dangled uselessly and grotesquely. Once the bleeding had stopped, Blanford planned to wrap the wrist and immobilize it in a sling. He had already packed gauze pads around White's shoulder and tightly bound it with bandages. He had also administered a hefty dose of morphine to ease White's intense pain, but the effects of shock still lingered.

"You're in good hands, White. Blanford makes a good nurse, although he hasn't got much of a figure. You try and hang on, White. We'll get you back to Dartmouth shortly, and a free pint of beer. Good lad; keep smiling."

"How is it up top, sir? Who's manning my guns? Can't rightly remember what happened," said White, in a strained whisper.

"Don't you worry about your guns. I'm afraid Blanford has to go back to the engine room shortly, White. There's a spot of trouble back there. But I think you'll be OK here. All right?"

"All right, sir. Don't you worry about me."

Wainwright would have liked to spend more time below decks, reassuring the crew and lending a hand to fix the center engine, but he had already been away from the bridge too long. They were still in the middle of a battle in which half-time breaks do not happen. He rushed up to the bridge to take control again.

Although the tanker had gone, the fuel oil from it had not. The slick was spreading out in a large circle, smoothing the sea, and one section of it was alight. The two MGBs had long since stopped firing, and were prowling around the edge of the oil. Suddenly, one of them went into the slick and stopped dangerously close to the fire. Wainwright observed this through his binoculars.

"What the devil's he doing? He'll blow himself up."

"Perhaps he's picking up survivors, skipper," said Matthews, standing behind the coxswain.

"By God, you're right, Billie! It's 5639, Demont's crew performing the heroics. Talk about love thine enemy; Frenchmen saving Germans. That's one for the books.

"Where's the SO and Richardson? What have they been up to? I go below-decks for five minutes and I become five years out of date."

"They went after the trawler that gave us a pasting. Richardson sank it with a torpedo. You can still see the burning debris. Look, where I'm pointing."

Wainwright followed Matthews's arm then raised his binoculars.

"So that's the remains of the bastard that killed Baker and almost did for White. I'm shedding no tears over you, mate.

"I think I can see the SO and Richardson coming to join us. I'm glad that oil is burning; we can almost see what we're doing. On the other hand, if there are anymore armed trawlers in the fog, they'll pop out to see who turned the lights on." No sooner had Wainwright said this when a trawler did appear, and then another one. They both started firing with everything they had; *son et lumière* again.

Richardson turned once more into the teeth of the enemy; he still had one torpedo left, and, by God, he was going to make good use of it. But it was not to be, for the concentrated fire of both trawlers was brought to bear on Richardson's boat, demolishing the bridge, the wheelhouse and then the whole boat, as shells found the magazine and the torpedo, still poised in its tube. The crews of the other boats could not believe their eyes. MTB 9340 just ceased to exist; blown to smithereens; ten men snuffed out in seconds.

A brief time elapsed before the British and French boats reacted, almost as though they were paying a silent homage to their lost comrades. But then they became Winston Churchill's bulldogs, snarling and biting through the waves, with but one thought in their minds - *destroy, destroy*.

The four boats closed quickly on the trawlers, firing as they went, except Wainwright's lagged the others because of its reduced power capability. Although Motor Mechanic Bartlett was working like a Trojan, so far he had not fixed the problem with the center engine, consequently, speed was limited to about 25 knots. Leading Stoker King had better luck; he had managed to disconnect the starboard rudder input shaft which allowed the rudder to float free. However, Coxswain Morris still had to provide an offset at the wheel for the modified rudder system.

Wainwright started to feel vulnerable as he brought up the rear of the attacking four boats, and, remembering his very recent nasty experience when he had shells rain down on his stern from the first trawler, he made a point of quickly scanning aft with his binoculars as he sped towards the enemy. His caution paid off.

"We've got company, Billie; about 1500 yards behind us. Three, no, no, make that five E-boats. That's a laugh, they must be the gang we were waiting for before we were so rudely interrupted. We need to let the others know about this little development, and fast. Send off a couple of signal cartridges then use the Aldis to flash the code for *Enemy Attacking Up Our Arse.*"

"I don't know the code for those exact words, skipper."

"Well, improvise, for God's sake. How about *Am in Danger of Sinking.* I know that one, it's *MP.* Hurry, hurry, Billie! Why did Telegraphist Baker have to die just when we need him.

"Hard a-port, Coxs'n! I'm breaking off our attack on the trawlers, such as it is. We've no guns and only one depth charge left; don't think we could contribute much anyway."

"Dunno, sir, you did pretty good with the first charge on the tanker," said Morris, as he put the wheel hard over and took 9339 through 180° to face the direction of the on-coming E-boats.

"That was a stroke of luck, not genius, Morris."

Wainwright let the crew below know what was happening. He tried to sound optimistic but he knew that five against one gave him and his crew little chance of survival. The best he could do would be to worry the E-boats by snapping at their heels, and then end up ramming one of them. That could possibly provide the time required for the other boats to see what was happening and act accordingly.

Matthews fired the signal cartridges successfully, and then flashed away with the Aldis signal lamp. That neither the SO's MTB nor the two MGBs saw the signal cartridges was not surprising for the air was filled with tracers in all directions. Two more colored lights were lost items.

Suddenly Wainwright remembered the badly wounded White forward on the messdeck. If they rammed an E-boat, that was not a good place to be.

"Anyone below, anyone at all," yelled Wainwright into the engine room voice pipe. "Get White amidships; wheelhouse or wardroom. It's going to get rough for'ard.

Acknowledge someone!" Wainwright did not have time to wait for an acknowledgment of this order; his brain was a jumble of thoughts which could only be spared a fraction of a second each.

With a closing speed of 60 knots, it took but a minute for Wainwright to reach the E-boats as they came at him in line abreast. He lined up with the center German and charged him as though they were knights battling in the lists for a queen's favor, except his lance was already broken. They held their course, seemingly intent on mutual destruction, but at the last minute the German flinched and they passed one another with inches to spare, crashing into each others foaming wake. Both bridges were deluged with the cold January sea that knocked the breath out of the occupants. But there was something strange going on; the German did not use his guns.

"Hard a-starboard, Coxs'n!" yelled Wainwright, desperately trying to make himself heard above the roar of the engines. Morris did not respond so he added his hand to the wheel and turned it until Morris understood what he wanted. As Wainwright came round in a wide arc, the Germans did the same and started a full frontal assault again, but this time the E-boat on the starboard flank opened up with its 20mm guns.

"I was wondering when you bastards would start using your guns," yelled Wainwright. "Are your fat little fingers frozen, then?" But nobody heard the sarcasm. Morris looked hard at Wainwright, wanting instructions.

"Same again, Coxs'n, but have a go at the bugger with the guns. Straight at him. Don't worry; God's on our side," said Wainwright with his mouth right in Morris's ear.

Should I ram him? Should I ram him? But I'll kill my crew if I do. They know the score. They signed up for this. We're all dead anyway. These chaotic thoughts rushed through Wainwright's mind in less than a second.

"Hold your course, Coxs'n. Steady, steady; you're swerving, man."

"Steering's playing up, sir. It's hard to hold her," yelled Morris.

Two hundred yards,...... one hundred yards,...... fifty yards. The guns stopped firing. Why? Then the boats smashed together with a horrendous cracking and splintering sound, bows rising in the air, enmeshed, embracing as though they wanted to dance with one another. Slowly the bows came back down into the sea, and with much creaking and groaning they parted, each drifting backwards a little as though to see what damage they had inflicted on their opponent, like boxers retreating to their respective corners to await the next round.

For a moment, silence fell, then the shouting began. The German crew yelled for one of the other E-boats to come alongside and heave a tow rope. One did; the rope was made fast on the stern, then the damaged E-boat was abandoned, the crew boarding the rescue boat while theirs was dragged into Cherbourg.

Wainwright ordered all his crew aft, and asked for reverse engines so as to minimize the downward cant of the smashed bow and full-scale flooding.

Wainwright's next thought was for White. Had he survived the impact or been crushed against a bulkhead? Blanford reported that White had been put in the wardroom and strapped down. He was safe although in a lot of pain.

On the bridge, Wainwright realized that his vessel was still a fighting boat and he was letting the enemy get away. As the distance between the crippled boats widened, the respective crews stared at one another, sullenly, in a state of shock. They looked like young boys who had been discovered by their headmaster doing something radically wrong and were awaiting their punishment.

"Break out the small arms, Mr Matthews," shouted Wainwright. "We're not dead yet. Give 'em a parting shot. What have we got that's lethal?"

"There's a .45 and a .303 in the wardroom, 1918 vintage."

"Get 'em, then! Get 'em! They're getting away!"

"Skipper, they've pretty well disappeared into the night, and the other E-boats have taken off as well. I can just see their white wakes. There's nobody to fire at."

"Blast! You're probably right, Billie. I guess our prime job is to stay afloat until one of our lads shows up. Send up another signal cartridge, will you. Also, flash the Aldis again. This time we really are in danger of sinking."

"Aye, aye, sir!"

The SO and the MGBs had been oblivious to Wainwright's actions, and the trawlers offered a really worthwhile enemy target until, that is, Charlie Wilcox, the CO of MGB 5631, spotted the E-boats and anticipated the imminent annihilation of Wainwright's 9339. Calling on the flotilla's code of independent action when the need arose, Wilcox broke off the trawler engagement and went at full speed towards Wainwright. His arrival was none too soon, for Wainwright and crew knew that their minutes afloat were numbered.

Wainwright's crew made a hurried transfer to the MGB, although loving care was exercised when moving the dead Baker and the wounded White.

But now the British boats were all running low on the means to wage war, so SO Cadogan sent the signal for all to return to base, knowing that they had done a good night's work. The cloak of night continued to be their friend, and by dawn they would be safely back in Dartmouth harbor. The German trawlers slipped back into the fog, bruised and battered, but game to fight another day. 9339, a tired boat, gave up the ghost and went to her grave at the bottom of the English Channel. There she lay in company with hundreds of other vessels that had sought peace from storm, shot and shell over the last two thousand years.

Somewhat sentimentally, Wainwright saluted his MTB as she left his view forever.

The E-boats that Wainwright had so valiantly engaged entered Cherbourg harbor with all their guns completely out of ammunition and their torpedo tubes empty. What had been good luck for Wainwright in encountering a debilitated enemy, had been bad luck for a British convoy that had been severely mauled by the five E-boats earlier in the night.

Chapter Thirty

Charlie Wilcox did not want to push his MGB too hard going back to Dartmouth, as he wanted to conserve fuel and also give the badly wounded Gunner White a fairly smooth ride. He set the speed to 25 knots which would allow them to reach base in about three and a half hours. The other two remaining boats, the SO's MTB 9312 and the Free French Navy's MGB 5639, also set course, in line astern, at 25 knots to allow group protection. All three boats were low on ammunition, so if they met the enemy it would be a one-sided battle, if not a slaughter. To compensate for this anxiety, each CO ordered a rum ration to be issued to every man. There were no complaints, although the crew on Wilcox's MGB, being almost double its usual size on account of carrying the survivors from Wainwright's boat, received only half measure. Their murmurings were quieted by Wilcox promising the other half ration on attaining base and a replenishing of the grog stocks.

The thoughts of the crews as they traveled home were numb, tired and colorless. The tenseness of the search for the enemy, the rage and chaos of the engagement and its sudden cessation, left the men drained of most of their normal emotions. It was not that they did not reflect on the losses of their dead comrades and how close they, themselves, had come to injury or death. They did reflect on these things, but with a calmness, an acceptance, an inevitability that loss is the principal property of war.

Finding their base at Dartmouth was not easy, for although the remains of the flotilla had only a hundred miles to travel, they were not sure of their exact starting position off the French coast. The fast and furious night action had taken the group backwards and forwards, in all directions, away from their last known accurate fix. It was unreasonable to expect a navigator to be able to plot the courses taken during an action, so the starting point for heading home was, at best, just a rough estimate. But navigators had to get used to this uncertainty. It was a normal situation in time of war. However, one thing was certain: if you went north across the Channel from France, sooner or later you would hit the south coast of England. The embarrassment came when you made landfall at a holiday resort like Bournemouth instead of your naval base eighty miles to the west. The Admiralty frowned on such a mistake as this.

But on this night, Mother Nature gave the flotilla a helping hand. When the boats were about five miles from the English coast, the cloud cover broke up, allowing the moon to shed light on the shape of the coastal landscape. Cliffs, wooded areas, and shoreline rocks started to become familiar to the navigator on the SO's leading boat. Then the radar station at Coleton Fishacre, on the headland east of Kingswear, communicated a fix to the navigator: *you are three miles due south of the Mew Stone.* They were almost home.

Ten minutes later the lead navigator proudly announced, "Mew Stone 100 yards on our bow, Captain."

"Thanks, Nav, I've got her. Change course to port, Coxs'n, and follow the coast into the estuary. You know the procedure from here," said SO Cadogan.

"Aye, aye, sir," responded the coxswain, pleased to show off his seamanship as they neared the harbor.

The wedge-shaped Mew Stone and its colony of seabirds were left behind the flotilla as it headed for the boom across the entrance to the harbor, near Dartmouth Castle. The boom, made of timber balks, was operated by a crew of men on a steam-boom defense boat whose job was to open the boom when given the correct signal by any "friendly" vessel.

Navigation in this area was aided by lighthouses on either side of the entrance and leading lights on the Kingswear side.

Inside the protective boom there was evidence of a very busy harbor. Ships and boats for all kinds of purposes were either anchored, tied up, or in transit. A small coastal convoy was getting up steam ready to depart on the next leg of its journey, having spent the night in the harbor's safe haven. There was activity on three trawlers that had been converted into minesweepers. A destroyer was slowly making its way downstream after maintenance at the Noss shipyard. Many launches, each manned by a pair of Wrens, were on a variety of missions: some were delivering sailing orders; others were transporting sailors to stores and depot ships for the acquisition of foodstuffs, marine equipment and all kinds of personal items. Launches were also used for ferrying officers to operational planning meetings, and taking Wrens back to their billets, immensely tired after a 24-hour shift. All this activity was taking place in the dark, for it was only 7:00 a.m. and sunrise was not until 8:55 a.m., local time. The darkness was 'false', made so by the non-standard clock-time. A special one-hour wartime advancement on Greenwich mean time was in effect during the winter.

Charlie Wilcox took his MGB to the Dartmouth South Embankment jetty in order to have the wounded Gunner White carried straight into the cottage hospital for immediate surgery, and to deposit the dead telegraphist, Baker, in the mortuary. Jimmy Wainwright, in a very somber mood, accompanied White until he was safely in the hands of a senior nurse and the surgeon on duty. Jimmy then had the chore of giving detailed information about White to another nurse for the inevitable hospital paperwork.

As Jimmy walked through the hospital he kept his eyes open hoping he would see his sister, Susan, who was a hard-working registered nurse on the wards. Other survivors from Jimmy's boat took the opportunity to go to the hospital's first-aid station for treatment of minor injuries, and to get a good dose of sympathy from two pretty nurses. Wilcox then took his crew and Wainwright's patched-up survivors in his

MGB over to the jetty by the Coastal Forces Headquarters in Kingswear.

The HQ was called HMS Cicala, although in reality it was not a ship at all but the top floor of the Royal Dart Hotel. This concept of having an hotel be one of 'His Majesty's Ships' totally confused the civilian population, but the proprietor did not mind at all, as his bar receipts clearly showed.

The crew were dismissed on the jetty, and the officers headed for some sustenance in their land-locked HQ.

* * * * *

By the time Wilcox and Wainwright entered the de-briefing office, scrambled eggs and tea had already been served to the officers from the other two boats of the flotilla, and two staff officers, namely, the CO Operations and an intelligence officer. Consequently, with food inside them they were feeling re-energized, unlike the late arrivals who looked on the point of collapse and were in no mood for friendly banter.

"No breakfast left for you, Jimmy, but there is some cold tea with plenty of bromide in it," quipped Jean-Paul Demont. "You should not have stayed so long squeezing the buttocks of those delicious nurses in the hospital."

"Ha, bloody ha! Froggie, you've got a one track mind. How can you think of sex so bloody early on a winter's morning, after a night of slopping around in a tub in the English Channel?" said Jimmy, as he slumped down onto a chair.

"It is very easy, my friend; a Frenchman is ready for it any time of the day or night, no matter the season of the year."

"There is a smart reply to that, but I'm too bloody tired to think of it."

Two Wrens entered the office carrying steaming mugs of tea and a plate piled high with scrambled eggs and sausages.

"For you late gentlemen, a special treat," said the first Wren, as she delicately served the food and gave Jimmy a wink of promise.

"*Mon Dieu*! What's going on here. You have favorites! *Mon Dieu*, we did not get the meat," complained Demont.

"Too bad, froggie. She only likes real English gentlemen," retorted Jimmy with a supercilious grin.

"But, hey, Jean-Paul, how did you get here so quickly? Didn't you have to go to the hospital first with the tanker survivors?"

"We were met by a launch with medics and an armed guard as soon as we passed the boom. The SO had radioed ahead for some quick service, so we did a transfer then came straight here," explained Jean-Paul.

"OK, OK, enough! Eat as you talk, we've wasted enough time; this is a de-briefing, remember," growled the CO Ops, Captain Gibson. "Usual format; the SO and each CO to describe last night's action in detail, as he saw it, then we'll discuss the differences and try to arrive at the real truth. OK? Right! Francis, off you go."

The SO, Lieutenant Commander Cadogan, proceeded to give a detailed account of the action, the successes, the mistakes and the losses. His tone was formal and unemotional, and reflected his disciplined RN training and career experience. His summary at the end of his report was clear and succinct.

"In conclusion, I would say that the action was successful, even though the main event of meeting a German convoy was not part of the original plan. The reward in sinking a 10,000 ton tanker with a full cargo of fuel, the destruction of a heavily armed and aggressive enemy trawler, and the damage inflicted on an E-boat, outweighed our losses. Although we lost two boats, we only lost one crew, which is certainly regrettable but to be expected from time to time."

With the exception of Jimmy Wainwright, the other boat commanders agreed, more or less, with Cadogan's report.

"With all due respect to the SO, I think he painted a too glowing picture of the night's action," stated Wainwright, seriously. "First, we had no intelligence about the German convoy coming out of the fog. We went out prepared for and expecting a battle with a large group of E-boats. As you know, such boats are causing heavy losses in our coastal convoys; convoys that are stopping our nation from starving to death, and giving us weapons with which to fight. When the E-boats arrived, our flotilla was scattered all over the map. Maybe we should not have attacked the convoy at the time, but let the RAF nail it today. Maybe we should have stayed as a group and concentrated on destroying all of the E-boats, which we could have done easily, for, as I discovered to my benefit, they were pretty well out of ammunition. We could have annihilated the bastards.

"Secondly, I believe our losses were substantial. We lost forty percent of our boats, two out of five. We lost eleven men, maybe twelve if my Gunner White doesn't pull through. And we almost lost another boat with its full compliment of men when our French hero here went sailing into a sea of flames to rescue three German survivors from the tanker. Jean-Paul, I commend your bravery; it was a selfless act, but nevertheless one that almost killed your whole crew and lost us another boat."

"Jimmy, not so swift! Are you not the black pot pissing on the kettle, or however it goes. Didn't you destroy *your* own boat and put *your* crew in danger by deliberately ramming that E-boat? Didn't *you* want to become the hero as well?" said Jean-Paul, accusingly.

"That was different. Someone had to keep the E-boats busy while you other three were deeply engaged with the armed trawlers. They were giving you a lot of trouble. Remember?" retorted Jimmy, piqued at the criticism.

The arguments and counter-arguments flowed backwards and forwards for some time. The CO Operations did not intervene straight away; he thought it beneficial to allow the young Sir Galahads to let off steam. They needed to anneal their stressed minds, minds that for the last fourteen hours had dealt not only with a clever human enemy but also with the unforgiving sea and its many moods.

The CO Ops relit his pipe for the sixth time, inhaled deeply and, with head canted backwards, slowly released the calming gray smoke towards the ceiling. Then he looked at each of the men seated around the table in turn. His thoughts took on a dark tone.

How young they all are. What average age? twenty-five, maybe? Tired out, stressed out, yet still with a spark of fun, projecting indestructibility, optimism for their own individual future. Yet I know how fragile their young lives are, like that of a candle flame in a draughty room. The sadness of those deaths that are near is in the shortness of their lives, lives that have not sampled all the joys that can be. No time to have had a hearth and home, no time to have loved a woman and fathered a child, no time to have found wisdom and contentment. Yet their condition is not new; each generation of young men has to repeat it every few years as commanded by their elders and betters. Elders and betters? My God, maniacs and lunatics, who unleash their lust for power and drag millions into oblivion. But I can't change that, me, a gray-haired old veteran of World War One with the scars to prove it. All I can do is wish these young Drakes 'Good Luck' and buy them a round in the bar.

"Time's up, gentlemen! Thank you for your reports. Please write them up officially within the next twenty-four hours. I know some of you have very short memories. And leave out the swear words, please."

The aging CO Ops leaned back in his chair, puffed his pipe and exhaled slowly, with a strange sigh.

Before the tired young seadogs had a chance to push away from the table, the Intelligence Officer, a shy but deliberate person, had a few words to say.

"Perhaps I can take up the final few minutes to mention a couple of things. Reverting back to the comment by Jimmy that you weren't warned about the presence of the convoy. I'm sorry about that but the fog you encountered stretched all the way up the coast to Rotterdam; a real pea-souper. There was no chance for reconnaissance aircraft to spot it. We still don't know where the convoy originated or when it left.

Neither did we have any message from our agents watching the ports in Holland or Belgium about convoy sailings. But, sadly, that could be because the agents we have in those areas are being located and picked up by the Gestapo in fairly large numbers at this time.

"Now, although you were forced to switch from your first objective, be absolutely assured that you did the right thing in attacking the convoy. You sank a large tanker that was probably heading for Brest, Lorient or Bordeaux with a full shipment of diesel fuel for the U-boat wolf packs. That tanker's cargo was worth more than the five E-boats, believe you me. Last year U-boats sent over four million tons of Allied shipping to the bottom of the Atlantic; twelve hundred and ninety-nine ships and their crews. Yes, I said four million tons; a disastrous amount, but keep your mouths shut about that figure. The British populace are depressed enough about the war. Without fuel the U-boats cannot leave their pens, so anything we can do to interrupt or stop the supply is very good news. We don't have confirmation yet of the tanker's size, but if it were 10,000 tons, it might have been carrying as much as 6 million gallons of diesel fuel. Given that a type IID U-boat has a fuel oil capacity in the region of 10,000 gallons, you cut off the fuel supply to an awful lot of them. In addition, even as I speak, Coastal Command aircraft are taking off to comb the area of last night's action, hoping to find more of the convoy you attacked, and, with luck, more fuel tankers to destroy.

"My second comment is about the bonus that might accrue from Jean-Paul's brave action in picking up tanker survivors. An altruistic act, no doubt, but one that could lead to useful intelligence data. Once the German seamen have sufficiently recovered from their ordeal by water and fire, they'll be interrogated, using friendly persuasion of course, with the aim of extracting any information that could bear military fruits. For example, disposition of enemy ships; how many and where docked; types of ships; port defenses; communication codes; ship armament; convoy sailing dates, et cetera. That's all, and thanks for your attention."

The CO Ops piped up again. "By God, I almost forgot! Everyone except Jimmy Wainwright is to be mustered for the next operation this afternoon by 1600hrs, with an SO's and COs's briefing in here at 1500hrs. Jimmy and his crew get some extra days off because we don't have a replacement boat for them immediately. Lucky sods!"

The officers departed to either their rooms on base or to billets in Kingswear or Dartmouth. Their tiredness had receded for the moment, and as they left the offices they became schoolboys once again, throwing playful punches at one another or placing arms across shoulders. They were, after all, very young.

Chapter Thirty-One

Jimmy Wainwright had just enough energy left to do two things before he collapsed into his bed at the Royal Dart Hotel. Writing his action report for the CO Ops was mandatory. He kept it short and factual. The second thing was more difficult: he had to write to the mother of Telegraphist Baker, who had been killed in action, and offer a mixture of sympathy for his passing and praise for his bravery. He had written such letters before, but the process did not come easier with repetition. He tried to make each letter different, to mention a particular attribute or characteristic of the deceased so that the letter was very much at the personal level and not a standard format. As it was, those suffering the loss of a loved one always received the official, dispassionate, military telegram first; that was the unsoftened blow to the heart.

Jimmy only slept for four hours, and that was but a fitful sleep. He left his bed, washed, shaved, and went down to the bar for a pint of beer and a sandwich. Because he had two whole days free of naval duties, he decided to go over to Dartmouth and stay with his sister. Together they owned a half-timbered, late eighteenth-century house on Ridge Hill, fairly close to the town center. They had inherited it from their parents. Staying at the old family home was always preferable to the confines of his small room in the Royal Dart Hotel, or HMS Cicala, the name preferred by the Admiralty.

Before summoning a Wren-driven launch to take him across the river, he decided to sit and view the harbor activity from a bench on the hard outside the hotel. The skies were clear and the late January sun had taken the bite out of the cold air, making it fresh not frigid. Nevertheless, Jimmy was well wrapped in his heavy navy duffel coat, and wore his old school woolen scarf, twice wrapped around his neck with the ends free, one in front and the other over his shoulder in a sporting fashion. On his head he wore, at a jaunty angle, a greasy black, peaked fisherman's cap that used to belong to his father. He sat with his gloveless hands thrust deeply into his coat pockets.

The harbor activity was just as frenetic as it was before dawn, but now Jimmy had a clearer picture of what was going on. The boats of his flotilla had already been up to the maintenance sheds where hull and decking repairs had been made, engines and guns checked and greased, and general household duties performed in the head and galley areas. The boats were now being refueled with 2,500 gallons of petrol near the three fuel tanks located below Hoodown Lane in north Kingswear. Torpedo sheds for the MTBs were situated on either side of the railway line that terminated in Kingswear, and local residents feared that if the Germans dropped a bomb on either shed Kingswear would be wiped off the map. Depth charges, ammunition, fresh water, a ration of rum and sundry foodstuffs all had to be brought on board before the boats were tied up at the Kingswear jetty ready for the coming night's action.

Although Jimmy could not see all the preparations from where he was sitting, the arrival in his vicinity of the officers and crews reminded him of the fact that he was left out of the next operation; he was a sailor without a boat. As the officers went into the hotel for briefing they had fun teasing Jimmy.

"What's up, Jimmy? Not feeling too good? Lost your sea legs?"

"Wainwright, you're a bloody slacker. Bet you're just going to sit around all day dreaming of Wrens you've never bedded."

"Hey, Jimmy, I hear your row-boat sank. Did you forget to put the cork in?"

Jimmy retorted in kind. "Why don't you lot just piss-off. Jealousy will get you nowhere. I'll change your nappies when you get back." Jimmy went back to his quiet thoughts, some of them troubling.

Perhaps he had been reckless in ramming the E-boat. Perhaps he should have put his men first and the war second. He thought of the painful letter he had written to Baker's mother. He had come close to having to write eight more, or none at all if he, himself, had bought it. But he was being paid to be reckless. He was one of the fighter pilots of the sea; twisting and turning, dancing through the waves, attacking the enemy head-on. Do or die, that was it. No other way.

Then he thought of the Germans in the tanker. How big a crew did it have? Twenty? Thirty? Forty? Perhaps he had drowned forty merchantmen, not military men, just men who go down to the sea in ships. Three saved, forty killed. Yet those killed were providing fuel to others who crept under the waves in vicious metal monsters to kill other merchant-men bringing food to Britain. So, who are the innocents? No one! Then why the war? Why any war? Poland, Holland, Belgium, France, Denmark, Norway; that's why; six reasons right there. Jimmy's thoughts had come full circle; he had provided himself the rationale for doing what he did on the sea at night.

He looked across the river to Dartmouth. The sun was shining on the picturesque houses, the narrow, winding, hilly streets, the castle, the churches and the beautiful countryside beyond. He wanted this, his birthplace, with its two thousand years of history, its countless maritime tales, its kindly people, to survive. That alone was reason enough to fight, and Dartmouth had always produced fighters. Up there on the biggest hill, dominating the town, stood the Britannia Royal Naval College, built in 1905, the modern-day source of naval cadets being transformed into officers, if not always gentlemen. All too soon they would be tested at sea; taste fear, show courage and maybe not return. But there is no doubt that they would fight. Then Jimmy's lofty thoughts returned to sea level. He needed a Wren with a launch and a nice smile to take him across the river.

* * * * *

Within a couple of hours Jimmy had crossed the Dart, walked up the steep hills from South Embankment to his house on Ridge Hill and opened the front door. He entered quietly in case his sister was still asleep. She was working the third shift at the hospital, midnight until 8:0 a.m., and normally went straight to bed after her night's work. Jimmy found her still in her pyjamas, drinking a cup of tea in the lounge, which she quickly put down on a side table and rose to greet him very affectionately.

"Thank God you're safe, Jimmy! I was worried out of my mind when news spread through the hospital that your flotilla had lost two boats. Nobody knew which two for certain. You know what second-hand information is like; mostly rumor. First it was the French boat and your boat. Then it wasn't your boat but Tony Richardson's; then it was Charlie Wilcox's and Francis Cadogan's. Matron told me to go straight home after my shift and not hang around the jetty trying to find out exactly what had happened. She said she'd telephone me as soon as she had definite news, but she never did. I tell you, I've had a very restless night. But that doesn't matter. You're here now and from the looks of you all in one piece. That's marvelous!"

Susan Wainwright was an attractive, twenty-three-year old, honey-blonde with a firm, well-proportioned figure. She normally wore her hair in a shortish page-boy style with a fringe in the front. This went well with her nurse's uniform and required little attention. Her cheeks were rosy-red and always gave her a slightly flushed appearance. Prominent dimples appeared whenever she laughed, which was quite frequently. She was average height, 5 feet 7 inches, and walked with a flowing grace, unlike her twin brother who affected a nautical rolling motion, unless he was drunk, when, for some reason, he walked normally.

Susan rushed at Jimmy and gave him another couple of huge hugs as small tears of joy parted from her sparkling eyes.

"Steady on Sue; that's a magnificent welcome, but the old body is a little battered and bruised right now. Easy on the ribs, I don't want a collapsed lung."

"Oh, I'm sorry, Jimmy. Let me see where it hurts the most. You need some expert nursing care, that's obvious."

"No, really Sue, it's not that bad. I just got thrown about a bit last night. Lots of hard objects on our boats, you know, and they tend to come up and hit you when you're not looking."

"Jimmy, the stoic! All right then, no pampering, just a cup of tea. How about I cook you some kippers and butter some homemade bread? Well, maybe not butter; let's say margarine."

"Sounds marvelous."

They both went into the spacious kitchen, and while Susan cooked she also chatted away, ten to the dozen. She was one of those conversationalists who could lace the most boring topic with histrionics and color. Jimmy loved listening to her. She had a sweet but exciting voice.

Jimmy had not been home for a week so there was quite a bit of local news to catch up on, although none on Susan's side that was too dramatic. She had a new boyfriend; an instructor up at the Britannia Naval College. Next door Mrs. Witcomb's spaniel had had five puppies. Constable Jones had arrested Freddie Bligh on suspicion of dealing in the black-market. Five cadets, dressed as civilians, who were off-limits in The Cherub pub on Higher Street, became drunk and disorderly. The landlord, who saw through their disguise, but against his better nature, had to summon the military police. They clapped the young sea dogs in irons and marched them back under close escort to Britannia. Their future as naval officers was put in jeopardy.

In its long history, dating back to medieval 1380, The Cherub hostelry had been the scene of many altercations, some relatively benign, like that of the high-spirited cadets, and some that caused blood to flow, and even death, when press-gangs burst in and carried off unwilling recruits to work the sailing ships.

Jimmy's news had to be somewhat self-censored. He was not supposed to describe, even to a close relative, details of his naval actions. This meant that the location where enemy engagements took place, the numbers and types of boats involved, and the losses sustained could not be divulged for fear that such information could get back to the enemy and be used to his advantage. Jimmy sometimes broke the rules with his sister when he wanted to get a point across. This was one of those times, a time when he needed to share his conscience with someone of known empathy.

"Your initial information was correct, Sue; my boat was sunk and I sank it. I rammed an E-boat, not accidentally, deliberately. I put my crew in grave danger. I could have killed everyone. In retrospect, I believe I acted recklessly, stupidly. Maybe my judgment is crumbling. Maybe I'm no longer fit for command."

Susan looked very closely at Jimmy's face for the first time since he had come home. It was a very tired face, deeply serious, devoid of its usual playfulness. His shoulders had slumped down as though his head had become a ton weight. There was a slight but distinct tremor in his hands as he held his teacup. He sipped the tea slowly, and stared vacantly straight ahead at the opposite kitchen wall. He related almost every detail of last night's excursion, and then fell into silence. Susan finished cooking the kippers and cut some bread. She put Jimmy's plate in front of him, took hers and sat beside him.

"Come on, Jimmy, eat up. Some home cooking to put you right."

Susan sensed a psychological change in Jimmy's state of mind, his feelings towards his job, towards the war. She knew he had had many enemy engagements before last night's, and, from what she knew of his previous battles, they were just as dangerous, just as bloody, just as nerve-shattering. But he had been doing this stressful job for nearly two years now. Whether it was convoy duty, or E-boat skirmishes, or harassing enemy destroyers and armed trawlers, the toll on his physical and mental system was building up. And then there was the sea and the weather, the other, ever-present enemies. Exceedingly long hours in wind, rain, fog and sleet, drifting and pounding through relentless waves that tossed and turned the little boats like corks, drained the strength from Jimmy and all the crews. But she knew that Jimmy would carry on until he either cracked-up or was killed. That was his nature. All she could do was lend him a sympathetic ear and see that when off-duty he relaxed and enjoyed himself. The Devonshire countryside was still there, the pubs were still there, and Wrens were in abundance; these pleasures provided an antidote to the periods of high stress.

"Sorry, Sue, I'm not very good company, am I?"

"You're doing fine, luv. Just a bit tired, that's all. Tonight it's early to bed for you, then tomorrow we'll have a ramble down a few muddy lanes in our Wellington boots and drink some Best Bitter in a cozy pub with a roaring wood fire."

"Sounds good, Sue. Kippers were delicious. I had thought about taking a hot bath, but I think I'll just head straight for bed instead, like the good nurse says."

"Wise man. Our boiler's on the blink. Water doesn't seem to get very hot these days, and you can only have three inches in the bath anyway. They say there's a war on."

"Really, I didn't know. Who are we fighting this time? Not more relatives of the royal family, I hope."

"No, a nasty little man called Hitler with a very bad bloodline," said Susan, through clenched teeth.

"Yes, I do believe I've heard of him. Don't worry, he won't last. He's too excitable."

Susan managed a small grin while Jimmy's mind drifted ahead.

"Don't work too hard at the hospital tonight. Oh, yes, a favor, Sue; could you check up on a Gunner White from my boat? I think you've met him a couple of times. Nice chap. He's badly wounded; Jerry took his left hand off and smashed his shoulder. Tell him I'll pop in tomorrow morning to see how he's doing. I'll do that while you're sleeping, before our little walk. Thanks for supper. See you tomorrow. Nighty-night, dear sister."

Jimmy slowly walked down the dimly lit hallway and up the stairs. As he mounted, each stair gave a different sounding creak. He remembered the difficulty he had as a teenager, coming in late at night, trying desperately to minimize the cracking and squeaking of the stairs to avoid detection by his parents. His father slept soundly, and even if he were awake and heard his stealthy son's slow progress, he would say nothing. His mother, on the other hand, could hear a pin drop at one hundred yards, and always uttered a soft, plaintive question: "Is that you, dear?" To which Jimmy had a few select answers: "No, Mum, it's the Plymouth ax murderer." Or, "No, it's only Father Christmas." Sometimes, "No, Paula, it's your brother Fred, just returned from the Belgian Congo."

The stairs, the slightly convex black wooden walls, the yellowing, cracked ceiling plaster and the splitting oak beams had endured, without much structural maintenance, since 1793. Because of its age and architecture, the house had character. The three bedrooms were small and each felt cozy and intimate. Downstairs, the pride of the house was the large lounge, called the drawing room in years gone past. It had a sweeping bay-window composed of small, leaded-glass panes. A segmented, cushioned bench followed the contour of the window with a boxed-in storage space underneath which was an area for long-forgotten bric-à-brac.

Jimmy lifted the simple latch on his bedroom door and entered, groping for the light switch as he almost tripped over the threshold. The room was icy cold, and although logs had been placed in the small firegrate, Jimmy was too tired to light them. He knew it would take at least twenty minutes to coax a fire into life. Shivering and cursing the English weather, he stripped down to his underwear and hurriedly climbed into his four-poster bed. He kept his socks on, of course. He persuaded himself that, even with cold sheets and a cold pillow, lying in his bed was preferable to standing on the bridge of an MTB with stinging sleet cutting his face and seawater getting inside his oilskins. Sleep came quickly.

Downstairs, Susan washed the dishes and went into the lounge to relax before walking to the hospital for the night's work. She thought about Gunner White from Jimmy's crew who had just lost a hand, and wondered how many more amputees would pass through her hospital; hundreds probably. How would they cope with the rest of their lives without all their limbs? How does a carpenter get by without arms? How does a footballer get by without legs? The government does not fix those kinds of problems, nor the depressed minds that go with them. At best, the wounded are fed, clothed and sheltered by a tolerant relative. At worst, they end up on the pavement selling matches for a few pennies, cold, wet and with nowhere to sleep. The heroes are quickly forgotten.

Susan did not like these black thoughts, for she could not stop the events that caused them. She had to cheer herself up. Perhaps music was the answer. She went over to the radiogram and put on a record that was very popular at the time, particularly with nurses and Wrens. Then she collapsed into her favorite chair. The dramatic opening bars of *The Warsaw Concerto* filled the room. The music took her back to a Saturday night last year in the Dartmouth cinema watching *Dangerous Moonlight,* a film about a Polish concert pianist who was also a dashing fighter pilot. Nominated by his squadron to fly the last fighter plane left, he escapes fromWarsaw as the bombs continue to fall. The pianist composes a concerto as a picture of a defiant but poignantly sad city, crushed but not extinguished, and plays it in American concert halls to arouse the American conscience. The romantic theme, although sentimental and short, triggered an emotional response from filmgoers throughout Britain. In Dartmouth, on warm summer evenings in 1941, the concerto could be heard agitating and then soothing the air coming from opened windows in the various houses occupied by Wrens. Susan tried to stop her eyes watering when she heard it, but to no avail.

She was now in a musical mood and took the next record from the stack on one of the bookcase shelves. She glanced at the label; Chopin's Étude in C Minor, Opus 10, better known as the "Revolutionary". She smiled at the coincidence; this time it was the Russian Army in 1831 that was laying waste to Warsaw, and stirring the patriotic zeal of Chopin to write an étude of condemnation and bitter regret for his exile. Poor Warsaw, the city with a very apt name.

But there was more coincidence to come. As Chopin was ending, Susan heard muffled explosions in the distance; the lights flickered and china on the sideboard gave a small rattle. *They're bombing Plymouth again, or trying to. Third time this week. Poor sods! I expect we'll get some of their overflow casualties tomorrow.* Susan pretended that the bombing did not worry her, but it did. Although it was Plymouth, twenty-five miles away, that was being plastered, she knew that Dartmouth's turn was coming. It was an obvious military target with ships of all kinds jamming the river; minelayers, minesweepers, destroyers, MTBs, MGBs, coal tenders, small convoys, and up at Coleton Fishacre the Royal Air Force had an important radar station, not to mention the Britannia Royal Naval College and its 600 cadets. A perfect target. What were the Germans waiting for?

Susan gazed idly around the room, looking lovingly at the antique furniture, the paintings, some done by her mother, a landscape artist. Her father's books, some rare, some first editions, sat neatly in a bookcase. Brassware and porcelain figurines adorned shelves and the mantelpiece.

She saw the beauty in the room, but then slowly her thoughts became worried and dark again, thoughts that were full of aggressiveness and out of character.

If this old house were to be destroyed, my anger would be ten times greater than Chopin's. I would travel to Berlin and personally disembowel Hitler, Goering, Himmler and the whole gang of Nazi butchers, then I would feed their wretched bodies to a pack of ravenous British bulldogs.

Susan realized that she was quite upset, but that in a few hours she would have to be cool, calm and professional as she tended her patients. She needed soothing music, not phrasing that evoked bombs and guns; some Debussy or Ravel would do the trick. She listened and regained a quiet mood.

At 11:30 p.m., she wrapped herself up well in a thick overcoat, scarf, woolen hat and gloves. The night was clear and a frost had already fallen from a starry sky. She walked briskly down Ridge Hill to the river and then along to the hospital, wondering what the long night would bring.

Chapter Thirty-Two

The following morning Jimmy Wainwright went to Ward 5 to see Gunner White, but he found him in a heavily drugged state. White had had the first of several operations and his survival was not assured. He had lost a lot of blood and infection was present in his left wrist where his hand had been severed. He was receiving massive doses of penicillin and morphine to combat the pain. In his semi-conscious state he was just able to discern Jimmy's presence and registered this with a weak smile. He could not make conversation so Jimmy just gave him words of encouragement and many good wishes on behalf of his crew. Jimmy told White that he had recommended him for a Distinguished Service Medal (DSM) for his gallantry in continuing to fire his guns even though he was badly wounded. White's face showed a slight sneer when he heard this, as though he wanted to say, *Thanks, Skipper, but I'd prefer to get my hand back on my arm than have a medal pinned on my chest.*

Jimmy said good-bye by giving White the thumbs-up sign and saying that he would come to see him again soon. Before leaving the hospital, Jimmy asked White's surgeon what the prognosis was for recovery. He said the next two days would be critical fighting the infection. If White got through that, there was a good chance he would recover, but further operations would be necessary. Jimmy left the hospital downcast, and the rainy weather that had come in over night did not improve his mood. He went home to make himself a sandwich and have a bottle of Watney's Brown Ale. He hoped that Susan would have had enough sleep by three o'clock so they could go for a walk before sunset at five, raining or not.

Susan had had a troubled, intermittent sleep, and by three thirty she knew that staying in bed any longer would not improve matters. She was ready for some fresh air. Just as Jimmy and Susan were about to leave the house for their walk close to four o'clock, the phone rang. Jimmy was to report immediately to the Operations Room annex in HMS Cicala. He thought this an ominous order.

* * * * *

"Take a seat Jimmy; glad you could make it," said Lieutenant Jack Walker, assistant to the CO Ops.

"You mean I had an option not to come?" said Jimmy, with a sly grin.

"Not exactly," said Walker. "I want to introduce Commander Braithwaite to you. Commander, this is Lieutenant James Wainwright, one of our top-class MTB COs."

Jimmy stood up briefly and shook hands. He did not know who Braithwaite was and wondered why he was in civilian clothes.

"Right," said Walker, "I'll get back next door and carry on planning tonight's action. I'll send Cicely in with some steaming hot tea. It's cold enough in here to freeze the balls off a brass monkey. See you later, Jimmy." Jimmy considered his balls to have adequate warmth, although he could not speak for the Commander's.

Jimmy and Braithwaite sat on opposite sides of a small table, close enough for Jimmy to pick up the scent of Braithwaite's breath; it was none too fresh and was laced with a mixture of tobacco and garlic. Braithwaite opened the cover of a pink folder and started reading the first page of its contents. It was Jimmy's personal file, and Jimmy immediately knew that this was going to be some kind of interview.

"Let me see. Born Dartmouth 1918 to Bill and Paula Wainwright, father a schoolmaster, mother an artist, both now deceased. Fourth generation, strong West Country stock, fishermen, farmers, etc. One twin sister, Susan. Educated in Dartmouth, good academics, average sportsman. Won commonership from Dartmouth grammar school to Jesus College, Oxford, where you read modern languages, French and German. Good, good, could be handy. Ummmm, did this, did that .... ummmm .... but, hello, hello, what's this, you left after completing only two years; didn't finish your degree. Why was that?"

"Look," said Jimmy, with a belligerent tone in his voice, "before I answer, can you enlighten me what this is all about? I haven't a clue who you are, what you do, why you're here and the relevance of going over my background. Are you going to give me a medal or a court martial? Is that it?"

"It's certainly not the latter, but from what the CO Ops told me about you sinking a tanker, receiving a medal is certainly on the cards. Now, your questions first. I thought they'd filled you in a bit."

"Whoever *they* are, haven't," said Jimmy, getting a little impatient.

"SOE, old chap, SOE. Special Operations Executive. Ever heard of us?"

"Of course I have, everyone in Dartmouth and Kingswear has. Your outfit has a couple of MGBs moored alongside our prized paddle steamer, *Westward-Ho,* in the middle of the Dart. Strange people come and go in the middle of the night. You dump them in France where they commit dastardly acts of sabotage."

Braithwaite was taken aback by Jimmy's knowledge of what was supposed to be a secret outfit. They sat in silence for a moment, and then Cicely brought the tea into the room. The tea ritual took a couple of minutes after which Braithwaite got back to the interview. "So you left Oxford prematurely?"

"Yes. I knew I'd be called up sooner or later so I thought I might as well volunteer. I toddled along to my friendly Royal Navy recruiting office, said I would make a very fine officer, and one week later I was marching up and down a parade ground with a rather rude man shouting obscenities at me. After three months of this, I found myself in an officer training school, which was far preferable to the parade ground; the food was still lousy, mind you. Strangely, I was given a commission after a few weeks and felt superior to everyone. This changed rapidly after I was posted to Coastal Forces, Portsmouth, a fully paid-up member of the RNVR. Active duty quickly gave me a dose of reality. Then in January 1941, I was moved to Dartmouth base, made a CO and carried on bashing around the Channel looking for Jerry. So now you know my life's history. What's next?"

"Would you like a change of pace, Lieutenant? I believe you've had a very strenuous two years; much stress, much discomfort; lost two boats, seen crew members killed and wounded. That kind of sustained action tends to fray the nerves, don't you think."

"There's nothing wrong with my nerves, and if you're leading up to offering me a desk job at the Admiralty, forget it," said Jimmy, on the attack.

"No, no, no, Lieutenant, I wouldn't insult you like that. Desk jobs are only for people like me. What we want you to do, willingly or unwillingly, is to join the clock and dagger flotilla right here on the Westward-ho. You already seem to know quite a bit about it. We think you'd fit in well, running agents to and fro to France, mainly to Brittany, and ferrying escaping Allied airmen back to England."

"You mean be a glorified taxi driver, sir?" said Jimmy, with a laugh.

"It's not so easy as it sounds. There may not be much shooting involved, or the launching of torpedoes, but the seamanship required is of the highest caliber. Don't worry, you'll have plenty of scary moments, believe me. I've been on one mission as an observer and nearly wet my pants. I'd say you're a good fit on two counts; your knowledge of the

French language is one, and your experience as a peacetime yachtsman along the Brittany coast is the other. I got the latter knowledge from CO Ops who seems to know more about you than what is in your personal file. Is it true you know every rock and reef, every beach and cliff along that coastline?"

"I would not go that far, sir, but yes, before the war I sailed and fished the Brittany coast quite extensively."

"Good, then there is not much more to be said on my part. You have two hours to think about it. We in SOE like to believe we run a democratic shop; you know, no coercion; not like the Navy. Call your CO by 1900 hrs with your decision. He'll affect the transfer and give you all the details for your next move.

"Good luck, Lieutenant. I expect to hear good things about you."

"Thank you, sir," said Jimmy, standing up and smiling, his mind in a whirl. Now that he had been put in the picture, he felt quite friendly towards Braithwaite.

* * * * *

Jimmy sat in silence as he ate the cottage pie made by Susan from scraps of old roast beef and potatoes with a little grated Cheddar cheese on top.

"Spill it, Jimmy! What are you wrestling with? You look serious and worried," said Susan.

"They want to get rid of me. Well, not exactly; it is strongly suggested that I change jobs." He looked at his watch. "I've another half an hour to make a decision, as long as the decision is, *Yes*. Right, here are the choices that amount to a choice of one." Jimmy proceeded to summarize his interview with Braithwaite.

"What should I do, Sue? Take the transfer?"

"Apart from the fact that you appear to have no option, I'd say it was a marginally safer job than what you are presently doing, so take it, definitely take it."

A big smile spread across Jimmy's face and his whole body relaxed, tension melting away.

"Thanks, Sue. Your feminine wisdom is much appreciated. I'll call the base CO right now, then I'll enjoy the prunes and custard even more." He gave Susan's shoulder a loving squeeze as he went into the hall to phone.

On his return, he chatted away in an excited fashion. The whole idea of the clandestine missions was beginning to really appeal to him. He believed the missions would call for much initiative, personal and professional skills quite different than the ones he presently used, and with very little worry about complicated machinery and armament. It might involve landing in France or even staying there for a few days. He would need to use his wits and his seamanship to beat the enemy. It all sounded rather fun.

"So, it's done, Sue! I'm to report to the SOE flotilla outfit in two days time."

Chapter Thirty-Three

Jimmy Wainwright started his new job by learning the details of transporting SOE agents across the Channel in a Motor Gun Boat. There was nothing new or special about the operation of the MGB itself, but an item he was not familiar with was the surf boat. The surf boat was used to carry the agent from the MGB, anchored offshore, to the landing place on the French beach, called the pinpoint. Any returning agents or escaping airmen would then embark the surf boat and be transported to the anxiously awaiting MGB. Journeys in the surf boat were extremely hazardous due to many factors. The pinpoints were chosen for their remoteness and ruggedness to dissuade enemy sea patrols from approaching the shore. Rocks and shoals made navigation difficult, and, when coupled with strong currents and rapid tides, even the most expert seaman was hard pressed to make a successful landfall. And then there was the weather. Winds and waves came charging in from the North Atlantic creating surf that was merciless, particularly when running against the tide.

When not on an SOE mission, Lieutenant Harrington, CO of MGB 5700, liked to practice surf boat landings on the Devonshire coast. Jimmy Wainwright was introduced to this rather special rowing boat on one such training exercise. The boat was wooden and clinker-built, with a straight bow and stern that allowed rapid turn around but gave considerable drag. Two pairs of muffled oars with rubber-covered crutches kept the rowing noise to a low level. A long sweep oar at the stern was used for steering, and at times when the breakers were troublesome a sea anchor could be dragged for stability.

Harrington liked to time all surf boat practices. Time was critical when landing an agent. He demanded that the boat get in and get out with all speed, for his MGB was a sitting duck when anchored offshore. For the exercise, he stationed his MGB half a mile east of the Mew Stone. The surf boat was to make a landing on the beach near Kelly's Cove.

"Come on men, get that boat in the water, pronto. You're not pushing off from the Henley boathouse on a Sunday afternoon. Move, move!" shouted Harrington. "And make sure you hit the right part of the beach or you'll be blown up by a mine. Remember, land between the two rows of barbed wire that run up the beach to the cliff. The wire has red ribbons on it; looks very pretty."

The boat was launched and the two ratings who would do the rowing stepped in and prepared their oars. Next in was Sub-Lieutenant Jackson followed by Lieutenant Wainwright. The Sub was to show Jimmy the techniques he used for getting to shore, although he only had limited experience himself. Normally there was only one officer on the surf boat, and he had to be an expert navigator.

The beach was about 1000 yards away and a moderate sea was running. The wind from the southwest was freshening and there was a strong out-going tide. It was hard work for the oarsmen, but they were big, beefy fellows and well up to the task. Jimmy took the steering oar and knew that he was being observed closely by Harrington through binoculars. It took him some time to get the feel of the steering, but the rowers helped him out by loading their strokes so as to keep the boat going with the swell and not broaching. All went well until they entered the surf close to the beach. Jimmy missed seeing a large, submerged rock that caught the hull of the boat, swinging it around broadside to the waves but then quickly releasing it. However, stability had been lost and the next wave capsized the boat thirty feet from the shore. All the crew were thrown into the water, uttering every swear word imaginable. Cold and very wet they waded ashore, but were relieved to see that the boat had made it in one piece, albeit upside down. Jimmy had a moment of extreme embarrassment, but quickly recovered by helping the men and the Sub right the boat. An inspection showed that the boat was still seaworthy.

The sea-soaked crew pushed the boat into the surf and jumped in, muttering very uncomplimentary remarks about Jimmy's helmsmanship. The ratings were pleased to be the rowers, for the strenuous exercise got their blood flowing again. Half way back to the MGB they took pity on the shivering officers and offered to exchange duties. This thoughtfulness took the officers by surprise, but they took the oars and gladly bent their backs. They went alongside the MGB without further incident as the crew gave them a rousing mixture of jeers and cheers. The soggy surf boaters went below to seek dry clothes and a hot cup of tea as they headed back to Dartmouth Harbor.

As the MGB tied up at the Westward-Ho base, a not-very-happy Harrington shouted to Wainwright and Jackson, "My office immediately!" The disconsolate pair followed Harrington closely, like scolded puppy dogs. In the office they stood at attention in front of his desk, waiting for what is known in military terms as *a good bollicking.*

"My God! I've never seen anything like it in all my born days. What the hell do you think you were playing at. Bloody amateurs! Incompetent, pathetic clowns! Sunday sailors, that's what I call you. All you're fit for is swanning around in a punt, and then I expect you'd lose the bloody pole. Jesus Christ!"

"Sir, it was entirely my fault, not Jackson's," explained Wainwright. "I failed to see a group of submerged rocks."

"I bet you did, and in broad daylight. It's going to be pitch black out there when we're doing the real thing. How are you going to make out then? Turn over a boat full of agents?"

The redness in Harrington's face from his risen temper slowly receded as he thought of the comical aspects of the capsizing, and saw the contrition of the two white-faced officers standing before him.

"OK, Wainwright, it was you're first time, I know. Everyone is allowed just one screw-up in my outfit, but only then during exercises. Enough said; tomorrow's another day. And I believe you did sink a tanker, Wainwright, by throwing a depth charge at it. You can't be all bad."

The landing exercise was repeated on each of the following three days and on the fourth it was done at night. Jimmy Wainwright did not make any more mistakes, in fact, he gained the full confidence of all crew members, including Harrington.

* * * * *

On February 11, Commander Braithwaite, who worked for the Deputy Director Operations Division (Irregular) at the Admiralty, informed the CO of SOE Operations Dartmouth that a cross-Channel delivery and pickup operation was planned for the night of February 14/15. Coded instructions would follow, and one MGB and crew should be worked up and confined to base. Close liaison with the C-in-C Plymouth and RAF Coastal Command at St Eval would be made.

Chapter Thirty-Four

By 1942, the increasing strength of RAF Bomber Command was evident from the number and size of the raids over Germany and the occupied countries. This led to more bombers and escort fighters being shot down and more surviving aircrew trying to escape back to England. The journey back could be long and hazardous, and was only possible at all because of the self-sacrificing help of the French, Belgian and Dutch Resistance and the involvement of brave members of the general population. Using the expertise of SOE agents, escape routes were set up whereby aircrew were handed on from one safe-house to another. Some disguised escapees traveled in broad daylight on trains or buses in the company of a Resistance member. Others had a much harder time, traveling at night on foot or using a stolen bicycle, still in their RAF uniform and knowing only roughly the location of the next safe-house.

While in London, SOE's DF Section requested Marcel to include his Tailor *réseau* in the escape network. This request had arisen from the glowing report of Squadron Leader James Alcock who had highly commended the daring and bravery of Marcel's group in organizing his escape back to England. At first, Marcel was reluctant to agree; his main interest was fighting Germans, not baby-sitting Allied airmen. After the *bigger picture* was explained to him, he saw that, without airmen for the bombers, the bombers could not smash the factories which fed the German war machine that controlled northern France. Marcel agreed to expand his group's activities on a permanent basis.

As soon as Marcel was returned to France, his réseau would become an official link in the escape network. In the meantime, unofficial rules applied, as Erwan was to find out on the morning of February 10 when he came across two men in uniform on his land. They were huddled together in a ditch; cold, wet and visible to anyone who happened to be in that particular field. Erwan was taken very much by surprise, and did not know how to handle this uncommon situation. He felt angry and perplexed. The airmen stood up. One gave Erwan a sheepish smile, the other clenched his fists as though to strike out, thinking everyone was his enemy. Erwan noticed that their uniforms were blue and had CANADA flashes on the shoulder seams. The smiling one had a full wings brevet and the other half a wing with a G in the center.

"*Bonjour, Monsieur. Je m'appelle Claude Fournier; Pilote; Numéro 43986,*" said the smiling airman.

One of them could speak French, in fact his home town was Montreal so his French was excellent. Erwan was relieved. His immediate thought was to get them back to his farm as quickly as possible. Strolling around in daylight was asking for trouble.

On the way back, Erwan ascertained that they were the only survivors from a Wellington medium bomber, shot down ten days ago over Le Mans, about eighty miles east of Rennes. For two days they hid in a wood where a young boy found them, and then, under cover of darkness, took them to a member of the Resistance who sheltered and fed them in the cellar of his cottage. There, the airmen learned of the escape network, and were told that they would be handed on to the next safe-house. Equipped with a small, hand-drawn map, a compass and a little food, they set out at night to try and find their next destination. Erwan's farm was to be their sixth stop. Miraculously they had made it, and *still* wearing their uniforms, which they insisted on keeping, for if captured in civilian clothes, they would be shot as spies.

Erwan was confused. Why was his farm part of an escape network? No one had told him this, yet the owner of the fifth safe-house had known of Erwan's Resistance activities and assumed he would provide safe refuge. At times like this, Erwan cursed Marcel for being hundreds of miles away. What was Erwan supposed to do with these fallen birds? Fournier did not know where the next safe-house was supposed to be; he was told that Erwan would have that knowledge. It was probably a quiet spot somewhere on the Channel coast, he thought.

Erwan showed them his barn. That was to be their home for the next few days until further arrangements could be made. But what arrangements? Another airlift? A walk to the coast for a boat pickup? Maybe make them honorary members of the Resistance? Obviously Erwan had to get some instructions from SOE. He needed to put Igor to work with his Morse key.

* * * * *

Later that day, Erwan walked down to Le Chien café in Basbijou hoping to meet both Igor and Annette. It was a Tuesday, the day when the three of them usually met there, ostensibly to just mix and socialize with the locals, but in fact to use that as a cover for Resistance activity information and planning. On Fridays they had the same loose arrangement, but with café La Chatte in Guillaume being the rendezvous. Erwan entered Le Chien and was pleased when he saw both Igor and Annette pouring over a chess board. He ordered a drink and joined them. Bit by bit, Erwan related his finding of the Canadian airmen. He requested Igor to inform SOE and ask for instructions. He also alerted Annette that he might need her help in leading the airmen to the next safe-house, wherever that might be.

Igor successfully contacted Grendon at midnight from one of his many transmission hideaways, and was told that instructions would be given the following night at the usual time. The encoded instructions were received on Wednesday night and contained a surprise. Marcel and Jean would arrive by boat at approximately 2200 hours on Saturday, February 14. The pinpoint would be Bonaparte Beach near Plouha. The Canadians were to be transported back to England in the same boat. A house on the cliffs above Bonaparte Beach was to be used as the holding location. Details of the house were given.

Realizing that there was not a great deal of time left until Saturday, Igor cycled over to Erwan's farm at first light. He found Erwan in the barn talking to the Canadians and excitedly told him the news. Erwan was overjoyed with SOE's instructions - Marcel was returning at last.

Erwan formulated a plan for Saturday. He and Annette would take the Canadians in his truck early on Saturday morning to the specified safe-house above Bonaparte Beach. He would cover the airmen with vegetables, and pretend he was making a run to St-Brieuc market if stopped by a German patrol. They would stay in the safe-house until nightfall, and then head down the cliffs close to the rendezvous time. Probably one of the people who lived in the safe-house would act as a guide down to the beach. Marcel and Jean would be disembarked and the Canadians would take their place in the boat. Erwan wondered what type of boat it would be - submarine, destroyer, fishing boat, rowing boat? He, Annette, Marcel and Jean would stay in the safe-house the rest of the night and return home the following morning. Nothing could be simpler.

Erwan thought about the brief description of the safe-house provided by SOE. It slowly dawned on him that it had to be the house belonging to the old lady who warned Annette and him about the mines on the cliff top just a couple of weeks ago. It was hard for Erwan to believe the coincidence, but he had to accept it.

Chapter Thirty-Five

Marcel and Jean's last week in England was a busy one, preparing not only for their return to France but also learning and discussing details at SOE HQ of *Operation Earthquake*, the blowing up of the German supply dump south of Rennes, an operation in which they had already agreed to participate. *Earthquake* was tentatively scheduled for the end of March. The exact date was dependent on the availability of a squadron of bombers for the air attack, and the ability of Marcel to organize a sufficient number of Resistance fighters for the coordinated ground attack.

Marcel and Jean arrived in Dartmouth on the Thursday prior to their Saturday departure, and were given a room in Westward-Ho. On Friday they were put through a rigorous SOE check of all clothing they were wearing and every other item they would be carrying back to France. Any labels on new clothes they had bought in England had to be ripped out. Personal items with *Made in England* on them had to be discarded. Their papers and permits were checked and double-checked by SOE personnel. They would be returning with upgraded arms and explosives, plus a number of new sabotage gadgets designed to cause the enemy much aggravation if not actual death. Usage and methods of maintenance of all these military objects were explained one final time. They also received two updated cyanide pills each. Jean made a joke about these, but Marcel's expression as he accepted them was one of grave seriousness.

* * * * *

On Saturday afternoon at 1500 hours, Harrington's crew assembled for briefing in the SOE Ops Room. Marcel and Jean sat in the back and were just referred to as *the passengers*. For security reasons they were not introduced by name, nor was their ultimate destination mentioned.

Harrington produced a small and a large scale map of the Brittany coastline, and a further one that showed only details of Bonaparte Beach and the immediate area. He described the characteristics of the beach and the navigation hazards to its approach; rocks, shoals, tide strength, mines and German guard posts on the overlooking cliffs. Jimmy Wainwright added his knowledge of the area. A weatherman pinned a weather chart on the wall and was non-committal in his prognosis for the next twenty-four hours. A deep low was coming in from the Atlantic and it contained an occluded front. Its speed of approach was difficult to gauge. It could possibly stall for a while, which would be good news, or it might affect their area of the Channel in the next six hours. If it were the latter, high winds, rain and sleet, and heavy seas could be expected. This announcement caused everyone in the room to let out a loud moan. Harrington finished the meeting with mention of the Canadian airmen to be guests on the return trip, and a few details about ship-to-shore communication. The meeting broke up, and the crew spent the next few hours in a number of diverse ways, all of which were tinged with an underlying anxiety that was not visible to a casual observer. Some slept, uncomfortably, in battered armchairs; some played cards; one wrote a letter; another read a thriller. Marcel and Jean slipped back to their cabins and thought of France.

At 1800 hours, the lines on MGB 5700 were let go and Lieutenant Harrington took her out of Dartmouth harbor. Once through the boom and out in the open sea, he called for 35 knots. The MGB proudly lifted her bow and charged into the gathering darkness, leaving a foaming wake of phosphorescence in a moderate swell. The low pressure system and its attendant foul weather had stalled for the moment, although the sky in the west was showing a few flimsy clouds. The new moon would not show itself until the following night, so the only celestial light came from the stars of the milky way; perfect conditions for throwing the cloak of darkness over the clandestine voyage.

Jean was thankful that a large sea swell had not developed; he was no sailor. Even so, the motion of the boat slowly overpowered his head and his stomach. After an hour below decks and with his pallor changing from pale yellow to pale green, he was advised to go up onto the bridge to allow a blast of cold air to sweep away his nausea. If it did not, he could conveniently direct the contents of his stomach over the side.

Sub-Lieutenant Jackson, the official navigator for the operation, and Lieutenant Wainwright busied themselves in the wheelhouse charting their course and making dead reckoning calculations. This would be Jackson's last trip on 5700; his posting had come through for a transfer to destroyers.

After three hours of cruising at maximum speed, Jackson informed Harrington that they were two miles from the anchorage point. Harrington ordered a switch to quiet engines and a speed of six knots. As they edged in to the anchorage area, Jackson and Jimmy did a final check on their position. They were able to take a visual bearing on the cliffs of *Pointe de la Tour* and to pinpoint *Le Taureau* rocks, although there was uncertainty about the latter because of the many groups of rocks along this part of the coast. A mile out from the shore, engines were stopped and a grass rope anchor dropped. In the event of a quick exit being required, the rope anchor could be hastily cut with a hatchet. A rope anchor could be lowered more quietly than a metal one; a distinct advantage in enemy waters.

As Jackson, Jimmy and the two nominated oarsmen prepared the surf boat, Marcel and Jean gathered up their equipment and supplies and went aft to get in it. With the aid of a rope ladder over the side, they clambered into the little boat to begin the most precarious part of the trip. Jackson pushed off and, with Jimmy on the steering oar, headed 215 degrees, according to Jackson's hand-held compass. The oarsmen pulled strongly but quietly against the tide and wondered whether they were headed for the right part of the beach, about a mile away. They also wondered whether they would be welcomed by friendly Resistance fighters or by the muzzles of German guns spitting fire.

* * * * *

The surf boat crew need not have worried about the land party. All had gone remarkably well. Early Saturday morning, Erwan and Annette had had no trouble driving to the safe-house on top of Bonaparte Beach cliffs with the Canadians hidden by mounds of vegetables in the back of the truck. Although cold, fatigued and hungry, the airmen's spirits were high; freedom was just across the water; but, when talking about the English Channel, the word *just* could easily deteriorate into *insurmountable barrier*. Catherine, the owner of the safe-house, insisted that her four guests remain well out of sight until nightfall.

At eight o'clock two young men arrived at the house, having cycled from Plouha where they lived and worked. One was Catherine's nephew; both were Resistance members. On this night, their job was to guide the group down the cliffs to the beach and return with Marcel and Jean. Erwan and Annette would be part of the group in order to provide recognition of the returning Resistance members, and give assistance in landing and carrying the supplies brought from England. The guides had a good knowledge of the location of mines and the best path to take, which depended on the weather and the physical abilities of the people to be guided. They were armed and ready to fight if absolutely necessary, but they realized that if any of the escapees or agents in their care were captured the conse-quences would be dire. Not only would the captured be tortured then killed but Catherine and her safe-house would, at the very least, be unavailable for future escapes, as would

231

Bonaparte Beach. Enemy avoidance was paramount in the climb down the cliffs.

In dark clothes and with blackened faces, the group set off at nine o'clock; the rendezvous was set for ten. They progressed slowly and with care. Because of the weakened state of the Canadians, each one was roped to a guide in case of a fall. Erwan and Annette brought up the rear, occasionally glancing behind to ensure that they were not surprised by a German night patrol. They made the beach without incident and hid, huddled together, behind some large rocks. They kept silent and still. The climb down had warmed them, but now the freshening wind and the inactivity drained that warmth. They longed for the boat to arrive.

* * * * *

Jimmy could see and hear the surf crashing on the beach. They were getting close now. It was time for a recognition signal. Jackson had a flashlight and sent the code letter repeatedly, hoping that the land party had been informed of this in an SOE transmission. The letter was an S, which in Morse was three short flashes. The response was supposed to be an O, three long flashes. There were no long flashes.

"Come on, come on, you Frogs! The Limeys have arrived. Show yourselves, for God's sake!" said Jackson, more or less to himself. Jackson flashed again. Nothing. His thoughts examined the possibilities of the situation. *What if we're entering a trap. What if the land group has gone to the wrong place or been betrayed. What if this isn't Bonaparte Beach. We're half an hour late; maybe the land group has packed up and gone home. Should I abort right now? There's just time to turn around and get the hell out of here. My decision, my decision. I'm in charge. I'm responsible............... No retreat! We're going in and that's final.*

Jimmy had his hands full. As the boat entered the breaking waves, it became harder and harder to steer, but Jimmy relished the challenge. He smiled to himself in the darkness and even let a few chuckles escape his lips. The oarsmen had aching arms and shoulders, and were sweating profusely in their oilskins. They could not see anything to laugh about. The slewing action of the waves put the boat in jeopardy of broaching, which could easily lead to a capsize. Jimmy did not want a repeat of the Kelly's Cove fiasco, so his determination to keep the boat more or less at right angles to the beach became as strong as steel. His oarsmen gave him full support; they were as determined as he not to get their feet wet. After one more heave by a wave, all the crew heard a welcome sound; a grating, grinding sound as the bottom of the boat crunched into loose shingle. They had hit the beach.

"Oarsmen keep her steady! Everyone else, out of the boat, and pull her up a bit," ordered Jackson. The bow line was wrapped around a conveniently placed rock to make the boat secure, then Marcel and Jean busied themselves lifting their supplies onto dry land. Jackson and Jimmy were worried; there was still no sign of the Resistance group. Although risky, Jackson decided to try flashing the code signal one more time. He flashed along the beach left and then again right.

"I see a faint response to the right," said Jimmy.

"I saw it too," confirmed Jackson. "Jimmy, why don't you take our two deliverables with you and check the light source. I see they've already got their Sten guns at the ready. Flash once if everything is OK. Here, take the flashlight."

"Will do." Jimmy looked at the hood around the periphery of the flashlight and thought that it might have prevented the land group from seeing the signal, unless they were viewing it from pretty well straight ahead. The hooded flashlight was really only meant for use on the MGB's bridge for looking at the compass or transmitted messages; the hood prevented a wide arc light being made which might be spotted by an enemy boat nearby. They had been using a good instrument in the wrong application.

Marcel and Jean shouldered their heavy packs, shook hands with Jackson and the oarsmen and followed Jimmy along the beach at a fast walking pace. After 200 yards they came to the group of rocks behind which Erwan's group was hiding. With a suddenness that surprised Jimmy, three figures silently appeared right in front of him. He froze on the spot for, even in the darkness, he could see that two of the figures had pistols trained on him.

"Welcome to Bonaparte Beach! The fishing is good this time of year," said the third figure in faltering English.

"Erwan, *mon ami, comment ça va*? It's good to see you. And never mind the fishing, how are your pigs?" said Marcel, stepping forward and embracing Erwan.

"The pigs have missed you but not the cows. They tell me it's good not to have their teats tortured by your rough hands. But I'm glad to see you, glad and relieved. It's hard work trying to run a réseau when you don't know what you're doing. And Jean, good to see you too. Your men are all alive but ready for some big action. They are a restless group; Philippe has a hard time controlling them - you know, wine, women and reckless acts of sabotage."

"And I'm one of the women, in case you've forgotten me," said Annette, coming forward from behind the rock. She embraced Marcel and Jean and applied kisses to their cheeks. Then she turned to the stranger, Jimmy, and embraced and kissed him too. "Forgive me," she said in English, "I didn't want you to feel left out. Welcome to France. A pity you can't stay. Maybe next time."

"*Peut-être, mademoiselle, et je peux parler français un peu,*" responded Jimmy, cautiously. He looked closely at Annette, but because of her heavy clothes and blackened face he could distinguish little about her. He *did* notice that she had a sweet, soothing voice after hearing her speak just a few words.

"Excuse me, these are our Canadian flyers, Flying Officer Claude Fournier and Sergeant Fred Bolton, and our guides, Christophe and Émile," said Erwan, concluding introductions. "But now we must hurry. It is not safe to stay on the beach too long. *Au revoir, Claude et Fred, bonne chance!*"

While the Canadians were giving profuse thanks to Erwan and Annette for all their help and kindness, Jimmy took his flashlight and gave a single flash to Jackson that all was well. The rearranged groups then went their separate ways, one back to the cliff face and the other along the beach to the surf boat.

* * * * *

The climb up the cliffs to the safe-house was strenuous because of the heavy load of supplies being carried. The inky darkness did not help, nor did the passing German night patrol that they almost stumbled into on the cliff road. Luckily the Germans were a noisy group, singing and laughing, which revealed their presence and gave time for the leading guide to order everyone to take cover in the undergrowth by the side of the road.

Once inside Catherine's house, the group was able to relax with a hot glass of cider. But that was not all; after the cider, Catherine produced a bottle of Cognac which warmed their souls and loosened their tongues. She thought the reunion of Erwan and Annette with Marcel and Jean was a special occasion, and she liked these people enough to raid her secret cellar. They did not retire to their makeshift beds until 3:00 a.m.. The next morning, with slightly heavy heads, they clambered into Erwan's truck and headed for home.

Chapter Thirty-Six

The launching of the surf boat back into the breaking waves was not a graceful affair. Getting wet was unavoidable. The Canadians almost missed the boat and had to be roughly dragged over the transom at the last minute by the burly oarsmen. This introduction to Royal Navy seamanship did not produce a lot of confidence. However, this quickly improved in the trip out to MGB 5700 when the strength of the oarsmen and Jimmy's steering skills became evident.

Finding the MGB was not easy. They used a course of 35 degrees, and knowledge that the anchorage was about one mile distant from the beach. Jackson had a walkie-talkie which he could have used to contact the boat in an emergency. However, at this point he did not want to risk a radio communication being detected by the Germans, so, not finding the MGB to be where it should have been according to his dead reckoning, he had no alternative but to conduct a square search. This was not popular with the oarsmen for it meant more strenuous exercise and they were already very tired. The wind continued to freshen and became laced with a cold rain.

Twenty minutes into the square search, Jimmy saw a light flash on their port bow. It was more than a flash; it was the MGB's code letter. The growing anxiety of the surf boat's crew and passengers disappeared in an instant when Jimmy changed course towards the light source; Jackson responded with his hooded flashlight. Within ten minutes the indistinct image of 5700 became a well-defined and very real MGB. After a further five minutes of hectic activity, conducted with a minimum of noise, the surf boat occupants were on board sipping hot cocoa, and Lieutenant Harrington was stealthily underway, heading for more friendly shores.

After five miles, the MGB was switched to her main engines, and with rising bows and foaming wake showed her grace and power. Harrington, ever vigilant, stood on the bridge scanning the darkness with binoculars pressed hard against his eye sockets. He knew he was still in enemy coastal waters and had to be prepared for an encounter at any time. He was looking astern when a voice bellowed above the roar of the engines:

"Flashing light dead ahead, sir. Closing fast. Moving to starb'd." Harrington turned around quickly and homed in on the light.

"Good work, Gunner. I've spotted it. Action stations all hands! Look lively! We've got company." *Damn and blast!* thought Harrington. *The last thing I want is an enforced gun battle. The crew's tired and I've got guests on board.*

"Signalman, get the Aldis ready. I'm beginning to recognize the silhouette of an E-boat, and that ain't good. We're going to try an fool them. Next time they send their single recognition letter, respond with three or four letters. That should confuse them for a while. Shake the Aldis up and down then maybe they'll think there's something wrong with it and give us the benefit of the doubt."

"Aye, aye, skipper."

The E-boat, now on a parallel but opposite course, was only 100 yards away. Harrington held his breath. The E-boat stopped signaling when the boats were almost opposite one another. *Surely they can make out that we're an MGB. Any moment now they're going to fire at us; I know it.* Harrington was right. A stream of 20 mm shells came from the E-boat across the MGB's bow. Was it a warning shot for them to heave to, or were the Germans just poor marksmen?

"Carry on flashing, Signalman, and every man on deck wave like mad," shouted Harrington, "there's still a chance we can avoid an engagement."

Harrington ground his teeth and firmed up his jaw; he desperately wanted to attack the E-boat but he knew the rules of SOE Operations:

Do not attack the enemy except in self defense.

In the wheelhouse Jimmy boiled over for a fight. It was against his nature, his training and his past experience to let this opportunity slip away. But he held his tongue; he was not the CO.

If just one shell hits my boat, I'm going after this bastard, thought Harrington, wishing that that would happen.

But it did not. The E-boat continued on its course at maximum speed without firing again. It obviously had a more important mission than establishing whether 5700 was friend or foe. With a relative separation speed of close to 80 knots, each boat was lost to the other in a matter of seconds. The night, the waves and the wind filled the area of the encounter as though it had never happened. Nature ignored these arrogant, petty, man-made disturbances in Her domain.

Four hours later 5700 entered the Dartmouth boom; the boat and her crew were proud of their night's work.

Chapter Thirty-Seven

Although Marcel had only been away from Erwan's farm for a month, the lack of physical activity in that time had softened him. Consequently, the first few days of hard labor in the fields made his back muscles ache and blisters form on the palms of his hands. He welcomed the fresh air of the countryside and its spaciousness. As he breathed its sweetness, he remembered that the population of London smoked like a chimney. In every public building a gray-blue haze filled the air and caused the smokers, and the few non-smokers, to cough and wheeze and have watering eyes. Gold Flake, Woodbines, Players, and an assortment of self-rolled cigarettes were puffed during every waking hour. Londoners smoked to steady their nerves, to snatch a little pleasure while the bombs fell. They deserved their cigarettes.

Apart from his farm work Marcel was kept busy with Resistance activities. With Erwan's help, he had to organize the farm as an official safe-house in the Brittany escape network. Hiding places in the various farm buildings had to be set up with mattresses, a change of clothes, a small stash of food and water, rudimentary medical supplies, and toilet facilities. The last amenity consisted of two buckets; one to wash in, the other for urination. Defecation by escaping airmen would be done in the farm outhouse, but *only* during the hours of darkness, so that they would not be observed crossing the farmyard.

Claudette did not like the new arrangements. Apart from the disruption to her daily farm routine and the increase in her household work, such as cooking and cleaning, she was fearful of being found out by the local Gestapo. She had heard stories about safe-houses being burnt to the ground and the occupants slaughtered. She was more than fearful, she was terrified, and, once again, she expressed her terror to Erwan in no uncertain terms. He was sympathetic to her fears, but explained to her that the men they gave shelter to were fighting to free France, and that some of their comrades had already died for France. Risks by the Breton people to help the Allies were necessary. The honor of France was at stake. Claudette did not care about honor; she cared about safety; to be dead with honor was still to be dead.

Marcel's biggest task was planning the ground attack on the supply dump south of Rennes. SOE London said he would need twenty men to be ready by the end of March. Marcel and Jean did not have twenty men; only twelve remained after the ambush during the arms drop of early January. Finding additional fighters in the dark winter days of 1942, when Breton morale was low, proved to be difficult. However, by expanding the radius of his search, Marcel found four more willing men and two possible women. The men were part of the Rennes *réseau*, and became temporarily assigned to Marcel. To obtain these men, Marcel had to divulge some of the details of *Operation Earthquake* to the Rennes circuit leader, whose code name was Georges. Initially the leader was very angry about not being chosen by London to control and fully participate in this major attack. After all, the supply dump was in his area. He had suspicions that Marcel was trying to takeover his territory and organization. Marcel had to be very persuasive that this was not the case. He just happened to be in London when SOE first came up with the idea.

London had given Marcel a layout map of the dump just before he returned to France. The layout showed the relative positions of the various major items; heavy tanks, lightly armored personnel carriers, shells, torpedoes, mines, dynamite, diesel fuel, trucks, and vehicle maintenance equipment. Miscellaneous caches of arms and ammunition were scattered amongst the bigger items. The map also included the railway extension that came off the main Rennes to St Nazaire line right into the dump. The map had been compiled from different sources of intelligence at no small cost; RAF reconnaissance flights (two planes shot down), an infiltrated agent (captured and killed three months ago), and observations by local inhabitants that were passed on to an operator in Rennes. SOE London deemed the map to be about eighty percent accurate. What seemed to be missing or unclear were the road access point and guard posts. Marcel and Jean decided that an extensive but surreptitious reconnoiter of the supply dump had to be made. But how?

Assuming the roads were open to vehicles other than German ones, they could drive around the dump's periphery in Erwan's truck, but that would look very suspicious.

Jean suggested a direct approach to the access point. He could bicycle up the access road to the entrance gate with strings of onions around his neck and towing a small cart filled with miscellaneous vegetables and a few bottles of calvados. As he tried to sell the guards at the gate his produce, he could make a mental note of the strength of the post; how many men, how well armed. He should also be able to see whether the wire fence on either side of the entrance was electrified or would be alarmed if cut. It was a bold plan but Jean felt confident about it. Marcel, on the other hand, thought he could be arrested on sight and taken into the dump for some rough interrogation. However, he agreed with Jean that his plan was worth the risk.

Marcel's additional plan required a moonlit night. He could walk the perimeter of the dump, observing when patrols were made either internal or external to the fencing. He could also look for weak spots in the fence, maybe even find a gap in the barbed wire, but he knew that would be wishful thinking; the German army was very thorough. Much of the periphery was right up against wooded areas, so Marcel would have good cover. It was decided that both plans would be carried out.

The Rennes *réseau* was contacted to provide information about any safe-house close to the dump. Marcel and Jean needed a temporary base for their survey operations, which could take three days or more. The village of Guichen, about seven miles south of Rennes, had a safe-house. From there the dump was a further five miles, and could be reached on a bicycle using quiet back roads.

* * * * *

On February 26, Jean made his way to Guichen, using a bicycle and pulling a small cart full of vegetables. It was a strenuous ride because of the load, but he covered the thirty miles in just under five hours. He was in good physical shape, thanks to the training course in Scotland. The safe-house in Guichen was a small cottage owned by the village butcher, Monsieur Chandon. Jean enjoyed a rump steak for dinner the day of his arrival, a delicacy he had not had for over a year. Staying with a butcher in time of war had distinct advantages. The following day he rode to the supply dump, feeling a little self-conscious with three strings of onions around his neck.

There was a lightly-manned guard post at the beginning of the access road, adjacent to the rural road that passed the dump. The rural road's surface had been upgraded by the Germans for their heavy traffic. Jean had to inveigle the two guards at this first post in order to go up the access road to the main gate. He employed a mixture of flattery, humor and good bargaining skills with the guards, overcoming language difficulties by supplementing French and German phrases with much body movement, particularly in the arms and hands. He could have been an Italian. The guards liked Jean's produce and bought a small selection. They were, however, reluctant to let him proceed up to the main gate. But then he produced a bottle of calvados and offered it as a gift. The bribe worked. He shook hands with the guards, mounted his bicycle and headed up the access road with a huge smile on his face.

When he reached the main gate, he immediately realized how heavily defended it was. The gate was *not* a simple counterweighted pole that could be raised and lowered by hand. It was steel mesh on a heavy frame, twelve feet high, forty feet wide and on motorized wheels. It was controlled from inside a large guard house, located on the right side of the gate. Outside the guard house were two machine-gun emplacements, one on each side of the road. One emplacement was a concrete pill-box with the muzzles of two guns poking menacingly out of a narrow slit. It would be impregnable in an attack with light arms. The other emplacement provided less protection to the gunners, being a stack of sandbags in a semi-circle four feet high.

Jean dismounted his bicycle fifty yards from the machine-guns, and waited. He almost lost his nerve and thought about a slow retreat, but he knew that he needed to get closer to see what was inside the guard house and what the buildings the other side of the fence were used for.

"'ello, 'ello, good Germans! I'm a poor farm worker selling a few vegetables. I need money to feed my family. Won't you buy, good Germans?" pleaded Jean. There was no response for a few seconds.

"Hello, hello, good Frenchman! You don't need money; feed the vegetables to your family," said one of the Germans behind the sandbags. *That is a logical reply*, thought Jean.

"But my family also needs meat to go with the vegetables. Let me come closer to show you how fresh my vegetables are." Jean took three steps forward.

"Halt, Frenchman. Don't move or you'll be shot."

Two Germans cautiously approached Jean; one examined the contents of the cart while the other held his rifle on Jean. As the vegetables were turned over with the soldier's bayonet, three bottles of calvados were revealed. The soldier laughed.

"You cook the vegetables in the calvados? Why do you French have to cook everything in alcohol. Water is for cooking; alcohol belongs in a glass, you peasant." Jean did not argue.

The soldiers conversed for a while, and then beckoned Jean to follow them right up to the gate. He could not believe his luck. At the gate, three more soldiers came out of the guard house and started mocking and taunting Jean, speaking German very quickly, unintelligible to Jean, but with a meaning that was obviously not friendly. Jean played along with them, but all the time his eyes searched the surroundings; the guard house, the fence, the other buildings.

Suddenly an officer appeared; he was furious when he saw and heard what was going on. The soldiers quickly went back to their posts to await disciplinary action. The officer ordered Jean to return down the access road after he had explained that under no circumstances do German soldiers make purchases from local inhabitants while on duty. Jean thought of pleading the precedent set by the two guards at the other end of the road, but decided against it; he might possibly need their help again.

Jean returned to Guichen, satisfied that he had learned enough about the viability of the Resistance entering the dump by the main gate. It would be impossible. The machine-gunners would stop anyone on foot. The gate was too strong to burst through with a heavy truck. There were at least ten armed soldiers in the large guard house and maybe another fifty in the buildings on the other side; those buildings were army barracks. Outside the barracks were two more machine-gun posts, and to one side, with its gun pointing at the gate, was a panzer tank. Also, Jean had caught a glimpse of insulators embedded in the termination of the fence near the guard house, meaning that the fence was electrified and probably alarmed. Floodlights were mounted on tall wooden poles around the whole complex. Jean concluded that blowing up the dump should be left solely to the RAF. A ground support group would be slaughtered.

Chapter Thirty-Eight

The following day, Marcel took a series of buses to arrive at the Guichen safe-house. Both he and Jean had to have a good cover story for what they were doing staying in Chandon's house, in case they were subjected to a spot check by the French police, or far worse, by the Gestapo.

Marcel's papers, which had passed inspection many times, had him defined as a farm-hand, born in Avignon, working for farm owner Erwan Cottereau of Basbijou. He was in the area looking for a better job, and renting a bed from Chandon for a few nights.

Jean's papers, forged by SOE when he was in London, had him defined as an itinerant vegetable seller, born in Caen. He was also renting a bed from Chandon until he was ready to travel farther west.

Marcel did not like what he heard from Jean about the impregnability of the supply dump, as they sat and talked in the unheated attic.

"Are you sure you're not exaggerating the strength of the German defenses at the main gate, Jean?" said Marcel.

"Of course I'm not. I know what I saw. If you don't believe me, go and see for yourself," said Jean, testily.

"OK, OK. Don't get upset; I believe you. So we need to find another way. I'm not giving up just because the main entrance is not possible. There's got to be a weak spot on the perimeter somewhere; we've just got to find it."

Marcel produced the SOE map of the dump that he kept in a false lining of his underpants.

"Look, there are two other breaks into the dump. Here is the railway line extension. How does it penetrate the fence? And here is some kind of water-way that joins the Vilaine river. SOE said they suspected it was a small canal or cut made by the Germans to bring barges into the dump, but no details were available. So what say you to a midnight prowl to these two places?"

"I'm game," said Jean. "And as we do so, we can examine the whole fence; look for watch towers; see what patrols are made. From what I've seen already, there's plenty of wooded cover up to about thirty feet from the fence. Mind you, it's a big dump; about a mile all round. It will probably take us two nights to check everything. We'll need to move quietly and carefully through the woods; and there might be some mines or trip wires."

"I doubt that there are mines," said Marcel "The woods are still pretty well privately owned, and the Germans try to keep local landowners moderately happy.

"So, until eight o'clock tonight when we venture forth, what shall we do? Cards? Wander the village looking for buxom maidens? Talk to our host about the intricacies of slicing up a side of beef? What do you suggest, Jean?"

"Well, if we're going to creep around the woods all night, I'm going to slip under my pile of disintegrating blankets and try to sleep. This attic is so cold that to do anything else would be misery. You can't play cards when your fingers are blue."

"I'm not tired, Jean, so I'll go down the ladder and talk to Monsieur Chandon. Maybe I should also try out the bicycle you've borrowed for me."

* * * * *

The ride down the country lanes on a night dimly lit by a quarter moon gave Marcel and Jean a feeling of detachment. Apart from their movement, the world was at peace; not a single sound could be heard. The crisp winter air nipped at their noses and earlobes, but the exercise kept their bodies warm and supple. They passed through La Belle Étoile and St- Senoux, then branched right into the woods that bordered the Vilaine river, which was flowing full and fast. Well before they came to the beginning of the access road to the dump, they dismounted their bicycles and walked west with them into the woods, where they found a place to conceal them and hopefully find them again.

They cautiously moved deeper into the woods, intent on getting their bearings by finding the dump fence. According to the SOE map, they should have been close to the railway branch line, and, after a further ten minutes, they did indeed come across it, more by good luck than judgment. They moved along the line just inside the trees and bushes, stopping frequently to listen for any foreign sounds. Suddenly the moonlight seemed to increase, except it was not the moon but arc lights adding a glow to the night sky. They were very close to the rail entrance.

It did not take long for Jean to see that the entrance was almost as heavily guarded as the access road gate. This meant that a lot of activity took place into and out of the dump via this entrance, maybe even on a daily basis. Marcel did not want to admit his disappointment at finding such strong defenses. They would need to hijack an armored train with 20 mm canons mounted on the front to burst into the dump. *Well, if that's what it will take, I'd better start visiting a few marshaling yards,* thought Marcel.

They quickly crossed over the line and continued north to locate the river cut into the dump. Instead of a navigable, well-maintained cut, they found an overgrown stream which they guessed eventually broadened out into a tributary of the Vilaine. The stream welled up outside the fence, being fed by an underground aquifer. *SOE, you need to redraw the map and tell the RAF to get a better camera!* thought Marcel.

It took another three hours to complete the circuit of the dump. Several times they lost their way when skirting around rock outcrops and losing contact with the fence. Also, they had to proceed at a snail's pace in order to minimize the cracking of branches under their feet. At one point they thought they heard search dogs barking, but they must have been way off on a distant farm. Sounds at night could be deceptive. It took them half an hour to find their bicycles, and another forty minutes to return to Guichen. The night had been tiring but informative. They collapsed into their beds, glad to be back in their attic home. Monsieur Chandon stirred in his sleep and smiled as he heard a string of swear words uttered by Jean as he climbed the attic ladder with much difficulty. His legs had turned to rubber.

* * * * *

The following day was Sunday, March 1, so it was a day of rest for Monsieur Chandon, that is to say, he did not have to open his butcher's shop and listen to complaints about the poor quality of whatever little meat he had. Being a house-proud, fifty-year old bachelor, he had set aside this Sunday to cleaning and polishing everything in his small domain. He started in the kitchen while Jean and Marcel took a late breakfast in the living room which, apart from the attic and a very small bedroom downstairs, was the only sizable room in the cottage.

"Well, Marcel, how do we get in? You're the one with the brains. You saw the formidable defenses. Tell me how?" said Jean, tearing a piece of bread from a stale baguette.

"I agree, it won't be easy."

"*Merde! C'est impossible! Impossible!*" said Jean, with anger in his eyes. "Tell the SOE to tell the RAF to go it alone. I've never really understood why they need our help anyway. They've got an ulterior motive; that's what I think, but I don't know what it could be. Maybe if the raid goes wrong, they want someone to blame, such as us. I can hear the top brass already saying: 'The Resistance failed to mark the target properly. Naturally we missed it. A poor show on the ground.' I've heard the RAF can't hit a barn door at twenty feet."

"Oh, they can. Maybe not from thirty feet, but twenty would be OK," said Marcel, sarcastically. "But seriously, the two main entrances are out of the question, and, as we saw last night, there doesn't seem to be a weak spot anywhere in the fence. It's electrified and alarmed. The trees and brush have been cut down for thirty feet outside the fence, so approaching the fence is a risk. There are high guard towers spaced around the full periphery, albeit quite far apart, maybe every 200 yards. As I said, it won't be easy."

Marcel stared thoughtfully at the white, bare wall opposite him. Jean continued to devour bread and drink cold milk. After a while Marcel said, "We'll have to go through the wire. There's no other way. Somehow we'll have to put a shunt around the wires we want to cut, so we don't get shocked or set the alarms off. Have you ever tried that, Jean?"

"Never! Never even heard of it. I'm not an electrical engineer."

Monsieur Chandon sauntered into the room and sat at their table, a mysterious, superior expression on his face.

"Excuse my impertinence, but I could not help overhearing some of your conversation. You weren't exactly whispering. So you want to get into the supply dump?"

"Who says we do?" said Jean.

"I've already been alerted by the Rennes circuit leader what you're up to, and it's not blowing up a few railway lines. This is a safe-house, you know; you're not here for a vacation; it's for something big."

Marcel looked coldly into Chandon's eyes. *How much should he be trusted? How much does he know already? Perhaps he's bluffing. Perhaps he knows nothing and is just fishing for information to sell to the Gestapo.*

"Well, Monsieur Chandon, you tell me what you know about what's going on, then we'll take it from there," said Marcel.

Chandon hesitated but then launched into all the details of *Operation Earthquake* that Marcel had told the Rennes leader. He also told a number of other facts about the Rennes circuit that only a trusted member would know. For now, Marcel was satisfied with Chandon's credentials.

"OK, Monsieur, you're right. The supply dump is our target. We want to make a very loud bang."

"And you need to get through the wire to do that?"

"There is no other way that we know of," said Marcel.

"Oh, but there is," said Chandon, smugly. "You don't go through the wire, you go under it; I mean *really* under it. A tunnel!" A silence followed while Chandon let the thought sink in.

"I said I wasn't an electrical engineer, neither am I a civil engineer," sneered Jean.

"Wait, wait, Jean, let Chandon explain further. I think he means what he says. Monsieur, please?"

"People tunnel into banks. People tunnel out of jails. Why not into supply dumps." Chandon paused, leaving his rhetorical question hanging in the air. "Almost a year ago, three young local men started a tunnel to get where you want to go. They were independent operators, not official members of the Resistance. Hot-heads, if you will. They started a tunnel but never finished it. They just disappeared off the face of the earth without a trace. Some say the Gestapo arrested them for some other act of terrorism, like blowing up a train or some army trucks. Others say they were taken to Germany for slave-labor. Yet others say they went south into Vichy France. Anyway, they never got into the supply dump, but I know how close they came to succeeding. I know where they started and I know where they finished."

"Eh? What do you mean? How could you?" said Marcel.

"One of the young men was my nephew. He showed me what they were doing; even used me as a consultant. I used to do construction work before becoming a butcher; even worked in a quarry once."

"Why didn't you tell the Rennes Resistance leader, Georges, about the attempted tunnel, even though it was unofficial? He might have wanted to carry on with it and send the dump sky high," said Marcel.

"I was on the point of doing just that after it looked as though the boys' disappearance was permanent."

"So what stopped you?" asked Jean.

"The fear of reprisals. I remembered the vicious reprisals by the Nazis against the inhabitants of Cadeau, the small village south of here. The Resistance had made attacks against German soldiers near the village. Fifteen villagers were shot. Three were women. Imagine the size of the reprisals if the Rennes Resistance blew up the whole supply dump. It would be catastrophic for all the civilians in the area. I would not want that on my conscience. Absolutely not!"

"Then why are you telling us now about the tunnel and the possible entry into the dump? What's changed?" asked Marcel.

"You know full well what's changed. The RAF is a partner; they will take the blame. Georges told me, and you told him," said Chandon.

"That is the *official* theory, I agree. In practice, things could, and likely will, go wrong. Some of our men could be killed inside the dump; their bodies would tell the Germans that the Resistance provided aid during the raid. There would be some reprisals."

"True, true. On the other hand, none of your men might be killed, so I say some risk can be accepted for a prize that is so big."

Jean and Marcel looked hard at Chandon. They had an uneasy feeling about this conversation; the way Chandon had kept knowledge of the tunnel from Georges; the switch in his opinion about reprisals and risks. But the biggest cause of their unease was the sudden disappearance of all three men who were working on the tunnel. *Was Chandon the only other person who knew about their activity and had possibly betrayed them to the Gestapo?*

"Do you want to consider this tunnel? If so, I think I can find the entrance again, and we can go tonight," said Chandon.

Marcel was hesitant, his imagination racing ahead to the possible sudden disappearance of two further Resistance fighters, Jean and he, courtesy of Chandon.

"You look worried, Marcel. What's the matter? You don't trust me?" said Chandon, laughing. Marcel did not reply. "Look, if you're interested, we have to go tonight. Tomorrow is Monday; I'll be in my shop."

"Give us a few details," demanded Jean. "Whereabouts is the entrance? How far from the fence? How was the tunneling done, and through what; granite, limestone, sandstone? What tools were used?"

"The entrance is in the woods, before you come to the access road, about 300 feet from the fence; well hidden by pines and some old beeches. Once you penetrate passed the trees, bushes and boulders, you'll be standing in a cavern with a ten foot high roof. Back in 1854 this was the beginning of a prosperous iron ore mine."

Marcel gave a hearty laugh.

"What's the matter? Have I said something funny?"

"No, no. It's just that Brittany seems to be full of old holes in the ground from which vast amounts of iron ore were extracted," explained Marcel.

"Well, that is true. So what? Anyway, the cavern extends in about 200 feet and stops at a limestone face. My nephew and friends tackled this with pickaxes and shovels, but very soon they hit a granite slab. They thought about using a little dynamite on this, but were worried about the noise and a cave-in if the blast were too big. I said I could get hold of a pneumatic drill for them, and they agreed to that. Of course, I also needed to get an air compressor and a gasoline engine to drive it. I scrounged and modified an old motorbike two-stroke. Worked like a charm! They conquered the granite. That was it. Then they disappeared.

"So, do you want to go tonight or not; it's up to you?"

"OK, we'll go. Agreed, Jean?" said Marcel.

"Agreed, but that means I'll lose another night's beauty sleep, and I'm ugly enough already."

"I won't argue with that!" said Marcel.

* * * * *

Once more Marcel and Jean cycled to the woods near the dump, but this time following Monsieur Chandon as their leader. It was much colder than the previous night, and even the exertion of cycling failed to warm their bodies sufficiently. Hands and feet, in particular, felt frozen, although they wore woolen socks and gloves. Chandon carried a small back-pack, containing a paraffin lamp, a compass, some thin rope, five wooden pegs, a hatchet and a silver flask full of calvados. None of them was armed.

Chandon found the mine entrance quickly, but it took some time for them to lift aside the brush and small dead trees used to conceal the entrance. Once inside, Chandon lit the lamp. They scrambled over loose rock that had been dragged back into the old cavern from the drilling until they found the end of the tunnel. The cross-section of the tunnel was much smaller than that of the old cavern, being about three feet by three feet, but big enough for one man to work at the face. It sloped slightly upwards, and, if continued, would eventually break through into the open. From the cavern, the tunnel had progressed seventy feet, so if Chandon's estimate was correct, the present end was only thirty feet from the fence. But this assumed that the tunnel had been dug in exactly the right direction, namely, at right-angles to the fence. Somehow that would have to be checked.

Chandon crawled to the end of the tunnel. Then he took his small hatchet and struck the face. There was a sharp, metallic sound.

"*Merde*! We're still in the granite. I was hoping for limestone. Still, we won't need shuttering on this stretch."

As Chandon backed away from the face, he wedged one of his wooden pegs between broken rocks and tied to it the thin rope he had brought. Farther back he placed another peg and wrapped the taut rope tightly around its top. Then he sighted his compass along the stretched rope to find its bearing. Marcel and Jean looked on, a little mystified.

"Are you sure your compass will give a good enough reading? Perhaps there is still enough iron ore around to throw the needle way off?" said Jean.

"Yes, to the first question. No, to the second. The reading is probably good to a degree or so. If we were on board ship or in an airplane, encased in metal, certainly there would be a big effect. Then you have to *swing the compass* to find the correction."

Chandon's intent was to place the rest of the pegs in line, out to the cavern's entrance and beyond. If in line, the rope's bearing should remain constant. From the last peg he could run the bearing up to the top of the rock that overhung the entrance, and from there he could sight the fence and see where the bearing intersected it. Crude but hopefully effective.

As they withdrew back into the cavern section, Chandon gave a cry of joy; he had spotted the drill, compressor and engine lying partially hidden under loose rock and dirt.

"*Mon Dieu*! What luck! I don't need to scrounge more tools; these look in working order. Been here for ten months, doing nothing," said Chandon, pulling them free from the rocks and dusting them off.

"*Eh bien, mes amis*, have you seen enough to figure out your big break-in plan? If so, let's get out of here and head for our beds."

Marcel and Jean made no argument about this. The cavern was beginning to unnerve Marcel. It had an evil atmosphere to it, not like the Brocéliande cave. This one dripped water from blood-colored seams where rusting remnants of iron ore still lay. The dampness and coldness killed their enthusiasm for staying longer, and the light from the swaying lantern made phantoms swoop down and pluck at their bodies. They did not relish returning to this place, but they knew they had to.

Before leaving, Chandon projected the rope's bearing up to the top of the rock over the entrance where Marcel stood moving a makeshift pole around to mark the projection. Chandon climbed up to the mark and swung the compass onto the bearing in the direction of the fence. The fence was only just discernible through the darkness and the trees, but Chandon seemed to be satisfied. He declared that the tunnel was going in the right direction. They scrambled back down to the entrance and covered it up as they had found it with brush, dead trees and rocks.

By midnight they were back in Chandon's cottage where they laid plans for continuing the tunnel to place its breakthrough forty feet inside the wire. They decided who should finish the tunnel, and discussed a thousand other details about the attack on the dump. Marcel was happy to have Chandon as a main participant; his suspicions of him had melted. All three retired to bed, warmed by copious quantities of calvados and an excitement for their mission that was not felt before. It might even succeed.

The following day, Monday, March 2, Jean, the itinerant vegetable seller, mounted his bicycle and headed west, ostensibly looking for business but in fact heading back to his cave in the Forêt de Paimpont. Marcel's traveling was much less strenuous; he took buses back to the farm at Basbijou.

Chapter Thirty-Nine

While Marcel and Jean were surveying the supply dump, two more Canadian airmen arrived at Erwan's farm seeking shelter and transport to the next safe-house. The escape process was repeated as before but with fewer problems. A pickup from Bonaparte beach was requested, and Harrington's MGB 5700 got the job. Annette, driving alone, took the airmen to Catherine's safe-house on the Plouha cliffs and assisted the guides, Christophe and Émile, in handing them over to Jimmy Wainwright's surf boat crew on the beach. The MGB sped back to Dartmouth without any enemy encounters. A smooth operation.

* * * * *

SOE activities at Dartmouth hit a slow patch, so Harrington's crew were given a week's leave. They did not complain. However, after a few days of doing home repairs and helping Susan with the household chores, Jimmy Wainwright became restless. He tried listening to records and re-reading Balzac's *The Chouans,* a tale of Royalist uprisings in Brittany against the post-Revolutionary Republic in 1799. He thought the novel to be particularly appropriate to his present involvement on the other side of the Channel. Being a French scholar, he read the book in the original French.

Jimmy's next book was one of local history that used to belong to his father. Although European history had been poured into him at school, his knowledge of what had been happening in his home town since 1066 was very sparse. He read the book from cover to cover, and really became quite excited by the rich tapestry of events that had taken place on his very doorstep.

He read that the Normans had first realized the value of the mouth of the Dart as a safe harbor for cross-Channel voyages, including the assembly and supply of ships setting off on the 2nd and 3rd Crusades in the 12th century. French technology built a dam across a tidal creek to power two grain mills which added to the town's growing prosperity. The dam eventually became the modern Foss Street.

Later, wine from Bordeaux made many merchants rich in the 14th century, and in 1341 King Edward III granted the town its Royal Charter. Dartmouth was now definitely on the map; a place of importance. The poet Chaucer visited the town in 1373, and was so impressed by its notorious seamen that he named one of the pilgrims in his Canterbury Tales *Shipman of Dartmouth,* a skilled sailor but also a ruthless pirate.

Jimmy loved old castles and knew quite a bit about Dartmouth's first one, completed in 1388 during the Hundred Years War with France. But what he did not know, until his reading of the local history book, was that a chain was stretched from the later 1488 castle across the river to Godmerock on the Kingswear side to stop enemy ships entering the harbor. That was almost six hundred years ago, and now, once more, there was a boom across the river's mouth for a similar purpose. This time it was to keep the Germans out, but to let the British and French vessels in. An enemy today is a friend tomorrow!

1620 saw the famous Mayflower and Speedwell sailing ships put in for repairs on their way to New England, where cod fishing banks were discovered that led to a new trade for Dartmouth merchants. Changing trades, changing fortunes came and went as the centuries rolled by. Sail gave way to steam, wine to fish, prosperity to poverty and back again.

In 1863 the Royal Navy brought stability to the Dartmouth economy by establishing its training center for naval cadets on the first *Britannia,* a ship in the middle of the river, followed by HMS Hindustan in 1865. But this, Jimmy knew already.

He returned the book to its correct place in the bookcase, and decided that Susan should be told of his new-found knowledge at some future date when she was in an historical mood.

* * * * *

It was a Saturday morning. Susan had had a good night's sleep because she had switched to the day-shift at the hospital for the previous week. For once, she and Jimmy were sitting together in the kitchen having breakfast at a reasonable hour.

"Sue, I've played all your records and finished *The Chouans.* Also, I now know all about Dartmouth since 1066, thanks to one of dad's old books, but enough listening and reading; I'm getting bored. What can we do for excitement?"

"My God, haven't you had enough excitement over the past two years to last you a lifetime," Susan responded.

"That's the trouble; once you've had a certain amount, you can't live without it. You need more, and more; it's like a drug, and addiction sets in."

"Is your new job not satisfying enough? I thought you'd welcome a rest from pure blood and gore. You still go to sea in your powerful little boat, and do heroic work bringing back to our shores brave airmen. That's got to be satisfying. What about the clandestine rendezvous's you make on desolate beaches under the noses of the enemy; that must be exciting. I bet you also meet mysterious French women resistors who entice Nazis into their bedroom and then plug them with a silencer as they smile enigmatically. Furtive, dark-haired, dangerous sirens."

"You have a vivid imagination, Sue. The only French woman I've met was not dressed to entice anyone, in fact, it was hard to tell whether the bulky image was male or female. Everything was black, including the face; it was the voice that had womanly tones. I've met her twice now but I don't know her name."

"Where did you have this amorous meeting," asked Susan.

"Can't tell you that; classified. You know that."

"Well, if you meet her again, ask her over for tea, if she's not too busy blowing up trains."

"Could you do that, Sue? I mean, if England becomes occupied, could you overcome your latent pacifism, join a group of resistors and go out and kill Germans. Could you do that?"

"It depends, I suppose, on how angry I became; on how the invaders affected me personally. For instance, if they shot or tortured you, or if they destroyed this beautiful house, that would cause me to reach for a gun, I suppose. I would sacrifice my pacifist principles, but it wouldn't be easy."

"So, although you belittle this nameless French girl I've met, if you knew her story, maybe you could understand her anger and her capability to kill the occupier; not that I know whether she kills or not, maybe she just helps escaping airmen.

"But seeing we're talking about her - and this is totally illogical - I have this strange feeling when I'm near her that I've met her before. It's bizarre. Some kind of magnetism, a spiritual link, a sixth sense, something inexplicable."

Susan burst out laughing.

"Surely you're not serious? Let me understand you. All you've seen of her is a blackened face and a lump of shapeless clothes. You don't know her name, where she lives, her hair color, her character, who her friends are, her relatives, her likes or her dislikes. You know absolutely nothing about her, yet you say you've met her before, that you already have a bond between you. What have you been drinking? This is not you, Jimmy, unless for some reason you've become a hopeless romantic, and that I doubt."

"Well, you can laugh if you like but the feeling is there. Perhaps it'll go away if I meet her again; perhaps she'll turn out to be a real cow."

"How many French girls or women have you ever known, Jimmy? I bet you met a few up at Oxford before the war. And those sailing holidays along the French coast; you must have gone ashore many times and sampled the local wine and other pleasures. Perhaps you've got a thing about them. Is it sexual or cerebral? Knowing you, I'd say it's the former."

"It's cerebral, of course. Every sailor knows that French girls are as cold as English ones," goaded Jimmy, expecting a stormy response.

"I won't respond to that except to say that I hope you die a miserable old bachelor without any teeth and a bladder infection. However, there is one French girl who I *know* you've met. Summer of 1935, my French pen-pal, Annette, came to stay with us for six weeks; the last summer that daddy was alive. You didn't seem to like her much to begin with; you were too masculine and opinionated. Consequently, we didn't do much together until the last week when we all went sailing up the Dart, and you, with one of your uncouth friends, deigned to play tennis with us. Actually, Annette thought you were a bit of a snob; always talking about your intention to go to Oxford. Don't you remember her? We were all the same age then, virginal seventeen-year olds."

"What do you mean, *virginal*? Speak for yourself; I knew a thing or two at seventeen."

"Really! I thought you said English girls were cold? Anyway, Annette was a small, feisty blonde; bit of a tomboy. Bluey-green eyes, good teeth, played the piano rather well. Now, do you remember her? You must do, it was only seven years ago."

"Not really. So many girls; so many girls in such a short time. Impossible to keep track."

"You bragging idiot," said Susan, laughing and hurling a cushion at Jimmy's face. "If I recall, you had so many because you couldn't keep just one interested for more than a couple of days."

"Not true; I went out with Debbie Pollock for four whole days. That's what you call a conquest."

"Poor girl! Back to Annette; I'm going to make you remember her. I bet I've a photo of us somewhere. Back in a minute."

Susan went into the living room and searched through the photo albums on the top shelf of the bookcase. She found what she wanted; her scrapbook for 1935. She returned to the kitchen and, with a triumphant flourish, placed the scrapbook at Jimmy's right elbow.

"There, look at that photo! Annette and I eating an ice-cream. Two very pretty and charming girls, and intelligent of course." Jimmy screwed up his eyes and pretended to concentrate very closely on the picture.

"Well, maybe I have just a vague recollection of her. She has a good figure, hasn't she. Quite buxom! Yes, I should remember her with a shape like that."

"Oh, shutup, you sex fiend."

Jimmy gave a diabolical laugh. "Wouldn't it be the most fantastic coincidence if this pen-pal of yours was the one on the beach. I mean, it is a possibility."

"Rubbish! Annette lived in Paris with her parents the last time I heard from her; that was late 1939. She'd just finished her degree at the Sorbonne, and was going to become a teacher at a Parisian gymnasium. Naturally, I haven't heard from her since; the Germans aren't too good at forwarding letters. What would take her from the lights of Paris to the cold, windswept peninsula of Brittany, where milking cows and fishing are the main occupations, and people speak a very strange language, like the Welsh?"

"Who said I'd been to the Brittany coast? That's classified!"

"Dear brother, nothing is classified in the Dartmouth pubs. You should know that. Anyway, time to forget your mysterious French woman. You'll probably never see her again. French agents don't last too long, from what I've heard."

"You're probably right," said Jimmy, with a touch of sadness in his voice. "But, changing the subject, I've a surprise for you. How about a wee bit of sailing up the Dart?"

"Sounds delicious, Jimmy, but Isabelle is all tucked away for the winter."

"Not now she isn't. I took her out of storage yesterday, and popped her into the water on our mooring at the end of Sandquay Road. I commandeered a couple of my Wren friends to help me pull the trailer and lift her into the river. It was just a question of rank, you know."

"That's cheeky! What did you promise them in return?"

"The usual; a trip around the moon and a pint of shandy. So, let's away and put on our jerseys and oilskins. I think there's going to be a bit of a blow."

Susan and Jimmy wrapped warmly, and, carrying the sails, a paddle and a baler, retrieved from the darkest corner in Jimmy's bedroom, they walked down Ridge Hill feeling very much alive in the bracing air.

* * * * *

It did not take them long to rig Isabelle, which was a Snipe Class one design racing dinghy, with a length-over-all of 15 feet 6 inches, and room for a crew of two.

"Sue, do you want to be skipper?" asked Jimmy.

"Certainly, as long as you promise to do what I tell you."

"Of course! Have you ever known me not to spring into action on your every word?" said Jimmy, with a big grin and a quick salute.

"In fact, it has been known more often than not, but today I'll stand no nonsense; I have a Captain Bligh feeling. One disobeyed command and I'll keel-haul you. Where's the wind?"

"Southerly, about a force 3, a gentle breeze but freshening, and it's clouding up rapidly."

Susan checked the tell-tales and thought Jimmy was right. The boat was moored against the quay with bow and stern lines, pointing upstream with a slack tide. After the main and jib sails were prepared and the daggerboard inserted, the moorings were dropped and Jimmy quickly raised the jib which set to the port side as it caught the wind. Skipper Susan on the tiller sailed the boat to leeward and brought her round head to wind. The jib luffed up and Jimmy hoisted the mainsail. They sailed close-hauled for a couple of minutes, and then turned upstream to run with the wind, being careful not to jibe.

They looked at one another and laughed out loud with the exhilaration of being free on the river. Life, at this moment, was good, and it became even better as they left the upper harbor, and all its ships of war, and crossed over into another world. Isabelle, pushed gently by a following wind, sailed quietly, save for the chuckling of the bow as it parted the water.

Passed Higher Noss Point, the woods on both river banks stood mainly leafless but not lifeless. Crows and rooks in abundance squawked and squabbled on tree tops, while red-breasted robins and proud thrushes stood more serenely on lower branches. A great blue heron, that stood as still as a statue in an area of reeds, awaiting to strike at any passing fish, suddenly took flight, showing the majesty of its slow-moving wings and long, delicate trailing legs. Wintry sunlight enhanced the bird's bluey-gray plumage as it ascended, laboriously.

Susan and Jimmy thought that talk was superfluous as their spirits melded into the world of nature. Except for a few sailing commands from Susan as they performed necessary tacking maneuvers, peace and tranquility fed their minds. But then it was time for something a little more demanding.

The river broadened out near Dittisham and gave the sailors the opportunity to put Isabelle through her paces, pretending to be in a cut-throat race with a whole fleet of

Snipe. They went through all the points of sailing, performing precarious jibes, heeling over until the deck was awash, bottoms hanging over the side, and letting volumes of cold water splash into their faces and take their breath away. This was living.

The exercise made them hungry, so they sailed back to Dittisham and moored at the Ferry Boat Inn, a cozy pub that sold solid sandwiches and a good pint of bitter.

After their lunch and well before low tide, they reluctantly sailed back into the world of aggression, danger and pain, but thankful that they had enjoyed a few hours of peace and innocence.

Chapter Forty

Marcel now had a single-minded focus; to complete the tunnel within a three-week time frame. He had the drilling equipment and he had enough men for the job, but the exact details of the process required more thought. He settled on a group of three as being the maximum number that could work together without getting in one another's way. But when should they work; during the day or at night? How many times could three men enter the woods, open up the cavern entrance and create noise with a pneumatic drill before being discovered by the Germans? But maybe noise would not be a problem. Maybe the sound would be completely deadened by the overlying rock and subsoil. Marcel reckoned that another seventy feet of tunneling was required; thirty to the fence and another forty to place an emerging man into the shadow of one of the weapon piles. That sounded easy, but how would the tunnelers doing the ground break-through know where they were? He shelved that problem for the moment; the only thing to do right now was to start the job and learn by trial and error.

Marcel decided it would be safer to work only at night. The first group would consist of himself, Chandon and one of Georges's men, Claude, who lived in the area. Chandon was needed on two counts. First, to make sure they could find the cavern entrance again; Marcel did not trust his memory after just one visit. Secondly, Chandon knew how to operate the compressor and drill and troubleshoot if it broke down. On subsequent shifts, all men on the ground attack team would be rotated in to share drilling duties so that they could become familiar with the tunnel and supply dump layout.

Annette, of course, knew of the impending *Operation Earthquake* and wanted to be part of the team. Marcel was against it. He considered that she lacked experience fighting with the enemy at close-quarters, which could well involve hand-to-hand combat. The operation would move at lightning speed once the RAF bombing started; there would be confusion, extreme danger, and split-second decisions to be made. He could not risk Annette being a weak link. She countered all his arguments with persistence, but he held firm. However, as a form of compromise, Marcel said that he would allow her to spend a night or two helping dig the tunnel in the days ahead. For now that satisfied her.

* * * * *

On Sunday, March 8, Marcel returned to Chandon's safe-house at Guichen where he met Claude, the third member of the first night-shift. At nightfall, they found their way to the tunnel cave without incident.

The tunneling work did not go well. There were continual breakdowns with the drilling system.

"*Merde, pas encore!*" swore Marcel. He painfully turned his head around and yelled back down the tunnel. "What the hell has gone wrong now?"

"It's the compressor; the outlet hose has come off again," replied Chandon, apologetically. "Give me one minute and I'll fix it."

Marcel, at the tunnel face, was pleased for the short rest. He lay prone on his stomach with the drill stretched out in front of him. It was hard, dirty work and he sweated profusely. His ears rang from the noise of the drill. His mouth and eyes were full of dust, and the muscles in his shoulders and arms ached with pain. He had trouble seeing what he was doing because of the poor light that came from a solitary candle that was lodged in a cutout he had made on the tunnel side. He really needed one of Chandon's paraffin lamps but there was no room to hang it. On top of all this discomfort there was bad air. The air back in the spacious cavern was fresh although a little damp. However, it failed to circulate down to the tunnel face where Marcel struggled. His air was stale and filled with the carbon dioxide exhausted from his own lungs, and only made tolerable by traces of garlic still on his breath from dinner.

"OK, Marcel, it's connected!" shouted Chandon. "Carry on enjoying yourself."

Directly behind Marcel, on his hands and knees, was Claude. As Marcel cracked the rock with the drill and broke it away with a small pickax, pushing the fragments behind him, Claude scooped the bits into a bucket. He took the bucket down the tunnel to the cavern and emptied it onto the excavated rock pile. Once this pile became too big for the cavern space, it would need to be dispersed in the forest in such a way that it was unnoticeable. Another group would take the best part of a shift doing that.

The equipment broke down another five times before the night was over, accompanied by a lot of swearing by Marcel. Chandon possessed patience in coaxing it back to life. As he did so, his brain came up with good practical modifications to improve the system's reliability. At one point, while Marcel was drilling, Chandon crept through the forest towards his estimate of where the end of the tunnel should presently be, and listened for the noise of the drill. He heard none, even though he stood there for a full five minutes. He was amazed by this but gladly accepted it. In fact, although the rock transmitted sound very easily, the overlaying spongy topsoil was a good absorber.

With this first effort, the tunnel was extended only four feet. Sixty-six to go!

* * * * *

The following days brought some improvement to the tunneling system. Chandon performed maintenance on the engine driving the compressor and replaced the compressor hose. He rigged up makeshift acoustic baffles around the engine to reduce the noise emanating from the cavern. He wrapped the drill exhaust ports with rags to help the driller's ears, and devised a means of circulating the air in the tunnel using hand-cranked bellows connected to a rubber tube laid on the tunnel floor. The bellows were borrowed from a local blacksmith. The system was not very elegant and required quite a bit of manpower, nevertheless, it was better than nothing.

By the end of the week, it was estimated that the tunnel had advanced by thirty feet, leaving another forty to be completed. Marcel thought that with their present average daily rate, completion might be possible within about another week; perhaps by March 22. However, this was contingent on the solution to two problems. First, was the upward inclination of the tunnel going to place the end of it in the subsoil fairly close to the ground's surface? In other words, was Marcel's trigonometric calculation for the required slope correct, and was the actual slope being made meeting this requirement? Secondly, how could they find out in advance where they were going to break through the surface?

* * * * *

On March 17, these problems were discussed during a meeting in Jean's cave in Fôret de Paimpont. It was Erwan who provided the solution to the second question. He suggested that once the tunnel was out of the rock and into the subsoil, a metal tube could be forced up through the soil until it just broke the surface by several inches. One of them could then crawl towards the fence and look for the tube, and hence determine whether the tunnel had gone far enough or needed to be extended.

"I've already got five steel tubes ready; half-inch diameter, one foot lengths, with internal and external threads on each end," said Erwan. "You hammer the first tube up and if it breaks the surface, OK, you're there. But if not, you screw another tube into the end of the first and poke up some more. You carry on doing that until you're through. I'm sure there's not more than five feet of subsoil to penetrate."

"Steel tubing is hard to come by and dies to cut threads. How did you do it?" asked Marcel. Erwan only answered with a chuckle, as though it were a private joke. "OK", continued Marcel, "so we've got the tube sticking out of the ground, and we hope we haven't impaled a German guard's foot in the process; that would not put him in a good mood. So how do we see the damn tube as we lie under cover from the other side of the fence, maybe sixty feet away and in the dark? Or do you propose we poke our periscope up in the daylight for all the world to see?"

"We use binoculars; special night binoculars, courtesy of the Royal Navy," said Jean.

"Really! And I suppose we just toddle down to our local camera shop and buy a pair," said Marcel.

"No need. I have a pair right here. Real beauties!" replied Jean, searching in one of his personal packs stored in the cave. He passed them around for all to admire. Marcel's mouth fell open in disbelief.

"You young bastard! You stole these off Harrington's boat on the way over to Bonaparte, didn't you?"

"Stole is too strong a word; I would say they're out on loan. I think they belonged to the surf boat officer, Lieutenant Wainwright. I'm sure he can easily get another pair. He didn't even miss them," said Jean without any guilt whatsoever.

"I'm not so worried about the theft as I am about your limited future if the Nazis catch you with them in your possession. Bang, bang, you're dead!" predicted Marcel, with a laugh. "I have to admit though, they'll certainly be useful to spot Erwan's tube marker.

"Now that we have the tunnel problems licked, well, in theory at least, we need to plan the raid itself," said Marcel. "I've a framework for the attack but I need your ideas to fill in the details. This is how I see it. The RAF bombers are due to arrive in the vicinity of the dump at 2100 hrs on a date not firmly fixed yet. Probably March 31 or April 1, around the time of the full moon. At 2040 hrs we remove the turf plug and wooden support from the tunnel's exit, and fourteen men move through the tunnel into the dump carrying plastic explosives, triggers and timers. In pairs, the men fan out to their appointed targets, and place the explosives. They stay concealed next to their targets until they hear the bombers arrive, as signaled by the lead plane dropping a string of incendiaries and a couple of 100 lb bombs into the Vilaine river just north of the dump. Then comes the tricky bit. Our men set the timers on the plastic for two minutes, and then run like hell back to the tunnel while the bombers circle awaiting our explosions to mark the dump. Two minutes should be enough to find the tunnel because the individual targets are all within 100 yards of it. The RAF sweep in and blow the dump to smithereens. We exit the tunnel and cavern into the woods, mount our bicycles and ride home to our beds. The whole thing's a piece of cake, as Squadron Leader James Alcock would say." Marcel paused to let his basic plan sink into Erwan's none-too-speedy brain and Jean's ever-critical one.

"Comments? Arguments?" asked Marcel.

"The RAF might be late or they might be early. What then?" said Jean.

"We'll wait in position inside the dump for half an hour. If they have still not arrived by then, we'll abort the mission; back down the tunnel and wait for another day. If they are early, they won't have our markers, and that would probably be disastrous for the local villagers who would probably have bombs rain down on them instead of on the dump."

"I don't like the idea of fourteen men trying to get down one tunnel at the same time with scores of German soldiers trying to shoot their arses off. We could have a big jam and have a big slaughter; could ruin a really nice night," said Erwan, with a pained expression on his face. Marcel thought about that good point.

"Well, Erwan, that's true. Definitely a good point, but that's just one thing that could go wrong, and I can't consider all of them. We're risk takers. That's our job. Right?"

"Look, you say fourteen men are actually going into the dump. What about the other two? You said we had a group of sixteen," queried Jean.

"That's right. Two will stay back in the tunnel as possible reinforcements and to help movement through the tunnel as the men return."

"I think that's a waste of two men. Why not use them on top to cut the wire in two places just as our saboteurs head for the tunnel. With explosions starting all around them, the Germans won't notice the wire cutters. That would provide three exits instead of only one." A slow smile spread over Marcel's face.

"Jean, you have a brilliant mind for a communist. We'll do what you suggest."

The three of them continued discussing and refining the plan for another hour, then Marcel and Erwan said they were hungry for supper and would leave for the farm unless Jean could show them some real hospitality.

"You want hospitality, you say? In my humble cave where I and three of my men still live a life of comfort and luxury? Louis XIV did not have it any better. He pissed into a bucket; we piss into a bucket," said Jean, proudly. "Look at our furnishings; sofa, table, chairs all hewn from the forest, padded with sheepskins; mattresses donated by a Rennes brothel still smelling of perfume and other undefined odors; cool earthenware jars and pots for our food and a wine barrel for our water. And here, hidden from view by an old blanket, a wine rack; so name your drink and we'll toast the success of *Operation Earthquake*. Calvados or red wine? The wine has a special flavor: the grapes were pressed by the strong feet of Marie Renard in her own bathtub."

"Jean, you are the perfect host. I'll take some red wine and a slice of that bread and goat's cheese. It looks mature enough, and the maggots give it a certain flavor," said Marcel.

Erwan took a swig of calvados, straight from the bottle. "Success to *Earthquake*! And may we all survive it." Then he took another swig, and another.

Erwan and Marcel returned to Basbijou, but little work was done on the farm during the remains of the day.

* * * * *

By March 23, Marcel thought the tunnel was long enough. So it was time to determine where its end was located. Erwan's tube method was applied. Jean approached the dump fence cautiously, his prize binoculars around his neck and Marcel at his side. A new moon diluted the darkness from being pitch-black to charcoal-gray, which helped Jean distinguish images on the other side of the fence. Even so, he had to strain his eyes very hard to pick out Erwan's metal tube protruding about six inches above the ground. Fortunately the ground was bare earth; all grasses, weeds and tree stumps had been stripped in the name of German tidiness. Erwan moved the tube up and down to aid its recognition.

"That's the tube; there's no mistaking it. Now Erwan, for God's sake stop moving the thing. It looks like a phallic symbol gone berserk. Just the kind of phenomenon a guard would rush to investigate," remarked Jean.

"I don't think Erwan can hear you; he's six feet under. But more to the point, the damn tunnel is short. I'd say we need another twenty feet to get farther into the dump. That spot is too exposed, and we should go a bit to the left to get closer to that pile of scrap metal. We can make a dash for that and get some nice cover before slinking off to our respective targets. I can't believe my calculations were that far off. *Merde alors*!" Marcel cursed himself profusely but then quickly regained his composure. Recrimination would not get the correction made.

"Come on, Jean, back down below. We know what we've to do. There's plenty of the night left for a good ten feet of digging."

Back in the tunnel they told Erwan the bad news. He seemed to expect it and blamed no one. But he had good news to counter the bad.

"I think we're about to leave the granite and enter a sandstone layer. The last foot has been a much softer mix, like aggregate. I don't think we have to use the drill anymore; we can gouge away with pick and shovel. Twenty feet will be no problem. Two or three more nights should do it."

"Fantastic news, Erwan. But, and there's always a but, if it's sandstone it's soft and weak. We'd better put shuttering in as support; we don't want a tunnel collapse at the last moment," cautioned Marcel.

* * * * *

Over the next three nights, the tunneling progressed rapidly, and after a further check with Erwan's tube the job was pronounced complete. Finally, the exit was carefully prepared with a wooden structure resembling a trap door, on top of which some hard packed dirt was placed consistent with the surrounding area. This device had to be quickly raised up from the tunnel in order to seal the surface hole. The chances of anyone standing on the concealed exit were remote, but if they did, the trap structure should hold.

On March 27, all the equipment needed for the attack was moved into the cavern; explosives, triggers, detonators, guns, hand-grenades, wire-cutters, some water, food and spare clothing. Final plans were put in place; when to assemble and where, who the attackers would be and how they would operate as pairs, backup persons, escape contingencies, dispersal. The plan was solid.

On March 28, Igor informed SOE Grendon who informed London that the French Resistance was ready for action. Just name the night.

* * * * *

At the beginning of the previous week when work on the tunnel reached its peak, Erwan had two further difficulties to deal with. Two more escaping RAF men arrived at his farm; a wounded bomber pilot and his tail gunner. The pilot was in a bad way with suspected broken bones. He needed to be returned to England as soon as possible. SOE was informed, and, conveniently, they already had an operation planned to pick up an agent from the Plouha safe-house on March 29. Erwan was instructed to get the RAF men to the same safe-house by that date. But Erwan was being pulled in all directions, not least by the fact that two of his cows were due to calf at any moment. He could not leave the farm and make a trip to Plouha; neither could Marcel who was still helping with the tunnel and busy making final plans for *Operation Earthquake*.

There was no alternative but to call upon Annette to run the gauntlet to Plouha alone. She hesitated in accepting the task with its inherent risks, but once she fully understood the situation, she agreed to go. Erwan's truck was packed with vegetables to hide the airmen. They were not too happy about the smell, but knew they were in no position to complain. Annette was going to risk her life for them. Her biggest concern was that the truck might break down; however, the tail gunner assured her that he was also an expert mechanic with much experience on all kinds of strange vehicles.

Chapter Forty-One

Harrington's MGB slipped through the Dartmouth boom at 2200 hrs on March 29 under a sky that was made for poets; serene, mystical, moonlit, and infinite. Harrington, however, did not have any time to compose a poem; he had been told that there was probably a U-boat lurking outside the boom trying to slip into the harbor. Earlier in the night, a vigilant radar operator on a destroyer returning from convoy duty had noticed an unaccounted object off their stern. As the destroyer moved towards the boom the reflection had seemed to move as well. But then it disappeared completely. All ships in the harbor were put on alert.

Although Harrington loved hunting U-boats, he had orders to be at Bonaparte Beach early the next morning at 0200 hrs to pick up a returning agent and two members of an RAF bomber crew, one of which was a wounded pilot. The Bonaparte run was becoming a regular event; a bit too regular for Harrington who believed the Germans would sooner or later discover that it was a pinpoint for SOE operations. There were other beaches along the coastline not yet used. He believed that no beach should be a pinpoint more than once every six months, long enough for the Germans to grow tired of watching it for SOE activity. But Harrington was only a messenger boy; what did he know about the intricacies, intellect and psychology of SOE planning. He left the Dartmouth approaches as quickly as possible. If there were a U-boat around, someone else would have to deal with it.

The sea was calm and the night air, although not balmy, was warm for the end of March. The English weather was being benign for once, but no British sailor ever trusted it to stay that way for long. MGB 5700 was making good progress and the crew were even enjoying the ride. Jimmy Wainwright was happy with his navigation, and looked forward to the surf boat fun he would have later on. He also wondered whether or not the same French girl would be on the beach, conducting the hand over as she had done on the previous trips.

For two hours, the speed of the boat was exhilarating, and then it happened; the Packard V-12 engine on the starboard side rapidly lost power and then stopped. Not long after, the port engine did the same thing and then the center engine gave up the ghost. MGB 5700 was dead in the water, and the reverie of the crew was quickly broken, particularly in the engine room.

"Petty Officer James," yelled Harrington down the voice tube, "what the hell's happened down there? Did somebody forget to fill our fuel tank? We're dead as a dodo. Switch to auxiliaries and at least give me 6 knots. Report as soon as you can."

"Aye, aye, sir. Right now there's nothing obvious. Bearings are cool; no electrical shorts."

"OK. Let me know if you need any help. The rest of the crew are willing and able."

"Aye, aye. Thank you, sir."

Except for those busy in the engine room, the rest of the crew experienced a creeping tenseness, although they did not show it openly. They knew that in the space of a few minutes they had become a wounded, if not sitting, duck. They could move but they could not fly. They wallowed in the middle of the Channel in the spotlight of the moon. They were not supposed to operate in strong moonlight; many things were not supposed to happen but they did, such as having all three main engines fail.

"Take the bridge, Lieutenant Wainwright; I'm going down to the engine room," said Harrington. Jimmy left the wheelhouse and took watch on the bridge, scanning the sea on all points with new binoculars he had had to buy after the previous pair had mysteriously disappeared.

"Any progress, Petty Officer James?" asked Harrington, as he observed the frantic activity in the engine room. "Do you know what the trouble is yet?"

"I believe I do, sir. I think it's the new fuel flow valves; I reckon they've all packed up. No fuel flow, no power!"

"Well, can you fix them or do we abort the mission and chug back to Dartmouth at 6 knots?"

"I don't reckon I can fix 'em. They're a new type; sort of experimental in fact, according to Maintenance."

"Bloody hell! Experimental? What the hell are we doing with experimental equipment on an active mission?" screamed Harrington, his face turning crimson and his hands forming clenched fists. "This is preposterous. My God, I'll get the maintenance chief court marshaled when I get back. Jesus Christ!"

"Sorry, sir, I thought you knew about the new valves. I believe they were mentioned on the maintenance checklist. Perhaps you didn't get a copy," said Petty Officer James, tentatively.

"I got a copy OK, but no item was flagged as experimental. If it had been I'd have screamed blue, bloody murder. OK, spilt milk. We'll have to abort."

"Maybe not, sir."

"What do you mean, James? Are we going to breakout the oars for some additional power?"

"That may not be necessary. You see we've still got the old valves on board. I insisted we keep them for a few trips, just in case. There's nothing wrong with them, just a bit old that's all."

A slow grin came over Harrington's face and his hands relaxed. "Petty Officer, I take back my evil thoughts of you. Get these engines going again and you can have my rum ration. Carry on."

It took twenty precious minutes until the engines roared into life again and allowed 5700 to continue her mission. By the time Harrington ordered the grass anchor to be dropped a half mile off shore, it was 0230 hrs. They were thirty minutes late.

Jimmy organized the launching of the surf boat, and, in addition to two oarsmen, he took along another crew man to help with the wounded pilot, the extent of whose injuries was not known. Jimmy was worried about the return trip through the surf, for if he capsized the boat the injured pilot would not stand much chance of survival in the waves. Jimmy gave instructions to the fourth crewman on how to flash the recognition signal using Morse. The instructions, however, were not needed because before the war the crewman's hobby was being a radio ham. The signal response from the beach was quick and definite, so Jimmy steered the boat through the surf which tonight was only moderate.

The welcoming party of Annette, the guides Christophe and Émile, the agent and the RAF men were out in the open, huddled in a group, cold and anxious. The verbal exchange was short and to the point, for fear that they might be being watched by persons unknown. Jimmy's main preoccupation was getting the pilot into the boat; he had a broken leg and a broken arm and required much assistance. Going out through the surf was a lot more difficult than riding it into shore, and as the boat lifted and plunged the whole crew sensed the pilot's broken bones grinding together and the pain he was having to endure. If the light had been better, they would have seen that he still carried a *stiff upper lip*.

Once through the surf, the oarsmen wasted no time in rowing to their MGB and coming alongside. After the bow line was secured, the agent quickly clambered up the rope ladder thrown over the side and went below. The struggle to get the pilot on board took some time, but was achieved successfully. Jimmy was the last one in the surf boat, remaining there to hand up the oars and the agent's pack. He had just finished doing this when the second disaster of the night broke open the bowels and organs of MGB 5700. An explosion of immense magnitude tore asunder the boat from bow to stern, sending a million flaming pieces into the sky;

wood, metal, glass, flesh, all rose up, reached their zenith and then, with energy spent, fell back into the quenching sea, hissing and boiling. A deadly torpedo from a U-boat had struck amidships on the port side.

Jimmy, in the surf boat, was on the starboard side, and because of his position was spared much of the blast. He was thrown forcibly into the bottom of the boat, hitting his head hard and losing consciousness. The boat turned over and broke its back. Jimmy's lifejacket bobbed him to the surface some thirty yards from the flaming wreck, and the cold sea shocked him into consciousness again. For several seconds he had no idea where he was or what had happened. In a dazed state, he kept blinking and rubbing his eyes to bring his surroundings into focus. Then he took action by instinctively swimming towards the debris of the boat in an effort to maybe save a fellow member of his crew. But the sea was on fire and forced Jimmy to stop and reconsider what he should do. He listened for the sound of anyone's voice. There was none. He scanned the surface of the water for floating bodies. There was none. He continued to gaze at the scene of total destruction, and a deep sadness took over his emotions, causing his eyes to water and his mouth to twitch. This feeling dissipated slowly into the need for self-preservation, and the realization that he was probably the only one left alive, and that it would be pointless for him to try and rescue the dead. He started to think rationally again.

Get out of the area, Wainwright. Whatever sank us is going to come and gloat over the kill; search the vicinity looking for survivors and maybe even finish them off. So swim, you idle bugger! Can I make the beach? Not too far. Should I take my sea-boots off? Hard to swim with them on, but I'll need them later, if there is a later. Don't get morbid on me. Save your strength. God, this water's cold!

It was the incoming tide that saved Jimmy, that is, the tide and Annette. She and the guides had just reached Catherine's house when the torpedo struck the MGB and lit up the sky. All three looked seaward and became mesmerized. They felt the pressure wave from the explosion on their faces and their bodies tensed. Annette was the first to react; she immediately headed back down to the beach, not knowing exactly what she could or should do, only that any survivors would need help. The guides were more cautious and waited near the house. They knew that before long German patrols would scour the beaches, and more E-boats would arrive to search off-shore. The guides assumed that it must have been an E-boat on patrol that had attacked the MGB. They gave no thought to the possibility of a U-boat being the killer.

Annette reached the beach, and, in an agitated state, walked backwards and forwards, looking intently into the surf; looking for something that might be human. Five minutes, then ten minutes went by; nothing. Was it hopeless? Should she abandon her vigil and retreat to safety? She turned away from the sea and started to walk towards the cliffs, but then decided to take one last look. It was that last look that saved Jimmy Wainwright's life.

There's somebody in the surf. Fifty yards out. No there isn't! Yes there is! Somebody is waving. Could be debris from the boat. No, that's an arm, that's a face. It's definitely a person!.................Oh, my God, he's being swept towards those rocks..............He's going to be smashed to pieces..........Oh, my God!..........Got to do something!

Annette hurriedly took off her shoes and discarded her heavy jacket. She waded into the sea and plunged through the first line of breaking waves, surfaced and swam strongly. Then came the heavier surf. She plunged again under the waves, and surfaced, and again, and again. As she did so, she desperately searched for a sign of the person she was trying to rescue. He was there, then he was gone. There and gone, there and gone. The rocks came closer, dark and menacing. Twenty yards to go. Annette prayed for strength and her determination peaked. She would get to the person at all costs. A frenzy, a madness gripped and helped her.

"It's all right, it's all right, I have you," said Annette, as she reached the almost lifeless and exhausted body. She put her left arm across his chest and held the front of his lifejacket. She kicked furiously with her legs and reached out and back with her right arm, endeavoring to do the side-stroke.

"Come on, Mr. Navyman, keep kicking and we'll make it. I'm only a weak woman so you must do your bit. This is no time for sleeping on the job."

Little by little they edged away from the rocks and reached shallow water, where a two-foot wave lifted their exhausted bodies and gently deposited them on the beach, as though they were a precious offering from Father Neptune. There they lay unable to move an inch farther, utterly spent. Soon they felt the strong arms of the guides, Christophe and Émile, lift them up and drag them up the beach onto dry shingle. After several minutes on their backs, Jimmy and Annette were able to sit up and look at one another. They burst out laughing. Tears flowed down Annette's cheeks and mingled with the salt water from her hair. Jimmy leaned over and threw his arms around her in as strong a hug as his body could muster in his weakened state. She kissed him on both cheeks, then kissed him again.

"Welcome back to France, again! Maybe you should stay this time."

They both laughed once more and continued until Christophe urged them to stand up and hurry off the beach. They quickly realized the precariousness of their position, and, with much assistance from the guides, scrambled up the cliffs. As they went their bodies shivered in sodden clothes, and Annette's bare feet lost all feeling. But her pride at what she had accomplished gave her inner warmth.

They reached Catherine's house safely, and went into the kitchen to shed their wet clothes. Catherine, herself, had stood out on the cliffs and watched Annette's brave rescue, although she sensed it rather than saw it, for the night allowed only shadowy images. As the beach party climbed the cliffs, Catherine had rummaged for two sets of dry clothes, and prepared some hot cider. Jimmy and Annette showered her with thanks as they gulped down the reviving drink, and laughed at one another as they saw each other's concoction of new clothes. Neither set was all male or all female but a mixture of the two. Catherine was a little hurt that her outfitting exercise produced such merriment. Did the recipients think she was a Parisian fashion salon?

This was the first time that Annette and Jimmy could look at one another in the light, albeit, only candlelight. Jimmy stared at the features of Annette's face and she at his. He thought her face was vaguely familiar, but he could not remember where he had seen it or when. He made no comment, in particular, he did not want to say the well-worn pickup phrase, 'Haven't I seen you somewhere before?'.

The guides slipped away to their homes in Plouha, leaving Annette to decide what to do with Jimmy. It was obvious to her that they could not remain long in Catherine's house. German patrols could be knocking at the door at any moment, and then search the house from top to bottom looking for survivors from MGB 5700. To stay would be to endanger the life and property of Catherine, a person who had risked so much already to help others. Annette decided to take Jimmy with her back to Erwan's farm that was well inland away from the anticipated search area. She would accept the dangers of the night drive in Erwan's truck; she had no option. By taking the back route and limiting use of the truck's lights, she thought they stood a chance of getting through.

What Annette did *not* know was that her assumption that the Germans would spring into a massive search operation was incorrect. Two guards in a cliff-top post had heard the explosion that sent 5700 skywards and saw the aftermath of flaming debris. But compared with other sinkings of large merchant ships, tankers or warships that they had seen out in the Channel, this was a minor incident. Nevertheless, they did phone their headquarters and report the event. The Guard HQ, in turn, showed no excitement at the report, as Coastal Forces Liaison had not transmitted any message about naval action in the area. The HQ put off any investigation until daylight hours.

The U-boat that had fired the fatal torpedo had done so partly because it did not want to return to its Cherbourg base with it on board after a lengthy Atlantic wolf-pack hunt. It was its last torpedo; torpedoes were for firing at the enemy and not for bringing back to base. The U-boat captain and his tired crew had hoped to find a final piece of easy action close in to the *friendly* French coast; he could not believe his eyes when there in his periscope sat an anchored MGB.

What was going on here; a Royal Navy fishing party with rum and pretty Wrens on board? thought the captain.

The MGB looked so alone and pathetic that the U-boat captain almost felt sorry as he fired his final fish at it. He felt even more sorry when he saw how devastating the explosion was, leaving little chance for survivors. He must have hit the main fuel tank. But the captain was more exhausted than his crew; exhausted, jaded and sickened by the weeks of destruction he and the pack had wrought in the wild seas of the North Atlantic. All he wanted to do was to quickly leave this last scene of sorrow and return to base for an endless sleep. He did not make a report of the MGB action until twenty-four hours later.

* * * * *

Annette and Jimmy reached Erwan's farm after a harrowing drive down dark and dangerous country lanes. They slipped into the barn unheard and unnoticed, found a cozy corner of hay, and, covered with some old horse blankets, fell fast asleep.

When Jimmy awoke, cold and stiff, a few hours later, the first thing he did was to take another close look at Annette's face, an attractive face that was so angelic and innocent in sleep. Recognition of her came to him in a surge of pleasure. Surely this was Annette, the girl in the photograph his sister had shown him some time ago? Of course, she was younger in the photograph; six or seven years younger, so she had lost the bloom of a sixteen-year old since then. Her face had become thinner and the bone structure more defined. Maturation and wartime rationing had probably caused this, but it was still a very pretty face, one he could spend hours looking at.

Should he wake her and confront her with his discovery? It would be a good opportunity to plant a tender kiss on her lips; a thank you kiss; he may not get another chance. He slowly bent over her sleeping body and lowered his face to hers. Her lips were warm but a little dry; he wet them slightly with his tongue and applied a lingering kiss with the gentlest of pressures. She did not stir so he applied another, a little more forcefully this time. She opened her eyes and stared with fright into his, only a foot away. She pushed herself up into a sitting position, her legs still straight out. For several moments she looked hard at Jimmy, not knowing who he was or what had happened. She shook her head to make her brain work. Slowly she gained comprehension.

"What did you just do to me?" Annette asked, with suspicion.

"Nothing," said Jimmy, a large grin spreading across his face.

"Oh, yes you did! What did you do? Tell me!"

"It was nothing, nothing at all."

"You're lying; I know you're lying. My lips are wet. Why are they wet?" Annette brushed her lips with the back of her hand, as though something unpleasant was on them. She continued to look at Jimmy askance.

"I believe you took advantage of me while I was sleeping. What kind of British officer are you?"

"A bad one, I admit."

"Well, next time you might have a shave first," said Annette, with a twinkle in her eye.

"I'll remember that, but first we must be properly introduced. I don't know your full name. What is it?" Annette hesitated.

"Normally it's safer when no names are used during brief encounters. But seeing our encounter will no longer be brief, I suppose you'll have to call me something. Mademoiselle Annette Renard is good enough. That name may be real or it may be false. I'll not tell you which it is."

"I'd say it is real. I've seen your photograph." Annette went white and exploded with anger.

"*Merde! Merde! Merde! Mon Dieu*! What bastard in SOE has a file on me? I'm not an agent; I'm only a Resistance fighter. SOE has no right to have my photograph. If that falls into the wrong hands, I'm dead. That's all the Gestapo would need, a name and a photo. I'd be picked up within twenty-four hours, and SOE wouldn't help me; Resistance fighters are expendable as far as they are concerned."

"Steady on! Steady on, Mademoiselle! I don't know what SOE has or has not on you; probably nothing. No, the photo I saw of you belonged to my sister, Susan. I believe it was taken in 1935 when you were visiting her in Dartmouth. A young girl called Annette Renard was her pen-pal. Now, does that ring a bell with you? Are you that same Annette?"

Annette said nothing for a full minute. She was struck dumb with amazement and confusion.

"This is incredible! I don't believe it! You're saying that you're Jimmy, Susan's nasty little brother? That's impossible! It's just too much of a coincidence."

"Impossible or not, it's true. I'm Lieutenant James Wainwright, RNVR, at your service. But you knew that already, didn't you?"

"No, I did not! As I said before, we're not given names or where contacts have come from. The less you know, the safer everyone is."

For the next twenty minutes, Annette and Jimmy shed their professional persona and slipped into the past. They talked of the summer when Jimmy was, at first, the height of annoyance to Annette and Susan, but then changed to being fun and a friend. They closed the intervening years with descriptions of what had happened to both families, and then dwelt on what the present wartime situation had brought them; the sorrow and despair, the fleeting moments of happiness and hope.

"Well, I think we've done enough talking for now. I'm famished so let's see if Erwan and Claudette can give us a little breakfast. I'm surprised Erwan hasn't been over into the barn already. He's a farmer and therefore an early riser; feeding, calving, plowing, hedging, he never stops. He wasn't expecting to provide sleeping accommodation for the Royal Navy, so he's in for a bit of a shock. You'll not get a good welcome from his wife, Claudette, but don't take it personally. She hates Erwan's involvement with the Resistance. And we'll need to see Marcel, whom you already know from delivering him back to *La Belle France.* He'll need to send an urgent message to SOE detailing the catastrophe with your MGB, and saying that you're the only presumed survivor and please send a battleship to come and pick you up."

"They may not send a battleship, in fact, I doubt whether they even have a spare rowing boat right now. I'd say I'm stranded for at least a couple of weeks, but I don't mind; they say 'a change is as good as a rest', and I like the present company."

Annette blushed a little at Jimmy's compliment, but then realized the consequences of having another person to hide and look after.

"We'll do our best to keep you alive, but it'll be an added burden on Marcel and Erwan who are already pushed to the limit. There's a big operation coming up that's going to be stressful."

"What kind of operation?" asked Jimmy.

"You don't need to know," replied Annette, curtly.

"OK. Sorry I asked." Jimmy was annoyed that he could not be trusted.

"Come on, Jimmy, you're a military man, you know how important it is to - how do you say? - 'keep the lid on' before any operation. Over here, in our line of work, it's doubly important. There are informers and spies everywhere. It's very hard to know whom you can trust. Nothing personal."

"I understand. I also understand that, like you, I'm famished. I could sink a good farm breakfast."

"Don't expect too much. The eggs are good but the coffee is terrible. You'd better bring your damp naval uniform with you; you won't be wearing that again. We'll get Erwan to burn it, and maybe he has some better spare clothes than the comical ones that Catherine gave you."

They carefully opened the barn door and checked that the coast was clear. Soon they were in the farmhouse kitchen making explanations to Erwan and Marcel. Claudette reluctantly prepared some food, her face as black as a thunder cloud.

Chapter Forty-Two

SS-Obersturmfuhrer Mann was a sadist. He knew he was a sadist and he enjoyed being a sadist. He delighted in carrying out reprisals against innocent French civilians for Resistance attacks. His whole body would quiver with satanic enjoyment when he gave the order "Fire!" to his squad of executioners, as they stood, with rifles raised, in front of a row of hostages, some terrified, some defiant. Before the killing, he would strut from hostage to hostage and stare into each face with venomous hatred, his face only inches from theirs. To female hostages he would give a sexual leer, and be so close that his stinking breath entered their nostrils like a poisonous gas. He pushed hard on the chests of the men, thrusting them back against a building wall and snapping their heads. Then came the obscenities uttered in high-pitched screams, his face red and contorted with anger. He considered that his talents for generating fear and terror in the French populace were wasted in the SS; he wanted a transfer to the Gestapo; he wanted to become a torture specialist.

Today, Mann was doing something that he was not very good at; using his brains and suffering physical discomfort. He was placing himself and a squad of twelve SS men in a potentially dangerous situation. They had orders to search a particular part of the Forêt de Paimpont for a Resistance hideout. The forest was thick, and the cold, damp weather ate into their bones as they moved at a snail's pace. Obersturm-fuhrer Mann did not like the situation. He liked the enemy to be already before him, unarmed and cowering. To have the enemy lurking behind any tree with a gun or a knife was definitely not to his liking. But orders had to be carried out.

"Where are we on the map, Hauptscharfuhrer Schmidt? Here or here?" asked Mann of his squad sergeant.

"Neither, Obersturmfuhrer. I believe we are in this gully, here," replied Schmidt, incredulous at Mann's incompetence.

"But we searched here over an hour ago. The map must be wrong or it's a decoy. We may be subject to an ambush." Mann's beginnings of panic could be heard in his voice.

"No, I think the map has been right so far. There's no reason to doubt it now," said Schmidt, wanting to keep his leader calm.

The map in question had arrived at the Gestapo headquarters in Rennes a few days ago. It came by mail without a covering letter. The Gestapo examined it carefully, suspicious that it was a fake, like the many other false communications they received. The drawing of the map was very amateurish and obviously done in haste, as though the drawer was scared of being discovered making it. However, for a person who knew the Forêt de Paimpont reasonably well, there were sufficient details on the map to find its salient point, an "X", with the words 'Resistance Hideout' next to it. But for a squad of SS soldiers the task was far from easy, that is why they had already spent four hours combing the woods and finding nothing. In addition to all his other faults, Mann lacked patience and was quick to blame others for not immediately finding "X".

"Schmidt, I want some results and I want them now. You are not reading the map correctly; give it to me!" Mann pretended to study the map with intelligence, and then gave orders for a sharp change in direction to the left. Schmidt slowly shook his head but kept quiet.

The squad moved cautiously but not quietly through the dense woods. All would have failed an Indian tracking class. After a further hour of wandering haphazardly on Mann's instructions, the group broke out into a clearing close to a large rock outcrop. They had accidentally stumbled on what they were looking for, but did not yet know it.

Mann called for a five-minute rest, but no sooner had he finished his command than a sharp crack was heard by the whole squad. Mann fell backwards, clutching his throat, blood pouring out between his fingers. The soldiers on open ground threw themselves reflexively into the prone position. Those near a rock or fallen timber took cover behind it, assuming the shot had come from somewhere higher up. A second shot rang out and Schmidt saw the flash of light that preceded it. He immediately opened fire, and ordered everyone to pour a hail of bullets into a bushy area surrounding what appeared to be a small opening to a cave. A figure, bent double, scurried from the bushes to a large rock fifteen feet from the cave entrance. From this rock, Philippe, the deputy leader of Jean's Resistance group, was able to pin the SS down for a while, hoping that his other comrades, deeper in the cave, would hear the firing and formulate a defensive plan. He knew his group had spoken of using the chimney exit from the cave in such a contingency, if they had the time.

Schmidt was an experienced soldier and thought quickly. He sent three of his men back into the woods to move around the rock outcrop and outflank Philippe's position. Philippe became hard pressed to return fire in two directions, and knew that his antiquated rifle would soon be out of ammunition. Meanwhile, Schmidt and two other SS advanced head-on to the cave entrance, gambling that if other Resistance fighters came out of the cave they could shoot them before they could be fired on. The gamble worked. Schmidt reached the cave and threw a hand-grenade into the entrance, then ducked to one side to await the explosion. Five seconds later the explosion forced all air out of the cave with a mighty, thunderous clap, followed by billowing clouds of rock particles, each a lethal bullet. Schmidt waited for the cloud to dissipate a little then threw another hand-grenade into the cave for good measure. The sound of the explosions reverberated through the forest, sending flocks of birds into the darkening sky, crying plaintively and warning all living things that danger was present. Philippe did not need the warning; he was dead already; a bullet had entered his heart, cleanly and almost painlessly.

An eerie silence prevailed for several minutes on the hillside around the cave, full of uncertainty and tenseness. Schmidt was the first to enter the cave and quickly moved to one side so as not to be a silhouette against the light outside. He could see nothing. The darkness was total and he feared that which he could not see. Eventually his eyes took on their night vision capabilities and objects slowly took shape, although the suspended rock dust prevented exact definition.

He saw three bodies, each lying as a rag-doll, lifeless and grotesque. Two clutched Sten guns, and part of their clothing had been ripped off by the blast. The third lay directly under a hole high up in the roof at the back of the cave. A soft beam of light filtered down to the body as though it were inviting the dead man to escape up it. No doubt the man had tried to climb the rock wall to this escape exit but had run out of time. Glancing around the cave, Schmidt saw the remnants of a sparse living area; a shredded mattress, tin cans, an enamel basin, a smashed table and chair, a couple of partially burned books, spoiled fruit and potatoes. It was the saddest of scenes; one that would make a normal person churn inside with a massive depression. But Schmidt was not normal, he was hardened to such scenes, a veteran of the winter campaign on the Russian front from where he had returned, wounded, but still capable of soldiering in a softer theater of war.

There was nothing further to be done in the cave, so Schmidt went outside and ordered a final sweep of the woods in the immediate area in case other Resistance fighters remained. Two soldiers carried Philippe's body into the cave and dumped it, unceremoniously. Mann's dead body posed a more difficult problem; should it just be left in the open or buried in a shallow grave? Schmidt looked down at Mann's upper body. He still clutched his neck and pints of blood covered his uniform. His eyes were open and rolled upwards, his mouth contorted with shock and surprise. He looked as ugly in death as he had been in life. Schmidt had despised Mann for his incompetence and his cowardice, so he gave him two swift kicks in the side as he decided what to do with his body.

"We'll carry the bastard back with us. HQ commanders will need to see how he died and that we didn't murder him. They'll probably give him a medal," said Schmidt to his squad, gathered around the body in a circle.

The squad were all for leaving Mann where he lay, instead of painfully hauling his corpse back through the woods in the dwindling daylight. But they kept their thoughts quiet.

* * * * *

Marcel had heard the gun fire and the two explosions when he was about a mile away from the cave. He immediately stopped walking, then left the forest path to take up cover in some densely packed pine trees. He stood still and listened. Apart from the flocks of squawking crows that flew overhead, the forest was quiet. Marcel's first thought was that German soldiers were on an exercise in the forest, maybe in teams, one against the other. But in that case, the gun fire would have been more prolonged, and why only two explosions which had seemed muffled, as though they had come from under ground. He decided to remain hidden for the time being and see what developed. As he waited he became more apprehensive; something was radically wrong; his stomach told him so.

After twenty minutes he heard voices coming from the direction of the path, then, through the trees, he caught a glimpse of a soldier, rifle at the ready, peering nervously left and right into the dense trees. More soldiers followed, strung out so as not to give a concentrated target to any enemy. Bringing up the rear, was a group of four carrying a makeshift stretcher and cursing under the weight of their burden. Marcel saw the bloody figure of SS Obersturmfuhrer

Mann on the stretcher, and knew that the gun fire had not been part of an exercise. He waited a further ten minutes before regaining the path and continuing on to the cave. His sense of foreboding was immense.

He reached the cave and cautiously entered, his heart in his mouth. He took a flashlight from his supply pack and swung it slowly around the floor, the walls and the ceiling. He counted four shapeless masses and went over to each one in turn. None had a pulse. None moved when gently shook. He stood up and gave a deep sigh and the sign of the cross. The bodies were those of Jean, Philippe, Pierre and Roger. Jean in particular would be greatly missed, not only as a fellow fighter but as a personal friend of Marcel's. Later on, Marcel would remember the good times they had shared in London; the sight-seeing, the drinking, the women friends, the jokes.

But this was no time to become maudlin and distracted. Four deaths in his circuit would cause a major operational problem in regard to carrying out *Operation Earthquake*. In fact, Marcel had come to the cave to make final plans for the operation. The previous night, Igor had heard from Grendon that *Earthquake* was set for the night of Sunday, April 5. Lancaster bombers would be over the target at 2100 hrs, unless Grendon advised otherwise. Weather could be a factor that changed this time. Marcel had to find four replacements quickly, and train them in the space of two days.

Although that was a major problem, he had a more immediate one; what should he do with the bodies in the cave? His options were clear. He could dig graves in the cave floor or the forest, but that would take a lot of time and effort, even if he had a serviceable shovel. He could go for help and return with proper tools for the burial. That would be risky because by morning the Germans would probably return with some sharpshooters, place them under cover, and watch the cave for the arrival of further Resistance fighters. Marcel decided that the best option would be to cover the bodies with loose rocks, to prevent scavenging by forest animals, then to return in a week or so, after *Earthquake*, to perform a decent burial.

Using just his hands, he covered the four bodies as best he could, and left the cave with their sorrowful souls still hovering in the dusty air. It would be completely dark within twenty minutes and Marcel was thankful for its protective cloak. As he walked, he wrestled with how to rebuild his team for the attack. He decided that Annette would definitely have to become a part of it; she already knew the plan and had seen the tunnel; she was enthusiastic and aggressive when she had to be. Early on in the search for a team, Georges, the Rennes Resistance leader, had mentioned the possibility of using two women fighters. Perhaps these brave persons could now be persuaded to be replacements; he was sure that Georges could vouch for their courage and capability. So that left one more to be found.

A flash of brilliance took Marcel to the name Lieutenant James Wainwright. Although he was an unknown quantity to Marcel, he believed he had seen plenty of action, albeit of quite a different, traditional kind. He looked athletic, and Marcel had seen a certain recklessness in Wainwright's eyes. Two days should be sufficient to teach him the rudiments of planting plastic explosives, firing a Sten and digging a knife into enemy ribs. Anyway, thought Marcel, Wainwright might as well do something useful while waiting for the Royal Navy to send another MGB over to pick him up.

Marcel's mind moved on to another grave worry as his thoughts tumbled around his head. *Betrayal! Another betrayal, and that makes three! First there was the arms drop ambush. Who tipped the Germans off? Who was responsible for the subsequent deaths of seven Resistance fighters. Secondly, how did the Gestapo pig Eichmann know that Annette would be walking on a particular path in the forest at a particular time on a particular day? Thirdly, there was today's disaster; how did the German's find the cave hideout so quickly? Jean had not mentioned seeing any past enemy activity in his part of the forest, yet suddenly a whole patrol of soldiers must have homed in on the location of the cave in a matter of hours. You cannot do that in such a densely wooded area as the Forêt de Paimpont unless you have a guide or maybe some written instructions. Someone is a collaborator, someone I know well, or who is just an acquaintance. Maybe another member of my circuit, or Jean's circuit, or even the Rennes circuit? Maybe a person often present in La Chatte, or Le Chien, eavesdropping on our planning meetings? Could even be Pierre Chirac, the owner of Le Chien; he's always asking questions, wanting to know what's going on. And he often talks at length to the Germans in his cafe as well. I'd say he was a suspect; definitely a suspect. But I don't really know. Mon Dieu! If we do have a collaborator in our midst, does that person know about Operation Earthquake? Are we already compromised? Good as dead? How do I tighten security, or is it too late? Merde! Merde!*

As soon as Marcel reached the farm, he took Erwan into the barn and told him and Wainwright about the slaughter in the cave hideout. Erwan took the bad news calmly; he was no stranger to loss and he, himself, had low expectations of surviving the war. Wainwright was beginning to realize the immense risks that ordinary French citizens were taking every day to help the Allies. For them, there was no reward, no medals and no end in sight.

Jimmy jumped at the chance to be a part of *Operation Earthquake*. At first he thought he should inform SOE Operations Dartmouth about his intended involvement and request permission, but then he envisaged the bureaucratic paperwork going up and down the chain of command; that would take a month, by which time the operation would have taken place. Best to keep quiet. It would be just a little moonlighting exercise for him.

Marcel visited Annette later that day, and she became very upset on hearing the news about Jean and his men. For her, each loss of a Resistance friend took a heavy toll on her emotions, but she knew that if she were now required to become an integral part of *Earthquake* she would have to shut the heartache out. She had two days to steel herself.

Marcel had good news from Georges. The two additions from his circuit were available, making nine men and three women. The group was set and ready.

Chapter Forty-Three

Squadron Leader James Alcock was declared fit for non-operational duty on February 15, and was posted to RAF Waddington in Lincolnshire. *Non-operational* meant that he was not yet cleared for flying again over enemy territory; a consequence of the wounds he had suffered in his last raid over St Nazaire. His left hand had healed well and his right collar bone had knitted back as strong as ever. Alcock had no doubts about his continued flying capability, even though two fingers were missing from his left land. After all, he knew of at least one pilot who flew without his original legs; he got on fine with steel ones, and they never bled.

He traveled by train to Waddington, a small town five miles south of Lincoln and thirty-six miles due west of the North Sea. The rustic locals of Waddington were glad that the seething metropolis of London, where most of the German bombs were falling, was a hundred and twenty miles to the south. The same sentiment was expressed by the residents of Lincoln who feared for the safety of their beloved cathedral that had defied fire and earthquake since its consecration in 1092. Its builder, Bishop Remigius, a Benedictine monk and supporter of William the Conqueror, was the first Norman bishop of medieval England.

As the train sped north out of the London suburbs towards Cambridge, James Alcock looked contentedly out of the window at the picturesque countryside which he loved so much. The rains had given a new vitality to the neat and orderly fields and pasture land. Lush greens had replaced the tired browns of last autumn, and early hedgerow flowers had started to bloom, giving a hint that spring was not so very far away. Only the deciduous trees, bereft of their leaves, lent a lingering winter starkness to the landscape.

James loved everything about trains; their rhythmic motion; the clatter and chatter as they went over points; the spinning wheels when they tried to accelerate too quickly and friction failed them. He loved to put his head out of the window as a young boy. He thrilled to the pressure of the rushing air on his face and the sudden darkness when entering a tunnel. The plume of steam and sooty smoke signified power to him. Sometimes he got a black smut in his eye, and he had to let his mother poke around with the twisted end of a handkerchief to retrieve the speck that felt like a boulder. In the train toilet, he liked to look down through the open tube as it flushed and see the railway sleepers whip passed at fantastic speed. He often wondered where the toilet paper ended up. There was something especially romantic about steam trains. He hoped they would never disappear.

The train slowed and then stopped just before getting into Cambridge, a frequent occurrence caused by bomb damage either here or farther up the line. The ticket collector wormed his way among the many passengers standing in the corridors, mostly servicemen and women, and announced to each compartment that the train would be delayed at least an hour, but quickly added "don't blame me, blame Adolf and his airborne hooligans." The responses ranged from hisses and boos to colorful expletives not fit for ladies to hear, although some WAAFs and Wrens were the ones making them.

The train eventually whistled and puffed into life again and crawled into Cambridge. Then followed an exodus to the tea trolley on platform 3 by the strongest and the fittest. James did not join the herd as he had come prepared with cheese sandwiches and a thermos of coffee. He offered to share these with the others in his compartment, but only one person accepted his offer, a sickly looking soldier of the Royal Engineers who looked as though he had not slept for a week. Maybe the others saw James's partial left hand, and, wondering what other body parts he was missing, felt embarrassed to accept a gift from a hero.

After Cambridge the train picked up speed. James went and stood in the corridor in order to give his seat to a pregnant young girl who, like the soldier, looked exhausted and full of cares. He wondered what her story was. Maybe she had just been bombed-out in London and was seeking shelter with a relative up north. Maybe her husband or boyfriend had just been killed in action, and she had no one to help her through her pregnancy or find a home for her. Maybe she had just finished a twelve-hour night shift in an armaments factory. James would have liked to help her further but that was impossible. His mood changed to one of melancholy, so he averted his eyes to the outside world, away from the faces of his fellow travelers.

Once through Peterborough, the train entered the fen country, an area of 400 square miles which lies between 0 and 25 feet above mean sea level. A low land of marshes and bogs, of rivers and cuts, of salt water and fresh water that needed to be defended against the encroachment of the North Sea; a battle that had gone on for centuries, similar to the one that the Dutch had fought and who fight it still.

James remembered his geography lessons as he gazed out over the treacherous expanses of the fens. The Romans first recognized the rich fertility of the soil and the potential for fine grazing, if only the water from the uplands could be continuously drained away. So they built a catch-water from Lincoln to Peterborough for the areas they were most interested in, close to the main Roman thoroughfares of King Street and Ermine Street. But the Romans left and barbarism returned. For two hundred years, Angles and Saxons from the continent raided the country and much of the fens fell into disuse. The raiders became the new "natives", the Anglo-Saxons. But they in turn had to deal with another set of raiders in the eighth and ninth centuries, the fierce but clever Danes, who with the Norwegians and Swedes were collectively known as the Vikings or Norsemen. The fens provided the Anglo-Saxons with a mostly impenetrable refuge in which to hide and survive. However, after Saxon King Alfred of Wessex, much to his surprise, defeated the Danes at the battle of Ethandune in 878 AD, the Anglo-Saxons and Danes learned to coexist, principally due to the establishment of Danelaw. Danelaw allowed the Danes to settle in the northern and eastern parts of England while the Anglo-Saxons stayed mainly in the south. But peace in the land did not endure, for in the eleventh century, the civilizing Normans came, and the fens once more protected the Anglo-Saxons and their way of life.

As James's eyes roamed over the fens, he wondered whether or not they would become a refuge again, a home for the British Resistance against the Nazi invaders. Historical precedent might have to be exercised.

The train pulled into Lincoln station where some RAF transport was waiting to take James to his new base.

* * * * *

December 1941 saw the arrival at RAF Waddington of a new, powerful bomber, the Avro Lancaster, which had been under development since the beginning of the year as a successor to the Avro Manchester. It was destined to become the backbone of the RAF's bombing campaign against the Nazi war machine. James Alcock had been sent to Waddington, along with many other experienced bomber and ground crew, to learn how to fly and maintain this latest flying wonder. He was attached initially to an HCU, a Heavy Conversion Unit, to learn, as quickly as possible, not only the Lancaster's flying idiosyncrasies but also the operational details of all the systems on the aircraft. As for every bomber pilot, he would be responsible for the safety of his crew, their efficiency and their morale. But these duties were nothing new to him, an old and experienced Halifax captain.

The Lancaster carried a crew of seven - a pilot, flight engineer, navigator, wireless operator, bombardier/front gunner, mid-upper gunner, and rear gunner. Long flights were an exhausting affair for the single pilot, but the flight engineer, who sat on a folding seat beside him, was given sufficient knowledge to fly the plane "straight and level", although with no formal pilot training he was never allowed to try a landing. Behind the pilot and flight engineer, the navigator had a curtained off compartment so that the lights he required would not give away the plane's position to enemy night-fighters. The wireless operator's station was in the rear part of the cockpit section, and he sat in the warmest part of the plane near the hot air outlets from the wings. On the other hand, the mid-upper and rear gunners had to suffer extreme cold in their isolated positions.

James Alcock, who was positively ancient at age twenty-eight, was lucky in having the particular crew allocated to him. They were very experienced, and knew that the key to survival was hard work, efficiency and compatibility, with the major factor of the last requirement being mutual respect. But respect does not come instantaneously; it comes, or does not come, after working together for a period of time. The HCU training allowed for a period of character melding and the ironing out of any personality clashes. The Lancaster became the crew's home for anything up to ten hours at a stretch; they were not the easiest of hours.

The new crews went through an intensive ground school given by knowledgeable design and maintenance instructors. This took a week, and then the fun began - exhaustively flying the beast. Specific, set air exercises had to be carried out, but captains, once they felt comfortable with the plane, could devise their own.

James pushed his crew hard. He was a stickler for accurate navigation, using every aid available, including astronavigation. He wanted his gunners to be quick at alerting him to enemy fighters and to shoot with precision and determination. He wanted his flight engineer to watch his engine instruments like a hawk for any incipient problems, and also to be able to keep the plane flying long enough for the rest of the crew to bale out if he became incapacitated by a bit of flak or a bullet. He expected his wireless operator to be fast at encoding and decoding messages from base, and to be another pair of eagle eyes in the astrodome searching for the enemy.

James concentrated on night flying exercises, for RAF Bomber Command were night people. He did high-level bombing runs over imaginary targets; he did low-level attacks over the fens at 200 feet, causing the crew's stomachs to churn and sweat to swamp their armpits. He did emergency drills; loss of three engines; fire in the cockpit; wounded rear gunner retrieval. His favorite exercise was corkscrewing - the principal avoidance technique for shaking off a fighter attacking from the rear. The crew hated this. Swinging around the sky and being subjected to 'g' forces sent their stomachs into revolt and heads into a turmoil. He worked his new crew to exhaustion, and then took them home for pints of beer and sausages in a local pub.

After two weeks, the HCU flushed out its latest graduates into operational squadrons. The conversion time was short because the squadrons were short, and the RAF had to step up the frequency of raids on German industrial targets. That was the paramount consideration.

James and his crew joined 4401 Squadron, and stayed at Waddington which pleased everyone. They liked the airfield with its concrete runways, the modern living quarters with central heating, the station cinema, the proximity of Lincoln with its beautiful cathedral, restaurants, shops, and entertainment, not to mention all the pretty girls who were very friendly. If only they did not have to be subjected to the nervous strain of climbing into their Lancaster every other night, life would have been pleasant enough.

James took 'C for Charlie', his Lancaster, to Essen on its first raid. Four squadrons were to be involved in the night attack; not a large number but sufficient to keep the ground crews busy preparing the aircraft. On a typical bomber station, ground crew personnel outnumbered air crew by about ten to one, and the men that took to the air greatly valued their skill and dedication, their long working hours out in all kinds of foul weather.

At 1900 hours 'C for Charlie' stood at the end of the runway awaiting the green flare for takeoff. James and the flight engineer had completed all checks and the crew sat nervously at their stations, their private thoughts laced with fear but their outward expressions showing a false calmness. James's thoughts were purely professional. His mind kept on running through the basic specifications of his new plane; wing span 102 ft, length 69 ft 4 in, height 19 ft 7 in, weight empty 36,900 lb, weight normal 53,000 lb, maximum speed 287 mph, service ceiling 24,500 ft, range 1,660 miles, four Rolls-Royce Merlin 24 engines at 1,280 hp each. On and on his mind went, repeating and repeating. Then he saw the 'go' signal, advanced the throttles and roared down the runway, deafening his crew and shaking their teeth. He was only 30 seconds behind the previous plane and picked up some of its slipstream. From his HCU training, James knew that the Lancaster had a strong tendency to swing to port on takeoff, so to counteract this he had advanced the port-outer throttle ahead of the others and got his tail up quickly to bring the rudders into play. He breathed a sigh of relief as the plane became airborne and started to climb out at 155 mph with its maximum bomb load of 14,000 lb.

"Pilot to crew, check in with me, please. I need to know that you're all still there and happy. Over!" said James. The crew responded in turn. All were happy except the tail gunner; he said his balls had frozen off already and wanted to go home.

"Sorry, Nobby, you're stuck with us for the duration. Don't worry about your balls; you won't need them this trip.

"OK, we're climbing to a cruise altitude of 16,000 ft where we'll rendezvous with the other squadrons. Gunners, test you guns once we're over the coast, and don't hit any of our colleagues. After we set course on the first leg, maintain radio silence except for night-fighter alerts. The enemy have colossal ears. Over and out."

The squadrons headed east over the North Sea until they reached the second leg turning point and then changed course onto a compass heading of 115 degrees. The flight plan called for crossing the Dutch coast just south of Haarlem then straight on the same heading to Essen, a distance of about 346 miles from Waddington, or a flying time of just over two and a half hours, depending on the actual winds and any evasive maneuvers that had to be carried out. The night was clear of clouds enabling navigators to get a good astrofix immediately after turning onto the second leg and another a half hour later. The point of Dutch coast crossing provided an even better fix, and a set up for the run to Essen.

The squadrons reduced their altitude to the bombing height of 10,000 ft, and the crews waited for their visit to hell to begin. The gunners constantly scanned up, down and around for enemy fighters but none appeared. They could not believe their luck. Where were the little bastards? As they neared Essen itself, the searchlight batteries came on with their blinding lights, making everything in the sky naked. Then the flak came up; tons of it; hot screaming metal that could devour planes and tear flesh apart without mercy. Two Lancasters became caught in cones of light and fell victim to the concentrated flak. One instantly exploded as its bomb load detonated, the other spiraled down in flames to meet the fatherland.

But the bombers had a job to do, and, in flights of three, came in steady on the bombing run, released their bombs onto the targeted factories then soared upwards, free of their load and still alive. The fear in each crew member abated but did not disappear; they still had to get home.

The squadrons formed up again for mutual protection, their numbers reduced. They hurried to cross the coast at near their maximum speed, 287 mph. Get home, get home, get home if you can, willed every flyer. Then the fighters pounced, Junkers 88's. They tore into the flights like hounds killing a fox. The planes scattered, guns blazing, pilots corkscrewing, twisting and turning, trying to shake the hounds off. Three more planes went down before the fighters were at the limit of their range or had lost contact with their prey.

'C for Charlie' was spared, the crew unscathed and almost euphoric as they circled the majestic Lincoln cathedral and came in for a perfect landing. They taxied to dispersal, gathered up the instruments of their trade and disembarked, fatigued but strangely happy, even Nobby whose testicles had unfrozen over the target. They headed for the debriefing building and the taste of a good cup of tea.

Chapter Forty-Four

On Sunday, April 5, Squadron 4401 was gathered in the briefing room to hear about the night's target. Since their first Essen raid, the squadron had been very busy; Berlin twice and Augsberg once; long, grueling trips. Losses had been heavy but James's crew had been lucky so far. Not one member had received as much as a scratch. But luck does not last forever, and the squadron was a little suspicious when they realized that they were the only squadron to be briefed. Something special must be in the works, thought Alcock, and special raids were normally especially dangerous.

Group Captain Townsend stood in front of a large map of England and France, with some tightly-stretched colored tape connecting various locations, starting at RAF Waddington. Button-headed pins with swastikas attached stood ominously on the map.

"Good afternoon, gentlemen. A special op for you tonight. You'll have the privilege of working with our friends in the French Resistance. No, don't get worried, we're not going to parachute all of you into a field full of cows. You and the Resistance are going to blow up a very big and important armaments dump full of tanks, torpedoes, bombs, shells, field guns, etc. We're calling it *Operation Earthquake*. What makes this op special are the tactics to be used. You'll be bombing in single file from a low level, only 150 feet, and you'll be bombing on markers provided by the Resistance. Actually, they'll provide more than markers; they'll set off explosions in various parts of the dump just before the first plane makes its run; but their explosions aren't likely to destroy more than a fraction of the dump. Your bombs will do most of the work.

"Question, Dickie?" Dickie was a pilot renowned for questions.

"Yes, sir. Why are we trying to commit suicide? Why can't we bomb from 10,000 feet with five or six squadrons? And why do we need the Resistance? We're big boys with big bombs." Several others shouted approval of Dickie's questions.

"Good questions, which I anticipated, incidentally. There are many little villages in the area of the dump, so accuracy is vital if French civilians are to be unharmed. We've had some mishaps recently when we've bombed from a medium altitude, resulting in French casualties. Using markers set on the ground and coming in very low should ensure that every bomb hits the target and nowhere else. Also, coming in low will make the German anti-aircraft gunners really upset. They won't be able to traverse fast enough to get you in their sights. You'll be over and away before they can say *Heil Hitler*. Attacking in single file, at suitable intervals, will prevent you blowing one another up with your own bombs. I suggest a ten-second interval, but Squadron Leader Alcock may need to modify that depending on conditions over the target. With ammunition exploding unpredictably all over the dump with a cascade effect, it'll get pretty hairy. But, you lads are used to that. Just exercise you initiative."

"Another stupid question, sir. Why can't the Resistance take along a few more bangers and do the whole job, then we could get a good night's sleep for a change?" George, the questioner, was a navigator who always came up with a different approach.

"Always thinking of your four-poster feather bed, George, and the WAAF that goes with it," replied Townsend, followed by some half-hearted laughter. "It's partly politics, George. There's an up and coming outfit called Special Operations Executive, SOE, which handles agents and sabotage in German occupied countries. Some of you already know them as an offshoot of SIS. In the interests of showing a united and cooperative front between all branches of the different services, we want to stage some combined operations. Such operations will impress Mr. Churchill and General de Gaulle. They might even be very effective. The Royal Navy is already helping out the SOE by landing agents on foreign shores, and some agents are setting up escape routes and safe-houses for our boys who carelessly get shot down. We are now going one step further, a combined, closely coordinated attack, by the RAF and SOE.

"Well, that's it. The operations, navigation, signals and met officers will now give their detailed briefings. Good luck!" The group captain picked up a fat brief case and left the room.

While Townsend had been talking, James Alcock had followed the path of the map ribbon to its southern-most point, the target area. He could see Rennes and the Vilaine river, familiar landmarks. A village called Guichen was situated close to the target pin which was about twelve miles south of Rennes. He also saw that the Forêt de Paimpont was not so very far from the target, maybe thirty miles. He knew the forest intimately, having spent several hours up one of its trees. He also knew the Resistance fighters who operated in that area, in particular, he knew that several of them had saved his life. Would those same fighters be involved in *Operation Earthquake*? If so, they had a very dangerous mission. He became anxious, almost fearful, that if the raid went wrong, he could conceivably cause the death of his Resistance friends. He swallowed hard and tried not to be so pessimistic, but the worry would not go away.

The operations officer gave further details of the target, trouble spots of flak and enemy fighter bases to be avoided. Flying low over the French coast would be necessary to avoid German radar. He then gave bomb load and fuse settings, engine start and takeoff times; how and when the French Resistance were to detonate their explosives; backup op leader in case Alcock bought it, and many other items important to the success of the raid.

The navigation and met officers gave a joint briefing. The headings to and from the target and expected wind speed and direction on each leg were explained. Navigators always gave a slight snigger when the met man gave them the winds as though they were gospel. The chance of them being right was about 20%. The met man did, however, gain rapt attention from everyone when he talked about expected base weather conditions.

"Our present visibility is down to 100 yards but this should improve to at least 1 mile by your 1800 hrs takeoff. Unfortunately the return news is not so good. There's a fog bank rolling in from the North Sea that's expected to be here by about 2200 hrs. It's likely to be a real pea-souper so expect a landing diversion to a base further west. You'll be informed, of course, as to where to go when you're about an hour out from Waddington. Because of the landing uncertainty, be very conscious of your fuel consumption on the flight home."

"That's easy for you to say," said George, "but when you've got a Junkers 88 going up your arse, you don't care about fuel consumption; you bash those throttle levers up and down when you corkscrew and your engines suck up the fuel like a new baby on his mother's tit."

"I like the imagery there, George, but please do your best to conserve," said the navigation officer. Remember, you're not going with a full fuel load because of the low flying you'll be doing. Over the target, we want you to be as light as possible, which will give you maximum maneuverability so you can avoid power lines, flak towers, and extra tall trees. For the same reason, your bomb load is minimal; two 1000-pounders, so make both count.

The signals officer stepped forward and read off a string of communication frequencies and codes for message traffic.

The briefing concluded and most crew members went back to their rooms to relax, read, listen to music or just fool around; doing anything to take their minds off what they had to do in a few hours time. Some, however, went out to their dispersed planes to talk to their respective ground crews about readiness, system modifications, and technical points that were worrying them. The ground crews were revered by the pilots, by everyone, in fact, who stepped into any aircraft.

Chapter Forty-Five

The morning of April 5 was acted out more or less normally by the Resistance members who were involved in the attack on the armaments dump. That is, they performed their Sunday activities as they usually did, be it working on the farm, doing maintenance jobs around the house, attending church or just being lazy. But whatever physical actions they were engaged in, their minds were elsewhere, being prodded and poked by fear and apprehension, just like the minds of the aircrews at Waddington.

Marcel and Erwan worked hard trimming hedges, rounding up five cows that had strayed too far afield, and fixing part of the barn roof that had broken loose. Jimmy Wainwright made himself useful by rearranging hay bales inside the barn, and then moved on to clean out part of the cowshed. About 2:0 p.m. they decided to quit for the day and try to get some sleep, knowing that they had to be alert and full of energy for the attack. They took their dirty working clothes and boots off in the farmhouse hall, and went into the kitchen to see if Claudette had something warm to eat.

But Claudette was not in the kitchen, in fact, Claudette did not respond to any of Erwan's calls as he walked around the house from room to room. However, Erwan thought nothing of her apparent disappearance; she had probably walked over to friends at a neighboring farm. He hoped, however, that she would be back before he, Marcel and Jimmy left in the truck to pick up Annette on their way to Chandon's house in Guichen. He wanted to give her a proper good-bye and try to reassure her that he would return safely.

At 4:0 p.m., Erwan went to the bedroom to put on warmer clothes to deal with the cold of the coming night. Claudette had still not returned home. He went to the wardrobe and received a shock; the dresses that were usually hanging there were gone, so were the shoes from the bottom of the wardrobe. He checked the dressing table drawers; empty. He sat down on the edge of their bed, confused and anxious. *What was going on? What had Claudette done?* he thought. Then he saw a folded piece of paper partially tucked behind the wall mirror. It had his name on it. He took it quickly and sat on the bed again. It took him no longer than a few seconds to read the note's contents but much longer to realize its consequences.

Erwan:
I am leaving you, but I still love you. I am terrified and cannot take the danger anymore. Forgive what I have done.
Good-bye - Claudette

Erwan read and re-read the note; stunned into a daze. Then the thoughts came tumbling into his brain and his heart began to sicken. He knew Claudette had been unhappy for the past two years. He knew she worried a great deal about his Resistance activities, and the use of the farm as a safe-house. Although she did not participate in sabotage or any overt activity, by association, by just being Erwan's wife, she was implicated. If Erwan was caught and shot, she also would be shot. That was where her terror lay.

But where has she gone, thought Erwan, *and how did she travel? Where is safer than here......... Perhaps Vichy France? Perhaps she's gone south? Has she ever mentioned any relatives down there?.........Avignon, she has a cousin in Avignon. That could be it.........And she has an uncle in Grasse.........Maybe there, but I don't know their addresses. I must try and find her address book and go after her. Sort things out. She's a good farmer's wife; works hard........But if I do that, what about the farm? I can't leave the farm. God, what am I to do?*

Marcel burst into the bedroom, agitated.

"Erwan, what the hell are you doing, sitting on the bed daydreaming? We've got to be off and get to Guichen before dark. What's up? Have you seen a ghost?"

He handed Marcel Claudette's note. Marcel showed shock by what it said but for a different reason. However, there was no time to elaborate on his thoughts, so he just offered Erwan some brief sympathy.

"I'm sorry, Erwan. You must be very upset. Maybe she hasn't gone far. Perhaps tomorrow we can find out more; why? where? that sort of thing."

"Thanks, Marcel. I think I understand her problem. Bad timing though."

"Yes, it is. Can you cope with tonight's raid? It's very important; the biggest thing we've ever done. I really need you, but........."

"Yes, I'm OK. Just shaken. Some action will take my mind off things."

"Good, then let's go and fire up your truck. Jimmy's already waiting and Annette will be getting anxious. I hope the eight others are on their way to the woods and the tunnel cave. I think it'll be a clear night with a good moon; good for bombers, that is, not so good for us."

Erwan was not really listening to Marcel; his mind was racing.

"Look we've got to make a quick stop at Antoine's farm. With Claudette gone, I'll need him to milk the cows and do the feeding. He's a good neighbor, as you know."

"OK, I understand," agreed Marcel.

* * * * *

Erwan drove carefully down the small lanes to Guichen, not pushing the truck too hard. The last thing he wanted was a breakdown, and the light was beginning to fade.

As they drove, Marcel's mind went back to Claudette's note and the sentence, "Forgive what I have done." *What did* *that **really** mean? Forgiveness for her leaving Erwan? That was Erwan's interpretation of it.*

But Marcel thought it could mean something else. *Could she want forgiveness for some kind of act she had performed; something far more disastrous than a disgruntled wife leaving her husband; something involving life and death? Could she be a traitor, an informer, a spy for the Germans?* Marcel did not want to believe this, but he had to admit that his suspicions had merit.

Claudette had often been around him and Erwan as they planned operations. She knew of the arms drop. She had seen Erwan's map showing the location of the cave where Jean and three of his men had been found and killed. She knew Annette and Marcel had taken supplies there on many occasions. Could she have leaked vital information to the Gestapo, either directly or through another informer, perhaps for money or some kind of protection? Did she tell Eichmann about the path that Annette took to get to the cave; the path which he followed and made an attempted rape of her? He did not like these thoughts but, nevertheless, they were there; he had to consider them. *And what of Operation Earthquake? How much did she know? Had she informed the Germans? Were they about to walk into a deadly ambush? Merde alors!*

Yet, this was Claudette he was having very evil thoughts about, the woman who fed him and washed his clothes, made his bed and cleaned his room. And another paradox; her beloved Erwan had almost been killed in the arms drop skirmish. Surely she had nothing to do with that ambush? Marcel decided to give her the benefit of the doubt. He had no proof of her betrayal, only conjecture. Besides, he needed a clear head during the next few hours; he wanted calmness and determination, not extra worries.

Annette had read Claudette's note also, and was developing feelings of guilt about her leaving Erwan. Her interpretation was colored by the romantic side of her nature. Had she sharpened the daggers of jealousy in Claudette's mind by playing the flirt with Erwan to the extent that Claudette was tearing her heart apart with anguish and rage each time she was in Annette's presence. Claudette wanted one hundred per cent attention and love from Erwan, but his feelings were split in two; they had been for years. Annette should have distanced herself more from Erwan, but, she had to admit, she enjoyed his attention. They had had a bond between them since childhood, and she did not think that it needed to be loosened because of Claudette; after all, love did not flow from her side even though it might from Erwan's. Perceived emotions can be twisted and turned by a third person, and now she realized that she had contributed to Claudette's unhappiness and loathing of her, and the breakup with Erwan.

She looked at Erwan's face as they bumped and jostled together along the lanes. It looked sad and uncertain, so she dug him in the ribs with her elbow and smiled her sweetest smile. He responded with a short laugh.

"What are you smiling about, Annette? Don't you know this is the last ride we'll be taking. Death is around the corner, waiting just for us!"

"Not for me, it isn't!" shouted Marcel, above the roar of the engine.

"Nor for me!" yelled Annette, with conviction.

"Well then, I'm not going alone. To hell with the grim reaper!" Erwan shed his melancholy, and burst into one of Edith Piaf's songs. Soon they were all singing.

Except for Jimmy. He was not with them in the truck's cab; he was in the back, partially covered with vegetables that had died a long time ago. He was cold and cramped and not in the singing mood. The vagaries of war had certainly dealt him a strange hand.

* * * * *

They reached Guichen without incident, and hurriedly picked up Monsieur Chandon. The plan was to drive the truck to within walking distance of the cave, and leave it hidden up a small cart track in the woods, ready for a quick escape.

Chapter Forty-Six

Night had fully fallen as they walked through the woods to the cave. Slivers of moonlight penetrated the canopy of trees as they went, stealthily, in single file, like hunters seeking an elusive prey. Marcel led the group of five, and Jimmy was placed in the middle as he had no idea of the way, and they could not afford to lose him.

Jimmy became distracted by the beauty of the trees standing in silhouette and the strange, threatening shapes formed by fallen trunks and branches. His inattention to the small path caused him to trip over a tree stump and make a revealing noise as he fell into the undergrowth. He was severely reprimanded by the others in the group.

As they got closer to the cave, the strong lights of the dump could be seen positioned at intervals on the other side of the wire fence. Even though there was no obvious activity inside the dump, hearts and breathing quickened with expectation. They thought of all the weapons of war piled up in the dump and felt warmed by the fact that they were going to destroy them. Annette, in particular, dwelt on the lives that would be saved and the pain that would be avoided. She was incensed that such weapons existed in the first place. She cursed all arms manufacturers.

They reached the cave entrance and scrambled inside to join the others who had already been there for an hour. They exchanged greetings and Jimmy, the unexpected participant, was introduced. Although he was generally welcomed, one or two fighters had reservations about this late substitute;

they had doubts about his credentials for doing sabotage work.

It was 2000 hrs.

The twelve fighters checked their weapons and the all-important explosive devices. Marcel then went over the plan of attack in detail. Afterwards, he tested each person as to their job and how it was to be carried out. He knew that people did not always listen to what they were told, or misinterpreted what they heard. Repetition and more repetition was the only cure for this.

Faces were blackened and articles of clothing nervously adjusted. They were ready but had some time to kill. At 2020 hrs, Claudine, one of the women from Georges's circuit, and Annette left the cave and crept towards the fence. Annette's job was to see if any German guards were patrolling in the vicinity, and, if not, to send Claudine back to Marcel with the message that all was clear. He would then prepare the tunnel exit by removing the turf plug support.

There were no guards to be seen, and the plug was removed without a problem. Annette stayed by the fence, ready with wire cutters to provide an additional escape route should the tunnel become unavailable or too slow an exit. She carefully placed her Sten gun by her side, but hoped that she would not have to use it.

At 2030 hrs Marcel urged the fighters down the tunnel towards the exit. Crawling ninety feet with explosives, timers and guns was not easy. It took fifteen minutes for nine men and one woman to emerge from the tunnel and to disperse in pairs to their individual targets. They were five minutes behind schedule. Claudine stayed in the cave to help the men on their return; some might be wounded. Jimmy's target was a juicy cache of torpedoes; items that he was very familiar with.

* * * * *

Twelve Lancasters of 4401 Squadron took to the air at 1800 hrs with Squadron Leader James Alcock leading them. They quickly rose to 5000 feet and formed up in tight flights of three. Close to the South Coast near Weymouth, the bombers dropped down to 200 feet, and a couple of RAF Spitfires provided fighter cover above them to counter any German night-fighters looking for prey. James loved the exhilaration of almost clipping the waves as they sped across the Channel. Not all crew members shared his sense of fun. The squadron crossed the French coast just west of St Malo. There was no flak. They had successfully sneaked in under the radar, but now navigation became difficult, flying so low and so fast. They needed to find the Vilaine River that ran close to Rennes, fly down it for twelve miles and there would be the dump.

* * * * *

The pairs of saboteurs successfully laid the charges in and around tanks, torpedoes, shells, mines and boxes of ammunition. The timers were set to two minutes, but had not yet been activated. The wait for the bombers was painful. Some fighters started to tremble, their nerves taut. They all sweated and mouths went dry.

"Come on, come on," growled Marcel to his partner. "Where are the bombers? Give us a sign. Where are those incendiaries that are supposed to be dropped in the river?"

A sign came; all the dump lights went out and the siren wailed. An alert coastal battery had phoned in to the German communication center in Rennes that enemy planes had crossed the coast. The beat of the Lancaster engines could now be heard, albeit very faintly. But with the lights out and the siren moaning that was a good enough confirmation signal for the saboteurs to activate the timers, and run quickly back to the tunnel. They had two minutes to avoid detection and scurry to ground like a sly fox.

Eight of them made it safely to the tunnel exit, but Jimmy and his partner, Pierre, were not so fortunate. From out of the darkness three German guards, who were hurrying to get to the dump air-raid shelter, ran right into them and all five fell to the ground. Pierre was the first to react; he drew his commando knife and thrust it hard under the ribs and into the heart of one of the guards. The other two guards got to their feet and tried to scramble away. Jimmy fired his Sten gun, but with an imperfect aim, and only shot one of them in the leg. The other guard turned and fired a short burst as Pierre lunged at him with his knife. Pierre died instantly. It was now one-on-one, the remaining unwounded guard versus Jimmy; about ten yards separated them. Jimmy pulled the trigger and a single shot went wide. It was supposed to be a burst. He pulled the trigger again, and again, but nothing happened; the gun had jammed. The guard snarled and fired just as Jimmy hurled himself sideways out of the line of fire. Jimmy rolled then quickly crawled on all fours behind a Kubelwagen. He had a reprieve, but for how long; his gun was useless and he did not have a knife, that left just his bare hands.

The firing immediately told Marcel that some of his men were in trouble. He stopped heading to the tunnel and moved in the direction of the shots, but that direction was only a guess. He shouted out, "help is coming," more as a distraction than a reality. Annette had also heard the shots and Marcel's shout. She, in fact, had seen the flashes from the firing and could direct Marcel if only she could see him. First, she had to get through the wire. Her cutters worked well and, gun in hand, she stepped through the gap.

Jimmy remained crouched behind the Kubelwagen which did not provide much protection, but it was better than nothing. He wondered when the first charge would detonate. *Surely two minutes must have past by now*, he thought, *probably the charges are duds, just like my bloody Sten gun........Bloody Hell! More trouble. Two more guards and one with a flashlight. This could be the end of Jimmy Wainwright.*

All three guards started to circle Jimmy's precarious position, moving in for the kill. But they did not reckon on Marcel's aggressive attack. He had homed in on the flashlight and quickly dispatched its owner with a single shot. He then wounded another guard, but in the process became an easy target for the third. Marcel pitched backwards with two bullets in his chest.

In another part of the dump, two charges went off almost simultaneously which acted as triggers for the detonation of shells, mines and ammunition. Explosions cascaded, one after the other, turning night into day. Blasts of hot air swept through the dump and knocked Annette off her feet. She recovered quickly, her adrenaline racing throughout her small body, giving her a tremendous urge for self-preservation. She saw Marcel on his back, moving slightly, and the wounded guard clutching his stomach. The third guard recovered from the blast of the explosions and raise his automatic. Annette fired but missed the target. She missed because the guard had moved his position; he was no longer standing but laying on the ground with Jimmy wrapped around his thighs. Jimmy had come from behind his cover and taken a flying leap at the guard. His rugby tackle was perfect; the best he had ever done. Jimmy took the German's gun and smashed the butt onto his head. He rolled over, unconscious, maybe permanently.

Dante's inferno suddenly became a reality. More charges went off, and the lead Lancaster roared overhead, almost close enough to touch. The noise, the fire, the blasts of burning, suffocating air, full of murderous metal fragments, created a scene of horror. Then more Lancasters arrived, in single line. One followed too closely to its predecessor and was caught by the explosion and fragments of a 1000 lb bomb. The second Lancaster's nose rose in the air like a swordfish on a sportsman's hook, hung, suspended, then cartwheeled into the adjacent woods and became a thunderous fireball.

Annette and Jimmy hugged the ground, not knowing what the best next move should be. They were mesmerized by the chaos around them, the intensity of the heat, and, in a perverted sense, by the powerful beauty.

"Come on, Annette, its time to leave. This is a dangerous place. We've got to carry Marcel out of this hellhole. He's very badly wounded, if not actually dead. Get his left arm over your shoulders while I take his right one, and drag for all you're worth."

"I don't know that I can make it," said Annette. "He's small but muscular; seems like he's a dead weight. Sorry, I don't mean dead."

"It's OK, I know what you mean.........Save your breath.........Just drag," shouted Jimmy.

"I'm trying my best..........Look, I've cut a hole in the wire fence. I can see it now. Over to the left.......Not far now."

"Good, Annette. One more last big effort...... God, I hope there aren't any more guards around. We're sitting ducks."

They reached the gap and with great difficulty maneuvered Marcel through it. They rested a little to gain strength for getting down into the cave, but help arrived in the form of Erwan and Igor. They were two of the six who had successfully crawled back through the tunnel, and who had been alerted by Claudine that Annette had cut her way through the fence and might be in trouble. Claudine had had the presence of mind to leave the cave when the big bangs started to check on Annette's safety.

Marcel was carefully carried down into the cave, but he showed no signs of life. Jimmy and Erwan examined his chest wounds. Jimmy slowly shook his head; he had seen quite a few men in their death throes before. Ten minutes later Marcel was dead.

* * * * *

With Marcel gone, Erwan automatically slipped into the role of leader without asking for a vote. The others responded well to him for they respected his experience in the Resistance and his quiet but determined nature.

321

"We have to get away from here as soon as we can, just in case the Germans think the RAF got some help from us on the ground, and start a massive area search. Mind you, I don't think they will because those Lancasters really plastered the dump. I know we left Pierre's dead body out there, but at the risk of sounding callous, I'd say he probably got torn to shreds by the bombs along with the German guards. The cuts made by Annette in the wire fence might leave evidence if that were the only break, but I'm sure most of the fence was blasted down anyway. What I'm saying is that I don't think we've left our mark anywhere in the dump, in fact, the dump has been obliterated."

"What about Marcel?" asked Annette. "We can't leave him here. We have to take him with us."

"Not possible. To carry him would be difficult. It would slow us down and we'd still have to find a place to bury him. Dangerous! No, we'll bury him right here in the cave. We have tools from the tunneling to make a good grave."

Annette was uneasy about this, but she saw it was the only practical way. She gave a small shudder as an ironic thought came to her mind. It was only a few days ago that Marcel buried Jean in the other cave, now here they were about to bury Marcel in a similar place, in a similar way.

Chandon, Igor, Jimmy and Annette remained with Erwan for the burial, and to return the cave to its original state. The other remaining Resistance members said their emotional farewells then left the cave. They independently melted into the woods to find their hidden bicycles and return to their homes under cover of darkness. Tomorrow they would need to cast off this night's activity as aberrant behavior, and resume a normal, mundane existence of mere survival.

A shallow grave was dug for Marcel and he was gently laid to rest. No words were said, but private thoughts prevailed as they stood in silence around the grave for a few moments.

Erwan wanted to seal up the tunnel exit to prevent the Germans finding it sometime in the future, after the dump had been cleared of its tons of mangled steel and iron. Small blocks of granite mixed with crumbled sandstone were shoveled into the end of the tunnel for a distance of about three feet, and the rest left for future archeologists to find and ponder over.

Chandon thought that they should take the drillings tools and air compressor with them back to the truck. Erwan vetoed the idea. He wanted to travel light and fast through the woods. The group's final job was to camouflage the cave's entrance as best they could with large boulders, brush and fallen tree trunks. The dump was still burning as they did this, and exploding shells and ammunition showered the black sky.

At the main entrance to the dump, fire fighting teams were forming up, and a few medical personnel were trying to cope with a multitude of wounded German soldiers in and around the barracks, which had been flattened by the blast from a 1000 lb bomb landing nearby. Confusion and panic best described the scene. But Erwan's group cared nothing about the predicament of the Germans; they welcomed it.

The truck was where it had been left. Erwan climbed in and prayed that the engine would start; it did, with a little coaxing. They took an indirect route back to Chandon's house in Guichen, so they were not subjected to road blocks that the Germans were already setting up.

It was almost midnight when they sat around Chandon's kitchen table drinking the last of his coffee, and toasting themselves and their dead comrades with the last of his brandy.

* * * * *

Ten Lancasters made it back to RAF Waddington. In addition to the one that crashed at the dump, another was lost to a persistent German night-fighter over the Channel. Two crews, fourteen men dead, but maybe several thousand lives had been saved by the destruction of the armaments dump. Squadron Leader James Alcock, who landed safely, would be given a bar to his DFC for leading the dangerous raid.

Chapter Forty-Seven

Erwan's group slept late, with the exception of Chandon who was up at six o'clock to do a full day's work at his butcher's shop. Erwan decided that it might be safer not to be on the roads that day, but better to wait another day at Chandon's before returning to Basbijou on Tuesday. He had arranged for Antoine, a neighboring farmer, to look after his livestock for a couple of days. Annette had no problem with staying, as she had arranged for her substitute teacher to look after her class that day. Igor was in no hurry to get back either. Jimmy, on the other hand, needed to have a message sent to SOE Dartmouth requesting a pickup as soon as possible. Igor said that he would do that at his next sked, Tuesday midnight.

* * * * *

It was when his truck reached the brow of the hill that overlooked Basbijou and the surrounding farmland that he first noticed it. He could see his farmhouse and the outbuildings quite clearly, but there was something wrong. Wisps of smoke were rising from the barn and two of its sides had fallen away. The white walls of the farmhouse were no longer white but blackish.

"Fire, there must have been a fire, and it's still smoldering. Oh, my God, the livestock! This is all I need. My God!" yelled Erwan to Annette. "I'd better go to Antoine's farm first and see if he saved my stock. Hang on, I'm going to move this old truck as fast as it'll go."

324

"This is terrible, Erwan. How did it start in the middle of Winter? I've got a bad feeling about this," said Annette.

Erwan swung into Antoine's farmyard on two wheels, and as he climbed out of the truck Antoine rushed out of the milking shed in a highly agitated state.

"They did it yesterday morning, the Germans, they set fire to your place, the bastards! Don't go up there. They may come back any moment. They're after you, Erwan. You're not safe in Basbijou; you've got to move away," said Antoine, very excitedly.

"What about my livestock? Where are my cows, the heifers, the sheep?"

"They scattered them. But I rounded many of them up earlier this morning. I've penned them; they're safe. I think they took your chickens, though. I thought the bastards were going to burn me down as well. They came into our farmhouse and turned the place upside down. My wife almost had a heart attack; she was terrified."

"I'm sorry, Antoine. I bet you hate having a member of the Resistance as a neighbor."

"No I don't! You're braver than I am. Fight back, that's what I say; but I'm a bit too old for that.

"Thank God your wife wasn't there yesterday. I reckon they were in a killing mood. Have you heard from Claudette yet? No, of course not; she's only been gone three days. But look, you've got to take my advice if you want to stay alive. All of you leave the area, right now. I suspect you've been involved in something big, but don't tell me; I'd be no good under torture."

"It's obvious the Germans have suspected us well before our last action," said Erwan. My farm has probably been under surveillance for some time, although I didn't know it; must be an informer in Basbijou."

"That's Annette in your truck, isn't it? She shouldn't go back home. She's linked to you. Ten to one the Gestapo will be waiting to pick her up. She should go with you and lay low. I know her aunt, so I can get word to her not to worry;

let her know that Annette is safe but won't be back anytime soon.

"And another thing; get rid of that truck. You had to register it with the Germans to get a permit, right? They'll be hunting for it. Wherever you head to, dump it half way and walk."

"You make sense, Antoine, but how can I leave my farm; it's been in my family for centuries?"

"I know, Erwan, but you've no choice. If you stay and rebuild, they'll come and get you before you've laid the first stone. You've had a good run with the Resistance. Many others have already paid the full price, so you should retire before you get another bullet in you. That one in the leg was a good warning.

"I'll willingly take on your livestock and your horse and plow. When you come back after the war, they'll still be here and so will your land. You'll start farming again one day."

Erwan anguished over his situation. To stay would mean death; he could see that, but where should he go? Maybe south to Avignon and try to find his wife? Not a good idea; the Vichy police would probably arrest him, or, worse still, send him to Germany as conscripted labor. His thoughts did not come quickly; he was completely dazed. Annette could see that he was troubled, so she left the truck and joined in the conversation after Antoine had summarized the situation again.

"Antoine's right, Erwan. We've *got* to leave right now. Look, we must take Jimmy back to Plouha, to the safe-house. He'll probably be picked up from Bonaparte beach. So I suggest *that* could be our safe-haven for a while. It's a fair distance from here. There's no reason why the Germans would search that far away for you. What do you say, Erwan?"

"OK, if it has to be, it has to be. I'm in your debt, Antoine. I won't forget your kindness. *Au revoir, et bon chance!*" They kissed cheeks and embraced.

"Please impress on my aunt that I'm safe and that I'll contact her soon. Thanks, Antoine; you're one in a million."

Antoine enjoyed Annette's kisses and hugged her longer than he did Erwan.

They went back to the truck and an anxious Igor. Jimmy was still in the back with the vegetables, and was pleased that they were headed back to Plouha. But first Igor needed to retrieve his paraset which was hidden in the bell tower of St Mary's Church, just outside Guillaume. The priest of the church did what he could for the Resistance.

* * * * *

Against Antoine's advice, Erwan decided to drive the truck all the way to Plouha and then to dispose of it. The most important thing was to distance himself and the others from his farm as quickly as possible. He accepted the risk of being caught at a road block. In the last few days risks had become commonplace. He was running on adrenaline and did not care about being cautious.

Igor became much happier when he had his paraset back in his possession. It was part of him, and to be separated from it for very long was like losing a limb. Jimmy was also happy to know that Igor could fire up his lifeline at midnight and request a rescue operation. He had had enough of France for the time being.

Miraculously, they reached the Plouha safe-house without incident, except for a period of five minutes when they seemed to be being trailed by a German soldier on a motorcycle. He must have thought they were on legitimate business, or he was just too lazy to stop them, for he suddenly disappeared down a side road five miles before St Brieuc.

Catherine was pleased to welcome the fleeing group to her cliff house, but she was visibly upset to learn that Marcel had been killed. She thought of all persons who passed through her house as temporary members of her family.

Late in the afternoon, Erwan drove off in his beloved truck to a swampy piece of land about two miles from the coast where Catherine thought he could dispose of it. It turned out to be an ideal area, for a small hill overlooked a large black bog surrounded by tall rushes. Erwan drove the truck to the top of the hill and pointed it straight at the bog. He revved the engine, slipped the clutch and jumped out. The truck splashed into the bog and disappeared under the surface. Erwan shrugged his shoulders; it was just another thing he had lost. First his wife, then Marcel, then his farm and now his faithful truck. He walked back to Catherine's house wondering what he should do next.

In the evening, a momentous decision had to be made. Igor needed to know what he should put in his message to SOE at the midnight sked. It was clear that Jimmy needed to be picked up as soon as possible. And it was Jimmy who first sowed the seed of an idea that involved taking both Erwan and Annette back to England with him. It took two hours for them to get used to this radical idea. They had assumed that they would stay with Catherine for, maybe, two weeks and then decide where to go. Annette thought of going to her mother in Paris. Erwan again considered going south into Vichy France and taking his chances there. Jimmy countered these ideas by saying that they could be much more useful to the war effort if they came to England and, there, were properly trained and recognized as SOE agents. They could then be returned to active duty in their beloved France and become very effective. Eventually, Jimmy's plan was accepted.

Igor's transmission went well at midnight. SOE responded to his request positively, as they had already planned to drop an agent in two night's time at Bonaparte beach. The WT operator for the St. Brieuc circuit had already been informed of the details. For this drop-off, use of Catherine's safe-house was not required. But now the plan had changed a little. Catherine knew the St. Brieuc operator, and she would obtain the rendezvous details so that Jimmy, Erwan and Annette could be ready and waiting.

Igor intended to make his way back to Guillaume and wait to hear whom his new boss would be, given that

Marcel's réseau had been decimated. While he waited, he would work for the priest at St. Mary's. He always had many odd jobs to be done, and he, or was it God, fed Igor very well.

Chapter Forty-Eight

At 2100 hrs on April 9, Christophe and Émile, the cliff guides, arrived at Catherine's house and led Erwan, Annette and Jimmy down to the beach, after they offered a thousand thanks to their much-loved hostess. The moon was in its last quarter and the sky was decorated with an infinite number of sparkling jewels. A northerly wind cut through the air and a moderate sea was running.

After half an hour in the lee of some large rocks, a series of flashes came from beyond the surf breaking on the beach. Christophe replied with the code letter and Jimmy strained his eyes to identify the surf boat that had been launched from an MGB. He wondered if he would know the crew and felt the excitement that they must be experiencing as they neared the beach.

The surf boat crew had some difficulty riding the surf. During one lunge forward the boat almost broached and capsized. Jimmy gave a laugh. As the boat ground to a halt on the beach, Jimmy ran forward with Erwan to help secure it. The agent stepped out and was immediately led away by the guides to one of the paths up the cliffs. Very few words were spoken until Erwan and Annette embarked, and then a torrent of French came from the crew. The Free French Navy had arrived.

Making progress back through the surf against the wind and tide was extremely slow and very tiring for the ratings doing the rowing. They were almost out of the surf when shots rang out from the top of the cliff. A German patrol started to scramble down the cliff face. Fortunately, they did this well away from the path that the guides and the agent were taking to the cliff top. By the time the German soldiers were on the beach, the surf boat was over a hundred yards off shore. The rowers had a big incentive; they were rowing for their lives. The soldiers started firing again, but it was a moving target, bobbing up and down. Nevertheless, two bullets smashed into the hull of the boat causing splinters to fly. One hole was below the waterline, and the sea began to bubble into the bottom of the boat. Erwan could see that one of the rowers was almost exhausted, so, after a brief exchange of words, he took his place. Erwan was strong and knew how to pull an oar with grace and speed. The boat's progress immediately improved.

Jimmy's old rival in recklessness, Lieutenant Jean-Paul Demont, was at anchor a mile off shore in MGB 5639. As soon as he heard firing he knew there was trouble brewing. He ordered the rope anchor to be cut and main engines started. Soon the MGB was roaring towards the surf boat, the crew all keyed up for a gun battle. In less than two minutes the MGB was alongside and the surf boat crew and passengers eagerly clambered on board. The surf boat, although damaged, was hauled onto the MGB's stern, and Demont wasted no time in heading out into the Channel. He knew that if the German patrol carried a walkie-talkie an E-boat might be dispatched to intercept them.

"You old devil, Demont, so you're working for SOE now, are you?" asked Jimmy as he shared the bridge with the coxswain and Jean-Paul.

"Not really, Jimmy. This is a special favor for you; a one-time expedition on my part. SOE have no official boats at Dartmouth since Harrington was lost, but a replacement is supposed to be on its way."

"Your surf boat crew handled themselves very well. When were they trained?"

"Yesterday. We French learn things very quickly. I believe it took you a week," said Demont, with a laugh. "But the girl, Jimmy, she's pretty. Where did you find her? Far too good-looking for you."

"Hands off, Demont. I'm her guardian."

Jimmy went below to warm himself in the wardroom with a hot mug of cocoa. Erwan and Annette were already there, trying to talk above the roar of the engines to members of the crew about life in England and Dartmouth in particular. When Jimmy entered, the crew went back to their duties, giving Annette saucy winks as they did so. Jimmy sat opposite Annette in silence for a while, very thoughtful, as though he were about to make several profound statements.

"We haven't talked about what you'll do after you've been interviewed and documented by the SOE staff in Dartmouth," shouted Jimmy, speaking in a staccato fashion in time with the thump, thump, thump of the boat's hull as it smacked its way through the sea swell.

"Well, I assume they'll let us stay for a while, and then whisk us up to London to start training. Isn't that what you said could happen, Jimmy? I really haven't thought beyond that. You know, take one day at a time," said Annette.

"I have another suggestion. Forget about working for the SOE; you've been through enough, and its very dangerous work back in France. I want you both to come and live with me and my sister, Susan. She'll be thrilled to bits to have you. Our house is certainly big enough, and Sue gets quite lonely when I'm away. Then, after a while, you could easily obtain a teaching position in the town. They're very short of teachers; all the male ones are off fighting the war.

"Erwan, Devon is full of small farms of all kinds. You'd be welcome on any one of them; farmers are also looking for help. So what do you say?" Jimmy repeated what he had just said to Erwan because some of it was lost in the noise of the engines. Then he waited for a reply.

They said nothing; this change of direction had stunned Annette. Slowly a smile spread over her face."

"Jimmy Wainwright, I do believe you have an ulterior motive."

"And what would that be?"

"As if you didn't know! You and I under the same roof? Anything could happen."

"Well, I wouldn't mind if it did," chuckled Jimmy. "What do you say? We've only an hour before we'll be docking." Annette hesitated. How could she decide her future in just an hour.

"Look, let's leave it like this. We'll go through the SOE interviews and establish our credentials. If they offer us a job, we'll certainly give it due consideration. While we're doing that, you could talk to Susan about your nice little plan, of which she knows nothing, and see how she reacts to what would be involved. Then we'll come and meet her once we're cleared, and make a decision that suits all concerned. Would you agree to that Erwan? Erwan?"

But Erwan was not really listening. His mind and body were in retreat; he was suddenly feeling immensely fatigued. The severe tension and strain of the last two weeks were taking their toll, and the realization of the losses he had suffered were just beginning to play havoc with his mind.

His wife had disappeared without saying where she could be found, or whether she ever wanted to live with him again. They had been companions for many years, toiling together on the family farm, sharing difficult times and bountiful times. Erwan knew that their love for one another had known peaks and valleys, but they had smoothed out the rough patches and stayed together. Now they had lost one another; the tenuous strands that had bound them had finally snapped. Erwan ached because of this.

He also thought of Marcel, and how he had been killed without seeing all his hard work in planning and organizing the dump raid achieve success. And although Erwan knew that the death of some of the Resistance fighters in his group was inevitable, he never thought Marcel would be one of them. Marcel had been a good leader; confident, clever, strong in body and determination. Moreover, Erwan had grown close to him as they worked the farm together, ate together, laughed together. A brotherly link had been forged between them. All that was now ended, leaving an emptiness in Erwan's soft nature to add to that of the loss of Claudette.

The third tragedy that plagued Erwan's mind was the destruction of his farm; land, buildings and livestock, with which he had been continuing a family tradition that was over a century old. He felt that he had betrayed his farming ancestors; he had lost their hard-won treasure; he had let the invader destroy it. For this, he anguished and wanted revenge.

"Erwan, Erwan, you haven't heard a word we've been saying, have you? Where have you been? Are you sure you're OK?" asked Annette, taking his hand and squeezing it.

"I'm OK. Really, I'm OK. Just a bit exhausted," replied Erwan, with a strong note of despondency in his voice. "Perhaps you could repeat what you were saying. Were you asking me a question?"

"What do you want to do when we get to England? Do you want SOE training as a full agent and return to France, or do you want to settle in England and farm?"

"I can't make any decisions right now, Annette. Just let me sleep. Maybe tomorrow I'll be able to think." Erwan let his head fall back against the wardroom wall, and closed his eyes. In seconds he was asleep, impervious to the boat's motion and the engines's roar.

Jimmy saw that further conversation about Annette's and Erwan's future should not be pursued at this time. Instead, he stared kindly into Annette's eyes and tried to understand her feelings. He knew that she must be as tired as Erwan, and was not surprised when she slumped across the small table and rested her head on her folded arms. She quickly slipped into a dreamless slumber.

Jimmy poured himself another cup of cocoa, and then went up on the bridge to feel the approach of England, hiding behind her cloak of darkness. He would be glad to get home again.

Epilogue

A dénouement is necessary in order not to leave the reader in a state of anguish at worst or perplexity at best.

Who was the traitor, if indeed there was one at all? Marcel had thought there was; Erwan's thoughts were inconclusive, and Annette's innocent nature could not conceive of anyone she knew being a collaborator.

She explained the German patrol being at the site of the first arms drop as pure coincidence. That Eichmann knew her path through the forest to the cave came from his expertise as a stalker. She had felt his presence in her vicinity on several occasions; while shopping in the village; returning home after school. Even on the day of the attempted rape, she had sensed his eyes upon her well before she entered the forest. The fact that the Germans had discovered the cave where Jean and some of his men were hiding, she attributed to German thoroughness. They had been systematically searching for hideouts throughout the whole forest. It was just a matter of time before they stumbled on Jean's. She had even suggested to Jean that he should change his location at frequent intervals. But he would not listen to her; he did not believe in her intuition.

Marcel had been right, but only half-right. There were two traitors, not just one. Claudette and Pierre Chirac, the owner of Le Chien café, collaborated together. She provided him with Resistance information, and he passed it on to the Gestapo. But why did they do this? How could they destroy, or attempt to destroy, the lives of fellow Bretons who were trying so hard to bring them freedom from oppression. It was the darkest type of betrayal. Was it a political act? Was it spawned by a personal emotion? Fear, hate, revenge, greed? Was it a complicated mixture of reasons?

For Pierre Chirac it was a question of protecting his livelihood. The Gestapo had threatened to close his café down unless he provided them with Resistance information, gleaned from the conversations of his customers or other sources. The method of closure would be permanent; a simple case of arson would be arranged, and there might be loss of life.

Claudette's motives were more complicated, and she barely knew what they really were. Her powers of self-analysis were limited, and when she tried such introspection she invariably ended up more confused than when she started. The information she passed to Chirac was intended to destroy Marcel's Resistance circuit but to leave Erwan unharmed. She wanted Erwan safe and secure. She wanted him as a loving husband and a hard-working farmer, not as a fighter for a lost cause. In particular, she wanted him all to herself. She did not want to share him. Her mind raged and her heart bled as she saw Annette and him drawn closer and closer together by the bonds of dangerous actions. If she were destroyed along with the circuit so much the better. She hated Annette.

When Claudette informed Chirac of the place and time of the arms drop, she also insisted that he tell the Gestapo and the Wehrmacht that if Erwan were captured he should be held for a short while and then released unharmed. As it happened, Claudette's naivity almost caused Erwan to be killed in the fire-fight that was not supposed to happen. Again, it was more by good luck than design that Erwan was not inside the cave when the SS found it. She had provided the map but never knew the exact day the SS would raid it. Her simple-mindedness had assumed that she would be informed of the date so she could keep Erwan busy on the farm.

Her bungled attempts to stop Erwan fighting, and to eliminate Annette, sent Claudette into a deep depression. She thought herself useless, a coward, a disgrace to her country. She had been responsible for the deaths of many brave Bretons, and she was no longer worthy to be Erwan's wife. She should commit suicide or flee south, away from the occupation. Claudette chose the latter escape, and as she journeyed by train to Grasse, to seek refuge and maybe understanding from an uncle, she felt the depths of guilt and despair.

* * * * *

And what of Major von Kruger? Was it really he who saved Annette from being brutally raped by Eichmann? It was.

On that late January afternoon, von Kruger had been visiting a particular church in the area of Folle Pensée, well known for its superb pipe organ. The priest allowed him to play it for half an hour, and admired his command of the instrument. On his way back to his Kubelwagen, von Kruger thought he noticed Annette taking a path into the forest. The light was not good, so he was not really certain whether it was she or not. Although some distance away, he was just about to try and attract her attention, when he saw another figure loom out of the graveyard. The figure followed Annette into the forest, but quite a way behind her so as not to be seen or heard. Von Kruger sensed that something evil was about to take place. He checked his revolver and quietly tracked the forest visitors. Von Kruger used the trunks of tall pine trees for cover, and although he could not prevent the cracking of small branches under his feet, the sinister figure ahead was so intent on tracking his prey that he was oblivious to noises behind him.

At a small clearing, the figure, which in fact was Eichmann of the Gestapo, revealed himself to Annette. After some words and Annette's abortive attempt to shoot him, Eichmann launched his brutal, sexual attack on her. Von Kruger could not believe what he was witnessing, as he

337

crouched, unseen, behind a fallen log. The anger at what his fellow countryman was doing swelled inside him until he could contain it no longer. He drew his revolver, and, using the log to steady his trembling arms, took careful aim and fired. His marksmanship was perfect; he did not have to fire twice.

The sound of the fatal shot died away, leaving von Kruger to make a difficult decision. Should he rush to Annette's side and aid her through the aftermath of her ordeal, or remain hidden until he could leave the scene undetected. He knew there would be massive complications if he stepped forward and declared himself the killer of Eichmann. With Annette having this knowledge, sooner or later it would leak back to the French civilian authorities and then to the Gestapo. He could see himself the target of a Wehrmacht firing squad, or lying wracked with pain from endless torture in a Gestapo prison cell. He was a brave man but not a stupid one. He watched and waited while Annette recovered her composure, and saw her drag Eichmann's body into the undergrowth as the twilight deepened into night. At this point, von Kruger slipped away unseen out of the forest, his secret still intact.

Three weeks later Major von Kruger was posted to the eastern front in Russia, in time for the German summer offensive. Later in the year, he was swallowed up by the battle of Stalingrad, very severely wounded, and invalided out of the army.